One Time Too Many

One Time Too Many

His Own Blood, Part 3

Richard Crombleholme

iUniverse, Inc.
Bloomington

One Time Too Many
His Own Blood, Part 3

iUniverse books may be ordered through booksellers or by contacting:

iUniverse
1663 Liberty Drive
Bloomington, IN 47403
www.iuniverse.com
1-800-Authors (1-800-288-4677)

ISBN: 978-1-4620-1569-6 (sc)
ISBN: 978-1-4620-1568-9 (hc)
ISBN: 978-1-4620-4370-5 (ebk)

Library of Congress Control Number: 2011913710

Printed in the United States of America

iUniverse rev. date: 08/27/2011

Contents

Also by Richard Crombleholme

HIS OWN BLOOD! This Time Is For The Son He Never Knew

AMERICA IN CONFLICT His Own Blood Part 2

You know who you are, you know what you are, a man who has done it all, achieved it all, played characters showing no mercy that are expendable, and is quite simply the best of the best!

This is for you, Sylvester Stallone.

Acknowledgment

---

*A*fter my wife and daughter had encouraged me to write the first novel, *His Own Blood! This Time Is For The Son He Never Knew,* the exciting sequel, titled, *America in Conflict His Own Blood Part 2* followed with plenty of action and excitement. The sequel announces a third book, when John Raven returns to train his final batch of elite soldiers in *One Time Too Many His Own Blood Part 3*. After spending much time with writing what I feel is the best of the trilogy, and trying to fulfil a personal ambition, the time has arrived to share this exciting story with you.

The people I would like to thank, you may also recognise from the previous books. These people are as follows:

- My wife Debbie Crombleholme
- My daughter Sarah Crombleholme
- James Noble
- Hayley Pomfret
- Alison Colquhoun

Each person played their own part in helping me achieve the sole objective of completing this exciting tale. I can now put it out to a host of different people hoping they will want to come back and read the fourth story sometime in the future. This is when Raven's son takes Louise with him

---

to visit Ricky Stevens' parents to give them his belongings and a photograph of Unit Invincible, which eventually leads to hidden conflict.

I would like to say thank you to a few of my colleagues from my place of work for letting me use their name for different characters you will find in this exciting story. These people are as follows:

- David Aindow
- Danny Armson
- Susan Berry
- Paul Burn
- David Higham
- Louise Mattinson
- Des O'Brien
- Graham Parker
- Peter Parr
- Lee Seager
- Gary Simpson
- Pete Wareing
- Stuart Wareing
- Martin Womack

Introduction

$\mathcal{C}$hristmas is a time of the year when people look forward to being with family, friends and loved ones. Exchanging gifts, attending parties and being merry is what usually happens. This Christmas is different, because an enemy of John Raven escapes fleeing to Iran threatening nuclear war against the United States. People living in the western world are nervous, making them worry and ask if this Christmas will be the last one they ever have the chance to celebrate.

The primary instigator responsible for all of this upheaval is James Cairns. He was formerly a Major in the United States Army when he was once also a good friend to General Hardaker. After finding out that he had performed espionage, involving treason to the highest level against his own nation, the U.S. military sent him to jail in Kuwait.

While Cairns had been in jail, he kept attending courses that involved I.T, to make the military think he was studying for when he was about to enter civilian life. What the military failed to realise, the devious mind of Cairns was scheming how to escape to Iran by making strong relations with President Modarres. At times, military personnel became suspicious, asking him questions but chose never to follow it through, which gave Cairns the freedom to plan his escape when the right time arrived. Spending time in a military jail, he soon became the ringleader holding a serious grudge against the two people, Captain Weller and John Raven that helped put him there.

The time had come to release James Cairns from jail when he had to attend a military court hearing and just remain silent to enable his release. His attitude had already become disruptive before he arrived at the military court, which Major Higham had confirmed to Judge Parker. The mention of John Raven's name enraged him so much, he lost the chance to become a freeman and begin a civilian life. Judge Parker gave the order to have him sent back to the United States and locked up for a further two years. Cairns became angry with Judge Parker's decision telling him, and the high ranking officers sitting next to him that one day Raven will die. This reminded General Hardaker when Cairns was shouting at Raven, "Soon it will be *one time too many!*" All while the military police officers were arresting him for working with President Rashaid and General Luchinski.

With holding a grievance against John Raven, General Hardaker thought it only right to have to tell Colonel Wareing about the arrangement. Hearing this news, made Colonel Wareing have to tell John Raven, with him requesting that when Cairns arrives back in the U.S. to tell him immediately.

After speaking about John Raven to Captain Weller, her son walked into the Colonel's office to remind them he was leaving to spend time with his girlfriend during the Christmas holiday. When John told them that he was going to propose to Louise, his mother, Captain Weller, became thrilled for him. Colonel Wareing wished him all the best for Christmas, and good luck with the proposal when he asks Louise one certain question.

In the past, John Raven had already mentioned that when he had trained his final batch of elite soldiers, called Unit Expendable, he would then retire from the military force for good. This pleased his father Richard, because all he ever wanted to do was spend time with him and catch up on the lost years while he had been fighting in different parts of the world. John reminded Captain Weller of her dark secret, she had kept for many years, before telling him about the son and daughter he never knew existed. Had he known about his children sooner, a different life to the one he has experienced need not have occurred. At times John couldn't help himself from showing his feelings to Captain Weller, when she reminded him that although it was many years later, she did eventually tell him the truth.

Sarah Jane and her mother, Captain Weller, had a few harsh words while speaking to each other on the telephone. Captain Weller asked her daughter if she had told her father about being one of the soldier's training with Unit Expendable. Knowing about the secret her mother had kept for many years, she didn't want to make the same mistake, so she decided to be honest. After telling her father the truth, she felt relieved when he had told her that he had already put her name forward unknown to her and thanked her for being truthful.

The time had come for John Raven to attend an induction, where he started to feel the pressure of training what he hoped would be his finest batch of elite U.S. Green Berets. Knowing that his career was almost ending, he became annoyed after a conversation with Captain Weller, when she told him that he was late, not dressed in proper clothing and appeared a disgrace. After a heated debate and an induction like no other, Captain Weller apologised to John for what she had said. John found it hard to accept the apology, which made Captain Weller keep apologising, frustrating John, when he just wanted to be left alone.

Using a military diversion the media wouldn't be aware of, meant that James Cairns could arrive back home in the U.S. without any harassment. Unfortunately, what the U.S. military had planned and what Cairns had planned were two different ideas, because it meant people getting killed, explosions occurring and Cairns finally escaping to be with his ally in Iran, who was President Modarres.

Colonel Wareing, after listening to further bad news from General Hardaker, felt as though he had no choice but to have to tell John Raven, when suddenly the future looked bleak.

After receiving the news from Colonel Wareing that Captain Weller had to travel to the Gulf and board U.S.S. Abraham Lincoln to perform high tech I.T duties, she accepted the decision gracefully especially at this special time of the year. With the little time left, she decided to do some Christmas shopping, buying presents for the family, aware that it would be a few months before she returns to the United States. She visited John, which made Richard become apprehensive when the military arrived, but felt relieved after telling him that she was visiting to give presents to the family before she left. She later asked John to drive her to Louise's house where their son was now staying, so she could also give him and Louise their Christmas presents. Raven agreed, wanting to spend time at Louise's and meet her father, Kirk Mattinson. He eventually found out that Louise had a brother called Enzio, who was once a Navy Seal. Unfortunately, for him, the Iranians had captured him, where there has been no contact for seven years. Captain Weller, thinking about her trip, worried how she would arrive home with John having a drink and deciding to stay the night at Louise's house. With John arranging for her to be back at the U.S. military base, she became sceptical. After accepting John will have her back at the U.S. military base, with help from a member of Unit Invincible, he did, and in style where she couldn't do enough to thank him.

After John had proposed to Louise, with Cairns appearing on television at the same moment, people begin to think and ask is there a future despite the threat from Iran wanting to launch nuclear missiles, creating World War 3. President Berry had a crisis with no choice but to have to call an emergency cabinet meeting to discuss all alternatives available. The conclusion resulted in President Berry and the Secretary of State, Sarah Johnson, flying to Iran on the 29th December to attend a meeting with President Modarres. With this meeting now arranged, she had made time when the world could at least enjoy Christmas. Serious events involving the New Year still needed discussing with the Iranians. A diplomatic solution would be best for everybody concerned.

Christmas Day is always special for everybody for their own reasons. Christmas Day for the Raven's became a nightmare, because after deciding that they didn't want to see Cairns' face on television and ruin their Christmas, Captain Weller phoned home from the U.S.S. Abraham Lincoln. She suspected hostile activity in the area from Iranian pirates in small boats making a nuisance of themselves. With being Christmas, and military personnel attending a party previously arranged on the warship meant the Iranian pirates could strike by quickly boarding U.S.S. Abraham Lincoln through the bulkhead door. They kidnapped Captain Weller, who had been standing on the deck speaking on the phone to her family. When the news reached John Raven, Christmas Day was never the same, because he became frustrated inwardly feeling as though he had to do something to be rid of the adrenalin now pumping through his body. He took his frustration out on creating a lethal weapon ready to use when needed. His father, Richard, noticed his frustration making him have to decide whether to give him his blessing and do what is right? This occurs when President Berry came to collect Raven and take him to Iran with her on Air Force One.

The enemy knew President Berry was coming with the Secretary of State after they had already planned to destroy Air Force One in extreme circumstances. Cairns became aware that John Raven was also aboard Air Force One. The motive for destruction became far greater, when Cairns' vendetta to kill Raven came to the forefront, when he wanted to make this man suffer for what he had now missed in his life.

When Air Force One landed, a huge explosion occurred on the runway making the plane tilt to one side with the wing scraping along the tarmac, heading for the large hole created by the vast explosion. With Air Force One being unable to stop, it dived down from the runway, crashing with an Iranian Metro underground train causing mass devastation all around.

When Cairns saw the devastation, he felt proud with such an achievement. He wanted to search Air Force One, which resulted in the capture of President Berry. Cairns ordered the enemy soldiers to search for Raven. In doing so, they eventually found Sarah Johnson, which made Raven have to hide and later do what he had to do. She gave herself up asking him in a low voice, if he would get her out and take her home. He nodded his head yes to her while listening to Cairns asking her who it was she was speaking to. Assuming it was Raven, he decided to throw hand grenades repeatedly at different places in the badly damaged fuselage of Air Force One. This made Raven have to move swiftly for his life before the remains of Air Force One exploded, which made the debris scatter everywhere and a huge inferno erupts.

Raven stopped, in the distance, to look back at the devastation, aware he had become involved in another war. At first, he was one man alone on a mission, eventually teaming up with members from Unit Expendable. With entering a new war, those words mentioned from Sarah Jane, who was *his own blood,* came back to haunt him when she previously said, "Don't make it *One Time Too Many.*"

A Traitor's Release

*A*fter the threat from Iraq and Russia had passed by, thanks to John Raven, Kuwait was perceived to be a much safer place to be at for the U.S. soldiers and the civilian people they were now protecting. That was at least until two military police officers were instructed to release from prison one of their own officers, Major Cairns, and escort him back to the military courtroom where he was going to find out the verdict on his future.

Footsteps could be heard, in the distance, making Cairns look up and glance at the door. For a moment, he paused from typing at the keyboard, which made one of the guards say, "Cairns! You ought to go back to your cell, because today is the day you find out your fate."

Cairns heard what the guard had said and moved his eyes, watching him closely. He blinked, replying, "I'm going nowhere until I have finished this!"

The guard, who was somewhat concerned, shouted back to Cairns in a disgruntled voice asking, "Finished what? You're fortunate be able to use a computer with what you have previously done. What is it; you're doing on that computer?"

Cairns stared hard, starting to snigger, which made the guard casually walk across and look at what Cairns was doing. Staring at the screen the guard asked, "Are you wasting everybody's time? You type, yet there is no text. You are an eccentric guy."

Cairns, cunningly narrowed his eyes, sniggering again, and replied, "I don't know about being eccentric, but I know I'm clever."

The guard placed his hand out wanting to turn off the monitor. Cairns stared menacingly at the guard grabbing his wrist tightly, saying, "I haven't finished my work yet!"

Not impressed by Cairns' actions, the guard stared back replying sternly, "Let go of my arm now!"

While easing his grip on the guard's arm, Cairns bawled out, "I need two more minutes! That's all, just two more minutes!"

The guard frowned, feeling suspicious while looking back at the screen. With seeing nothing, made him ask with concern, "What are you up to, Cairns?"

Before Cairns could answer, Major Higham walked into the room speaking sternly, "Cairns! The military police are on their way to escort you back to the court where you will be left to find out what fate has in store for you."

Cairns heard what Major Higham had mentioned, while releasing his grip on the guard's arm. Looking at the guard and then at Major Higham, he replied, "I will just shut down my computer and log off for the last time."

Major Higham, looking down at him replying, "With what you have done to your fellowmen, you shouldn't be allowed to use one of these machines again."

Cairns, while listening to the Major's last comment, narrowed his eyes slightly, knowing inwardly that Major Higham was indeed relating about the treason he had performed against his own country. Thinking back to how he had been captured, still feeling much hatred for John Raven, he slowly turned to listen to the Major say, "You will most probably end up back in civilian life, when the force will want to give you a head start in something you seem to be good at and will most likely use to your advantage after entering back into civilian life."

Cairns, smirking replied, "That's possible."

Major Higham, who was glaring at Cairns, remembering what he had been placed in jail for, said, "Shut the computer down immediately and go back to your cell."

The guard watched his reaction, with Cairns just nodding his head in agreement. Major Higham turned with the guard starting to walk away from Cairns. Cairns highlighted the white text showing on a white background, and selected black from the paint palette making the text visible.

Major Higham, who was standing at the door speaking with the guard, paused for a moment and shouted across the room at Cairns, "Cairns! Move your butt now!"

Cairns placed his cursor on the send button and sent the e-mail, watching it travel. He had just typed to the Iranian president through a third party, which made him produce an evil grin. He then went into his sent item box to delete the message. Next, as requested by the Major, started to shut down the computer where there was no trace of his actions.

The guard casually walked over to Cairns, noticing the computer had now been switched off, making him say, "Today could be a new beginning."

Cairns sat there just looking straight ahead nodding his head agreeing. He then stood up waiting for the guard to escort him back to his cell, knowing that he had finished everything to ensure he had the future he had planned meticulously while being inside this military jail.

In the blurring heat, the M.P. officers travelled to the military prison in Kuwait. They were discussing that they could not understand why Major Cairns performed acts of treason against his own nation. He risked his family, his high profile job, his pension and his future for the greed of more money than he could imagine. All this, which had been offered to him previously by the Iraqi president, and General Luchinski, for inside information received about U.S. soldiers, who were embarking on many missions to try and rescue their colleagues.

Captain Weller, only found out about his wrong doings, when she started to ask questions to different people at

One of the M.P. officers, called Scott Sinclair replied, "We are sir. We have instructions to escort him back to the military courtroom."

Major Higham pushed his chair back deciding to stand up, yet still giving a stern look to the military police officers, he said, "People like this, who are traitors against their own country should never be released!"

The military police officers were nodding their heads agreeing as they proceeded to follow Major Higham to Cairns' cell. Walking to the cell Cairns was being held at, other prisoners watching in anticipation started to shout and jeer. Cairns ignored the shouting by remaining seated on the bed with his head down still looking at the photo of his family, with his long scraggy hair hanging over his face. In the distance, he could hear the footsteps becoming louder, but still he didn't move. He sat there with a sorrowful face looking at his family while thinking back to his foolish actions, which was for them, so they could enjoy what he thought would be a better life.

Major Higham, followed by the military police officers arrived at Cairns' cell. A guard standing nearby was ordered to unlock the caged door. In doing so, he too stared at Cairns as he searched through his bundle of keys, feeling disgust with the previous acts of treason he had performed. With all this happening, Cairns didn't raise his head; he kept it lowered with his hair hanging down in front of his face.

When the caged door had been unlocked, the bolt clattered has it was pulled across horizontally so that the door could now open. The prison officer, followed by the two military police officers, walked into the cell looking down at America's most hated man. They all looked at him sitting there on the bed with his head lowered, refusing to acknowledge the military personnel standing in front of him.

Major Higham asked Cairns with concern, "Why are you not wearing your military uniform?"

Cairns didn't answer. He just sat there with his head lowered still looking at the photograph, making John Radford, who was the other M.P. officer say, "He isn't worthy of wearing the U.S. military uniform anymore!"

Cairns heard the snide comment made by Radford, but chose to keep silent and remain seated with his head lowered still staring at the photograph of his family, he had so sadly lost.

Major Higham gave an arrogant stare to his colleagues, and then turned to look back at Cairns, replying, "If he has to go to the courtroom representing the U.S. Green Berets, I want him to look smart and presentable! This man has already received special privileges, including using a computer, attending several courses, and letting him grow his hair when he refused to eat food. Without any negotiation, he will enter that courtroom in a respectable way!"

The military police officers didn't respond to Higham's last remark. They just watched Cairns move his head ever so slightly with his hair hanging over his face, listening to him say, "I left the force the day I was put in here! I'm dressed for court, because they're only going to lecture me, telling me what I could have achieved. I won't need to hear it! I won't be putting my uniform on ever again! Understood?"

Major Higham stood there frosty faced after listening to Cairns' outburst. He moved his eyes away from Cairns' face, noticing that he was looking at the photo of his family. He pulled from his pocket a newspaper cutting, walked a little closer towards Cairns, gracefully handing it over to him to look at. Not sure what it was, Cairns placed the photograph of his family down onto the bed to accept the newspaper cutting and start unfolding it. When a picture of John Raven had been showed, it infuriated him when he realised who it was. In anger, he stood up tearing the newspaper article of Raven up into bits in temper. He looked back wide eyed through his hair, paused for a few seconds, raised his arm and pointed his finger at all the military personnel, saying in an angry voice, "You just don't get it!"

The three men holding stern faces were waiting in anticipation for whatever else Cairns may have to say to them. Cairns pointed at the newspaper he had just torn up and said in an angry voice, "If it hadn't been for him and that bitch, Captain Weller, I wouldn't be here today. One day, revenge will be so sweet! I have already told him some considerable time ago when I had been arrested for working with President Rashaid and General Luchinski, that soon it will be one time too many. John Raven's day of reckoning is coming!"

All the military personnel stared at Cairns wide eyed at how he could insult a well-known legendary soldier, making Radford become protective and have to say, "John Raven is an elite U.S. Green Beret whom the United States of America is proud to call up on several occasions!"

Cairns, slowly turned his head to face Radford, looking through his scraggy hair, paused, produced a menacing stare, replying in a disgruntled way saying, "Raven will die!"

Hearing this, all the military personnel narrowed their eyes angrily, but chose to keep their hidden emotions that were now flowing through their body under control. Major Higham took another couple of paces closer to Cairns while glaring at him, making Cairns say, "You don't frighten me, soldier!"

Major Cairns didn't reply at first. He looked sternly into Cairns' face hard, deciding to reply back to his outburst by saying, "If you want to get out of here, I suggest that you place your military uniform on!"

Cairns thought for a few seconds, glanced at the military personnel, reluctantly deciding to give in. He nodded his head slowly deciding to agree, knowing that his actions could affect the outcome of his future. The military police officers grabbed Cairns, escorted him to the showers, and told the staff there to clean him up. They sniggered as they watched Cairns being hosed down from head to toe while moving along the shower section. When he had finished, he walked out of the other side with Sinclair, still glaring at him, offering Cairns a towel and then pushed it into his stomach, wanting him to take it from him. Cairns noticed the M.P. officer had a little arrogance showing. He gave a short sharp stare back, before starting to dry himself with the towel.

The military police officers escorted Cairns back to his cell, waiting patiently for him to get dressed appropriately for his court appearance. Cairns went to the mirror, placed his hands through his hair, then started to comb it neatly and place it into a pony-tail. Watching these actions made Sinclair say in disgust, "You ought to take a long hard look at yourself when you look in the mirror!"

Cairns heard the remark but chose to ignore it. Instead, he looked at his reflection for a few seconds slowly starting to produce an evil grin, knowing what he had planned for the future. He turned to face the military policemen, piercing them with his eyes and said, "I never thought I would wear this rag again. Let's go! I'm ready!"

He then walked back to his cell to collect his belongings saying to Sinclair and Radford, "Okay! Let the party begin!"

Major Higham was already walking back to assess the progress of Cairns knowing that people were now waiting at the courtroom for his presence. Cairns, being escorted by Sinclair and Radford following behind, walked out of his cell with his bag. They made their way back to Major Higham, who was waiting. He stood still, watching Cairns walk by him un-nerved, and then nodded to Radford and Sinclair, before following behind them. They all listened to the jeers and chants as they escorted Cairns to their vehicle that would take him to the military courtroom, when he was going to find out what indeed his destiny now involved.

Military Court Appearance

$\mathcal{A}$s Sinclair drove the military jeep that was now travelling to court, Radford, who was sitting beside Cairns, and thinking of the soldiers he had betrayed asked, "Why did you do it?"

After hearing Sinclair's question, Major Higham, who was sitting in the front passenger seat, looked back to face Cairns to listen to what his reply might be. Cairns, just as before, held his head low just staring at the jeeps' floor amid his own thoughts. With this, Radford asked again, but abruptly, "So, why did you do it?"

Cairns started to lift his head detecting the military police officer had now a strong tone in his voice. Turning his head slowly to face Radford, he gave an evil stare, and in a sarcastic sadistic way he answered Radford's question by asking, "Do what?"

Major Higham knew that Cairns wouldn't answer Radford's question truthfully, suspecting that he would be awkward. With this, Major Higham ordered Radford in a stern voice, "Leave it Radford!"

Cairns, listening to every word, immediately wanted to join the conversation by saying, "Yes Radford, leave it!"

He then turned his head to stare at Major Higham through his scraggy hair. Major Higham stared back at him feeling disgust, shaking his head in disbelief at what was once a respected officer had now become. He then turned back to the front windscreen holding a face of discontent.

Major Cairns, who was looking straight ahead said, "That's right! Keep that gross face of yours well out of my face!"

Sinclair glimpsed in the corner of his eye at Major Higham to see what his reaction would be. Major Higham nodded to Sinclair, making him realise that although he had heard Cairns' comment, he wisely chose to ignore it.

Radford turned his head, glaring at Cairns with the small outburst he had just performed. Wisely, he too chose not to rise to Cairns intimidating remarks. Instead, he slowly turned his head away starting to wonder what will indeed happen when they finally arrive at the courtroom.

Sinclair started to slow down has he approached the court. Military police officers on duty outside the court saw Cairns sitting in the back of the jeep. Seeing him made them feel hidden sorrow for the soldiers he had betrayed. It brought back memories for many other soldiers, knowing they could never forgive Cairns for his previous acts of treason that he had performed against his own nation.

The military police officers standing at the doorway were watching Major Higham and Sinclair climb out of the jeep. They made their way forwards to Major Higham and Sinclair to help escort Cairns to the courtroom. Noticing the military police officers coming towards them all, Radford turned to Cairns and said, "Okay, move it!"

Cairns, just staring at the courtroom building in front of him, ignored Radford's comment. He remained seated amid his own thoughts, remembering who he was and what he has now become. He soon became aware that this was going to be the end of his military career for good.

Radford stood up becoming agitated with Cairns' behaviour. He looked down at Cairns and said, "Cairns! Move it!"

Cairns, detecting a tone in Radford's voice, moved his head slowly. He looked up at him through his scraggy hair and said, "Don't you ever raise your voice to me again!"

Radford ignored Cairns' reply by grabbing his arm, where he shrugged his hand away. Major Higham noticing that

Cairns was going to be difficult, signalled to his colleagues to restrain and escort him into the courtroom to hear what his destiny now had to offer.

Major Higham walked up the concrete steps to hold the door open for the four military police officers who were escorting Cairns into the courtroom. The door slammed shut making administrative military personnel working close by, watch in anticipation, feeling angry with remembering what this once respected soldier had done too many of their colleagues. As they watched him walk with the military police officers, they would question themselves, why would he perform such evil deeds, when he was climbing the ranks with ease?

Cairns saw many influential people, aware that all eyes were now on him. He casually moved his head in different directions, looking through his long scraggy hair that had fallen over his face. Still walking, he produced an evil menacing stare, looking at them all, making them feel uncomfortable and want to turn away.

Radford grabbed Cairns' shoulder to hurry him along some more, which made Cairns rebel by pushing his arm away and create a scuffle in the corridor. Radford pushed Cairns against the wall holding his throat tightly while staring hard into his face. Major Higham immediately shouted, "Enough!"

Radford ignored his superior officer, as he gripped Cairns' neck tightly with more pressure, making him rest the back of his head against the wall. Cairns, also holding a face of anger, croaked, "Go on! Do it?"

Major Higham, again shouted, "That's enough Radford!"

He told the other three military police officers to release Cairns from Radford's grip. They hustled with Radford, until he finally let go of Cairns. When Cairns became free from Radford, he turned to Major Higham to ask, "Just what kind of military police unit are you running here?"

Major Higham, while feeling angry narrowed his eyes at Cairns' comment, choosing to ignore it. He turned to face Radford, and said in a disgruntled voice, "Go and wait for me in my office now!"

Radford, feeling a little shocked at the Major's outburst, replied, "But . . . ."

Major Higham, who wasn't in the mood for a debate, raised his voice and said, "Just do it!"

Radford, feeling embarrassed with his actions, reluctantly turned around obeying the Major's order. Cairns, producing an evil grin, pointed his finger at Radford wanting to patronise him, and shouted, "See! That's what you get when you're not a good boy!"

Radford stopped walking, turned around to stare at Cairns still pointing his finger at him. Cairns, watching Radford's facial expression with intent, raised his eyebrows, nodded his head agreeing to his gesture, which he assumed meant one day soon.

Major Higham, aware that needless tension was rising, shouted to Radford once more, "Go!"

He then grabbed Cairns' shoulder; quickly marched him into the courtroom and escorted him to the front where Judge Parker and the high ranking officers were now waiting. Cairns noticed General Hardaker, who was once a good friend to him before being arrested for acts of treason. He responded to him by giving him a respected nod of the head, which General Hardaker reluctantly responded to by raising his hand deciding to remember him, has what he was and not what he has now become.

The military police officers released Cairns, saluted to the high ranking officers in the courtroom, and remained standing next to him waiting for the judge to say a few words.

Cairns, feeling alone, knew that all around this courtroom were many pairs of eyes watching and waiting to hear what he already knew.

Judge Graham Parker, looked down at Cairns with a solemn face, feeling disappointed at what he had now become. He could not call him by his military title because it didn't feel right; instead while shaking his head slowly from side to side still feeling disappointment he said, "James Cairns."

Cairns held his head low not wanting to respond to the judge. Other officers sat in the courtroom were watching a broken man who had nothing. Judge Parker looked down on Cairns with a deep thought and said, "James Cairns, now there is a name to remember."

One of the officers listening immediately shouted, "But not in the same way as John Raven!"

Judge Parker wasn't happy with the sudden outburst. Cairns turned his head slightly to look across at the soldier who had bawled out Raven's name. The adrenalin started to rise inside his body, knowing it was Raven and Captain Weller, who had ruined his military career. They found out the truth about U.S. soldiers entering Iraq and becoming prisoners of war. Cairns, thought back to when he had previously performed acts of treason after John Raven's Unit Invincible embarked on a dangerous mission in Iraq. Regrettably, for the U.S. the enemy captured members of Unit Invincible because Cairns had leaked confidential information to the enemy. Thinking back made him breathe heavy, especially with hearing John Raven's name again.

Judge Parker, aware of Raven's military achievements, turned to everybody in the courtroom. He paused for a few seconds feeling proud, and said, "Raven is a formidable soldier, where everyone in this courtroom will agree that he is indeed the best of the best."

Hearing this comment made Cairns laugh out aloud, and then spit on the floor, making Judge Parker stare down, feeling angry and want to ask, "Where has yourself-respect gone?"

Cairns refused to lift his head to look at Judge Parker. He could only visualise the person he hated the most, just wanting revenge! Judge Parker, still looking down at Cairns said, "You do know that Raven nearly lost his life when he and his son fought to save President Berry when the United States of America was in conflict?"

Cairns sniggered at the thought of Raven killed in action. Judge Parker, however, while looking down at Cairns with a hint of disappointment showing on his face carried on saying, "John Raven did come through his last ordeal, where he is I'm glad to say, still alive."

General Hardaker, at this point was also thinking back remembering how Raven came so close to death. He recalled Colonel Wareing in despair contacting him for help to have Raven taken to a U.S. medical military unit in South Korea. Looking up at Judge Parker pausing for a moment, he decided to say, "John Raven is analysing his final unit were few people know it is Unit Expendable."

After hearing these words spoken by General Hardaker, Cairns raised his head, looking across bewildered to what was once his good friend. General Hardaker, looking straight back at him feeling hidden sorrow, reminded him by saying, "You too could have commanded the same respect that John Raven has received, if only you had gone about it in the right way."

Cairns had heard enough. He walked quickly away from the military police officers, where they immediately followed, grabbing his arms tightly making Cairns shout out aloud, "John Raven this, John Raven that, I'm sick of listening to his Godforsaken name!"

He shrugged the military police officers, telling them to take their hands-off him, which they refused to do. Judge Parker, feeling annoyed at Cairns outburst said to the military police officers, "Take him back to his position!"

While the military police officers dragged Cairns, he turned his head to look at what was once his good friend, General Hardaker. He scowled and then spoke with meaning by saying, "I promise you; soon it will be *One Time Too Many* for your beloved soldier!"

General Hardaker frowned at Cairns' comment, knowing that he had previously heard him blurt these words out to Raven, which made him wonder whether releasing Cairns was the right action to perform. Starting to feel anxious about his last comment, General Hardaker replied, "Explain what you mean, when you say, one time too many."

Cairns, for a few seconds gave a solemn look at the General, who was still waiting for a reply, which made him say to Cairns, "Well? I'm waiting for an answer!"

Cairns moved his head away, gave a prolonged blink, turned back to the high ranking officers inside the courtroom and replied, "We know who John Raven is and what he has become involved in."

Judge Parker, frowning said, "Please elaborate."

Cairns, sniggering while thinking back to Raven punching him in the face replied, "You need me to tell you? He is supposed to be the supreme soldier."

General Hardaker interrupted him by saying, "He is the supreme soldier who just happens to be the best of the best."

Intrigued, Judge Parker placed his hand up, which made the General stop from saying anything further. Suspecting that those words, one time too many were involving a threat of some sort made him say, "Cairns, explain what you mean when you say, one time too many, because you're diverting from the original question."

Cairns visualised Raven for a few seconds, and replied, "The first was for him. The second was for his nation. The third was for his friend. The fourth time was for a group of missionaries, do I have to go on?"

Many officers inside the courtroom were frowning while listening to what Cairns was saying, which made Judge Parker reply, "Yes! Carry on I need to hear this."

Cairns sighed, and then said, "After Raven returned home, he received a visit by Colonel Wareing and Captain Weller. They were both eager in wanting him to come back to carry on with the late Colonel Lewis' work, by training elite soldiers from Unit Invincible. They became involved in my ordeal, destroying all my plans I made for the future. Raven sent members of Unit Invincible into Iraq to fight my contacts, President Rashaid and General Luchinski, who also had a serious vendetta against Raven for killing his uncle in Afghanistan many years ago."

With Cairns deciding to pause, it made General Hardaker say, "It still doesn't explain the motive for one time too many."

Judge Parker raised his hand to stop General Hardaker from saying anything further and said, "Carry on Cairns."

Cairns sighed once more, replying, "You probably know the rest!"

Judge Parker said, "You're right. We probably do, but we want to listen to your version."

Cairns closed his eyes recalling Raven hitting him hard in the face. The memory wouldn't go away. When Cairns opened his eyes, he replied, "Raven became involved when Captain Weller decided to tell him a dark secret she had kept for many years, when this time was for the son he never knew."

Everybody in the courtroom listened with intent at what Cairns was saying, which made Judge Parker say, "Carry on Cairns."

Cairns, still frowning, replied, "When I was at the U.S. military jail in Kuwait for my acts of treason, I heard that Raven became involved in another war when America was in conflict. The primary instigator was the Asian boy, Azar Sajadi, when he had once given the necklace to him many years ago. He had grown up to become a terrorist with members of Hermes and came face to face with Raven many years on. I heard that this war almost took his life, which makes me want to ask, how far can you push one soldier? Surely there is going to come a time when it will be one time too many."

Judge Parker listened hard to Cairns, replying, "Perhaps one time too many can come to us all in whatever we undertake. The way you implied these words was in a way of revenge, and because of this, it will be through you and you alone that it will be one time too many for John Raven."

Cairns sniggered, which made Judge Parker ask, "Am I right?"

Cairns replied, "All I know is that soon it will be one time too many."

Judge Parker turned to see that many high ranking officers were speaking among themselves about what Cairns had just told them. Judge Parker, after careful thought stared at Cairns and then asked, "You mentioned that soon it will be one time too many, what have you been planning?"

Cairns spat on the floor again, which made Judge Parker, say in an angry voice, "Don't do that inside my courtroom!"

Radford grabbed Cairns' arm, which made him move wanting to shrug him off. Judge Parker, looking down at Cairns, aware of the special privileges given to him, ordered the military police officers to take the computer he had been using for investigation. Cairns smirked, knowing that it was too late for them to find anything.

General Hardaker sat there shaking his head in total disbelief as Cairns bawled out these words, "One time too many!"

Judge Parker stared at him, which made Cairns say, "Your famous soldier is going to die one day soon!"

Judge Parker wanting to know more replied, "How?"

Cairns grinned before replying to the judge, and then said, "He will die because you are all too stupid to see when a soldier has gone to hell, only to return and do it again and again! There will come a time when people will say it was one time too many."

Judge Parker feeling concerned, asked, "Why, because you had planned it?"

Cairns replied, "Who knows what the future holds?"

The courtroom was becoming rather rowdy, which made Judge Parker, unimpressed with the outburst, decide to bang his hammer down and shout, "Silence in court!"

Cairns, aware that he was trying the patience of everybody, decided to be tactical and say, "Your honour, I don't pretend when I say I don't like John Raven! Why must I have to listen to his achievements on my release? I'm here for me and me alone, hoping that you the court can find it in your heart to enable me to remain in the job I do enjoy the most. But you're not going to do what I want, are you?"

Before answering Cairns' question, Judge Parker leant down to speak with General Hardaker to listen to his comments. He then sat back up to face Cairns and reply to his question. "With what you have done, and you do know what you have done don't you?"

Cairns remained silent. Judge Parker, while holding a stern face carried onto say, "You performed treason against the U.S. which means you could never be reinstated to your original military position."

Cairns already knew this and just wanted to know what his destiny now held. Just as before, he glanced at General Hardaker, who was giving a sombre look of disappointment at what was once a well-respected work colleague. With this, Cairns lowered his head, clasped his hands together just waiting for Judge Parker to tell him the inevitable news he already knew.

Judge Parker, after listening to the comments Cairns had made earlier about Raven having to die, looked down on him with concern. It made him want to ask Major Higham a question, "In your professional opinion do you think this man should live a normal everyday civilian life?"

Major Higham, before answering turned to look at Cairns, then slowly back at the Judge, thinking about what his reply would be. He gave a sigh, then spoke, "Your Honour, I'm sure you would agree that this man is a dangerous, devious person, where I think he will be a threat to our fellow countrymen and women."

Cairns still standing there with his hands clasped together and his head lowered heard what Major Higham had just told Judge Parker, which made him produce an evil grin. Judge Parker, who was thinking about the Major's opinion, noticed the smirk on Cairns' face, which made him feel angry. He shouted to Cairns. "Look at me!"

Cairns refused to raise his head, making Judge Parker shout once more. "Cairns!"

Just as before, Cairns ignored him by standing there with his head lowered. Judge Parker, who was now aware Cairns was going to be awkward, looked at his high ranking colleagues sat nearby and then looked down once more at Cairns, where he said, "Well Cairns! You refuse to co-operate and want to make this difficult! I have no alternative, but to send you to a U.S. military jail for a further two years, rather than set you free and be able to live a civilian life."

Cairns started to raise his head making Judge Parker ask, "Do I have your attention now?"

Cairns stared at Judge Parker in the eye replying, "You do what you have to do, and I will do what I have to do!"

Judge Parker narrowed his eyes at Cairns after he could see there was no remorse. He had made a decision and said, "Cairns you give me no option but to have you escorted to the United States. You will be held prisoner for a further two years at a military compound. Maybe in two years' time your attitude will have changed, and we may be able to discuss your future."

Cairns didn't show any emotion; he stood there choosing to accept whatever Judge Parker had to say to him, knowing that the future he had planned was different to the one Judge Parker had just arranged.

Judge Parker, feeling disappointed in having to perform these actions, ordered the military police officers to take him away and have him escorted to the U.S. as soon as possible. The military police saluted, grabbed their prisoner, turned him around and started to escort him out of the courtroom. Cairns, while walking, looked back at General Hardaker, where he put his finger on his throat and moved it from side to side. General Hardaker shook his head from side to side feeling utter disappointment from what he thought was once a good friend. While walking to the back of the courtroom, Cairns bawled out, "John Raven will die!"

Everybody in the courtroom glared at Cairns feeling anger as he was being escorted out of the building. General Hardaker stood up to tell Judge Parker that John Raven may have to be warned that somebody has a serious vendetta against him. Judge Parker replied, "I'm sure Raven can look after himself."

Knowing that Raven only just survived his last ordeal, he replied, "I ought to let Colonel Wareing know of what has been arranged."

Judge Parker while recalling events that had just occurred in his courtroom, nodded his head agreeing saying, "It would do no harm for the right people to know of what is about to take place."

General Hardaker, while watching the military police escort Cairns to the back of the building, turned to the Judge and said, "No matter how long you know somebody, you never know who that person is."

Judge Parker and General Hardaker discussed the court hearing, while turning to watch Cairns step out of the door with the military police officers. Each had their own thoughts of what was once a respected officer.

Admiration

S ince John Raven had returned from his war in North Korea, when it almost killed him, Colonel Wareing made a personal promise to himself. Hating to admit that time had finally caught up with John Raven; no further military action requiring fighting by him was needed. His knowledge and experience of wars he had previously been involved in would be an asset to pass onto future military units. All they needed, was ambition of becoming like himself, the elite combat fighting machine, that when pushed, will be able to deliver and most important of all, survive!

It was a cold December day with Christmas approaching rapidly. Some soldiers at the U.S. military base were looking forward to leaving when they could be with their loved ones at this special time of the year.

Colonel Wareing stood at the window in his office, moved the venetian blinds slightly and watched elite soldiers interacting from two different units that John Raven had trained since his return from North Korea. He gave a wry grin feeling proud of them knowing who had trained them to become an extra special soldier. Slowly, he turned to the pictures hanging on the wall, looking at Colonel Lewis and John Raven. Casually, he walked over to study the picture of Raven in more detail, while nodding his head agreeing, he said quietly, "I hate to admit it, but you're the best of the best."

While looking at the picture of Raven, he turned holding a solemn face to look at the picture of Colonel Lewis. He started to remember the good times, the bad times and the disagreements, with most of them happening in his own office. Recalling memories made him look down at the floor, take a drag on his cigar and casually blow the smoke away. He slowly raised his head looking up at Colonel Lewis, recalling some more memories he had shared with what was once a legendary officer. Amid his own thoughts, the telephone rang making him turn around sharply, immediately picking up the receiver to answer it by saying, "Colonel Wareing speaking."

General Hardaker, was on the phone and replied, "Hello Colonel, are you well?"

Colonel Wareing acknowledged the General exchanging pleasantries before arriving at the focal point of the conversation. With working long hours, General Hardaker placed his finger and thumb over the bridge of his nose stroking his tear ducts with his finger. He then placed his hand down onto the desk, glanced out of the window, noticing the military police officers were escorting Cairns away to prepare for his journey back to the United States. Feeling disappointed in what was once a loyal colleague; General Hardaker asked Colonel Wareing a question. "Do you remember Major Cairns?"

Colonel Wareing immediately thought back to the time when the military police arrested Major Cairns at the Kuwaiti control centre for taking part in espionage. Emotions with anger and frustration were high that day, because some U.S. soldiers previously captured, had lost their lives needlessly. Raven; also hit Major Cairns hard in the face with his fist in temper after realising that he had performed the ultimate betrayal. Colonel Wareing replied back to General Hardaker, "How could I forget that weasel!"

General Hardaker, without hesitation told the Colonel that Cairns would be travelling to the United States in two days and held in a secure military compound for the next two years. After this period of time has passed by, Judge

Parker will receive an evaluation report, and depending on his attitude, possibly released.

Colonel Wareing, listened hard to what the General had to say, and replied to him. "So the weasel is coming home?"

The General answered, "Yes."

He then thought back to Cairns' outburst in the courtroom, carrying onto say, "Cairns has a serious vendetta against John Raven."

Colonel Wareing gave a half-hearted laugh, replying to his superior officer by asking, "Who hasn't?"

General Hardaker signed the release papers for Cairns. He paused for a moment after listening to Colonel Wareing's reply. Concerned for Raven, he said, "He has much hatred for John Raven, that much so he has even bawled out aloud that he will die."

Colonel Wareing chuckled, and replied, "He has been through much worse situations and warzones than Cairns himself."

General Hardaker recalled how Cairns appeared when he had bawled these words out, and decided to end the telephone conversation by saying, "Watch your man! Don't under estimate Cairns because he has had time in a military jail to instigate his revenge. I will be in touch with you in a couple of days to give you an update on Cairns' situation."

Colonel Wareing agreed with the General's proposal, which then left them to say goodbye and end the conversation. For a few moments the Colonel held the receiver in his hand thinking about what the General had told him, when Cairns wanted the final revenge, which was to kill Raven. Slowly, he placed the receiver down onto the hook, stood up, turned around and looked at those pictures of Colonel Lewis and John Raven that were hanging on the wall.

Captain Weller was walking down the corridor acknowledging different people, telling them that she too like them was looking forward to the Christmas holiday. Approaching Colonel Wareing's office, she noticed the door had been left open and with this saw Colonel Wareing looking at those pictures hung on the wall once again. She stopped in her stride deciding to change direction and knock on the Colonel's door. The Colonel looked casually watching her walk in with a grin on her face after seeing him looking at both of those pictures, which made her say, "They have that effect on you."

Colonel Wareing greeted her, as he looked at the pictures, nodding his head agreeing, turned back to the Captain to say, "They're legends in their own right."

As Captain Weller walked closer to the Colonel's desk, she replied, "You've probably looked at those pictures many times, and each time you have had many thoughts. The last time I saw you study those pictures; Raven went on to fight in North Korea."

Colonel Wareing grinned, looked at Captain Weller and said, "I remember it well! I thought the son of a bitch had died when the last conflict just seemed too much to take!"

Captain Weller moved her eyes away recalling the time when her son had brought President Berry safely back home to the United States, then go through the torture of not knowing whether Raven had survived his latest battle. Colonel Wareing suspected Captain Weller was reliving Raven's last war, and said, "I so dearly wanted to ask him to come back and fight in North Korea. Only I didn't need to because he knew I wanted it, and chose to do it anyway. It did take the pressure away from me."

Captain Weller agreed and asked, "How does he do that? I felt the same way when I felt compelled to ask him to take over training Unit Invincible when Colonel Lewis had so sadly died of a heart attack."

Colonel Wareing looked back at the pictures, and then after taking another drag on his cigar, blew the smoke up into the air. Captain Weller coughed a little as she gently waved the smoke away. Colonel Wareing turned to face her, while placing his cigar down in the ashtray, and said, "Look what Raven has done for us since his last ordeal. He has trained two elite military units and made those soldiers into elite Green Berets. Colonel Lewis would be extremely proud of his prod jet."

Captain Weller glanced at the pictures, remembering that one was once her superior officer. The other was an ex-lover and father to her son, John Weller, and daughter, Sarah Jane, and then replied, "I hate to say it sir, but you're right."

Colonel Wareing's eyes narrowed slightly with the thought of Raven going back into war once more, remembering how close to death he had come to on his last mission. With this he replied back to Captain Weller by saying in a stern voice. "Raven's fighting days are over for good!"

Captain Weller wanted to believe what Colonel Wareing had just told her, but wisely chose not to say anything. Inwardly, she just agreed with him.

A knock on the door made Wareing and Weller look, and then the Colonel shout, "Enter!"

John Weller walked in, acknowledged his mother, Captain Weller, and Colonel Wareing by saluting to them. He was then told to stand at ease. He just like many others glanced at the pictures hung on the wall behind Colonel Wareing's desk, but chose to keep his thoughts to himself. John Weller came to the Colonel, telling him that his holiday leave set for Christmas was almost up on him and to ask permission that it was still okay to have. Colonel Wareing without hesitation replied to John, "Absolutely, do you have anything special planned for the Christmas period?"

John placed his hand into his pocket and brought a small box out making Captain Weller put her hands to her mouth in disbelief. Noticing his mother's reaction, he calmly said, "You know how much I love Louise? I'm going to ask her to marry me."

Captain Weller gave her son a hug and patted his back feeling proud of him. She whispered into his ear, "You have an honest young woman there, don't lose her."

She then released him, while watching Colonel Wareing walk slowly from behind his desk to congratulate him, wishing him all the best. He looked at him, grinned and remembered how he once was to what he has now become making him say, "You've done well, almost a chip off the old block."

John Weller listened to those words, knowing what the Colonel meant. He said nothing; instead he just nodded his head agreeing while thinking of his legendary father. The Colonel, who suspected that he was thinking back to his father said, "Go, you have a huge task ahead of you when you decide to ask Louise to marry you."

John chuckled, and then turned to walk out of the Colonel's office. Captain Weller called out to him, "Good luck John."

John turned back around and replied, "Thanks."

He walked out of the office, making his mother, Captain Weller, act spontaneously. She rushed out of the office to walk with her son, thinking it would be a good idea to offer some advice to him, with what he is about to ask Louise.

Colonel Wareing went to close the door, and then walked back to his desk thinking about what General Hardaker had said earlier, when they were speaking on the phone. Looking at the picture of John Raven hanging on the wall once again, he showed immense admiration. Looking at his rugged lines, he decided to ring him to warn him of whom is about to be released and brought back to the United States.

Home Life

_C_olonel Wareing took the phone, stood up, and walked over to the window once more watching some of the elite soldiers Raven had trained. It made him feel proud that he could bring the best and possibly more out of them. Slowly, he started to press the buttons, waiting eagerly for Raven to answer the phone.

John's father, Richard Raven, answered the phone by saying, "Hello."

Colonel Wareing, who knew Richard could be a stubborn old mule replied, "Hi Richard, it's Colonel Wareing here."

Richard gave a groan realising it was the military, reluctantly asking abruptly, "What do you want?"

Colonel Wareing moved away from the window, walking back to his desk. He sat down and asked, "Can I speak with John?"

Richard, who became defensive, asked, "Why? His military days are now over!"

Colonel Wareing rolled his eyes slightly with half expecting what Richard's reaction toward the military would be. He sighed, deciding to humour him by saying, "I couldn't agree more, although he has been of high value training elite units for us."

Richard, who will never accept that John will leave the force for good, paused for a few seconds and then asked, "You're not going to take him back into war are you?"

Colonel Wareing gave a half-hearted chuckle, replying, "Richard. John Raven's fighting days are over. I promise you. North Korea was the last time."

Richard wanted to believe the Colonel, replying in a solemn voice, "I would like to believe you, but can't."

Colonel Wareing moved the phone into his other hand, holding it at his other ear. He sighed, replying to Richard, "Believe it! It's over! Now can I please speak with John?"

Richard, who was slowly starting to believe the Colonel, replied, "I'll go and get him."

Colonel Wareing gave a quiet sigh of relief while listening to Richard in the background calling for John. With no response, Richard again shouted, "John!"

As Richard walked away from the house, he could hear clattering and banging, in the distance. Assuming he must be working, he put the phone back to his ear, telling the Colonel, "It sounds like John is busy."

The Colonel tactfully asked Richard to give him another call. Richard placed the portable phone down by his side, calling out once more, "John!"

He walked, shouting John's name again. Clanging and banging became louder, which Colonel Wareing could now hear on the phone. Richard walked into the barn, noticing his son working hard by heating and banging a horseshoe into shape for one of their horses. Inside the barn, it was like a hot furnace, which made Raven start to sweat with the intense heat. Raven moved the heated torch, placed the horseshoe onto the iron, and immediately started to bang it with the hammer once more.

Richard walked over, shouting, "John!"

Raven stopped banging, stood up straight, slowly turning around to face his father. Richard stared at John, noticing the sweat rolling down his face and chest, and then held his hand out to give John the phone. Graciously, John took the phone, slowly placing it to his ear and said, "Yo."

Colonel Wareing answered by asking, "Hello John, how are you?"

John replied in one word, "Good."

Richard moved around the barn starting to cool the horseshoe down John had just shaped, while trying to listen to what the military also wanted John for.

The Colonel had decided to have some small talk with John before telling him the news about Major Cairns. They would laugh and joke and then become serious. The Colonel moved the phone to his other ear, asking John, "Do you still want to call your next batch of Green Berets Unit Expendable?"

John heard the question while watching his father cool down the horseshoe, remembering when he had asked him a similar question once before. After thinking, he replied to the Colonel, "Yes sir."

Richard turned around feeling concerned, watching John aware the conversation was becoming officially military orientated. He waited eagerly at what John was about to say. John glimpsed at his father, while carrying onto say, "Sir, just has I have once told my father, I will now tell you the same. When I have trained a Unit called Expendable, that's it, I'm done, I will gracefully retire."

Richard, who was watching his son speak to the Colonel, produced a wry smile nodding his head agreeing with him after deciding to leave the military for good when he had trained Unit Expendable.

Colonel Wareing became stunned, replying with a sense of denial, "We have to let you go sometime."

John just gave a wry grin saying, "Yeah."

The Colonel asked, "What will you do?"

John looking across to his father, who was eagerly watching him, replied, "I'll live day by day."

Colonel Wareing picked up the cigar he had left in the ashtray earlier. He relit it, blowing smoke up to the ceiling, feeling disappointed that Raven had now decided to leave the military force for good. Listening to John's reply he said, "I guess you will John."

He paused for a few seconds, and then repeated himself by saying, "I guess you will."

John, suspecting the Colonel was disappointed with deciding to leave the force, wanted to humour him by saying, "I'll always be here if you want to come and visit, but no missions, and no more training anymore units. Unit Expendable is the last time."

Richard Raven heard the dogs barking causing him to move away from the workbench, and take notice that Sarah Jane had arrived home in her car. Going over to greet Sarah Jane, Richard patted John's arm feeling pleased with hearing what he had just told the Colonel.

Colonel Wareing replied to John's offer by saying, "Thanks John. I understand that I will always be welcome in your home. Who knows, Richard may even welcome me now with you deciding to leave the military."

John chuckled, nodding his head agreeing while watching his father walk back inside the barn with his daughter, Sarah Jane, replying, "He isn't that bad."

The Colonel gave a snigger, telling John that his father had received what he so dearly wanted, for him to leave the force and be with his family for the rest of his time. Listening to the Colonel, John gave a casual blink, wanting to remind him by saying, "It had to happen sometime."

"You're right." The Colonel replied. Holding his hand to his forehead, thinking of previous missions gone by with Raven, he became silent for a few seconds. Coming back to his senses, he decided to tell John about Major Cairns transfer from Kuwait and placed into a military compound in the United States.

Richard and Sarah Jane walked inside the barn, with the family's dogs following. The Alsatian, named Sadie, that Sarah had befriended and brought home from North Korea had once fought with Raven during his last mission, giving him new scars on his face. She walked over always appearing sheepishly at John. Holding the phone to his ear he gave a hard stare, but gave her a pat on the head when she then tried to lick his hand.

Sarah Jane turned to her grandfather to say, "When the North Korean soldiers captured me, you would never have known that my father had been in a ferocious fight with that dog."

As John spoke to the Colonel on the phone about Cairns, he overheard Sarah Jane speaking a little about his last mission. He placed his hand over the mouthpiece, turned to Sarah Jane and said sternly, "Sarah Jane, enough!"

Richard watched John's reaction, causing him to frown. John patted the dog's heads before turning away to lean on the workbench nearby. He carried on talking to the Colonel about Cairns, remembering how he had performed treason, and wanted him captured while on a mission in Iraq. Raven thought of what could happen if they ever came face-to-face again.

Colonel Wareing sighed, reluctantly deciding to tell Raven that Cairns did have a personal vendetta against him, stating that he will die. Hearing these words, Raven stared ahead of him, ignoring his father and daughter, thinking of the past, where his adrenalin started to flow. Managing to contain himself for the sake of his family, he replied to the Colonel, "He should never have been allowed to set foot on American soil again!"

Colonel Wareing placed his cigar down in the ashtray and replied, "I'm with you there all the way, but it isn't up to us."

John, interested in the result of Cairns' future, asked the Colonel, "What happens when Cairns is released from the military compound here in the U.S?"

Colonel Wareing sniggered in disbelief, replying to Raven's question, "Had Cairns shown a much better attitude in court, the military was going to offer him a new beginning."

John interrupted the Colonel by asking, "By doing what?"

Colonel Wareing replied, "I'm about to tell you. They were going to give him a new identity when they released him into civilian life."

John, feeling mystified asked, "You were going to do that after he had betrayed his own country?"

Colonel Wareing replied, "It was a serious choice, but when Cairns became provoked at the mention of your name, it was obvious that he needed time to cool down and think about how he does want to spend his future. In two years when possibly released from the U.S. military compound, he may have a different attitude about freedom, life, and even you."

John remained silent, wanting to study the conversation for a few seconds, while thinking back to the past. Sarah Jane, noticing that her father had become deep in thought, touched his arm tenderly, making her want to ask, "Dad, are you okay?"

Slowly, John moved his head to his side, and with his eyes wide open, looked down at Sarah Jane nodding yes. Richard blurted out aloud, "Only the military could make John react like that!"

Hearing his father speak like this made John turn away and carry on speaking with the Colonel. After some thought, he said to Colonel Wareing, "When Cairns arrives back in the U.S. I would like to visit him."

Colonel Wareing sat up in disbelief with the thought of having these two people meet again. Concerned he asked, "Are you sure John?"

Raven had already made his mind up and replied, "Make it happen!"

Colonel Wareing, detecting a sharp tone in Raven's voice, was about to reply to him, when somebody knocked on his office door. After placing his hand over the mouthpiece, he shouted, "Enter."

Captain Weller walked inside the office, walked across to the Colonel, aware that he was on the phone, and said in a low voice, "There is the file for Unit Expendable."

John heard her speak, suspecting that it was Captain Weller. With this, he asked the Colonel, "Can I speak with Debbie for a few moments?"

Colonel Wareing replied, "Sure."

He looked up at Captain Weller, holding the phone out for her to take. Accepting the phone, she asked the Colonel, "Who is it?"

Colonel Wareing replied, "John."

She placed her hair behind her ear and asked, "Hi John, how are you?"

John replied, "Good."

She glimpsed at the folder on Colonel Wareing's desk, while asking, "Are you ready for training your next group of elite soldiers?"

John gave a wry smirk, replying, "You know, I want to tell you before Colonel Wareing probably will. After I have accomplished my task with Unit Expendable, that's it, I'm done."

Captain Weller frowned causing her to ask with concern, "Done, what do you mean?"

Colonel Wareing, suspecting what they were speaking about said, "It's time to let our boy go."

Captain Weller heard what Colonel Wareing had just told her, but before John could reply to her, she asked, "Are you leaving the force for good?"

John looked at his father and daughter, who were watching and replied, "My time has finally come to say enough is enough."

Sarah Jane listening to her father speak didn't understand what he was talking about and with this, turned to her grandfather to ask, "What does Dad mean when he says he has had enough?"

Richard feeling pleased, turned to Sarah Jane, placed his arm around her and replied, "My boy has finally seen the light, and is now going to leave the military when he has trained his last unit."

Sarah Jane turned away from her grandfather, to look at her well-known father, producing a smile of content remembering the question she once asked him when they were standing at Tony Hindle's grave. Fearing for his life, she tried to make him promise that it wouldn't be one time too many, when at the time, he just couldn't make that promise. With now knowing her father was planning on leaving the force, meant that she had received the best Christmas present ever. She turned to her grandfather and said, "Soon it will be over."

Richard turned to her, placed his arm around her again replying, "I have to agree with you, Christmas has come early for us."

John noticing that Sarah Jane and his father appeared pleased about the news he was retiring from the military, carried on his conversation with Captain Weller. When she had finally accepted that he had made up his mind about wanting to leave the force, she decided to change the subject and speak to John about Christmas. She asked him, "Are you looking forward to Christmas?"

John replied, "Christmas is for kids!"

Sarah Jane heard John's response and shouted across, "Well, I still want a good present from you."

John glimpsed back, gave a wry smile, nodding his head agreeing to her.

One of the dogs went to sit beside Richard, which made him stroke her head and gently pat her. He looked across at John and said, "John, John!"

John stopped speaking with Captain Weller for a few seconds, held his hand over the mouthpiece and turned to his father asking, "What?"

Richard, feeling pleased replied, "Would Debbie like to come to our house for Christmas dinner?"

John became stunned at his father's question. Richard, chuckling carried onto say, "It's Christmas."

John moved his eyes away nodding his head agreeing, deciding to ask Captain Weller in a solemn voice, if she would like to have Christmas dinner with the family. Captain Weller, surprised by the question, replied, "We haven't eaten together since I stayed at your house, when we went out for a meal."

She gave a half-hearted laugh and carried on saying, "It was the time I wanted to ask you to take over the training of Unit Invincible from Colonel Lewis."

The mention of Colonel Lewis, brought memories back where he could never forget what he had helped him achieve over the years. The knowledge he had received, he was now able to pass onto soldiers he thought would become that elite Green Beret. With thinking about Colonel Lewis, Captain Weller asked, "Are you okay John?"

John just replied, "Yeah I'm okay. He's gone but never forgotten."

Captain Weller gave a smile, looked across to Colonel Wareing, who was sitting down at his desk, and said, "I agree John; he was always a tough act to follow but guess what? You did it! Do you remember when you questioned yourself if you had the ability to follow in his footsteps?"

John smirked as he thought back to when he had first decided to take over the training of Unit Invincible. Captain Weller carried on saying, "John you did well and our kids have done well with your guidance. You're going to be a tough act to follow when you're gone."

John modestly replied, "I'm sure you will choose my successor wisely. Anyway, back to my question, will you be visiting during the Christmas period?"

Captain Weller, knowing that she may have to go on a mission replied, "I'll see what I can do."

Trying to break some of the disappointment John was feeling, especially with his father wanting to invite her, she thought it may be a good idea to tell him of the news she had received earlier from her son? Thinking about John Weller, who was now travelling to see his girlfriend, Louise, she smiled and then said, "You know our son is going to propose to Louise while he is away on leave?"

For a few moments John paused, eventually asking, "Why would he want to go and do that?"

Captain Weller looked down at Colonel Wareing sitting at his desk starting to look at the file: Unit Expendable. Turning away from the Colonel, unsure about Raven's reply, she asked with concern, "Are you not happy for John, that he has found a decent young woman?"

John thought back to when he and Debbie were once together and replied, "The military and a married relationship are never going to work! One will have to succeed the other."

Captain Weller started to think back to when she and John were together and said sternly, "Tell me about it! They're not us though, give them a chance!"

John stared in front of him, wondering what the future now held for his son. Wisely, he chose to blank the conversation making Captain Weller say angrily, "That's it, same old John. You bottle up all of your own thoughts!"

John's eyes widened, as he looked down at the floor feeling hidden anger with hearing such a remark. Especially when many years had passed by before he found out the truth about the existence of his son and twin daughter.

Sarah Jane could see the angry stare in her father's eyes. She remembered it after seeing him in battle when he had come to rescue her from being held captive in North Korea. Knowing that his mood was beginning to swing rapidly, she walked away from her grandfather towards her father. Looking up towards him, she saw his hair hanging from the side down onto his face. Feeling concerned, she asked, "Are you okay Dad?"

John's eyes glared a little remembering the secret Captain Weller had kept from him for so long. Realising his daughter had asked him a question, he decided he didn't want to say anything else to Captain Weller, and gently held his arm out handing the phone to Sarah Jane. She held the phone to her ear and said, "Hello Mother, what have you said to Dad to make him become in such a bad mood?"

Captain Weller gave a half-hearted laugh, asking, "I've put him in a bad mood?"

Sarah Jane watched John and her grandfather who was following behind walk outside the barn when she said, "For him to react like that you must have hit a raw nerve, which must mean John and me, when he never knew we existed."

Captain Weller narrowed her eyes at the thought of that one secret she could never tell John, feeling guilty for all the lost years when he didn't see the twins grow up. Her eyes glazed over slightly as she replied, "At least you do now know who your father is, and you can still spend time with him. I can't change the past, and I do regret not telling you much sooner."

Captain Weller turned back around watching Colonel Wareing turning the pages over from the file called Unit Expendable. She saw a photo of Sarah Jane, making the Colonel look up at the Captain. Suspecting what his thoughts were, she asked Sarah Jane, "While we're on the subject of secrets, have you told your father that you and Hayley Pomfret are the female elite soldiers joining Unit Expendable?"

Sarah Jane thought for a few seconds, looked across at her father standing outside leaning on the fence, and replied, "I can't find the right time to tell him."

Captain Weller said, "Sounds familiar, there is never going to be a right time! Tell him before he arrives here for the induction. He always knew you wanted to be that elite soldier, like him. Don't make the same mistake I did."

Sarah Jane reluctantly nodded her head agreeing, saying, "You're right Mum, I will tell him."

Captain Weller glancing at the file once more on Colonel Wareing's desk replied, "Trust me, it's the right thing to do."

Sarah Jane agreed and said, "Okay Mum, hope to see you over Christmas."

Captain Weller replied, "Bye."

She then handed the phone back to Colonel Wareing asking, "When is John coming in order to do the induction for Unit Expendable?"

Colonel Wareing who had left the page opened on Sarah Jane's profile ignored Captain Weller's question and asked, "John doesn't yet know that your daughter is going to be a member of Unit Expendable?"

Captain Weller shook her head saying no, and then replied, "How do you tell him when Sarah Jane is the apple of his eye?"

Colonel Wareing closed the folder, looked up to Captain Weller and said, "I hope your daughter has the guts to tell John before the induction because if she hasn't, it could become an agitated meeting."

Captain Weller thinking about how John may react after Sarah Jane tells him the truth about becoming a member of Unit Expendable said, "So do I."

She then turned to walk out of Colonel Wareing's office, repeating herself by saying once more in a low voice, "So do I Colonel, so do I."

The Colonel gave a solemn look, watching her leave his office, then looked at the folder with the title, Unit Expendable and muttered, "You have a challenge this time John."

Being Honest

S arah Jane, after finishing her conversation with her mother, held the phone down by her side while walking across to her father and grandfather. The dogs trotted to her, making her bend down to pat one of them. Walking towards her father, she held one thought, *should I tell him the truth?* Richard saw Sarah Jane coming closer, and asked, "Is your Mother okay?"

Raven, leaning on the fence amid his own thoughts, turned, looked at his father and waited for Sarah Jane's reply. Sarah Jane paused before answering to her grandfather. She noticed her father's eyes were like daggers. Deciding to look away from him, she turned to her grandfather to reply, "She's okay."

Raven produced a disgusted look and turned to look straight ahead beyond the open fields. Sarah Jane thought about telling him about being a member of Unit Expendable. She came to the decision; there would never be a right time to tell him the truth. She handed the phone to Richard asking, "Will you leave Dad and me alone for a few minutes?"

John turned, frowning at his father, wondering what it might be that Sarah Jane wanted to tell him. Richard nodded, agreeing and slowly started to walk back to the house with a couple of the dogs following. Sadie, the dog that had befriended Sarah Jane, remained close by and sat beside her. John turned, leant back on the fence, and looked straight ahead once more. Sarah Jane came to stand next to her father, where she too also leaned against the fence, looking ahead, making her say, "It's a gorgeous view."

John's stony face started to mellow a little, making him nod his head agreeing. Sarah Jane looked up at her father, making her wonder, whether to tell him the truth. Her eyes glazed over a little, which made her look away sharply. John, casually turned his head, looking down at her and asked, "What's wrong?"

Sarah Jane knew the moment had come to do what is right? For a few seconds, she thought about the importance, slowly starting to say, "Dad, do you remember when I kept telling you that I wanted to come back to the force and be like you?"

John listened, thinking back to the many times she had said these words, which caused friction on many occasions. It was only when he was at the football game watching the Arizona Cardinals play the New York Giants, he could feel in his heart, he had to let her go and live her own life. Right or wrong, she had to find out for herself. Accepting the decision he had made then, he turned and rather than reply to her, he looked straight ahead once more waiting for whatever else Sarah Jane might have to say.

Sarah Jane, still looking up at her well-known father said, "Dad, I want you to be proud of me."

Raven replied immediately, "I already am."

Sarah Jane then asked, "What do I have to do to impress you?"

Raven, still gazing out at the vast open fields, gave a casual blink. Thinking back to *America in Conflict* he replied, "I'm already impressed with the way you handled yourself after your brother, and I freed you from that horrific ordeal you suffered in North Korea."

Sarah, thought back to that horrific time and said, "To be like you, this still isn't enough!"

John turned, looking down at her sternly and replied, "I've told you before, be anything but me!"

Sarah sighed, saying, "I am you. You're my own blood and through you, I live! I want you to be so proud of me."

Again John replied, "I already am!"

Sarah Jane, who knew she had to come to the main point of the conversation asked, "Dad, with my previous military record, my name was put forward to become an elite member of Unit Expendable."

John replied, "Yeah. I know."

Sarah Jane's face became puzzled making her ask, "You know? How do you know?"

John turned away again, looking straight ahead while replying, "I put your name forward, with Hayley Pomfret."

Sarah Jane, who wasn't expecting this reaction from her father asked, "Why?"

John without hesitation replied, "Because it's what you want, and I have finally accepted it where you have my blessing."

Sarah Jane smiled, came closer to her father, and gave him a hug. John knowing what the training involved said, "It's going to be a tough time for you!"

Sarah Jane said, "I will be ready for anything and everything!"

John just replied, "Yeah. You will need to be."

Sarah Jane felt relieved after a huge burden had been lifted from her shoulder when she had told her Dad the truth. What she failed to realise, was that her father had tested her, and she had passed the first test, by being honest.

Sarah Jane started to walk away, feeling much better about herself. John, watching shouted in a gentle voice, "Sarah Jane."

She turned to look back at her father, who said, "Thanks for telling me."

Sarah Jane produced a wry grin replying, "When you've trained Unit Expendable, at least I can stop saying to you, please don't make it one time too many."

John remembered the times she used to ask him to promise not to make it one time too many. He could not make such a promise because of whom he was. He knew that after training Unit Expendable, finally he could fulfil that promise. However, then would he?

Visiting Special Friends

$\mathcal{J}$ohn Weller was now travelling by train, looking forward to being able to see his girlfriend, Louise Mattinson, after having some long awaited leave. Occasionally, he would look up from the paper he was reading to glance out of the window wondering, what Louise's reply would be when he decides to propose to her. Turning back to read the paper, he couldn't help but notice other passengers on more than one occasion glancing at him. He suspected people hadn't forgotten the time he had brought the President of the United States home safely when she had been captured in North Korea. He turned over the page of the newspaper, immediately making him grin when he saw a picture of President Susan Berry next to the headline:

President Berry is Losing Patience with Iran!

With having a close acquaintance with President Berry, he started to read the article about the Iranian president refusing to co-operate with the American's. Concern was growing about large quantities of plutonium entering Iran at an alarming rate, making the western world feel uneasy and nervous. President Berry had warned the Iranian leader time after time that this influx of plutonium had to stop. After consultation with leaders from other countries that agreed to her actions, she had decided to place sanctions on Iran making them a country exile to the rest of the world.

John Weller-Raven looked up from the paper remembering the time he had brought President Berry home. Amid his own thoughts thinking back to America in conflict, he saw in the corner of his eye an old man sitting across from him, who recognised him on television after his heroic return from North Korea. The old man spoke to Weller-Raven by saying, "I speak for every person here in the United States. What you did when you brought President Berry home from North Korea, was a brave heroic action I doubt will never be repeated."

John narrowed his eyes slightly, said nothing, and just decided to listen to the old man saying, "Although we have many fine soldiers, I feel we do need more like you."

John, inwardly felt pleased knowing he was being noticed and starting to get the same recognition as his legendary father. Placing the newspaper down, he replied, "We're all the same because any one of us will fight to defend our country."

Other passengers sitting nearby on the train were watching and listening to the conversation, but chose to say nothing. Instead, they preferred to listen to the old man speaking with John, who they had accepted in their heart as an all new American hero. At times it brought smiles to their faces, when he gave modest replies to the old man.

The train started to slow down making John stand and collect his green bag that displayed his name in large green letters. If some people weren't sure who he was, they did after they saw his name displayed on his bag. John placed it over his shoulder, still looking down at the old man who had been sitting across from him. He placed out his hand, gently clasping his hand to shake it. The old man looked up to him and said, "Take care kid."

John releasing his grip from the old man nodded his head agreeing and replied, "Thank you."

He turned away to walk down the passageway noticing people again looking at him and beginning to whisper among themselves. Some of the passengers responded to him by nodding their head agreeing with him. In response to them all, John casually raised his hand as he walked on by to stand at the door waiting for the train to stop.

When the train entered the station, loud screeching sound of brakes was heard by people standing on the platform has it slowed down. John waited for the train to stop before opening the door. He stepped off the train, followed by other passengers onto the busy platform. John looked around, searching through the crowd that was rushing about the platform, but couldn't see his girlfriend, Louise, who had arranged to meet him. With this, he brought his mobile phone from his pocket, looked at the picture of them when they were sat in the BMW M3 together and started to type a message.

The guard blew his whistle, which made John look up and take notice of the train he had just stepped off rumble and slowly begin to move forward. He saw the old man at the window he had been speaking with on the train looking at him, sensing inwardly there was something unique about this soldier. In acknowledgment, John nodded his head graciously agreeing back to him. He then looked back down at his phone wanting to carry on typing his text, making Louise, who had just arrived, and who was now standing beside him, ask, "Who are you texting?"

John looked up to notice Louise, immediately giving her a big hug, and then kissed her on the lips. Feeling pleased to be able to see her once more he said, "It's good to see you again."

Louise, looking up at John replied, "It's good to see you again. I've missed you."

John, while listening to Louise's reply, deleted the message he had started to type, making her ask, "So, who were you texting?"

John, after placing his phone back in his pocket, looked at her, replying, "Who else but you. I was going to ask if you had arrived at the railway station."

Louise who was looking radiant, dressed casual in jeans, a woolly jumper, woolly hat, and designer coat turned to him and said, "I just went to that newsagent for a fizzy drink and a chocolate bar."

John looked across at the newsagent Louise had visited, recalling that he had once visited the same shop when he came close to conflict with a group of Asians. Keeping his thoughts about the past to himself, he became silent choosing to look away as he walked beside Louise. Becoming silent made Louise ask, "Do you want me to get you a Mars bar?"

Louise turned away from John to go back to the shop she had just visited. Reluctantly, John slowly followed, deciding to wait outside the shop for her to return.

The shopkeeper asked Louise had she forgotten something with her returning so soon. Louise brought out her purse from her handbag replying, "No, I'm buying these items for my boyfriend who is standing outside next to the shop window."

The shopkeeper looked, noticing John's green bag displaying his name, making him remember what he did when he last visited his shop. John turned to see if Louise was now coming out of the shop, but saw her talking to the shopkeeper while he was giving her change back to her. He too noticed John looking through the window and decided to walk outside with Louise, making John give a stare only his father could have given.

Louise gave the can of coke and Mars bar to John where he thanked her. John feeling the ice cool can of cola in his hand, pulled the ring back making it hiss from the gas escaping and take a gulp to quench his thirst. The shopkeeper now sure that it was John wanted to shake his hand, knowing what he had previously done for the United States. Louise, taking a sip of her cola watched the actions of the shopkeeper, which made her feel proud of him. John glanced in the corner of his eye at her and then held out his hand in return to shake the shopkeeper's hand. The shopkeeper patted his shoulder with his other hand and said, "The United States of America is proud of you."

John looked into the face of the shopkeeper remembering his previous battle and just replied modestly, "Thanks."

Louise frowned, but chose to say nothing at this point. The shopkeeper let go of John's hand and said, "I too am so proud of you because you brought President Berry back home safe."

Louise turned away looking down at the ground thinking back to when she saw the real John Weller-Raven show what he is capable of. John suspected this, thanked the shopkeeper, turned, gently held Louise's hand and started to walk away from the railway station, continuing to the car park. When they walked, they seemed subdued amid their own thoughts, remembering actions performed previously. John taking a sip of his cola squeezed Louise's hand tenderly, asking with concern, "Are you okay?"

Louise, who was looking straight ahead, was also having flashbacks from when John had killed a couple of terrorists at the football match, when the Arizona Cardinals played the New York Giants. She slowly turned, looked up to him and said, "Nobody would believe what you're capable of if I hadn't seen it with my own eyes."

Just like his father, John gave a sharp blink and then replied, "We've been over this many times Louise. I am what I am!"

Louise stopped walking for a moment, wanting to release her grip from John's hand, making him also stop in his stride and look down at her with concern. Bringing a smile to her face she said, "I fell in love with a kind gentle man, but you have a dark side, making you dangerous!"

John frowned, closed his eyes for a few seconds and replied in a low voice, "I know."

After replying to Louise, John wanted to change the subject. As they walked to Louise's car, he said, "Nice car."

Louise chuckled, replying, "I knew you would like it."

John starting to laugh, while thinking back to his sister's driving skills and said, "I hope you don't drive like Sarah Jane."

Louise pressed the key fob, unlocked the central locking on the car and pulled the door open. She jumped inside the Mini Cooper S, waiting for John to put his bag onto the backseat, and get in the passenger seat. After placing his seatbelt on, he saw Louise just looking at him, making him ask, "What?"

Louise smirked at him, replying, "Give me some credit; I don't drive like your sister. She is just a maniac!"

John narrowed his eyes slightly while Louise reversed the car out of the parking space and then defended his sister by saying, "She did have a good reason to drive the way she did."

Louise, now driving down the ramps to the ticket machine, pressed the switch for the door window to slide down. She braked slowly; stopping, picked her ticket up placed next to the gearstick, and positioned it into the ticket machine to make the arm rise automatically, so they could leave the car park correctly. Driving towards the give way sign, she stopped, looked both ways at the traffic, and replied to John by saying, "That day when you were involved in that chase with the terrorists, it was just downright idiotic!"

John looked at Louise as she drove, and replied, "It seemed right at the time, with the President of the United States being kidnapped."

Louise put her signal on to change lanes and started to move the steering wheel. After getting into the correct lane, she said with a concerned voice, "Yes, but you were nearly killed with the actions Sarah Jane performed."

John knew that Sarah Jane and Louise didn't get on together, making him respond to her last remark by saying, "I would have done the same for you."

Louise took her eye off the road for a couple of seconds, noticing John looking out of the passenger window watching people walk with bags that probably had Christmas presents for their loved ones. She smiled at him saying, "I know, you probably would."

She turned back, looking out of the front windscreen while driving straight on. Occasionally she would look in her mirror at the traffic following her while speaking with John. In the distance ahead of them, John saw a flower shop, which made him ask Louise if she could stop the car while he bought a bunch of flowers. Louise gave a smile, thinking the flowers were for her and said, "Sure."

She placed her signal on, pulling into the layby to park the car used for vans and trucks to load and unload goods for these shops. Louise asked, "Do you want me to come with you?"

John smiled at her, replying, "No, I will be just two ticks."

John opened the door, climbed out of the car and started to walk over to the flower shop. Louise leaned forward on the steering wheel, placing her hand on her forehead stroking her blonde hair, thinking to herself, how can a guy like that become the warrior she once saw. For her, at times it was difficult to accept. She watched John inside the shop handing the money over to the assistant making her grin thinking the flowers were for her. The assistant came back with two bunches of flowers. There was one bunch of red roses, and one bunch of yellow roses, making Louise frown, and suddenly realise about his good friend, Tony Hindle, who had now passed away.

Watching John inside the shop talking to the assistant made Louise think, he is a good and decent man. Deciding to think about all the positives John had, she became startled when a police officer tapped on her car window loudly. Turning to face what she could now see as the police, she sensibly pressed the button to lower the electric window. The police officer who was sitting on a motorbike next to where she was parked said to her in a stern voice, "You can't park there!"

Using her feminine charm, she gave a big beaming smile to the police officer sitting on the bike. He ignored her charm by starting to write out a parking ticket for her. Louise noticing his actions, decided to say, "I'm just waiting for my boyfriend over there in that shop."

The police officer looked over to the flower store, noticed John Weller inside chatting with the assistant, and then turned back to Louise and said, "You still cannot park there!"

Louise, who was slowly starting to become disgruntled replied, "I'll only be two minutes."

The police officer gave a stern look, as he gave her the parking ticket, and then said, "This area is for loading and unloading only. Move on!"

Becoming agitated, Louise threw the ticket down on the passenger seat and reluctantly turned the key to start the engine to begin moving away. John who was walking towards the shop door, noticed Louise driving away in the red and white Mini Cooper S, making him wonder had he done something wrong. The shop assistant also noticed the car had now driven away. With concern she asked, "Has she gone and left you?"

John turned back to face the shop assistant unsure of why Louise had driven away and replied, "I hope she hasn't jumped to the wrong conclusion with me speaking with you for so long."

The shop assistant gave a half-hearted laugh replying, "Men can't handle me!"

John glancing out through the window to see if Louise had circled, turned back to ask, "Oh, and why can men not handle you?"

Again she sniggered, while John glanced through the window once more for Louise. Looking at John, she said, "I know who you are. You're the soldier who brought our president back home safe."

John didn't seem interested in that comment because he had heard it all before. However, the shop assistant, whose name is Hayley, carried on saying, "This is my parent's business. I too am a soldier; I have to report for an induction when I will be joining another female elite soldier called Sarah Jane."

John turned around sharply to face her but chose to say nothing. Hayley moved from the counter to walk to the door to see if John's girlfriend was driving back to collect him, but there was still no sign of Louise. Hayley turned from the window to face John and said, "Well soldier boy. It looks as though she has left you!"

John opened the door, while looking back at Hayley, and in revenge, replied, "Unit Expendable is going to have it severe under John Raven!"

Hayley's face suddenly became serious with the comment John had just made to her. He then walked out, which made her look at him with concern, knowing he was right about the next unit to be trained under John Raven was Unit Expendable. She opened the door to follow him, asking, "Can I introduce myself properly?"

John, while staring at her said nothing. Hayley carried onto say, "I'm Hayley Pomfret, and I would like to get to know you better."

John, who again was looking for Louise's red Mini Cooper S, turned to stare at her, while taking notice of her long brunette hair and replied, "Perhaps you will someday."

He turned around to walk away, with Hayley just watching him. She shouted, "What about your girlfriend?"

John stopped walking, pointed to the necklace he was wearing, and replied, "She will know where I am, because it was where she gave me this necklace."

Holding two bunches of flowers in his hand, he thought perhaps it would best to walk to the cemetery, with knowing it wasn't too far away. This way he could pay his respects to the best friend he once had and has now so sadly lost.

Anger started showing on Louise's face, with having to drive through a one-way system, and be able to come back and meet John. She muttered about the asshole police officer that was up his own backside. Hayley, who was now walking back to the shop, saw the red Mini Cooper coming down the road, making her turn around to rush to the kerb side waving her arms to catch Louise's attention. Louise, startled, noticed her, pulling in sharply. She pressed the button to lower the passenger window to speak with the shop assistant. Hayley asked like she didn't already know, "Are you looking for John?"

Louise asked outright, "Where is he?"

Hayley smirked, replying, "You have a good man there."

Louise banged her hand on the steering wheel in frustration while asking again, "Where did he go?"

Hayley gave a chuckle, replying, "You don't know your man at all!"

Louise, by now was wishing she hadn't pulled up for John to be able to buy flowers, glared at the assistant and asked, "Will you tell me where he went to?"

Hayley gave a half-hearted laugh while noticing the police coming down the road once more. Cunningly, she decided to lean inside the passenger window to say, "He has gone to the place he received the necklace from you."

"Shit!" Louise replied. Becoming flustered, she checked her mirror, and started pulling out of the layby, immediately noticing the police had pulled up beside her once more. She contained her anger, turned to the police officer and said, "I'm sorry officer. I'm leaving now."

The police officer noticed the first parking ticket on the passenger seat, which made him say, "You don't seem to learn lady."

Again Louise said, "I'm sorry officer. I've only been here one minute."

The shop assistant feeling sorry for her, decided to speak to the police officer by saying, "Officer, she was just asking where her boyfriend had gone?"

The police officer chuckled as he replied to Hayley, "Why has she lost him?"

Louise, just about managing to keep her anger contained, was becoming annoyed with this situation. She turned away to look out of the front windscreen trying to contain her anger. Wisely, she moved her eyes to look at the officer once more, repeating herself by saying, "I'm sorry."

The police officer looked away from the shop assistant down at Louise inside the Mini Cooper S, aware she was acting sincere. After watching her reaction for a few seconds, he said, "Go, but watch where you park in the future!"

Louise placed the gearstick into first gear, revved the engine, and slowly started to pull away. She turned to watch Hayley walking back into the shop and muttered, "Bitch!"

With knowing where John has gone, she started to make her own way to the cemetery to meet with him once more.

Speeding down the road she saw him, in the distance, walking down a passage that created a shortcut to the cemetery. With missing him, it made her bang the steering wheel again with her hand in frustration. It meant she now had to drive to the main gate, and then drive through the cemetery at a slow speed until she arrived at Tony Hindle's grave.

John had arrived at the cemetery, walking briskly to Tony's grave, starting to recall some of the times he had spent with his best friend. The most horrific time was witnessing Tony having his kneecap drilled, when they were captured in Iraq while serving on a mission for their country. John crouched down gently placing the yellow roses onto his gravestone. Holding the other bunch of flowers that were for Louise, he looked up to the sky, feeling a cold shiver go through his body. With his right hand, he held the necklace holding the green emerald his father had once worn, remembering that it was Louise, who gave it to him where he was now standing. He looked away from the sky to where Tony had been laid to rest. Still missing him, he spoke in a low solemn voice, "You were right Tony, when you said that I would be free from my father's military shadow, I just wish you too could have seen it."

John felt a shiver go through his body once more, sensing his presence was nearby. He released the grip on his necklace and placed his hand to his forehead, while good and bad memories flashed by through his mind.

Louise had entered the cemetery, slowly driving to Tony's grave. In the distance, she saw John resting his hand on his forehead, suspecting he was reliving some of the memories he had shared with his best friend. Seeing John like this made her lose some of the anger, she had been feeling moments before. Her fringe fell down onto her forehead, where she too thought back to when he had been stood in that same position, just wishing his best friend was still alive. Louise stopped the car close by to Tony's grave, and for a few moments just watched John pay his respects to the friend he had so sadly lost. Watching him, brought memories flooding back to her of *America in Conflict* when John killed many terrorists, so she could be safe. What haunted her most was when John killed the first terrorist by slicing his throat with the knife his father had once owned. Blood spurt from the terrorist onto her face and clothes, something she could never forget, even if she wanted to. After this terrible day, when she felt shocked, weak, and in total disarray, memories of John's mother and father came flooding back into her mind. They kept telling her that if John had not performed the actions he had taken, she would without doubt have been killed. Remembering this thought that she was now alive, made her look across towards him in a solemn way. She opened the car door gently, climbed out of the car, closing it discreetly. John heard the car door close, which made him turn around and see that Louise was walking towards him. She raised her eyebrows to him, gave him a cheeky smile and casually raised her hand to notice him. John, feeling relieved that she had found him, walked across to her, placed his arms around her and gave her a big hug.

Louise, as she hugged John, stared at Tony's grave for a few seconds and then said to John, "You're the highlight of my day."

John pulled away from Louise feeling surprised, asking, "Isn't it me that is supposed to say that to you?"

Louise looked up to John, kissed him on the cheek and replied to him by saying, "I love you John, but I despise the soldier in you."

John, after listening to that remark felt hidden emotions because he now wondered what her reply would be when he finally decided to propose to her. Louise patted his arm tenderly and asked, "Are those for me?"

John looked at the red roses he was holding in his left hand, smiled, and gave them to her. Louise brought a huge smile to her face, kissed John on the lips and said, "Thank you."

John felt a shiver go through his body again. It was like Tony was nearby, making him turn and look once more at his grave. In a sombre voice, he said to Louise, "I miss him."

Louise held John's hand, clasping it tightly and then rested her head on John's shoulder, making him place his arm around her and say, "I love you."

Hearing those words made her look up to him and say, "I want to do something."

Slowly, she pulled away from John, wanting to walk closer to Tony's grave and crouch down. She pulled two roses from the bunch she had been given by John, crouched down and placed them down on top of the yellow roses. John watched, feeling proud of her. She looked up and said to John, "Red is for you and Tony, because I know you did spill your own blood."

John gave a sincere look, as he decided to walk a few paces closer and crouch down beside her. He placed his arm around her and said, "He's gone but not forgotten."

They placed their palms on Tony's grave, closed their eyes, and for a few minutes kept their own thoughts private to themselves. Louise opened her eyes first, put her hand on John's waist and said, "It's getting dark and colder. We should go now."

John opened his eyes noticing dusk was now appearing. In the distance, he saw people walking and dogs barking, which made him briefly recall the time his father had a ferocious fight with a dog that almost killed him when he was in North Korea. Louise stood up shivering, making John glimpse up to her. He turned to Tony's grave and said, "See you mate."

He stood up, which made Louise place her arm through his arm and say, "I'm getting cold."

John, remembering that this was the place Louise gave him the necklace he was now wearing, thought for a few seconds about whether to propose and give Louise the engagement ring he had bought for her. It seemed right and Tony would have approved. After all it was Tony, who helped John and Louise become together as a couple.

Louise rested her head on John's arm, making him turn and look down at her. For a few more seconds he thought to himself, it's now or never. In a solemn voice, he said, "Louise."

She looked up at him to reply, "Yes."

Still looking into her face, he paused for a few seconds before speaking. This made Louise ask, "John, what do you want?"

Still looking into her face, that had a cheeky grin and a dimple he could never forget, he so dearly wanted to propose to her. Fearing rejection, he declined for the sole reason of Louise saying earlier that although she loved him, she despised the soldier.

Rather concerned, Louise asked, "What do you want John?"

John looked up at the sky noticing it was almost dark. Averting from what he did want to ask, he replied, "It's getting dark, I think we should go now."

Louise, not knowing what John wanted to ask her, said, "I agree. It's getting cold too, let's go. We can come and visit Tony another day."

John had one final look at his long lost friend and then turned to walk back to the car with Louise, wanting to ask, "So where did you drive off to earlier?"

Louise pressed the key fob to unlock the doors, feeling in a much better mood and replied, "The police told me to move on."

John opened the passenger door, noticing the parking ticket on the seat, which made him grin. Louise saw him grinning and said, "It's not funny! If it hadn't been for that bit of fluff in the flower shop talking to you, I probably wouldn't have received this parking ticket!"

John remembered Hayley at the flower shop aware that he may meet with her again, with now knowing his father will be training her alongside his sister to become an elite member of Unit Expendable. Watching Louise start the engine, switch on the lights and begin to drive away out of the cemetery, tactfully, he chose not to tell Louise this information. Instead they spoke about Christmas that was almost up on them, Tony's partner, Rachel, and John's father, John Raven where Louise always had the utmost respect for him for helping her come through her trauma of *America in Conflict*.

Work Pressures

*J*ohn Raven was outside exercising the dogs feeling the brisk cold air hitting his face. Frost on the grass crunched when he walked to collect the ball and throw it for the dogs to chase. Each time he would pat the dog wanting to give the ball to him. Taking time-out with the dog's, made him repeat the action, having the dogs chase after the ball once more.

John's father, Richard, came outside with a hot drink and gave it to John. Knowing where he had to visit today, he asked, "John, when you have trained Unit Expendable, will it be the end?"

Not wanting to discuss the military, John narrowed his eyes while placing his cup down. He picked up the ball again making the dogs become more excited. Aware of his father's question, he threw the ball, which the dogs immediately gave chase for. Still thinking about his father's question, he turned to him replying, "After Unit Expendable. That's it! I'm done."

Richard, feeling pleased, said, "You don't know how happy that makes me feel."

Just as before, John threw the ball again for the dogs to chase as he spoke with his father. He picked up his cup, taking a sip of the warm coffee and said, "After Unit Expendable, nothing will want me to come back and fight anymore. I will have done it all, hoping that I have passed what I know onto America's finest soldiers."

As Richard listened to John speaking, he bent down to take the ball away from Roxy's mouth. Raven grinned as he watched his father tease the dogs with the ball. The dogs started to bark, making Richard throw the ball for the dogs to sprint after. Richard noticed Sarah Jane was now walking to her car smartly dressed in military uniform, which made him ask John, "Are you not taking Sarah Jane to attend the induction?"

John slowly moved his head producing a solemn look at his daughter, replying, "I don't want the other members to know I'm her father, and to be honest I don't even want her to be there!"

Richard grinned at John, saying, "Now you know how I feel! Today you have become me."

Sarah Jane gave a casual wave to her father and grandfather making them notice how well presented she looked for her induction. They raised their hand back to her in acknowledgment as John replied to his father, "Yes, and perhaps just like her brother, she has become me."

John took another sip of his coffee, glimpsed at his watch while taking notice of Sarah Jane driving her car out of the garage and down the long driveway. He turned to his father and said, "I should go too."

He took another gulp of the coffee, swallowed it, and handed the cup to his father to take back into the house. He walked over to his car, and climbed into the BMW X5. He placed the key into the ignition, to start the engine, deciding to leave it running to defrost the front windscreen. Waiting patiently for the windscreen to clear, his phone rang, which made him pull it out from his pocket and see who was ringing him. Noticing that it was his son wanting to contact him, he answered by saying, "Hello John."

John, who was in the kitchen at Louise's house helping to make breakfast replied, "Good luck today with the induction, and don't be too hard on my sister."

Raven gave a wry grin while watching the ice melting on the front windscreen and replied, "How could I be hard on your sister?"

Louise came into the kitchen and saw John speaking on the phone, which made her ask, "Who are you speaking to?"

John placed his hand over the mouthpiece, replying to her, "My father."

John took his hand away from the mouthpiece and answered his father by saying, "She has a lot to live up to and will no doubt want to become an elite member of Unit Expendable."

Raven lowered his head slightly, reluctantly replying, "No doubt! I do also recall you wanting to do the same thing when you were in training with Unit Invincible."

John thought back remembering the times he wanted to break free from his father's military shadow. Remaining quiet for a few seconds made Louise, standing nearby ask, "Are you okay?"

Glancing at her, he nodded his head agreeing while replying to his father, "Look after Sarah Jane, she is going to need you more than I did."

Raven placed the windscreen wipers on to clear the windscreen from the ice that had almost melted away and said, "Sarah Jane is tougher than you think, you haven't forgotten what happened in North Korea?"

John went to sit down, looked outside the window at the perfect winter picture he could see outside, leaving Louise to carry on making the breakfast and replied to his father by saying, "How could I forget North Korea?"

Raven said, "You never will! Trust me your sister will be okay, I'm there to make sure of that."

John agreed, hoping that when the training does start, she will persevere because his father will show no mercy even though she is his daughter.

Raven glanced at his watch once more to check the time, while recalling the news from Captain Weller that John was going to propose to Louise. He asked, "Have you popped the question yet?"

Listening to his father ask this question made John get up from the chair and walk over to Louise, hold her waist gently, kiss her cheek, and then make off outside with a bacon sandwich. He stood on the steps outside, paused for a few seconds thinking about what Louise had told him earlier. He gave a sigh replying to his father. "Louise does love me; I know that, but she despises the soldier in me."

Raven widened his eyes slightly, and said, "Trust me; you can't always have everything in life. Choose wisely."

Louise also came outside eating her bacon sandwich wanting to stand with John. When he saw her, he placed his arm around her asking, "Do I live for nothing and die for something or do I live for something and die for nothing?"

With hearing this question, Raven paused for a few seconds, and then replied to his son by saying, "Only you can answer this question."

Louise was feeling cold with only wearing her dressing gown. John, aware of this asked her to go back inside the house to the warmth. Taking another bite of her sandwich, she pulled away from John, to walk back inside the house with her father asking, "Who's he talking to on the phone?"

Louise, as she was eating another mouthful of her sandwich, replied, "His father, John Raven."

John turned to smile at Louise standing at the window, as he carried on speaking with his father. Raven decided to admit to his son by saying, "After Unit Expendable, my time with the military is done. I'm finished."

John was a little surprised by this remark, which made him ask, "You're leaving?"

Raven, noticing the ice had now melted on the hood, revved the engine slightly, flicked the windscreen wipers on again, and replied, "It's time. Anyway I have to meet these elite soldiers and perform an induction ready for when their training takes place after Christmas. Take care John, speak soon."

John disconnected by pressing the red button on his phone, and placed it back into his pocket, standing there trying to absorb his famous father is finally retiring from the military force.

Louise's father, Kirk, noticed John in deep thought, and asked Louise, "Is John okay? He looks as though he has something huge on his mind."

Louise looked out of the window once more to see John standing on the same steps she had once been sat on, when she admitted for the first time to her father, that she did indeed love him. At the time, all she could think about was John, alone, aboard Air Force One fighting for his country and wanting to protect the President of the United States, wondering whether she would ever see him again. To see John on those same steps in deep thought made her go outside and want to ask, "What's the matter John?"

He turned to face Louise, trying to disguise the truth by replying, "Nothing at all."

Louise knew when John wasn't telling the truth and said, "You're a weary liar, what's the matter?"

John turned back around facing the driveway, and in a sombre voice, replied, "My father is going to retire from the U.S. military after training Unit Expendable."

Louise smiled with glee as she started walking closer to stand beside him and asked, "Isn't this good?"

John, thinking of his legendary father replied, "I can't imagine my father not being involved with the military anymore."

Louise went to place her hand on John's arm and say, "Perhaps he has now accepted his time has come to call it a day. On his last mission that you shared with him, he so nearly didn't make it home."

John lowered his head, starting to frown, knowing that Louise was right about the fact that he did almost die. To have survived his last battle was a miracle to say the least. Deciding not to linger, aware that his father will no longer be on the force soon, he raised his head, turned to face Louise and asked her, "What would you like to do today?"

Being a woman and wanting to do something women like to do, she replied, "We could go for Christmas shopping."

John replied, "Okay, but I would also like to visit Rachel after we have been shopping."

Louise looked up at John starry eyed, kissed him, and said, "I will go and get ready."

She hurried inside leaving John to stand there on the steps with that one thought that his father has now decided to call it a day, and retire from the U.S. military. Knowing this, John pulled the phone from his pocket, scrolled through his contact list, selected his father, and pressed dial. He placed the phone to his ear, waiting patiently for him to answer. Louise came back into the kitchen after having a quick shower and saw John holding the phone to his ear, making her open the door discreetly, and shout, "John! Are you going to get ready?"

John turned around to see Louise with a towel wrapped around her hair and a bath towel wrapped around her body. Waiting for his father to answer the phone, he replied to Louise, "I won't be long; I will probably be ready before you."

Raven, who was now driving to the U.S. military base, used the hands free kit to answer the phone by saying, "Hello John."

The traffic lights changed to red making Raven have to brake and stop. He glanced at his watch again to check the time while listening to his son reply, "Father, with wanting to propose to Louise, should I leave the U.S. military too?"

Raven, listening to the radio playing low in the background, studied John's question while waiting for the lights to turn green. He came to the conclusion that his reply had to be honest, which made him reply in a solemn voice, "Do what your instincts tell you."

The lights changed to green making Raven rev the engine and start to pull away quickly. Driving with the flow of traffic, he listened to his son speaking to him. Raven, on several occasions repeated himself, telling John to do what his instincts told him. Although John heard, it took a few times for this remark to register. When it finally did, he asked, "How will I know?"

Raven gave a casual blink, looked straight ahead out of the front windscreen as he drove and briefly thought about his past for a few seconds, later replying, "You will know because it will feel right."

Weller walked down the steps to stand on the ground and said, "I hope when the time comes, I do make the right choice."

Raven heard Louise calling John's name, detecting that she had become annoyed that he hadn't yet gotten ready. Realising this, he said, "Stop dwelling! Enjoy your time with Louise, and I will see you both in a few days when you visit our house."

John turned around, raised his hand to Louise to apologise, quickly replying to his father. "Louise is standing on the steps with her arms folded, and it looks as though I'm going to be told off."

Raven chuckled saying, "Good luck."

He disconnected the call using the hands free kit, and carried on driving to the U.S. military base listening to the radio with a Christmas song fading out. When the DJ spoke, he announced to listeners that they were going to the newsroom for the latest update. The newscaster mentioned President Berry, announcing her plans with Iran, who is now becoming a nuclear threat to the western world. As Raven approached more traffic lights, he listened intensely to the report, until his phone rang once more, making him say, "Not again!"

He pressed the button on his hands free kit and answered, "Raven."

Captain Weller, rather concerned, asked, "Where are you? You're late!"

Raven watched the traffic lights turn green, revved the engine and pulled away once more, and replied to Captain Weller, "I'm turning into the U.S. military base now."

He pulled up at the soldier on patrol inside the cabin, asking him to raise the barrier, so he could drive inside the

U.S. base and park his car. Raven climbed out of his car, glancing around the U.S. military base, knowing the end was now near. From the passenger seat, he picked up his headband, looking at it for a few seconds while caressing it, remembering who had given it to him.

Colonel Wareing, who was standing at the window, called Captain Weller over and said, "Look at Raven, he isn't in uniform, what's he playing at?"

Raven, holding the headband once worn by a samurai decided to wrap it around his head and tie it tightly. Colonel Wareing narrowed his eyes, suspecting that Raven was missing the warzone. Captain Weller watched Raven turnaround, noticing that he was unshaven and appeared menacing as he walked to the main building. Colonel Wareing didn't look too happy, with now knowing that Raven hadn't made any effort to wear his military uniform. He watched him outside, speak with some of the soldiers he had trained, when no matter what he wore, they always treated him with the utmost respect.

Raven trotted up the steps, walked through the door, and saw one of the few remaining members of Unit Invincible coming towards him. Ricky Stevens became elated when he saw John Raven, making him want to rush to greet him and shake his hand. Raven after shaking his hand, well aware that he was the real reason for coming back into combat to help him regain his confidence as a pilot, asked, "Are you okay Ricky?"

Stevens, feeling pleased to be able to see his mentor once more, nodded yes, understanding what Raven's question was about. With this, he glanced and saw the U.S. military administrative personnel working close by, was also watching Raven and speaking among themselves about his appearance. Stevens didn't hesitate any longer, because he said to Raven, "I never had the chance to say thanks for what you did, helping me to regain my confidence when Lee Ashworth was killed in extreme circumstances. I'm just sorry I got you into another warzone."

Raven chuckled slightly, replying, "Don't be sorry. I'm still here, and besides, we still also have an excellent pilot our country can be proud of."

Stevens reluctantly agreed with Raven, by saying, "Thanks."

Raven, feeling proud of Stevens, told him that he should be ready for anything and give everything if his country ever needed him. Stevens agreed, promising him that he would never let him down. Raven produced a menacing stare, and then patted the top of his arm in appreciation after hearing that remark.

Captain Weller had stormed out of Colonel Wareing's office holding a frosty face, hurrying to meet Raven, who was chatting with a member from Unit Invincible. She called out, "John!"

While John was speaking with Stevens, he paused, looked to his side and saw Captain Weller rushing to him, with what seemed a little attitude. Stevens also noticed Captain Weller, where she appeared rather annoyed, which made him say to Raven, "I had better go. This doesn't look too good."

Raven understood Stevens' remark, nodding his head agreeing. As he watched him walk by, Raven patted him on his back and said, "See you around kid."

Captain Weller, who was holding a face of fury, slapped John's arm making some of the U.S. military personnel place their faces down and grin among themselves. She asked, "What are you playing at?"

Raven ignored her by starting to walk, deciding to remain silent. Captain Weller became more frustrated, asking again, "John, just what are you doing? I've seen you dressed like this when you have returned from warzones!"

Raven's eyes moved to the left, piercing her as they carried on walking straight ahead down the long corridor, while approaching Colonel Wareing's office. Just as before, John remained silent, refusing to speak to Captain Weller. The silence from John made Captain Weller say, "Colonel Wareing will not like the way you have presented yourself, which to be honest you do look a disgrace!"

Hearing these words, Raven stopped walking, narrowed his eyes in anger and stared hard at Captain Weller, still choosing to say nothing. Feeling disgusted at what she had just said, he turned around to start walking in the opposite direction back towards the main door. Captain Weller placed her hand to her forehead wondering what she had brought on herself. It would have been easier to let Colonel Wareing lecture Raven about how he had presented himself. Watching Raven walk further away, she called out, "John!"

Military personnel looked on, where she immediately told them to carry on with their administrative duties. She then called out again, "John!"

John didn't respond to her call, which made her trot after him quickly. John heard the sound of her footsteps coming closer, making his stride become much slower. He turned immediately scowling at Captain Weller, waiting to hear what she had to say. Looking up at John, she said in a solemn voice, "I'm sorry for what I just said, about you being a disgrace."

Raven, feeling annoyed, glared into the face of Captain Weller, before replying, "Who the fuck are you to lecture me and call me a disgrace, when you know the warzones I've experienced!"

Captain Weller lowered her head down in shame, replying once more, "Sorry."

Still feeling annoyed, Raven turned back, saying to the Captain, "Come on! Let's go and see Wareing!"

Captain Weller stood there just watching Raven for a few seconds walk back in the direction of Colonel Wareing's office wondering if Raven was now losing the respect for the military. She trotted to catch up with him, wanting to say once again, "I'm sorry."

Raven, this time glimpsed in the corner of his right eye at her and with a disgruntled voice, replied, "Save it!"

Captain Weller raised her eyebrows slightly and carried on the conversation by saying, "But I . . ."

Raven, still annoyed, interrupted with what she wanted to say. In a stern voice, he replied, "Why don't you just shut your arrogant mouth for once, and let me do it my way!"

Not feeling too impressed with the way she had been spoken to, Captain Weller walked a little quicker to be in front of Raven. She pointed her finger at him, replying to his outburst, by sarcastically saying, "Who do you think you are, Frank Sinatra?"

Raven didn't reply, he chose just to walk behind Captain Weller, where the least said the better it was for everyone. Captain Weller arrived at Colonel Wareing's office, knocked on the door left open, and walked straight inside making Colonel Wareing look with a face of disappointment and stand. John Raven followed in behind her, making the Colonel shake his head in disagreement while placing his cigar down into the ashtray, and then raise his arm and ask Raven, "What are you playing at?"

Captain Weller went to stand at the front of Colonel Wareing's desk feeling disappointed. Her disagreement made her place her head down, because it reminded her of when Colonel Wareing and the late Colonel Lewis had furious arguments in this same room. Raven gave a menacing stare at Captain Weller, not wanting to forget her words mentioned earlier, "You're a disgrace!" as long as he lived. He then slowly turned to face Colonel Wareing, and asked, "What?"

Detecting an attitude, Colonel Wareing asked, "You haven't forgotten how to salute an officer, have you?"

Raven remained silent, moved his eyes focusing them on his own mentor, the picture of Colonel Lewis hanging on the wall behind Colonel Wareing's desk. Slowly, he raised his arm to salute Colonel Wareing as requested.

Colonel Wareing looked at Raven, picked up the file called Unit Expendable and threw it at him, making some of the sheets separate and land onto the floor. Colonel Wareing, glaring hard at Raven with how he had presented himself, said, "Pick them up!"

Raven, holding a face of discontent, slowly crouched down to pick up the sheets of paper holding information about members from Unit Expendable. Colonel Wareing, feeling disappointed said, "I never agreed with Colonel Lewis's last unit, when he decided to call it Unit Invincible.

It's as though history is repeating itself, because I'm not happy with you calling what would be your final batch of elite soldiers, called Unit Expendable!"

Still crouched down holding some of the papers, Raven looked up and replied, "Sir. Trust me."

Captain Weller watched Raven crouched picking the sheets of paper up and then listened to Colonel Wareing say, "You just had to go to one step further didn't you?"

Raven stood up, held the file beside him and asked, "What do you mean?"

Colonel Wareing stared back at Raven, replying in a disgruntled voice, "The title Unit Expendable places pressure on these elite soldiers, even before they have done anything!"

"That's how I want it!" Raven replied.

Colonel Wareing said, "Keep the name, and you will regret it!"

Raven shook his head from side to side in disagreement replying, "Sir. They will be my finest batch of elite Green Berets. Trust me!"

Captain Weller entered the conversation wanting to ask Raven, "How can we trust you, when you have walked in here looking almost the same way you did when you fought in North Korea?"

Raven, aware of Captain Weller's opinion, turned to her and said, "You've already said too much!"

Colonel Wareing started to frown as he glanced at her leaning on the front of his desk. He then watched Raven throw the file, Unit Expendable at her, which just as before, some of the sheets separated and fell to the floor, making Captain Weller crouch down to pick them up. She saw her daughter Sarah Jane, wondering if this was the cause of Raven's strange behaviour. Feeling annoyed, she held Sarah Jane's profile, showing him her details, and asked, "Is she the reason you're in such a foul mood? After all you never wanted her to come back to the military!"

Raven studied the picture of Sarah Jane, admitting that he had put her name forward because he knew it was what his daughter so dearly wanted, hoping that she could impress her mother and most of all, him. Captain Weller lowered her head dwelling on Raven's last remark, as she carried on picking up the sheets of paper and placed them back into the file. She stood up, placed the file down onto Colonel Wareing's desk, while briefly looking at the pictures of Colonel Lewis and John Raven hanging on the wall. Colonel Wareing noticed what she was looking at, and turned to bring the picture of John Raven from the wall and held it in front of him, while asking Raven, "Do you see anything different here?"

John knew what the Colonel meant, and just as before replied, "Sir, trust me."

Colonel Wareing, who was feeling bad tempered, threw the picture to the other side of the office, creating an almighty crash that was heard by the military personnel outside. Broken glass scattered around the office. Captain Weller appeared shocked with the Colonel's actions. Raven, although feeling annoyed on the inside, contained himself on the outside and just turned to the military personnel entering Colonel Wareing's office, aware that they were about to clean up the mess, which made him say, "Leave it!"

Colonel Wareing frowned at Raven's instruction. Raven suspected his reaction would be of confusion, making him, while watching the military personnel's movements, put his hand up at the Colonel. Captain Weller, also watching Raven's actions, looked at the Colonel in amazement, and then listened to Raven say, "Go and bring the members of Unit Expendable!"

The military personnel looked at the Colonel, where he nodded his head in agreement. One of the military personnel had already started to sweep the glass up making Raven walk across to grab her hand and say, "I told you to leave it!"

He then made her drop what she had just swept up and stood on the broken glass to make the pieces become much smaller.

Colonel Wareing and Captain Weller were staring hard at Raven's strange behaviour has he scattered the glass. Raven saw them watching, but carried on suspecting that this is where Unit Expendable would be standing when they entered Colonel Wareing's office.

Colonel Wareing, feeling disappointment shook his head from side to side in disbelief. Captain Weller, who knew she had already said too much earlier, decided to keep her thoughts to herself. Raven turned to them saying, "Trust me."

Colonel Wareing, in a sombre voice replied, "Today a legend just died."

Raven's eyes pierced Colonel Wareing and Captain Weller, and repeated himself by saying, "Trust me."

Induction

*C*olonel Wareing was still staring hard at John Raven as he moved away from his desk to see if the military personnel were bringing members of Unit Expendable to his office. Walking up the corridor towards the Colonel standing outside his office, he saw Alison Colquhoun, escorting the next batch of elite soldiers to him. Captain Weller gave a snide look at Raven as she went past him to join the Colonel and welcome Unit Expendable. Raven, standing there with his arms down by his side, glanced once more at the picture of his mentor, Colonel Lewis, wishing he had been here today to support him in his latest task.

As Alison came closer to the Colonel, she stopped to salute him. All the elite soldiers standing behind her repeated the same action, which he told them all to stand at ease. He thanked Alison for bringing the soldiers and then asked her to bring out the file, Operation Gulf Warrior, and place it onto his desk. She totally understood, saluted, and left the Colonel, nodding her head noticing Captain Weller.

Colonel Wareing glimpsed inside his office to see Raven standing there with his arms down by his side, suspecting he was amid his own thoughts as he looked at the picture of Colonel Lewis hanging on the wall. Captain Weller went back inside the office and said to John, "Turn around and be ready to greet Unit Expendable!"

Raven ignored her, deciding to remain standing there in the same position, enraging the Captain, which made her ask, "John, did you hear me?"

John moved his eyes, piercing her with them; making her look away and watch the eight soldiers walk in one by one and stand in a line next to the broken glass. Colonel Wareing came inside the office, closed the door, deciding to keep the friction from the heated debate that occurred moments before hidden from the new batch of elite soldiers. He walked across the room to John saying, "John, here is Unit Expendable."

One of the soldiers spoke, which everybody in the room heard him say, "Who's the American bum stood there?"

Colonel Wareing looked at Raven, who by now had narrowed his eyes feeling anger. Holding his tongue, he turned around to face the soldiers making them gasp, to see that it was indeed, John Raven. Colonel Wareing went to stand by Captain Weller and said, "They're all yours John."

Raven, not wanting to speak with the officers, nodded his head once agreeing, while walking closer to the soldiers. With his menacing appearance, the soldiers became intimidated as he slowly walked down the line making eye contact with every member of Unit Expendable. Captain Weller was watching him closely has he approached the two women, who were standing together at the end of the line. Raven's expression didn't change when he approached Sarah Jane, who was his own blood and his daughter. She remained professional, understanding her legendary father was now in work mode. Walking by her, he stared at the woman on the end of the line, where she asked, "Do you know John Weller?"

Sarah Jane moved her eyes to look at her new colleague, and then watched her father's reaction to the question about her brother. Raven glared at her with his eyes piercing her, and with a strong voice asked, "Did I ask you to speak?"

Hayley, feeling embarrassed replied "No."

Raven in a stern voice asked, "No what?"

Hayley's eyes glazed over with noticing how overpowering Raven can be, and replied, "No sir!"

One of the soldiers standing in the line spoke up saying, "Leave the chick alone. Pick on somebody your own size!"

Captain Weller watched Raven turn his head slowly, giving a look that could kill to the soldier who had just spoken out of turn, and who was also glaring back at him. Raven decided not to say anything to the outspoken soldier yet. Instead, he chose to remain standing in front of Hayley, turning to face her softening his look. Sarah Jane watching events closely, could see her father emerging from the beast who lies within him.

Captain Weller, while watching Raven, spoke in a low voice to the Colonel standing next to her saying, "Something tells me that history is about to repeat itself here."

Colonel Wareing, who was also keeping a watchful eye on Raven, agreed with Captain Weller, replying, "It sure is going to be interesting."

Raven looking down at the female soldier, asked her name. The soldier who had spoken out earlier started to kick away the glass, making Raven look away from Hayley and ask the soldier further down the line, "Did I tell you to do that?"

The soldier became embarrassed as he watched Raven briskly walk to him and slide the glass with his foot back to where it had been originally left. Colonel Wareing frowned and would intervene if need be, but for now chose to let Raven, has done previously, to do it his way. Raven stared at the soldier, knowing it was him who had spoken out of turn earlier. Without saying a word, the soldier felt intimidated just by his sheer presence. Raven walked back to the end of the line asking the first female soldier, "What's your name?"

She looked up at Raven, standing to attention, replying, "Hayley Pomfret, sir."

Raven placed his hand out to shake her hand, with her taking notice of the headband he was wearing when she clasped his hand. Raven said to her, "Welcome to Unit Expendable. Do you think you can go the distance?"

The soldier who had spoken out earlier decided to speak out of turn again, saying, "She's a stupid woman who shouldn't be here!"

Colonel Wareing and Captain Weller watched at what John's reaction would be to this sudden outburst. He remained cool choosing to ignore the latest outburst from what he suspected has the possibility of a bad apple in the group.

Captain Weller, while still watching Raven, said to the Colonel, "If I know John, he won't let him get away with that."

Colonel Wareing put his finger to his mouth replying, "I've seen this before with Unit Invincible, when Colonel Lewis was in command."

Captain Weller turned to face the Colonel, listening to him carry on saying, "We know what happened then don't we?"

Captain Weller didn't answer. She turned back to watch Raven shaking hands with Sarah Jane, who unknown to her colleagues was his and Captain Weller's daughter. Raven, slowly moved down the line to the next person asking, "What's your name?"

The soldier taking notice of Raven's appearance stood to attention, saluted, replying, "Lieutenant Peter Parr."

Raven, paused by just staring into the face of Parr for a few seconds, and then asked, "Were you born to lead?"

Lieutenant Parr looked straight back into the face of Raven, replying, "It's an honour to be a part of Unit Expendable and be able to help in leading an elite unit of Green Berets."

Raven almost produced a wry smile as he placed his hand out, wanting to shake hands with him, while tapping his shoulder with his opposite hand. Pulling his hand away he said, "It's going to be tough, but Unit Expendable will be the best!"

Hayley, who had just met Raven, immediately thought back to the time she had met John Weller in her parent's flower shop recalling him saying that Unit Expendable would have it severe under John Raven. It was now she started realising for sure, when this was only the induction.

Sarah Jane moved her eyes, watching her father move further down the line shaking hands with Lee Seager, who was proud to be a member of Unit Expendable. Raven moved his head slightly to look at the next member in line, noticing that standing next to him was the troublemaker, who had been outspoken on many occasions. Raven, moved up to the next person making him feel intimidated. Before Raven could ask him his name, the soldier, standing to attention said, "It's an honour sir!"

Raven watched the soldier and frowned. There was a knock at the door, which made Colonel Wareing move, while saying to Raven, "Hang on, because I need to hear what this soldier has to say."

As he waited to resume with the introductions, Raven stared at the outspoken soldier who was next in line. Colonel Wareing was heard by everyone in the room saying thank you to Alison Colquhoun. He walked back and placed the file, Operation Gulf Warrior onto his desk, and then turned to Raven to say, "Carry on John."

Raven, refusing to acknowledge the Colonel, slowly moved his eyes away from the outspoken soldier, wanting to focus back onto the soldier who had just mentioned that it was an honour. Raven asked in a stern voice, "An honour to be in Unit Expendable?"

The soldier replied, "Yes, and be able to meet the same person, the legendary soldier, who gave my mother a photograph many years ago when you fought for our country with my brother."

Colonel Wareing and Captain Weller watching closely became intrigued with this soldier's comment, wondering what Raven's reaction would be. Remaining calm, Raven thought back to when he had handed a photograph to his friend's mother when she had told him that he had died of cancer. He glanced across to the Captain making the soldier say, "You had a personal war shortly after when a police officer tried to run you out of town."

Raven raised his eyes to look at him aware the soldier speaking was the small boy his mother had sent inside when she spoke with him many years ago. Captain Weller moved away from the desk and went to the soldier, politely holding her hand out, asking, "May I?"

The soldier placed his hand out offering the picture to the Captain. The outspoken soldier standing next to him also put his hand out, clasped the picture from the Captain's hand, making her gasp a little in shock. He looked at the photo, waved his arm about and asked "What's this trash?"

Raven, who was already feeling annoyed, pulled his knife out of its holster with his right hand and held it tight, while grabbing the soldier by his neck with his left hand. Captain Weller, feeling concerned, said, "John!"

Colonel Wareing, watching closely, also said, "Raven, you're out of order!"

Sarah Jane, standing further down the line watching intensely, listened to her father saying, "You and I have a fucking problem!"

The outspoken soldier replied, "Fuck you!"

Raven dragged the soldier forward with him staring wide-eyed into Raven's face. Raven with his lip hanging down pushed him towards the door, placed his knife away, opened the door and threw him outside into the corridor saying sternly, "Fuck off! I have no time for idiots like you!"

The soldier landed badly on the floor. Raven bent down to take the photo from his hand and went back inside the office. Colonel Wareing stormed across the office, past Raven, and saw the soldier getting up, starting to limp down the corridor, and shouted, "Williams! Get back here now!"

Williams stopped, looked at the Colonel for a few seconds, but chose to ignore him by carrying on walking away from him. Colonel Wareing shouted again, "Williams!"

He stopped in his stride, turned around noticing the Colonel's stern face. Wisely, he chose to walk back to the Colonel, making him look inside his office at Raven and then close the door. The Colonel after closing the door said to Williams, "You and I ought to have a little chat in Captain Weller's office. Follow me!"

Inside the Colonel's office, Raven studied the photo remembering his friend and colleague from Unit Storm, and the time the police drew first blood against him. Slowly, he raised his head, placed his hand out and gracefully gave the photo back to the soldier, saying, "It was an honour to have fought with your brother."

Sarah Jane felt compelled to move slightly wanting to look at the photo that showed a much younger version of her father. Raven saw that she had moved out of position and glared at her. Understanding her father, wisely she went back to stand next to Hayley, saying in a quiet voice, "He's a bastard!"

Raven, who had heard Sarah Jane's comment, stopped speaking and looked back down the line glaring at both women. Captain Weller, fearing the worst for their daughter, with knowing what Raven can be like said, "Remember John, it's only their induction."

Raven turned his head to face Captain Weller, and then still holding a stern face, turned back to face both women saying, "I want you to do twenty five press ups now!"

Hayley, feeling rather stunned said, "I haven't done anything!"

Raven replied, "You smirked! That's fifty press ups now!"

Sarah Jane said, "There is glass on the floor."

Raven started coming closer to the women, which made Sarah Jane look at her mother, Captain Weller, shaking her head from side to side. Raven stood in front of the women and said, "That has now been raised to seventy press ups! In war, there is no dress rehearsal, you have to be ready for anything and give everything and learn there is no pain!"

Hayley and Sarah Jane looked at each other in dismay, which made Raven say, "Unless you begin doing those press ups in the next ten seconds, I will raise it to one hundred!"

Sarah Jane and Hayley reluctantly crouched down, placed themselves into position and started doing the press ups. Raven, looking down on them, noticed blood starting to run from their hands resting on the broken glass. In a stern voice, he said, "Here, I am a bastard!"

Captain Weller, who had walked across the office to stand next to the women, was counting the press ups Raven had ordered. Raven saw the blood running down their hands, making Captain Weller say, "John, this is madness!"

Raven, who was also counting the press ups the women were doing replied, "They do seventy five press ups no matter what their hands look like!"

Captain Weller gave a look of disgust at Raven, knowing he was inflicting a mild dose of torture on them. He turned away to walk down the line and carry on speaking with the soldier who had shown him the photograph. He glanced at the women to make sure they were still doing their press ups. Captain Weller, who was counting, gave a prolonged blink, deciding to look away in disgust. Raven ignored the Captain's reaction by turning to face the soldier asking, "I now know your surname is Templeton with fighting in battle with your brother, but what is your first name?"

The soldier glimpsed at Hayley and Sarah Jane still doing press ups noticing the blood on their hands. Raven aware of whom he was, decided not to place any pressure on him. Instead, he just waited for a few seconds for a reply. When Templeton looked back at Raven, he replied, "My name is Scott Templeton sir."

Raven shook his hand, while giving him a friendly pat on his shoulder with his other hand. Templeton, while letting go of Raven's hand said, "Sir, do you recall my brother doing that same exercise many years ago, when Colonel Lewis had trained them?"

Before answering Templeton's question, he looked down the line at the women, and moved his fingers into his palm twice at Captain Weller, signalling for them to stop and stand up. Raven turned back to face Templeton, recalling that moment he had just mentioned and said, "To be the best, you have to be trained by the best! Your brother and I were trained by the best!"

Raven then patted Templeton's shoulder again before continuing onto the next elite member of Unit Expendable. He looked back down the line at the women, aware that blood was dripping onto the floor. Feeling undeterred, he moved onto the next soldier asking, "What's your name?"

The elite soldier standing to attention replied, "Russell Lerner, sir."

Raven chatted for a few minutes with Lerner, and made him welcome to Unit Expendable. Colonel Wareing opened his office door to walk back inside with Williams, making Raven turn and say, "He's had his chance!"

Colonel Wareing noticed the blood on Sarah Jane's and Hayley's hands and said in a disgruntled voice, "For Christ's sake, John!"

Williams, who had received a severe lecture from Colonel Wareing apologised for his behaviour to Raven. For a few seconds Raven thought, making the Colonel say, "I've given him another chance because he reminds me of what John Weller was like when Unit Invincible was being trained. He also reminds me of one of the best soldiers I've come to know and who also behaved with a cocky attitude in his younger days. You! They became formidable soldiers. I would like you to consider giving Williams another chance."

Raven stood there silent thinking. There was another knock at the door, which made Colonel Wareing look at Captain Weller, for her to walk over and open it. Alison Colquhoun walked inside with another soldier telling the Colonel, John Radford had now arrived. Raven turned around with the headband hanging onto his shoulder feeling annoyed that a soldier had arrived late. The Colonel saw Raven's reaction and told Radford to stand next to Williams.

Raven, before moving onto the next person thought about the Colonel's comment he had just made. He looked back at the women, aware that they were both standing in line focused. He glimpsed down at their hands ignoring that blood still dripping onto the floor. Casually, he walked further down the line to the next person asking the same question, "What's your name?"

Just as all the other soldiers before him had done, he stood to attention replying, "Simon Ashworth, sir."

Hearing the name Ashworth, made Raven frown, then ask, "Are you related to Lee Ashworth?"

Ashworth replied, "Yes sir. My cousin died for his country, where I will do the same if called up on."

Raven, feeling proud, nodded his head agreeing, but said nothing. He shook Ashworth's hand, deciding to move onto the troublemaker called Williams. Raven stood there glaring hard into William's eyes, piercing them. Colonel Wareing and Captain Weller were watching what Raven's actions were going to be after what had occurred earlier. Raven and Williams were eyeballing each other, which made the Colonel walk over and say, "Trust me John. He will make the grade to become that elite soldier."

Raven moved his eyes slowly away from Williams to look at the Colonel for a few seconds, to listen to the Colonel say, "He knows that if he steps out of line again, he's out."

After listening to what the Colonel had just said, Raven moved his eyes wanting to focus on Williams. With a stern voice, he asked, "Your name?"

Before answering, Williams glanced at Colonel Wareing, and then back at Raven, eventually replying, "Kevin Williams, sir."

Raven decided not to shake his hand. Instead he said, "To win my respect, you must earn it! Do you think you can do it, knowing that it will be hard?"

Williams knew he had provoked the wrong person and replied, "I can only try."

Raven turned, still looking at Williams and walked a few paces up to the next soldier in line. He glanced at the Colonel, looked at his watch and asked the soldier who had arrived late, "What are you getting for Christmas, a new watch?"

Captain Weller looked away with a wry grin for a few seconds after hearing John's sarcastic comment. She then turned back watching John looking at Radford sternly.

Radford, who had been given an opportunity to leave the military police and join Unit Expendable by Major Higham, suspected that Raven wasn't best pleased with him being late. Aware of this he said, "I can explain . . . ."

Raven interrupted him by saying sternly, "Save it!"

Raven walked away from Radford, giving a snide stare at the officers watching, as he went to the Colonel's desk to pick up the folder, Unit Expendable. Radford, feeling deflated, shouted across to Raven, "Don't you want to know my name?"

Raven had his back faced to the soldier while reading Radford's profile. In an arrogant voice, he replied by asking, "Did I ask for it?"

Captain Weller turned to face John, frowning with concern, because although she always knew Raven was hard, she had never seen him act in such a ruthless way at an induction. Raven saw her and moved his eyes away feeling disgust from what had been discussed earlier. He turned around to face all the members of Unit Expendable, taking notice of Sarah Jane and Hayley's hands dripping with blood onto the floor. His face softened as he walked over to them. He looked into Sarah Jane's eyes hoping for a reaction, but she remained focused, which made her mother, Captain Weller, proud. Raven grabbed Sarah Jane's hand gently, making her look at him in a way only a daughter could. Raven released her hand, and then repeated the same action with Hayley Pomfret. Feeling concerned, he asked them, "Do you feel the pain?"

Hayley was about to reply, but Sarah Jane gave her a nudge replying, "There is no pain sir."

Raven gave a snide stare to his daughter after hearing this comment. He placed his hand on her shoulder and said, "Welcome to Unit Expendable. Go and clean yourselves up."

The other members standing in the line just listened, when at times they kept looking across to Colonel Wareing and Captain Weller, who was watching Raven's actions with great intent. Raven was about to speak, when Sarah Jane turned to say, "Sir. It's an honour to be able to serve under your command."

Raven chose to say nothing. Instead, he nodded his head slowly, agreeing. Captain Weller, who was watching closely, had to fight back the tears. Knowing the motherly instinct was starting to take over, she turned to the Colonel and said, "I'll go with them to help clean them up."

Colonel Wareing agreed with the Captain while placing his finger to his mouth, deciding to keep his thoughts to himself, as he watched Raven speak with the remaining members of Unit Expendable. Raven spoke to the soldiers telling them what he expected from them, and that he would like nothing else, except for them all to become an elite member of Unit Expendable.

The elite soldiers stood in line, listening hard to every word Raven had to say. He paused for a few seconds, looked down at the glass and then to each soldier. He asked in a sombre voice, "When you saw me for the first time dressed like this, what did you think?"

The Colonel narrowed his eyes slightly wondering where Raven was heading with this question. He waited patiently for at least one member of Unit Expendable to answer his question, but they decided to remain silent. Raven turned giving an arrogant stare at the Colonel, reminding him of the disagreement they had earlier. Turning to face the members of Unit Expendable once more, he said, "We know what Williams' opinion of me is, don't we Williams?"

Williams, not sure whether to reply to the question asked, "Sir?"

Raven, deciding to ease the pressure off Williams, for the moment, reminded them all what he had asked earlier when he said, "Who's the American bum stood there?"

Facing Williams, he asked, "Isn't that right Williams?"

Williams regretfully answered by replying in a sombre voice, "Yes sir. I'm . . ."

Raven suspecting that he was going to apologise raised his hand to make him stop talking and said, "Save it!"

Hayley and Sarah Jane came back into the room and went to stand back in their original positions. Captain Weller closed the door, walked over to stand next to the Colonel, where she was about to speak, but was hushed by his hand preferring to hear what Raven had to say. Raven turned to the women asking, "Are you two okay?"

They both replied in unison, "Yes sir."

Raven took a few paces while looking at the officers leaning against the desk, and then turned to face Unit Expendable once more to say, "I dressed like this for a reason!"

Colonel Wareing and Captain Weller frowned with confusion, but chose not to interrupt him. Raven recalled memories to *America in Conflict* saying, "I was dressed like this during my last conflict, which I have to say was one of the toughest encounters I have ever had to endure. I wanted to show you the soldier I once was."

Captain Weller interrupted him by saying, "You're still an elite soldier."

Raven turned, producing a menacing stare at both officers for a few seconds recalling the friction that had occurred earlier. He turned back to face the soldiers, took off his headband, he was wearing and caressed it. Remembering who had given it to him, he said to them all, "When I was given this, I was told a warrior, who was once a samurai had worn this headband. It was then I knew I had received the extra inspiration I needed to fulfil my mission. I want you to go beyond your limits and become what I hope will be the best of my elite groups I have trained since taking over from Colonel Lewis. I would like Unit Expendable to have no fear, to feel no pain, to die for something and to live for nothing if need be. I want Unit Expendable to be feared, respected, and to be the best of the best!"

Colonel Wareing as he listened to Raven speak looked down at the floor regretting his actions when he had thrown the picture of Raven onto the floor. With his head lowered, he listened to Raven carry onto ask, "Do you think you can do this for me when the serious training begins?"

Colonel Wareing listened to the soldier's all reply in unison by saying, "Yes sir."

Raven turned to face Colonel Wareing and Captain Weller, giving a snide stare at them. He turned back to face Unit

Expendable saying, "Appearances can be deceptive! I am now going to present myself in a proper way to you by changing into some decent clothing. Meanwhile I would like you to lie down on the floor and do press ups on the broken glass until I return."

Colonel Wareing feeling confused with Raven's instructions, asked, "John?"

Captain Weller, while watching the members of Unit Expendable crouch into position became concerned for the women, especially with Sarah Jane being her daughter, and asked, "Surely you don't want the women to go through this exercise again?"

Raven walked towards the door, but with hearing the Captain's comment, he stopped, paused, turned around, noticing the soldiers had done has he had ordered. Remembering his own experiences in war, he said, "In war, there are no rehearsals, we can't pick and choose how a war will be fought, and how much pain will be incurred. They all carry on doing what I have asked until I get back!"

Raven opened the door and walked out of the Colonel's office to get changed into clothes that were more presentable to wear at an induction. When Raven arrived at his own room, he turned the radio on to listen to some music before he went for a shave and a shower. The sound from the radio became muffled as the water splashed down onto him. Raven didn't take much notice of the radio. He was thinking about Unit Expendable in Colonel Wareing's office, hoping they would be still doing the task set by him before he left to change into decent clothing.

Raven turned off the shower and stepped out to dry himself with a towel. The radio that was on in the background had gone to the news bulletin. Raven listened to the newscaster telling American people that relations with Iran had now reached breaking point; because of the fact, they had been constantly ignoring the western world about their nuclear plans. Whilst getting dressed, Raven said in a low voice, "It's a sad world!"

Raven, after getting changed into clean military clothing was much more presentable. He went across the room to pick up the headband once worn by a samurai. Holding it, he caressed it, while thinking back briefly to the time he spoke with the old man, when he had arrived at his village that was nearby to the Korean jungle. Flashbacks came flooding back into his mind, of how he remembered his daughter, Sarah Jane, when she had been beaten, tortured, and then after escaping helped him fight to escape. He gave a casual blink, placed the headband into his pocket and picked up his knife, once owned by Colonel Lewis. Looking at the lethal weapon, he thought back to his mentor, remembering how he had been taught.

Captain Weller feeling concerned for the members of Unit Expendable that were performing press ups on glass, decided to leave Colonel Wareing's office to go and look for Raven. When she arrived at Raven's room, she knocked once and walked straight in to see that Raven was holding the knife he had used many times to kill and be able to survive. Concerned, she asked, "John, don't you think you should come back to the Colonel's office now?"

Raven, while holding the knife, slowly turned to face her, knowing he had made a decision. He placed the knife back into the holster and said, "It's time!"

Captain Weller, noticing how well presented John now was, replied, "You scare me at times."

Raven didn't reply, instead he walked over to the radio to switch it off, but after hearing Major Cairns name, he chose to stand there and listen. Captain Weller took a few paces over to him, wanting to speak once more. Aware of this, John placed his hand up, letting her know that he wanted to listen to the newscaster announcing that Major Cairns, who was once a respected officer is now going to be sent back home to the United States in disgrace.

Captain Weller, who had also heard the breaking news looked at John asking, "Do you think your past is coming back to haunt you?"

John switched the radio off, replying, "Cairns got what he deserved!"

He then walked across the room, turned to the Captain, who was standing next to the radio and said, "Come on. Let's go!"

Captain Weller walked across the room to John and out of his room, where he then locked the door. Concerned for John, Captain Weller asked, "Are you okay John, you seem on edge?"

John chose not to reply to her with having a confrontation earlier. Instead, as they were walking back to the Colonel's office, he remained silent. Captain Weller could see his attitude, and behaviour seemed different, and with this said, "Unit Expendable doesn't have to be your last group of elite soldiers."

Raven moved his eyes slightly, glimpsing at her as they carried on walking. In a disgruntled voice, he replied, "After Unit Expendable, it's over!"

Captain Weller watched Raven turn his head away suspecting he was still annoyed with her about what she had said to him earlier. Remembering him for whom he is, she said, "John, I'm sorry about what happened earlier."

As they carried on making their way back to Colonel Wareing's office, Raven chose not to look at her when he replied sternly, "Save it!"

Captain Weller decided not to speak to him again. She had apologised, hoping that John Raven was man enough to accept it. As they walked to the Colonel's office, military personnel staff would look at them, noticing how well presented John Raven now appeared. Just as before, he chose to ignore them focusing on the task. Becoming provoked with Raven's behaviour, Captain Weller slapped his arm saying, "You can be a stubborn old mule!"

Raven, who had clearly heard the Captain's comment, carried on walking just looking in front of him choosing to remain silent and say nothing to her. Her facial expression changed with it now appearing frosty, knowing that John may never forgive her for telling him that he was a disgrace.

Raven knocked once on the Colonel's door and placed his hand on the handle to open the door. Captain Weller placed her hand onto John's hand holding the handle, and said in a solemn voice, "John. I'm sorry for what I said earlier."

John narrowed his eyes slightly, thinking about what she had just said as he looked down at her with his piercing eyes. Looking back up to him, Captain Weller said once more, "I'm sorry. Okay?"

John turned away after hearing Colonel Wareing shout, "Enter!"

John opened the door, but before he could walk inside, Captain Weller said, "John, no matter what you think of me, will you be there for our daughter, Sarah Jane?"

With nobody entering the Colonel's office immediately, Colonel Wareing walked briskly across the office, opening the door sharply. He saw standing there; Raven nodding his head agreeing to Captain Weller's question. Colonel Wareing said, "It's you! Well, are you going to stop this charade you have created here in my office?"

Raven and Captain Weller went inside the Colonel's office, noticing that some members of Unit Expendable had given up with the task, he had set. Other members carried on doing what he had requested, hoping to get on the right side of Raven when the real training begins. Raven felt proud after noticing his daughter Sarah Jane had persevered by carrying on doing more press ups on the broken glass, but couldn't help but notice the blood dripping once more from her hands. He told the remaining soldiers who wanted to impress him to stop and stand up. The other soldiers who were instructed to stop by Colonel Wareing also stood up waiting anxiously for their leader and commanding officer to speak. Raven stood there well presented, glancing at all their hands. With concern he asked Hayley, "Do you think you can go the distance?"

Hayley replied, "I'm sorry I gave up, but I do want to improve and be an elite member of Unit Expendable."

Raven paused, thought for a few seconds, nodded his head reluctantly agreeing and said to them all, "If you can trust me enough, you will all become that elite soldier you so want to be."

They all stood there feeling proud of what Raven had just mentioned. Colonel Wareing and Captain Weller watched the blood from some of the soldier's hands drip onto the floor and then watch Raven pull the knife out of his holster. Colonel Wareing in a concerned voice, said, "John!"

Raven, ignored him by gripping the knife handle tightly and started weaving it through the air. All the members of Unit Expendable were watching with intent at Raven's actions, but chose to say nothing. Raven put his arm down by his side, holding the knife firmly. He looked at Williams, asking, "Do you still think I'm that American bum, Williams?"

Williams placed his head down, making Raven say, "Williams! Answer the question!"

Captain Weller, feeling concerned, said, "John, please."

Williams held his head up, replying, "Sir. I'm sorry for what I said earlier. I now know appearances can be deceptive and realise that when I'm in battle, I should trust nobody."

Raven gave a wry grin saying, "To survive you must trust nobody, whatever their appearance may be."

Williams, felt hidden glee that Raven agreed with him, which made him want to say, "Sir."

Raven looked back at him, with his eyes piercing him, while waiting for what else Williams had to say. The Colonel and the Captain were watching with anticipation waiting for what Williams was about to say. Williams said, "Sir, it's an honour to be able to serve and have the opportunity to fight someday with the sister of John Weller-Raven and the daughter of you."

Hayley turned feeling surprised to glance at Sarah Jane, who was standing next to her remaining focused. Captain Weller looked across at her, giving a wry smile. Raven, however, looked stern at Williams, gripping the handle of his knife much more tightly. Simon Ashworth spoke up saying, "Sir. We recognised her from the chase she was involved in with her brother, when President Berry had been kidnapped at the American football game she had attended."

He turned his head away from Raven and said, "Cool driving, Sarah Jane."

Sarah Jane looked across at her father, producing a wry grin as she casually raised her hand in acknowledgment to give Ashworth the thumbs up. Raven smirked, making Captain Weller say to the Colonel, "I think a burden has just been lifted from him."

Colonel Wareing, watching events closely replied, "Possibly."

Raven pulled the knife he was holding in front of him and said, "I wanted to give this weapon to one of you. With you knowing who Sarah Jane is, and because she already knows that her brother, John Weller, owns my original knife, it leaves me no choice but to give it to her."

Raven took a few paces holding the knife with two hands and gently passed it with sincerity to Sarah Jane saying, "I hope you will be as successful as your brother."

She held her hand out to take the knife from him, thanking him. He looked across to both officers leaning on the desk, has he unbuckled his holster saying, "I meant it when I said Unit Expendable will be my last batch of elite soldiers whom I will train."

Sarah Jane held out her other hand to accept from her father, the holster for the knife to be inserted into. As she placed it around her waist and put the knife into the holster, she listened to her father say, "After training what I hope will become my finest batch of Green Berets, that's it, I'm done! It's over!"

Sarah Jane had already heard him say previously he was leaving the force for good when he had trained Unit Expendable, but didn't want to believe it. After receiving something precious to him, she now knew this time was the last time. Raven turned to Unit Expendable and said, "It was good to meet you. Go and get cleaned up, have a nice Christmas and be here on time in the New Year."

Radford gave a cheeky grin making Raven say, "Clear, Radford?"

Radford agreed by saying, "Yes sir."

Raven stood there watching them all leave the Colonel's office when he heard Hayley say to Sarah Jane, "You're a dark horse! I don't suppose you could arrange a date with your brother could you?"

Sarah Jane, who already knew her brother John, had a girlfriend called Louise, replied, "I'll see what I can do."

When Unit Expendable had left the room, Raven went to close the door. He turned back to see that Colonel Wareing wasn't best pleased. The Colonel went to stand behind his desk asking Raven sternly, "Just what the hell was all that about?"

Raven gave a casual blink, looked away from the Colonel, glancing at Captain Weller remembering her sincere apology. Colonel Wareing, who was feeling rather angry asked, "So what was all that about, a huge ego problem?"

Raven, just as he had said before replied, "Sir, trust me."

Colonel Wareing said, "Trust you, when you perform actions like this, and in my office too!"

The phone rang interrupting the Colonel from speaking any further to Raven. He answered the phone by saying, "Colonel Wareing speaking."

Raven turned away feeling as though enough had been said and started to walk away to make his way out of the Colonel's office.

General Hardaker was on the other end of the phone wanting to tell Colonel Wareing that Cairns will be sent back to the United States tomorrow. Colonel Wareing placed his hand over the mouthpiece and said, "John. Cairns will be brought back to the United States tomorrow."

Raven, feeling a little despondent stopped walking away, turned around to face the Colonel replying, "I'll see you in the New Year."

The Colonel responded to him by raising his hand as he carried on speaking to General Hardaker on the phone. Thinking of his son, John, and daughter, Sarah Jane, he stopped to ask Captain Weller, "Will you be coming to our house sometime during the Christmas period?"

Captain Weller smiled at John, suspecting he had forgiven her for what she said earlier. Colonel Wareing also heard John's question, which made him place his hand over the mouthpiece again and say. "Captain Weller is being sent as a replacement to one of our aircraft carriers in the Gulf to perform hi tech I.T duties."

Raven frowned asking, "Don't they have a command and control ship that controls the fleet for all communications, computers and intelligence?"

Colonel Wareing raised his hand wanting to speak with General Hardaker again, which made Raven glimpse at Captain Weller. She looked away from Raven with concern towards the Colonel, immediately asking, "Is this what the folder, Operation Gulf Warrior is about?"

Colonel Wareing placed his hand up letting her know he was still speaking with General Hardaker on the phone. Raven turned around feeling bitterly disappointed and walked out of Colonel Wareing's office making Captain Weller shout, "John."

Raven ignored her, choosing to carry on walking down the long corridor feeling glad to be almost away from it all.

Military Diversion

$\mathcal{G}$eneral Hardaker placed the phone down becoming anxious after hearing the media now knew about James Cairns release to the United States, where he will spend the next two years at a secure military compound. He thought about the serious situation that occurred and implications it may have on his return to the United States. Aware the American people could only feel hatred for this man, and knowing a riot may occur on Cairns' return to the United States, he thought it would be best to create a military diversion and confuse all the media. He picked up the phone, starting to press the buttons to call one of his senior officers. He held the phone to his ear, listening to it ring, while waiting for it to be answered. Colonel Armstrong answered the phone by saying, "Colonel Armstrong speaking."

General Hardaker replied to Colonel Armstrong exchanging pleasantries before discussing the real reason for the phone call. Concerned at the result of what might occur back home in the United States, he ordered the Colonel to have the military police officer's dress in civilian clothing. Cairns had to be also dressed in the same clothing while being taken back to the U.S. using American Airlines opposed to military transport. The Colonel agreed to the instruction by saying, "Cairns isn't worthy of flying on one of our planes with what he has previously done."

General Hardaker thought for a few seconds, later replying, "I would prefer to keep this low-key. The less the media know, the better it will be for us all."

Colonel Armstrong agreed by telling the General he would pass on the order for the military police to have a car ready to escort Cairns to the airport as soon as possible.

Cairns sat on the bed inside his cell anxiously waiting for his release to a secure military compound in the United States. He was hoping everything previously planned with the Iranians was arranged, so he could be free to have his revenge against people who had persecuted him the most. His blackberry phone beeped, telling him that he had received an email. He pulled it out from inside the mattress to read the email. It was a message from the Iranians, confirming their own diversion was now in place to rescue and take him back to Iran. What the Iranians needed to know and kept asking him, was the date he would be travelling. Cairns while producing an evil grin typed an email back saying, *soon my friend.*

In the distance, he heard footsteps, which made him look with concern. He turned off his blackberry phone, casually slipping it into his pocket. The military police opened Cairns' caged cell door and walked inside. One of the M.P. officers threw civilian clothing onto his bed, while the other stood at the door watching precariously. He was told that he had thirty minutes to change out of his military clothing and into the civilian clothing the military police had just brought him. He would then be taken to the Kuwaiti airport, and flown to the United States. Cairns produced an evil smirk, because he knew the time for his release was close. He turned to the military police asking, "Now you don't want to be perverse and watch me change my clothing do you?"

The military police officers glared at Cairns, reluctantly deciding to walk out of the cell. One of the military police officers turned back to him to say, "Hurry up Cairns!"

Cairns gave an evil look to the military police, nodding his head agreeing, waiting for them to go. He started to take off his shirt, while watching the military police walk further away to speak with Major Higham. Keeping a watchful eye on them, he pulled his blackberry phone from his pocket, frantically wanting to email President Modarres to confirm that his release would be in the next hour. After getting the confirmation the Iranian president so dearly wanted to know, he sent the message to his own terrorist group, telling them to take their positions. The Iranian president e-mailed Cairns telling him that to enable him to become a freeman, innocent people will surely die. When Cairns read the Iranian president's reply, he chuckled and typed an email straight back to him saying, "Good!"

He turned off his blackberry phone and placed it into his pocket. The military police officers were casually walking back up to Cairns' cell, with one of them asking, "Are you almost ready?"

Cairns turned to them, asking, "You don't expect me to wear this tie do you?"

Sinclair, who was one of the military policemen waiting to escort Cairns replied, "Just wear everything given to you!"

Cairns recognised Sinclair, which made him ask, "Where is your feisty friend? Radford I think his name is!"

Sinclair produced a chuckle making Cairns frown and ask, "What's funny?"

Sinclair looked at the military police officer standing next to him and replied, "Oh, if only he knew."

Cairns placed his collar down and then reluctantly pulled his tie up to the top button. He casually put on the suit jacket, picked up his baggage and walked with the military police officers, asking, "Knew what?"

Sinclair, suspecting his reply would infuriate Cairns, replied, "Radford has now left us and is being trained as an elite member of Unit Expendable under John Raven's command."

Cairns moved his head to the side glaring at Sinclair with the sheer mention of John Raven's name. The military police followed him, wanting to escort him out of the building. His friends he had made shouted and cheered has Cairns left the building, with him now aware that soon he would be a free man, he just didn't know how.

When the military police officers arrived outside with Cairns, four more of their colleagues dressed in civilian clothing accompanied them and continued to their black Range Rover Vogue cars parked close by. As they walked closer to the cars, Cairns asked Sinclair, "Do you have any children?"

Sinclair replied sternly, "Why do you ask?"

Cairns producing an evil glare, replying, "It's the time of the year that children enjoy the most, and I expect the two children you have, will be relishing you being at home this Christmas."

Sinclair frowned with concern, knowing that Cairns had spoken with the correct information, when he mentioned that he had two children. How, he wasn't sure, and with this chose to remain silent. Cairns placed his hand through his hair, deciding to taunt Sinclair some more by saying, "It's a shame you're not going to be there to share this Christmas with them!"

Sinclair became angry immediately wanting to protect his children and replied, "Touch my kids, and I'll personally kill you!"

Cairns moved his head away, looking straight ahead and said, "I like a man who is ambitious!"

Sinclair carried on walking beside Cairns thinking about when he had mentioned his family. One of the military police officers walking behind him tried to assure him by saying, "Ignore him, he's just trying to irritate you."

Sinclair didn't reply. He remained focused with the task, just walking toward the black 4x4 cars. General Hardaker stood next to the rear door of the second Range Rover, opening it for what was once a good friend. Cairns stopped before climbing inside the car to face the General, who was looking back at him with disappointment showing on his face. In a sombre voice, he said to Cairns, "You could have progressed much further if you hadn't performed those foolish actions."

Cairns sighed, choosing to look away from the General, and then climb inside the car, followed by two military police officers. Sinclair walked around the car to climb into the driver's seat and waited for his colleague, Andrew Ferguson, to climb into the front passenger seat after he had finished speaking with the General. Sinclair noticing the car in front of him had started its engine, and was waiting to travel. The General glanced, immediately telling Ferguson to get into the car and start their journey back to the United States. Ferguson opened the passenger door; Sinclair turned the key making the huge V8 engine turn over and growl. General Hardaker held the car door, and said to Sinclair, "Remain in close radio contact at all times."

Sinclair and Ferguson agreed, making Cairns, listening, look at the military police officers who were sitting beside him in the back of the car. Cairns produced an evil grin, making General Hardaker say, "I hope you find the man I once knew that was a friend."

Cairns, who had always respected General Hardaker, replied by saying, "People change."

General Hardaker, feeling disappointed with Cairns and his actions replied, "When people do change, it's usually for the better!"

Cairns, sitting on the backseat looked down at the General, while closing the passenger door. Ferguson pressed the button to lower the window and spoke to the General by saying, "We will keep in contact."

General Hardaker said, "Often I might add, now go, be on your way."

Sinclair flashed his headlamps to the driver in front, signalling for the journey to start. The driver of the first car revved the engine, slowly pulling away with Sinclair following and General Hardaker watching, while Ferguson was raising the window on the passenger door.

Conflict

$\mathcal{T}$ he military police drove their Range Rovers through busy traffic in Kuwait, without the sirens blurring. They did display the red and blue led flashing lights placed at the front on the grille, making other motorists aware that these military vehicles had a demanding presence. Cairns, sitting in the back of the Range Rover staring straight ahead out of the front windscreen, knew that sometime soon something was about to happen. Ferguson noticed how quiet Cairns had become and said, "It's not like you to be so quiet."

Sinclair, who was driving, clearly heard Ferguson's comment while also noticing that Cairns had become quiet. Sinclair briefly looked behind him for a couple of seconds to see Cairns sitting there focused. Sinclair, while following the car in front said to Ferguson, "Something doesn't feel right."

Cairns moved his eyes to watch Sinclair's reaction, and then turned to watch Ferguson picking up the radio to give his first report about the trip. General Hardaker, who was speaking with Colonel Armstrong at the control centre, heard the call and immediately went to pick up the radio asking, "What is the status of your journey?"

Ferguson replied to the General, saying, "There is heavy traffic in places, but we should reach the airport in the next 30 minutes."

General Hardaker said, "I'm glad to hear that everything is going smoothly, keep in touch with Colonel Armstrong every ten minutes with an update report."

Ferguson accepted the General's request; turned off the radio and then looked behind him once more to notice Cairns was now holding a serious stern look on his face. One of the military police officers sitting next to Cairns asked, "What made you perform those acts of treason against your own country?"

Cairns thought back to when he had arranged for large sums of money to be transferred to his account from President Rashaid and his accomplice, General Luchinski. It was payment in return for inside information, resulting in the capture of some of the United States elite soldiers. Cairns grinned, replying, "Money!"

Sinclair listening in the front while driving, asked, "You already had a large salary and was climbing through the ranks with ease. Why did you become a traitor against your own people?"

Cairns, while thinking of his escape chose to answer calmly by saying, "At the time it seemed like the right thing to do, but as you're aware, people can make mistakes!"

The military police officer sitting next to Cairns replied, "Yes, but your mistake was huge and unforgivable!"

Cairns sighed, while noticing at the traffic lights, people wanting to wash car windscreens in exchange for money. The Range Rover in front of Sinclair crept forward towards the traffic signals, continuing to go through while the lights were still displaying red. Ferguson lowered his window down, placing his hand out to make sure the traffic did remain stopped while they travelled through. The men wanting to wash windscreens were joined by more people also shouting and bawling at the military police, which made Cairns smirk. Colonel Armstrong aware that Ferguson was late with his next update report contacted him leaving Ferguson to have to tell him of the developments and hostility surrounding them. Over the radio, he heard people shouting and kicking the car trying to damage it as they slowly drove through what had now become a barricade. Ferguson brought out his gun, making Sinclair say with a concerned voice, "Put the gun away Andy, it's only the local people wanting to make some money."

Ferguson put down his gun on the centre console, which Cairns took notice of. Colonel Armstrong, who was still on the radio aware of the hostility, asked again, "What is the current status of your journey?"

Ferguson replied, "Nothing we can't handle."

Ferguson then turned off the radio, which made Colonel Armstrong have to contact General Hardaker with an update of recent events.

The V8 engine from the Range Rover's revved hard as they accelerated away from the people who were creating a scene. Some of the people involved in the disturbance saw Cairns sitting in the back of the second Range Rover. This made them start to use their mobile phone, contacting their colleagues elsewhere to confirm that Cairns is travelling in the second Range Rover.

Cairns, who remained silent throughout this ordeal, said to Sinclair and Ferguson in a sarcastic way, "Perhaps it might have been better for them to have washed your windscreen."

Sinclair replied, "You ought to know the procedure better than anybody! We don't stop for anything or anyone!"

Cairns placed his hand through his hair, casually looking at the military police officers sitting at either side of him and then at the gun placed on the centre console next to the handbrake. He suspected that an escape plan was near, and knew he had to be ready when it was about to take place.

Cairns turned his head to look out of the window, smirking again, while watching the oncoming traffic pass by. Keeping his thoughts private, he turned back, glimpsing at the gun once more that had been placed next to the handbrake, which seemed so inviting to use. Sinclair became aware of more traffic on the road, kept watching in anticipation. He asked Ferguson to radio the car in front. Ferguson detecting some anxiety in Sinclair's voice asked, "Why?"

Sinclair replied, "Do it because something doesn't feel right."

Cairns, still watching closely, remained silent. The military police officers sitting beside him looked at him with stern faces. Ferguson picked the radio up to contact the military police officers driving the Range Rover in front of them. Feeling apprehension, he flicked the switch, calling to one of his colleagues, where they responded to Ferguson by reporting that no further obstacles were in front of them, and that it should be a safe journey to the airport. Ferguson, feeling relieved decided to radio Colonel Armstrong to report with an update. Sinclair interrupted him, asking, "What the hell is happening there?"

Colonel Armstrong heard Sinclair's outburst, making him become somewhat concerned and want to ask, "Is everything okay?"

Ferguson didn't reply because he was mesmerised by the articulated vehicle that had changed lanes to collide with the first military police Range Rover. Watching the vehicle in front swerve from side to side, Sinclair held back creating a much larger space between the two vehicles. Colonel Armstrong, rather concerned, asked again, "Ferguson! What's happened?"

Ferguson, watching in dismay did not reply. Sinclair snatched the radio from Ferguson's hand, flicked the switch and replied, "Sir, we have a situation!"

Sinclair threw the radio down, with everybody sitting in the car hearing Colonel Armstrong say, "Please explain!"

Sinclair and Ferguson ignored the Colonel's request. What seemed important at this time was survival. Ferguson lowered the electric window after noticing two Mercedes Benz AMG cars do a sharp 360 degree turn, narrowly missing other road users, and then start in pursuit of the military Range Rovers.

The articulated lorry kept weaving from side to side making the driver in the first Range Rover turn the steering wheel in the opposite direction.

Ferguson said, "He's going to collide with them and possibly us. Do something!"

One of the military police officers sitting in the first car lowered the window, and didn't hesitate in firing his gun at the people driving the articulated lorry rapidly approaching them.

The Mercedes AMG cars that had done a 360 degree turn moments before were now behind Sinclair's vehicle. One of the cars pulled out onto the opposite side of the road making an innocent driver have to swerve. Other motorists using the same lane chose to slow down, pulling in for their safety. The Mercedes AMG dodged a couple of vehicles and then made impact side on with Sinclair's Range Rover. Colonel Armstrong became frantic on the radio, asking, "Just what the hell is happening?"

Neither Sinclair nor Ferguson replied because of the situation that developed. Colonel Armstrong, who had become annoyed, was aware something serious had occurred. He ordered two soldiers to fly a military helicopter to explore just what indeed had happened, and to report to him using the radio immediately.

People in the Mercedes AMG lowered their windows, firing their guns at the military Range Rover. Ferguson shouted, "We're under attack!"

Sinclair, who was watching the crisis developing in front replied, "Do you think I don't already know this?"

Ferguson reached out for his gun, while telling his colleagues sitting in the back to also fire at what seemed to be the unknown enemy travelling in the Mercedes AMG cars. They ducked for cover for a few seconds, and then retaliated by shooting back with sub machine guns. Ferguson was hit with one of the bullets, causing blood to spill out of his body, badly staining his uniform. Sinclair, who was starting to swerve from side to side grabbed Ferguson by the chest using one hand, and said, "Hold on buddy!"

He glared at Cairns, who was sitting on the backseat cool and calm, and said in an angry voice, "You bastard!"

Cairns didn't reply, instead he just produced an evil grin. Sinclair concerned for Ferguson, shouted, "Hold on!"

Colonel Armstrong could be heard on the radio in the background, saying, "Sinclair, a U.S. military helicopter will be with you in minutes to help resolve the situation you have become involved in."

Hearing this, Cairns frowned.

The articulated lorry travelling at a speed made a huge impact with the first military Range Rover, crushing its front bumper and bonnet, before sending it up into the air. Sinclair pulled the hand brake hard, causing the Range Rover to skid and turn ninety degrees. The terrorists in the Mercedes AMG vehicles were still shooting at the military police, where they retaliated by firing back. Sinclair drove into the opposite lane, colliding with one of the terrorist's car, by denting the front wing and driving into a new estate being built. The Range Rover sent up into the air came crashing down creating a huge explosion, remaining there to burn to a shell in a huge fireball.

Sinclair knew that his colleagues inside that vehicle would have been dead up on impact with the lorry. One of the military police officers feeling anger for his colleagues, turned, placing his gun onto the side of Cairns' head and said, "All this is caused by you isn't it? The United States finest traitor scores again!"

Sinclair reminded them that they were still under attack from the terrorists who were following with one sole purpose, to free Cairns! Military police were hanging out of their windows shooting back at the terrorists. Cairns quickly leaned across, opened the door and pushed one of the military police officers out of the car, leaving the terrorist to drive over his body, killing him instantly. Sinclair's Range Rover was being pounded with bullets, with several hitting the other military police officer, leaving him to hang out of the window, dead. With one of the rear doors swinging open and closed, Cairns had to duck for cover between the front seats. He grabbed the radio on the floor, flicked the switch and asked Colonel Armstrong, "Isn't revenge sweet?"

Colonel Armstrong and a host of other people who had now joined him at the control centre knew that Cairns had planned a mission to escape. Feeling angry, Colonel Armstrong, radioed the pilots of the military helicopter saying, "Bring him back to base no matter what!"

One of the pilots replied to the Colonel by asking, "Do you want us to fire missiles?"

Colonel Armstrong aware that General Hardaker was now walking towards him answered back to the pilot, "Use whatever you have to! Just bring that son of a bitch back here!"

General Hardaker didn't speak, he watched his Colonel take charge of what had become a hostile situation.

Sinclair, who was weaving from side to side, while trying to drive and avoid workers on the site, grabbed Cairns' hair, pulled his head up, and smacked it back down repeatedly onto the centre console next to the gearstick. As Sinclair picked him up once more, he noticed blood dripping from Cairns' mouth. Cairns, while placing one hand out to support him, lunged at Sinclair, punching him hard in the chest with his other hand. Sinclair became badly winded, losing control of the vehicle. The U.S. military helicopter had now arrived on the scene with the pilots noticing the damaged Range Rover was under heavy attack from the terrorists driving the Mercedes AMG cars. The co-pilot radioed to Colonel Armstrong, where he just turned to briefly look at General Hardaker standing close by holding a stern face. Turning away from the General, he ordered the pilot to destroy the terrorist vehicles. Without hesitation the pilot released a heat seeking missile in pursuit of one of the AMG cars. For a few seconds, the terrorists stopped shooting, realising what had now joined the battle. They heard the speed of the missile travelling through the air, which hit their car, killing them all instantly after creating a huge inferno.

Sinclair, still trying to keep control of the car, had let go of Cairns' hair. He skidded while positioning the steering on opposite lock, making the back end of the Range Rover snake into the opposite direction. He hit a cluster of timber framed houses, making them collapse. Scaffolding and building materials started to fall onto the Range Rover. Roof tiles and more timber fell onto the car roof, badly denting it. Sinclair became agitated, with not being sure where he was driving anymore. The terrorists driving the second Mercedes AMG car became trapped in the timber that had fallen. In frustration, they fired their submachine guns at the Range Rover, while watching Sinclair climb out of the timber using the 4 wheel drive option to travel once more on the building site that had now become a warzone.

One of the terrorists aware that he could no longer follow Sinclair's car, radioed the driver of the articulated lorry blocking the road. He told him to drop both sides of the trailer and have the pilot launch the Iranian Harrier the terrorists had been hiding. The terrorists started to flee from their car still shooting at the American helicopter. In retaliation, they fired another missile at the terrorist's car, making a huge explosion, and creating an almighty inferno, resulting in many houses being built on the site catching fire. Some of the workers who had previously ducked for cover, decided to run for their lives. The U.S. pilots opened fire using their machine guns at the enemy, who were now waving their arms in anticipation to the pilot flying the Iranian Harrier.

The U.S. pilots in the helicopter saw the Harrier fly past them at high speed and then bank flying into position for a prime attack on the U.S. helicopter. The Iranian pilot locked onto the helicopter, firing two missiles that travelled at speed through the air. The U.S. pilot tried to diversify, by changing direction, but it was too late! The missiles made impact with the helicopter, one after the other, creating a huge explosion and fireball that followed in the sky, which immediately became orange. The burnt wreckage from the helicopter fell from the sky onto an abandoned builder's merchant's wagon, creating another explosion, which also set fire and started to burn to a shell.

The terrorists, who had fled from their car, waved their arms in the air firing shots from their guns. They turned in glee, watching the Iranian pilot fly in pursuit of Sinclair and Cairns, who were still travelling somewhere on the building site. The Iranian pilot saw the badly damaged black Range Rover, suspecting that Cairns must be inside this vehicle, which made him fire at them using only his machine guns to try and demobilise it without killing Cairns. Sinclair, showing anger in his face as he slowly drove the vehicle over wreckage, pulled his gun out turning to briefly face Cairns and said, "I ought to kill you here and now!"

The Iranian pilot pounded the Range Rover with bullets from the machine guns below either wing, which distracted Sinclair, making him drop his gun, so he could concentrate on his driving. The Iranian Harrier flying low flew by at a high speed, banking once more ready to make a further attack. He then released a couple of missiles, destroying all the remaining properties on this prestige building site that were being built. Fires erupted, followed by clouds of smoke; Sinclair couldn't see where he was driving and drove one side of the vehicle up an embankment causing it to roll over onto its roof. Cairns braced himself and then lunged forwards to take Sinclair's gun, and crawled out of the door left open earlier. Sinclair grabbed his ankle in desperation to try and stop him from escaping. Cairns turned back, shooting him in the chest and then repeatedly in the face, killing him instantly. He scampered out of the Range Rover, eventually able to stand up and stagger away into the smoke, eagerly looking for the Harrier jet. He could hear the power of the engines it had, but couldn't see it because of all the fire and smoke around contaminating the air. Feeling apprehension and anxiety, suspecting that the American's would now send a squadron of military aircraft to attack the Iranian Harrier jet, he waved his arm frantically to try and clear the smoke. In the distance, he saw the wing realising that the pilot had landed and was waiting for him. Cairns stood there for a few seconds looking at the carnage created, and said in a low voice, "It's time to have my revenge!"

He staggered over the bricks, timber and sand to the Harrier jet, where the pilot saw him and waved his hand frantically telling him to hurry to him. With this, he released the cock pit, waiting anxiously for him to climb into the co-pilots seat. The Iranian pilot said to him, "Welcome aboard Major Cairns."

Cairns, feeling relieved to have lived through this escape plan replied, "Thanks. Take me to my new home!"

The Iranian pilot didn't hesitate; he continued by manoeuvring the thrusters into position so the Harrier jet could take off vertically. As the Harrier jet started to ascend, Cairns, while looking down at the devastation below had one thought, which was, free at last. He looked around the sky to see if the U.S. had sent a squadron, but saw nothing. The Iranian pilot radioed to the Iranian president confirming that he had Cairns inside his jet sitting behind him. President Atash Modarres gave a wry grin and said to Cairns, "Welcome to freedom my friend."

Cairns nodded his head agreeing, replying, "We have much to discuss now."

President Modarres, feeling pleased with how the plan had progressed, said, "I look forward to it!"

He flicked the radio off, leaving the Iranian pilot to ignite the afterburners and fly away to Cairns' new home with his influential new friends in Iran. As he was travelling, he still had one thought, which was John Raven, and how he will have his long awaited revenge against him.

Aftermath

$\mathcal{F}$erguson, who was still inside the overturned military police Range Rover kept coming in and out of consciousness. His vision became blurred while trying to focus around him. Still feeling the pain from his wound he placed his hand on to his chest, feeling more great pain, which made him, close his eyes once more. Starting to drift back out of consciousness, the radio could be heard with eager voices calling Sinclair and Ferguson's names. Rather wearily, Ferguson slowly opened his eyes and heard a muffled sound coming from the radio.

Colonel Armstrong kept trying to contact any of the military police officers in the 4x4's or the pilots in the helicopter. He felt apprehensive sensing something serious must have happened. With knowing Cairns when he was once a Major, General Hardaker appeared frosty faced and ordered the Colonel to have four F35 fighter planes circle the area where the conflict had taken place. Without hesitation, Colonel Armstrong relayed the order for the pilots on red alert to be kitted up ready for a dogfight in the sky. Suspecting there could be casualties, Colonel Armstrong ordered a team of medics to fly in a military helicopter and look for survivors who were travelling on this journey.

People rushed around in the control centre attending to their duties, while the General and the Colonel stood watching feeling apprehensive. A military worker confirmed to the officers, the F35 fighter planes were now travelling to the scene of conflict. One of the military workers called out, "Sir!"

Hearing such a tone, the General and the Colonel gave a startled look. Colonel Armstrong walked briskly over to the worker asking, "What is it?"

The worker, hoping it was one of our boys, said, "Sir. I think the person on the other end is one of ours, but he doesn't sound too good."

Colonel Armstrong took the radio and said, "Soldier, identify yourself."

With his eyes slowly opening and then starting to close again, Ferguson couldn't find the strength to speak, which made the Colonel ask again in a much sterner voice, "Soldier! Identify yourself."

Starting to open his eyes once more, Ferguson heard the Colonel's voice and with difficulty brought the radio to his mouth saying in a weary tired voice, " . . . Taken him."

Colonel Armstrong immediately asked, "Who has taken Cairns?"

No reply came from Ferguson. General Hardaker walked over to take the radio from Colonel Armstrong and said, "Help is coming, hold on!"

Ferguson, groaning said, "Yes sir."

One of the military administrative workers also listening said to the officers, "He doesn't sound good at all."

Colonel Armstrong, aware of this picked up another radio, wanting to contact the medics flying in the U.S. helicopter, warning them time was precious and that one of their own colleagues could be seriously injured and possibly close to dying.

The squadron leader flying in the F35 fighter planes contacted the control centre and reported the devastation that had occurred in the area where the conflict had taken place. Colonel Armstrong fearing the worst told the squadron leader and the three other pilots to circle the area within a one-hundred and fifty mile radius and to report anything thought to be suspicious back to base immediately. General

Hardaker put the radio down by his side and turned to Colonel Armstrong, narrowed his eyes, and then said, "Face facts! Cairns escaped!"

Colonel Armstrong, remembering his last words mentioned over the radio, which were "Isn't revenge sweet!" suspected it, but didn't want to accept it. With this he contacted the pilots in the F35 fighter planes asking, "Can you see anything?"

The squadron leader replied, "Except for the damage at the point of conflict, there is no sign of Cairns."

Feeling frustrated, Colonel Armstrong said, "Keep looking, they must be out there somewhere!"

The pilots in the helicopter could see the infernos created earlier making them wonder, just what did happen here. Three of the medics rushed through the fading smoke next to the burning fires to search for military casualties and civilians. Another soldier reported to Colonel Armstrong about the devastation created, as damaged motor vehicles were burning to a shell. He told Colonel Armstrong that a huge articulated lorry with its sides lowered at either side was badly damaged at the front, and blocking both sides of the road. Colonel Armstrong placed the radio onto the loud speaker, making General Hardaker ask, "In your opinion, is this lorry large enough to carry a military helicopter or fighter plane so it could fly to safety?"

The soldier studied the lorry, assessing the length of the trailer, and replied, "Sir. It could be possible if the wings had been folded."

General Hardaker turned to Colonel Armstrong and said. "Cairns escaped using military transport, but who is the enemy?"

Colonel Armstrong stood their frosty faced, remaining silent with not being able to answer the General's question. General Hardaker paused, and then said to the soldier, "Go and join your colleagues, and bring back as many survivors as you can. This also includes civilians."

General Hardaker thought back to when Cairns had been arrested by military police in the same control room a few years earlier, when he had performed treason against John

Raven's first batch of elite soldiers from Unit Invincible. Remembering his devious actions performed on a computer, he said to the Colonel, "We ought to check Cairns' computer and what his actions have included while studying I.T for when he was about to be released into civilian life."

Colonel Armstrong in a concerned voice, said, "Surely, he hasn't been planning while going to these lessons, has he?"

General Hardaker didn't reply, instead he remained quiet knowing how what was once a respected officer could now become an evil, scheming sadistic man.

One of the medics contacted the control centre making them aware that they had found Ferguson. Colonel Armstrong looked with concern replying, "Is he alive?"

The medic whose name was Ron Crenna, said with concern, "He's alive, but in a bad way."

Colonel Armstrong asked, "Are there any other survivors?"

Feeling dejected, Crenna replied, "Sir, all the military police travelling, except for Ferguson are dead."

Colonel Armstrong clenched his fist and said, "Damn it!"

Feeling saddened by the events, Crenna carried onto say, "Sir, we're going to bring back a few civilians, so they can be questioned later."

Starting to feel angry, Colonel Armstrong agreed with Crenna and carried on saying, "Good work Ron. Bring Ferguson back to base as soon as you can, because his condition sounds critical."

Two of the medics moved Ferguson, making him groan with the pain he had endured. Crenna, aware that Ferguson must be suffering, said, "Hold on, we'll get you back to base as soon as we can."

Ferguson occasionally kept opening and closing his eyes just nodded his head slowly agreeing. Crenna and his colleague Patterson carried Ferguson and hurried back to the helicopter, gently placing him inside. Crenna turned, looking behind at the wreckage, noticing that some of his colleagues helping injured workers, who had been working on the building site.

He waved his arm in anticipation, knowing that Ferguson's state of health was serious. They had to get in the air soon if Ferguson was to remain alive. Again he waved his arm making his colleagues move much more quickly. Crenna turned to Patterson saying, "Start the engines. We have to leave as soon as these people are aboard!"

Patterson finished dressing Ferguson's wound and then rushed into the cockpit to start the engines, making the rotary blades slowly rotate, and gather momentum quickly. Crenna watched his two colleagues climb into the helicopter with the injured workers and then turned back to Ferguson and said, "Try to hold on. We're going back to base now."

Ferguson opened his eyes wearily, nodding his head once more agreeing. Crenna climbed in and went to sit in the cockpit with Patterson, telling him to take off and fly back to base immediately. When they had climbed into the air, the squadron of F35 fighter planes joined them, escorting them back to base. Crenna asked the squadron leader, "Did you see anything?"

The squadron leader held the radio feeling disappointment and replied, "No! Cairns must have escaped!"

Crenna flicked the switch wanting to contact base to confirm that he was flying back to base with a military escort from the F35 fighter planes. Colonel Armstrong, concerned for Ferguson, asked, "How is Ferguson?"

Crenna looked behind at him, turned back while holding the radio to his mouth and replied, "Critical."

Colonel Amstrong placed the radio down by his side, thought for a few seconds and then ordered a couple of military ambulances to be driven to where the helicopter would be landing. General Hardaker, who had been watching closely said, "I ought to call Colonel Wareing to let him know what has happened and that Cairns will not be arriving in the United States."

Everybody watched General Hardaker turn and walk away feeling deflated. As everybody watched General Hardaker leave, they all shared the same thought, which was, what happened to Cairns, and who's taken him?

Communications

$\mathcal{G}$eneral Hardaker walked past his personal assistant, where she noticed that he seemed annoyed. Sensing this, she asked, "Is everything okay, sir?"

General Hardaker, still thinking about what had happened earlier, stopped, turned back to face his assistant, and replied, "Jackie, can you get me Colonel Wareing on the phone. I need to discuss something urgently with him."

Jackie didn't hesitate; she started to dial the number straight away, as the General walked into his office to sit down behind his desk wondering what to do about the serious crisis that had occurred. The phone beeped, which made the General pick up the receiver and listen to Jackie tell him that Colonel Wareing was now on the phone. The General thanked her, leaving her to place the phone down so the General could speak with Colonel Wareing.

General Hardaker gave a huge sigh asking, "Why isn't life ever simple?"

Colonel Wareing sniggered replying, "Then there wouldn't be any challenge. How are you General?"

General Hardaker narrowed his eyes slightly, thinking about Cairns, aware that he had become a major challenge for him. Before mentioning Cairns had escaped, General Hardaker thought best to be rid of the pleasantries before discussing the real matter of the conversation. Colonel Wareing was first to bring up the subject of Cairns' trip home, making the General have to reluctantly say, "He won't be travelling back to the United States. He has escaped!"

Colonel Wareing frowned in disbelief, asking in a sombre voice, "How did this occur?"

General Hardaker, feeling angry about this crisis, which had been planned meticulously, replied, "Cairns is a clever devious man, and for him to have escaped, he must have arranged it."

Colonel Wareing, asked with concern, "Who with?"

General Hardaker sighed again, and replied, "That's the annoying point! We don't yet know!"

Colonel Wareing frowned while changing hands to hold the phone and said, "There will probably be an inquest about what happened."

General Hardaker closed his eyes for a moment, replying to the Colonel, "I know there will have to be an inquest. We have brought witnesses from the scene of the conflict, hoping to ask one of our own soldier's questions about events that took place when Cairns escaped."

Colonel Wareing listened hard to what the General was telling him, and asked, "Who would want this man?"

General Hardaker thought again, remembering how he had previously performed acts of treason against his own country to help leaders of the Middle East. He mentioned this to the Colonel, telling him Raven had managed to get rid of the cancer in Iraq when President Rashaid and General Luchinski had conspired in trying to take all Kuwait's wealth. They agreed, ruling out Iraq being involved with Cairns' release, but Colonel Wareing did say, "Iran has been in the news a lot today, with President Berry often seen to be having a war of words with their leader."

General Hardaker replied, "No, surely not! He couldn't have gone there, could he?"

Colonel Wareing put his hand to his forehead thinking of the effects that could occur if James Cairns used his knowledge and influence with the Iranians. There was a knock at the door, which made Colonel Wareing say, "Excuse me General."

He shouted, "Enter."

Captain Weller walked inside the office holding her bags while watching the Colonel place his hand up to her, letting her know that he was speaking with somebody on the phone. She waited in anticipation as she listened to the Colonel speak on the phone, causing her to frown after hearing the words, Cairns and Iran mentioned more than once. Colonel Wareing looked up to her, placed his hand out for her to take a seat while carrying on having his conversation with the General. She sat down waiting patiently for Colonel Wareing to end his conversation, and gazed at the picture of Colonel Lewis and the empty space that now appeared after the Colonel had thrown the picture of John Raven in temper. When Colonel Wareing mentioned he ought to let Raven know of what has happened, Captain Weller looked away from the picture and sharply at the Colonel holding a face of concern while waiting eagerly for him to end his call.

Colonel Wareing thanked General Hardaker for letting him know about the crisis involving Cairns, which made him pause for a few seconds and then say, "Colonel, look after Raven, because Cairns does have a serious vendetta against him."

Colonel Wareing, knowing that John Raven will retire from the U.S. military soon, replied, "Sir. Trust me! Raven can look after himself. I don't know whether you're aware, but Raven is retiring after he has finished training Unit Expendable."

Captain Weller looked down at the floor thinking what life around the U.S. base would be like once John Raven had left the military for good.

General Hardaker contradicted Colonel Wareing, replying, "Colonel Lewis's boy will never leave the military completely, somewhere inside him, there will always be that warrior who will eventually want to fight once more."

"You're wrong sir, this time John has finally accepted time has caught up with him, and he is bowing out gracefully. I do have to admit the son of a bitch is still the best of the best!"

Captain Weller looked up at the Colonel after hearing the way he spoke about John, and produced a wry smile knowing that he was right.

General Hardaker not convinced that John will leave the military said, "Who knows what the future holds? When you decide to tell John what has happened to Cairns, he may be in a different frame of mind."

Colonel Wareing looked behind his chair at the wall where John's picture once hung beside his good friend, Colonel Lewis, and casually replied to the General, "Possibly."

They exchanged pleasantries again and said goodbye to each other. Colonel Wareing placed the receiver down and looked across towards Captain Weller and said, "Just one moment Captain. I have to correct something I do regret doing."

Captain Weller stood up, walked over to the window, moved the venetian blinds, and watched the soldiers parading around even on a cold December day. While watching the soldiers she imagined the time John Raven came back to the force after being asked to do so by the military on a special terms basis. At the time he agreed to carry on training Colonel Lewis' last elite batch of Green Berets that were called Unit Invincible.

Colonel Wareing spoke on the phone wanting to order the finest picture he could ever imagine of John Raven. Captain Weller turned around, listening to him describing how he wanted this new picture to look and to show that he is still the legend of today and the soldier of tomorrow. The people Colonel Wareing was speaking with told him that to produce the finished article of what he had described, they would need several images. Colonel Wareing agreed confirming that he would have it arranged, wanting nothing less than the best to be produced when it will once again hang on his wall beside Colonel Lewis.

When he placed the phone down, Captain Weller said, "I'm proud of you and John would be proud of you."

The Colonel looked to his side watching Captain Weller walk and take her seat once more. He then asked, "With what happened in this room, the last time he was here, do you really think so?"

Captain Weller produced a wry grin with wanting to speak about John, replying, "You know John; he'll get over the friction that occurred in this room because he's a much bigger person than that to hold a grudge. Sure, he can be a stubborn mule, but somewhere inside that man, he does have a heart of gold."

Colonel Wareing reluctantly nodded his head agreeing while listening to Captain Weller carrying on to say, "You only need to watch how he is with Sarah Jane and John, when they're around. They're a huge reason for him starting to mellow."

Colonel Wareing gave a half-laugh, which made Captain Weller frown at him and then listen to him reply, "Mellow! What was all that about in my office when he made members of Unit Expendable do press ups on broken glass? He even made Sarah Jane perform the same exercise for Christ's sake!"

Captain Weller defended John replying, "There is a reason for everything with John. We may not know now, but I'm sure we will soon."

Colonel Wareing narrowed his eyes after hearing Captain Weller's comment and asked, "Do you still have feelings for the old dog?"

Captain Weller laughed a little as she replied. "John was a part of my life, and yes I still do have feelings for him, but not in the way you think. That side of things is finished."

Colonel Wareing, feeling as though he had heard enough small talk opened his drawer to bring out the folder, Operation Gulf Warrior, and place it onto his desk. Captain Weller for a brief moment stared at the folder and asked, "When do I have to travel to perform my duties?"

Colonel Wareing before answering the Captain's question opened the folder, looked down to read the report and then slowly looked up to the Captain replying, "The day after tomorrow."

Captain Weller feeling disappointed with having to cancel Christmas with her family said, "I guess Christmas will have to be placed on hold this year?"

Colonel Wareing, who also felt her disappointment, holding a sombre face replied, "It wasn't my decision Debbie. It came from the top. One of the senior I.T personnel posted on the aircraft carrier, U.S.S. Abraham Lincoln is seriously ill and has to be replaced as soon as possible. Your duties will be explained when you arrive."

Captain Weller appeared a little disappointed to say the least, which made Colonel Wareing say, "Look on the bright side, at least spring will have arrived when you come home."

Captain Weller nodded her head agreeing and then asked, "What time do I leave?"

Colonel Wareing looked down at the report and then back at her replying, "07.00am Tuesday morning."

Captain Weller decided to react in a professional way by saying, "I had better pack a few things. Oh, and I want to see John before I leave."

Colonel Wareing picked up the phone wanting to make another phone call. Before dialling the number, he replied to Captain Weller, "That's fine; just don't be late for the departure on Tuesday morning."

Captain Weller, feeling bitterly disappointed listened to every word Colonel Wareing had just mentioned, and while watching him dial the numbers, she said, "Okay Colonel, bye."

Colonel Wareing raised his hand in acknowledgment while holding the phone to his ear, and watched Captain Weller walk from his office. Colonel Wareing stood at his desk listening to the phone constantly ringing in his ear. He was about to give up and place the phone down when Raven answered the phone by saying, "Yo."

Colonel Wareing replied, "John, its Colonel Wareing."

Raven who wasn't in the mood for a conversation with the Colonel after what had previously happened in his office, replied, "I know!"

Colonel Wareing detected with John's voice, he still held a grudge about what had happened previously, and with this said, "I'm sorry about what happened in my office John."

John held the phone tightly, narrowing his eyes slightly and replied, "Yeah!"

Colonel Wareing aware that John was making it hard for him said in a disgruntled voice, "You're not making this easy for me John!"

John didn't respond to that comment, instead he asked, "What can I do for you?"

Colonel Wareing, who still detected a tone in John's voice said, "I think it's only right that you should know that Cairns escaped while travelling back to the United States."

John, while holding the phone tightly went quiet making the Colonel ask, "John, did you hear me?"

John, who was trying to absorb what had just been told to him, replied, "Yeah, I heard! What are you going to do about it?"

Colonel Wareing decided to ignore John's attitude, replying, "We're not sure yet, I just thought I ought to let you know, that's all."

John's father, Richard Raven, walked into the lounge asking, "Who's on the phone John?"

John ignored his father's question and carried on speaking with the Colonel by asking, "Where has Cairns gone?"

Colonel Wareing closed his eyes feeling embarrassed, replying, "We don't yet know."

Richard walked over to John, handing him a cup of coffee. John stared at his father nodding his head in appreciation toward him, took a sip, and then carried on his conversation with the Colonel by asking, "Who is responsible for Cairns escaping?"

Colonel Wareing sat down feeling frustrated at questions being put to him that he could not answer. Placing his hand to his forehead, he replied, "John, we don't know anything, all we do know is that Cairns has escaped, and he does have a personal vendetta against you."

Listening to these words made John become quiet for a few seconds before replying to the Colonel in a stern voice, "Bring it on, I'll be ready!"

Richard, while taking a sip of coffee looked across at his son with concern, suspecting the military were trying once more to get their claws into him.

Colonel Wareing brought a wry smile to his face hearing John say these words. Feeling as though he wasn't able to discuss the topic amicably with him, he decided to end the conversation by saying, "I just thought I ought to let you know."

John glanced across to his father and replied, "Yeah, thanks!"

Colonel Wareing started to feel as though he was starting to lose the good friendship he had with John, which made him repeat himself once more by saying, "I'm sorry about what happened previously in my office."

John gave a casual blink, replying, "Yeah! You said!"

Colonel Wareing now held a frosty face and decided to diversify with the conversation by saying, "Debbie is coming to visit you before she leaves on Tuesday. Be nice to her John. We are sorry for what happened."

John immediately replied, "Will you stop saying sorry!"

Colonel Wareing thinking back to the heated discussion that took place in his office said, "I got it wrong . . . ."

John interrupted him by saying, "You did!"

Colonel Wareing said again, "John, I got it wrong, but at the same time you're making it hard for me too!"

John narrowed his eyes and said nothing, leaving Colonel Wareing to say goodbye. Before the Colonel hung up, John said, "Colonel."

Colonel Wareing placed the phone back to his ear and answered, "Yes."

John replied in a sombre voice, "Thanks for letting me know."

Colonel Wareing held the phone to his ear where the signal had disappeared making him place the phone back down on the hook wondering had he now lost what was once a good friend.

Emotions

Captain Weller had prepared her kit and was ready for departure the following day when she would board the aircraft carrier, U.S.S. Abraham Lincoln, positioned somewhere in the Gulf. Today, however, will be spent with members of her family, before she travelled away, knowing that she would be absent from them for a few months.

Debbie placed her bags with Christmas presents for the family into the trunk and then went to climb inside the car to start her journey. As she drove with the flow of traffic, she noticed different people doing their Christmas shopping, which made her produce a wry smile. Seeing this made her want to do some more shopping, so before travelling to visit John Raven, she decided to park the car and visit a few more shops. She looked through a window outside a jewellery store at a watch, wondering if Raven will like it, after always wearing the same black watch for years gone by. Casually, she walked inside waiting for a shop attendant to become free. As she waited, she browsed at other items, with a gold necklace catching her eye. An attendant became free and walked across to her, where she asked in a polite way, "Can I help you?"

Debbie looked up replying, "Yes. May I have a closer look at the gold necklace on display and the watch over there in the window?"

"Certainly you can." The attendant replied.

Debbie watched her bring the gold necklace out of the glass cabinet and place it on the counter for her to look at, while she went to get the watch on display in the main window. Looking at the necklace, she thought of her daughter, Sarah Jane, and knew for sure that she would like this piece of jewellery.

The shop attendant walked back to Debbie, watching her looking at the necklace closely. Before placing the watch down she asked, "Is the necklace for anybody special?"

Debbie casually looked up to face the shop attendant, smiled, and replied, "Yes. It's for my daughter."

The shop attendant who was anxious for a sale said in a vibrant way, "I'm sure she will be thrilled with this at Christmas."

Debbie picked up the necklace, and held it for a few moments. She noticed people coming in and out of the shop and then turned to the attendant replying, "You're right, I will take it. Will you gift wrap it for me?"

The shop attendant smiled replying, "Of course I will. Would you also like to buy the watch?"

The shop attendant started to gift wrap the necklace, occasionally watching Debbie, holding the watch to study it some more. Looking across to the attendant, she said, "It's a class watch."

The attendant, who was just placing a bow on the necklace smirked saying, "Oh yes. It's an Omega. James Bond wears this style of watch."

Debbie grinned, thinking about John Raven and replied, "Trust me; this is for a person who is twice the man of James Bond."

With Debbie saying this, made the shop attendant ask politely, "So, you will also want to buy this too?"

She nodded her head agreeing while saying, "It isn't going to do my credit card statement much good, but they're worth it."

The shop attendant grinned as she started to gift wrap the watch and replied, "Christmas can be expensive."

Debbie opened her handbag and brought out her purse. She watched the attendant wrap the red Omega box as she brought her Visa card out of her purse. The shop attendant finished wrapping the present by placing a bow on top of the box, and then placed her hand out to take the card from Debbie to pay for the goods. The shop attendant gave her two gift tags to fill in while she processed her card. Debbie brought a pen from her handbag and filled the gift tags in wishing Sarah Jane and John Raven a Merry Christmas and apologising for not being available on Christmas Day. When the card transaction was done, she gave Debbie her card and receipt and said, "Thank you. Have a nice Christmas."

Debbie thought about her journey to the Gulf and replied, "Thank you. I will."

The shop attendant watched her carry her bags and walk out of the shop, which made the manager walk over to her and say, "That person you just served was a classy woman."

The attendant carried on watching her walk into the distance, while chuckling at the manager, then moved away to serve another customer replying, "You're just hoping aren't you?"

Debbie visited a few more shops, buying more Christmas presents for other people she knew that were close to her. She walked a different way back to her car noticing a lingerie shop on the opposite side of the road. She waited with other people for the traffic to stop before crossing the road with them to head for the lingerie store. When she walked inside to look at the underwear, a female attendant approached her asking, "What colour of underwear do you prefer?"

Debbie looked away from the underwear, replying, "I will take three pairs of those black knickers, three of those black bras, and two of those black strapless bras. I will also take the same in white."

The attendant replied, "No problem. I will just go and get these items for you."

Debbie waited at the counter for the attendant to place the garments into a bag before taking the card from her to pay for the goods. Debbie walked out of the shop, turned left and started to walk back to the car park to collect her car.

As she walked, she heard a humble voice from somebody sitting on the ground keep repeating himself by asking, "Can you spare a couple of dollars?"

Debbie walked slowly, starting to watch people with their Christmas shopping frantically pass by a person who just seemed to have had some bad luck to be in such a position. She stopped walking, paused, and decided to place her hand inside her handbag to bring out her purse. Looking at the person sitting on the floor with a jacket wrapped around him to keep him warm; she opened her purse and brought out five dollars. As she approached the man sitting on the ground, she closed the purse and placed it back inside her handbag. People would glimpse, judging her as she approached the tramp sitting on the pavement. She heard snide remarks from different people passing by say, "It's his fault for being in this position." Others would say, "Don't waste your money; he will only use it on drugs, booze, or cigarettes!"

Feeling sorry for the man sitting on the ground, Debbie ignored all those snide comments, making her look and think, it's Christmas, if you can't help somebody at this time of the year, when can you help somebody? The man sitting on the cold pavement asked in a humble voice, "Miss, can you spare a couple of dollars?"

Looking gracefully down at the man, she took a few more paces and leaned forward to give to him the five dollars she had just taken out of her purse. The man thanked her, making her start to feel sorry for him. She crouched down wanting to ask, "How did you get into a position like this?"

The man looked straight ahead before answering, reflecting on his life for a few moments. He slowly looked up at Debbie, genuinely concerned about him briefly replying, "I had a dream."

Debbie with concern, asked, "Did you achieve it?"

The man before answering the question started to think back to his normal life before suffering the hardship he was now enduring, replied, "I longed every day that he would call."

Debbie frowned asking, "Who?"

Feeling sadness, the man went quiet, which made Debbie ask, "What's your name?"

The man turned focusing on the present day with people walking past him and Debbie and replied, "Gerard."

Debbie stood up and said, "I'm going to buy you a hot drink."

Gerard raised his hand in appreciation saying, "Thank you."

Debbie went to walk across the road to a fast-food outlet. She went inside and ordered a hot drink and a sandwich. Whilst waiting for her order to be processed, she looked out of the window at Gerard sitting on the ground starting to wonder what he meant when he had mentioned those words about who would call. The attendant came back to Debbie with her order, where she graciously brought out her purse once more to pay for it. She took the hot sandwich and drink to Gerard, who was watching from the other side of the road. She handed the sandwich and drink to him, where he accepted it graciously saying, "Thank you. You're a good woman."

Debbie didn't reply to that comment. She just thought back to the time she held a dark secret for many years. She then held his hand tenderly saying, "Hold onto your dream. It may just happen."

Gerard looked up at her, paused thinking about her kindness, and later said, "Merry Christmas."

Smiling at Gerard, she replied, "I'm sure you will receive that call. You take care and try to enjoy your Christmas."

Gerard taking a sip of his hot drink nodded his head agreeing with her and said once more, "Thank you."

Debbie turned away, starting to walk to the car park reflecting on what had just happened. When she reached her car, she placed the bags into the trunk, and then climbed into the driver's seat. She placed the key into the ignition and turned it making the engine turn over and start. Slowly, she reversed out of her parking place and drove forward continuing down a couple of levels, to the attendant, who was waiting to take her ticket before raising the barrier for her to drive out of the car park. When she had paid the car park attendant, she drove following the traffic at a sensible speed listening to the radio in the background. Christmas songs from the past and present were being played on the radio. When one song with the title, *True Colours* was starting to play, it brought back memories of when Louise was sitting next to her feeling distraught with seeing her son, John Weller-Raven, reveal the person for whom he is. She turned the volume down because it reminded her of *America In Conflict* when she had to witness different emotions around her, while trying to remain professional. As the song played in the background, she had a flashback when she placed her gun into the mouth of a terrorist, who had been constantly outspoken and had hit a raw nerve, making her react in this way. She remembered Colonel Wareing climbing from his Harrier jet, taking off his helmet as he briskly walked over to her. She spoke quietly in the car repeating those same words, she had mentioned to the Blade, "I'm no whore!"

The song called *True Colours* was fading out causing the disc jockey to speak over the music, which made Debbie think about Gerard, who she had briefly met earlier, hoping that he would get his call one day soon. Debbie turned the volume up wanting to listen to the radio some more while driving to John Raven's house feeling better the song had now finished. Driving with the flow of traffic, she signalled to turn right, drove four hundred yards up the road and then signalled to turn left, driving straight on following the curves of the road. Driving closer to John's house she noticed some mail hanging from Richard's mailbox. With this she signalled, and pulled over to stop, climb out and went to the old mailbox showing the name, R Raven. She looked at the name on the mailbox, bringing a wry smile to her face, as she collected the mail and climbed back inside her car. With leaving the engine running, she just needed to release the handbrake and pull away slowly, where she turned left down Richard and John's long driveway. The sound of the gravel and the snow crunched as she parked the car. The dogs realising a visitor had arrived ran out to see who had come. Richard saw Debbie collecting some bags from the trunk and then watched her making her way to the front door immediately asking, "Is this a military call or a personal call?"

As Debbie walked closer, she gave a half-hearted laugh replying, "Richard, you will never change! I'm here on a personal call for the family, not with the military."

When Debbie had reached Richard and stood in front of him, Richard, who looked at her sternly, asked, "You do know John is leaving the military soon?"

Debbie gave one of the bags and the mail to Richard to carry inside the house and replied, "Yes. I do know, and he will be missed."

Richard stopped walking to look behind him at Debbie, and said, "Promise me that none of you will ask him to come back and fight again."

Debbie shook her head from side to side saying, "Richard. It's over! When he has trained Unit Expendable, he is going to retire from the military for good."

Richard turned back to walk towards the lounge replying, "You've made me a happy man."

Debbie followed, feeling relieved that something did make Raven senior happy. Richard opened the door, walked inside the lounge and said to Sarah Jane, who was sitting on the sofa and John, sitting in the chair, "We have a visitor."

They looked at the door watching who was about to walk inside the lounge. When Sarah Jane saw that it was her mother, she got up wanting to greet her with Debbie immediately saying, "Show me your hands."

Raven's eyes narrowed slightly at that comment, but he chose to say nothing. As Debbie hugged Sarah Jane, John asked, "So what do we owe the pleasure?"

Sarah Jane let go of her mother, turned around to face her father and said, "Dad, don't be nasty!"

Richard asked her to take a seat, which she did. She composed herself as she looked across at John, with Sarah

Jane and Richard wanting to listen in anticipation with what she was about to say. In a sombre voice she asked, "Do you remember when you asked me if I would like to visit you over the Christmas period?"

John slowly nodded his head agreeing and listened to Debbie say, "Colonel Wareing told you that I have to fly out to perform hi tech I.T duties on one of our aircraft carriers. Well, I have to travel tomorrow and won't be back at least until spring next year."

Sarah Jane letting her emotions take over, said, "I'm going to miss you Mum."

John glimpsed at his father standing nearby, but chose to remain silent. Debbie turned to Sarah Jane and said, "At times you will have to be posted to different parts of the world. Ask your father, he has done it all."

John listened to Debbie speaking and moved those piercing eyes to focus on his daughter to watch what her reaction would be. Sarah Jane glimpsed at her father to see the menacing stare looking back at her. She then turned away to speak with her mother, asking, "You will keep in touch won't you?"

Debbie being a considerate mother replied, "You know I will."

She then leaned forward to place her hand into one of the bags and brought out a Christmas present and gave it to Richard. He immediately said, "You didn't need to buy me anything."

Debbie glanced at John and then looked up at Richard to say, "It's Christmas and you're family."

John moved his eyes, watching everything going on around him. Debbie then said, "You can open it now if you like. Christmas is only a few days away."

Richard, who was feeling rather excited, turned to Sarah Jane asking, "What do you think, should I wait until Christmas Day or should I open it now?"

John started to smirk, as Sarah Jane replied, "Open it while Mum's here, she would like that."

Richard glimpsed at John sitting in the chair, where he nodded his head agreeing. Captain Weller smiled at him and placed her hand out to give him his present, making him ask, "This is for me?"

Sarah Jane looked across starry-eyed at her father, who was reading the gift tag, where it said, To John, best of the best, Merry Christmas, sorry I won't be here xxx. John produced a wry grin when he read the gift tag, and then started slowly to rip the wrapping paper open. Debbie watched in anticipation, hoping that he would like the present she had bought him. When John could see the red box that showed the Omega logo, he said, "You shouldn't have, you've spent far too much."

He pulled away the rest of the paper and held the box; carefully opening it to look at what he already knew was a class watch. Sarah Jane said, "Try it on Dad."

John took off his black watch and put it on the chair arm. He gently placed the new watch on to his wrist and said, "It feels different."

Debbie asked, "Do you like it?"

John nodded his head agreeing and said, "Thanks."

Richard placed his arm on John's shoulder and said, "Son. You were getting ready for a new watch. You've had that one for many years."

Once again, John nodded his head agreeing. He then took off the new watch and said that he would wear it after he had finished training Unit Expendable. He placed it back inside the box and listened to Sarah Jane, who was watching her father's reaction, ask, "You do like the watch, don't you Dad?"

John stood up, and took the box to place it underneath the Christmas tree. As he was crouched down, he looked back at Sarah Jane replying, "You know I do."

Sarah Jane narrowed her eyes slightly suspecting different, but chose to say nothing for fear of hurting her mother's feelings. Debbie gave a half-hearted smile as she turned to Richard to ask, "Was your present okay?"

Richard replied, "Buying socks for somebody at Christmas has always been a safe bet. Thank you."

Debbie looked back at John, who was starting to stand up taking notice of a few more unopened presents next to the tree. She looked at the Christmas tree with the decorations flickering, and then at John. Surprised, she asked, "Did you decorate the tree?"

John smirked, which made Debbie say, "I thought not! Some things never change!"

Hearing those words made John look down at her starting to remember the past they once shared, which made him walk outside for a bit of fresh air. After watching him walk out of the room, Debbie placed her hand into her bag for Sarah Jane's present. Sarah Jane's reaction was to give her mother a hug and then say, "Thank you."

Richard walked over to the window and saw John throwing the ball for the dogs to chase. Debbie watched Sarah Jane unwrap her present, and then glanced at Richard watching John outside play with the dogs. Debbie said, "He will be lost when he finally leaves the U.S. military for good."

Once over, Richard would have turned around and snapped at her for making such a remark. Not this time, he just stood there at the window watching his son throw the ball for the dogs to chase. In a solemn voice, he replied, "I know, but it does feel good knowing he will be home forever in a few weeks."

Debbie smiled as she walked over to stand beside him, while still taking notice of John outside, she asked, "Are you mellowing Richard?"

Richard sniggered at Debbie's question. He then turned to Sarah Jane, who was trying on her necklace and said, "That's nice."

Sarah Jane agreed, and went over to her mother to give her another hug and say thank you once more. Debbie patted her back tenderly replying, "I'm glad you like it. It makes it all worthwhile."

She looked back outside the window to see the gentle side of John Raven, and then turned to Sarah Jane, taking her hands to look at the wounds that had been created through John's arrogance. Feeling sorry for Sarah, she said, "When your training officially starts, your father is going to come down hard on you, make no mistake about that! Just persevere, and remember that you're his daughter, who will not quit, because believe me, he will try to break you."

Sarah Jane placed her hands behind her neck to unclip the necklace. She too looked outside at her father, thinking how could a man who appeared so calm and gentle, turn into the raging beast most men would fear. Richard who had been listening to the brief conversation between Sarah Jane and Debbie, glimpsed at his son asking, "Is he that bad?"

Debbie replied, "He's much worse! Isn't that right Sarah?"

Sarah, who was now placing the necklace next to her father's new watch, replied, "When he's on duty, he's a different man. I already knew this after I saw him in action, when he and my brother came to rescue me and the President of the United States."

Debbie listened to Sarah's reply with intent, but with fearing she wasn't as strong as her brother, she said, "Sarah, Colonel Lewis taught all his units he had trained, there was no pain. Believe this Sarah, and trust in your inner instincts, because when pain arrives, and it will, blank it and tell yourself there is indeed no pain."

Richard, who was still listening, asked, "What kind of people are you?"

Sarah Jane could see her grandfather was becoming upset and walked over to him to give him a hug and look up to him and say, "We're the best, but do you know what? Being a Raven is even better than I had imagined."

Richard put his arms around her and gave her a hug, replying, "That's my girl."

Debbie looked through the window at John once more, and then turned back to watch Sarah Jane with her grandfather and thought that Sarah Jane was a chip off the old block. She walked over to the chair John had been sitting in earlier and picked up his own watch, starting to slowly caress it. She turned to face Richard and Sarah and said gracefully, "There are many memories with this watch."

She kept hold of the watch, and then went to collect her bag, telling Richard and Sarah Jane that she must leave because she had to go and visit her son, John, and his girlfriend, Louise. Sarah Jane became a little frustrated with the fact she had to leave so soon. Debbie frowned at her saying, "Sarah Jane. I have to leave tomorrow, and I have so much to do."

Sarah Jane feeling guilty replied, "I haven't done my Christmas shopping yet."

Debbie gave a half-hearted laugh and said, "I can see that you're picking up some of your father's bad habits by waiting until the last minute."

Sarah Jane said, "No! I wanted to buy you this bracelet I had seen, and now I can't give it to you. I feel bad with accepting the necklace you have given to me."

Debbie placed her hand out to Sarah Jane to reassure her while saying, "Sarah Jane, the best thing you could give me this Christmas is to become an elite member of Unit Expendable."

Sarah Jane remained quiet, glanced at her grandfather, and then nodded her head agreeing with her mother, replying, "I'll do it for you no matter how much pain is inflicted on me."

Debbie squeezed her hand tenderly, as she said, "That's my girl, because you're also my girl too."

Sarah Jane's eyes started to glaze over, which made her say, "I love you Mum."

Debbie started to feel her own eyes starting to glaze over and become upset. She turned to Richard and said, "See what kids do to you."

Richard, who was listening hard to every word said, chose to say nothing. Instead, he placed his hand gently on Debbie's back and slowly walked with her outside. John saw the rest of the family coming outside, which made him ask, "Are you leaving Debbie?"

Debbie placed her hand out giving John his own watch back and replied to him, while watching him place it onto his wrist, "I have to visit John and Louise before I leave tomorrow."

John gave a solemn stare when he heard their names and said, "Thanks for the present; I'm sorry, I didn't get you anything."

Debbie gave a half-hearted laugh replying, "Nothing changes! You're still the same old John!"

Listening to the tone in Debbie's voice, John stood there feeling perplexed. Debbie walked by him, thumping him gently on his arm saying, "Do you know what you can give me for Christmas?"

John turned narrowing his eyes staring at Debbie, feeling intrigued while waiting for the answer about to be revealed. Looking at John, she chuckled before carrying onto say, "You appear uptight John."

John's eyes remained narrowed, as he crouched down to pick the ball up and throw it for the dogs to chase. With his back facing Debbie, he said, "You were saying?"

Debbie, who was containing her anger with John after turning his back on her replied, "John, John!"

Richard intervened saying, "Son. Debbie is speaking to you!"

Slowly, he turned around with his piercing eyes to face Debbie, who was also holding a frosty face waiting for her to speak. She looked back into his face, where she could still see the legendary soldier everybody else just wants to be. Her face softened when she asked, "Where did it all go wrong?"

Sarah Jane watched them both to see what their reaction was going to be. John gave a prolonged blink choosing not to reply. Instead, he started to turn away again, making Debbie say, "That wasn't what I wanted to ask."

John turned back, asking, "So what did you want to ask?"

Holding a much softer face, Debbie replied, "I was going to ask will you drive me to Louise's house with John staying there for a few days?"

John didn't speak. He thought for a few seconds, making Debbie say in a stern voice, "You'll never change John!"

John just nodded his head agreeing, making her ask, "Yes you will take me, or yes you will never change?"

John replied in a solemn voice, "I'll take you to Louise's house."

"Good, I'll just get my bags from my car and place them in your car."

Debbie said goodbye to Sarah Jane and Richard and started walking over to her own car. John, who was following, turned to his father and daughter and said, "I'll see you both later."

Richard and Sarah Jane watched them both, with Sarah Jane saying to her grandfather, "I'm impressed with Mum, with how she can handle Dad at times."

Richard chuckled, placed his arm around his granddaughter and then started to walk back inside the house out of the cold brisk December weather, replying, "Your Dad isn't that bad."

Sarah Jane heard her grandfather's words, but chose to say nothing and just keep walking holding one thought, no pain.

Travelling

$\mathcal{J}$ohn closed the car door, inserted the key into the ignition, quickly turning it to make the engine turn over and start. Debbie opened the passenger door, climbed inside the 4x4, sitting beside John and then pulled the seat belt across her chest to buckle herself in. After Debbie had closed the door, John slowly started to drive forward while looking at the dogs following his father and Sarah Jane back inside the house. John beeped his horn, which made Richard and Sarah Jane turn around to wave at them. Debbie gave a casual wave back to them and then turned to watch out of the front windscreen. She started to worry about her daughter, making her want to ask John, "You will go easy on Sarah Jane, when the serious training with Unit Expendable begins?"

John, who had his arm resting next to the window has he held the steering wheel ignored the question by asking Debbie, "It's chilly, are you warm enough?"

Debbie turned her head staring at him for a few seconds, which John had noticed in the corner of his right eye. She nudged his arm saying, "You will look after her and protect her, won't you?"

John, who didn't want to discuss Unit Expendable replied, "Forget work!"

Debbie turned to look out of the front windscreen again. She paused for a few seconds and then spoke in a different tone by saying, "It's not work! It's our daughter,

I'm concerned about with you always feeling as though you have to produce the best with being taught by the best. I know she will be in for a rough ride!"

John started to brake and slowdown has he approached a set of traffic lights. He took his hand away from the steering wheel, rested his head on his hand and scratched his forehead replying, "Probably."

John's reply enraged Debbie, making her say in an angry voice, "You only have one daughter!"

John took his hand away from his forehead and placed it back onto the steering wheel. He then turned to face Debbie, replying, "I know I only have one daughter! It's just a pity, I didn't get to know her or my son sooner! Perhaps my life may have been a whole lot different!"

Debbie looked away holding a frosty face with being reminded of the dark secret she had held for many years before telling John the truth. The lights changed to amber, followed by green, making John rev the engine and move forward following the traffic travelling in front of him. Debbie rested her arm next to the passenger window and then rested her head on to her hand feeling hurt and rather fed up. Watching the traffic in front of her, she replied to John's comment by saying, "I know I didn't tell you sooner about John and Sarah Jane, and I'll always regret that until the day I die."

She turned to face John deciding to place her hand on his and carried on saying, "At least I did tell you the truth."

John remained quiet, casually blinking, thinking about how he did eventually find out about John Weller being his son. As he drove, he remembered Debbie has a frantic desperate mother concerned about her son, after being captured by the Russians and the Iraqi's. Remembering when he had received the truth for the first time, and then deciding to drive off into the desert feeling angry, he said, "Sorry."

Debbie asked, "For what?"

Taking his eyes away from the road, John turned, glancing at her for a few seconds and replied, "For walking out when you told me the truth about our son."

Hearing these words made Debbie's face mellow, where she gave a wry smile and said, "There were so many times I wanted to tell you, but I just couldn't find the right moment."

John, thinking back to when he had to come back into battle once more, when this time was for the son he never knew, also gave a wry smirk, making Debbie ask, "What are you grinning at?"

John, who was driving along the road sensibly, following the traffic in an orderly fashion said, "You tried to tell me about our son, and yet you couldn't have picked a worse time."

Debbie gave a prolonged blink has she started to think back to when her son had been captured, and how she helped John Raven escape. Visualising all the carnage, she replied, "I'll always be eternally grateful for what you did for our son when he suffered in Iraq and Sarah Jane when she was captured in North Korea. You know I've said this on many occasions, but you're the best of the best!"

John didn't know how to reply to Debbie, so he just answered in one word by saying, "Perhaps."

Debbie was about to speak when John stopped her by turning the volume up on the radio, wanting to listen to people discussing Iran and how they had now become a nuclear threat to the western world. Debbie, who was listening too said, "World War 3 will take place through nations in the Middle East."

John nodded his head reluctantly agreeing and carried on driving while listening to the radio, which made Debbie say, "God forbid! If World War 3 ever does arrive, at least you won't be a part of it anymore because you've done your time."

Whilst placing his signal on, John thought about what Debbie had just mentioned. He slowed down starting to turn left and then accelerate away replying, "You're right. I've done my time."

Debbie gave a cheeky smirk, reminding him that he had said those words before, making him confirm that after he had trained Unit Expendable; his military days would be finally over for good. Debbie wasn't convinced, and realising if she chose to contradict that fact it may create friction, she chose to say nothing about it. For a few miles, she and John listened to the radio with people putting their opinions forward about Iran and Russia, who were becoming a powerful ally. Plenty of music featuring a host of Christmas songs was also being played, making John say, "I'm looking forward to Christmas this year."

Debbie immediately replied in a harsh voice, asking, "Why, because I'm not here to share it with you?"

John gave a huge sigh, making him feel as though whatever he said would be received in the wrong way. Debbie detected John wasn't best pleased about the comment she had just made, and decided to change the conversation. With this she asked, "When you had trained your previous units, what were you looking for?"

For a few seconds, John glanced at the dash, briefly recalling his mentor, Colonel Lewis, and then replied, "One of the things Colonel Lewis always taught us all was to feel no pain."

Debbie interrupted him by saying, "Which you have also done."

As he gradually turned the steering wheel to overtake a Greyhound coach, John nodded his head agreeing and carried on saying. "When I did take over from Colonel Lewis at his request, I always felt I was in pursuit of perfection. With Unit Expendable I want perfection to come as standard."

Holding a face of concern, Debbie replied, "That's a big call."

In the distance, John saw a roundabout, which made him start to brake and slow down while saying. "Unit Expendable will have to go beyond their limits to achieve what I want from them. They're going to be my last group of elite soldiers whom I do want to be the best."

Debbie gave a loving smile replying, "You know what? Nobody will be as good as you."

John raised his eyebrows while saying, "I don't know about that, if our son hadn't arrived to save me when I was rescuing Sarah Jane, I might not have lived to tell the tale. In fact, I nearly didn't."

Debbie felt proud with John and Sarah Jane now knowing who their father is and replied, "Perhaps you're right, and you've realised the time has come to quit while you're ahead."

Still resting his arm next to the window while holding the steering wheel with his finger and thumb, he briefly visualised some of the conflicts he had been involved in replying, "Perhaps."

Visualising some of the conflicts he had faced while cruising along the road, he asked Debbie in a stern voice, "Do you know what my biggest disappointment is?"

Debbie turned her head slowly to face him holding a frown, replying, "No. What was it?"

John placed his hand around the steering wheel, holding it tightly has he started to think back. Watching his facial expression and the way he was now gripping the steering wheel, Debbie asked again, "John! What was your biggest disappointment?"

John narrowed his eyes, thinking back to the time he fought for the gallant Afghan people and a young Azar Sajadi, who wanted to take his knife and play with it. He remembered Azar asking him how many miles it would take for him to walk home, with him replying, about two years. He remembered the time he told Azar to go back, when he ignored him, choosing to be brave and enter the Russian fort. In return for his bravery, he gave to him the necklace, he had once worn, which had always reminded him of a beautiful oriental young woman. Ignoring Debbie's question, he gave a chuckle making Debbie just stare at him. John said out aloud, "Expendable."

Debbie, becoming confused, asked, "What?"

Approaching the traffic lights, John started to brake and slow down, stopping behind the car in front. He noticed the traffic crossing the busy road, travelling in both directions and turned to look at Debbie showing a perplexed face.

Knowing what she wanted to know, he said, "Years ago, somebody once told me that I wasn't expendable."

Debbie raised her eyebrows asking, "Who might that have been?"

John started thinking to the time when he and other members of the military visited Tony Hindle and were enjoying a barbeque. He recalled the question asked by his son, did you ever give a necklace to an Afghan boy. He narrowed his eyes feeling disappointment in what the boy had grown up to become. Driving along the road, he gave a prolonged blink, which made Debbie, who was still waiting for an answer tap his arm gently. John moved his eyes, frowning with recalling the past replying, "Do you remember when we were at Tony's and John asked me a question about the necklace he now owns?"

Debbie, feeling intrigued with the question, immediately answered, "Yes. You gave it to Azar for the bravery he had shown."

John, noticing the lights were about to change, nodded his head agreeing. Watching the traffic in front of him start to move, he revved the engine and moved forward starting to follow while saying. "The person I had taken this necklace from when I was sitting next to her on a boat reminded me that I wasn't expendable."

Debbie, still feeling intrigued replied, "Perhaps she was right. Being expendable could mean that you're not coming back."

After hearing that comment, in the corner of his eye, John glanced while saying, "It's ironic I should call my final batch of elite Green Berets, Unit Expendable."

Listening to John talk about what had happened in his life made her place her hand on his arm and say, "I'm sure Unit Expendable will be your finest batch of soldiers."

Modestly, John replied, "Possibly."

Debbie, now realising the necklace had once belonged to a woman asked, "The woman on the boat you spoke to. Was she a good friend?"

John, visualising her beauty, smirked, replying, "Do you mean where we once a couple? We were planning to be because she was going to travel to the U.S. with me. I always remember her telling me with a face of happiness that I had made a good choice, knowing that I will bring her back to the United States."

Concerned, Debbie asked, "Then what happened?"

John's eyes widened as he thought back to when he had so sadly lost her. He held the steering wheel tightly replying in a disgruntled voice. "Enemy soldiers killed her by shooting at her several times!"

Debbie asked, "Did you love her?"

John turned to face her, using his eyes to pierce her with his stare. He chose not to answer her question and carried on driving, which made her ask, "What did you do when she was killed?"

Reliving the nightmare, John raised his cheekbones, creating lines around his eyes. Recalling his ordeal, he replied, "I killed the enemy!"

Debbie wasn't surprised at John's reply, which made her ask, "What happened to the woman?"

Driving along the road watching people that were living for today and preparing for Christmas, he replied in a soft voice, "I buried her and took the necklace she wore to remind me of her. Years on, I gave the same necklace to Azar for the bravery he had shown when I went into battle to rescue Colonel Lewis."

Debbie, listening with intent replied, "I remember you telling us about that at the barbeque we attended at Tony's."

John slowly nodded his head agreeing with her and carried on saying, "To have witnessed that Azar had grown up into a terrorist filled me up with huge disappointment."

Realising John must have come face-to-face with Azar many years on, must have been a strange situation for him. Suspecting this, she asked, "Did you kill Azar?"

John glanced at her, replying, "Don't you remember? You were there on the Korean bridge when the terrorists were being released from your helicopter and about to be exchanged for President Susan Berry."

Reminding Debbie of what had happened, made her ask, "Do you regret killing Azar?"

John immediately answered her in a disgruntled voice, "No!"

He placed the signal on to pull into park the car, which made Debbie ask, "What are you doing?"

As he stopped the engine, released his seat belt and placed the hand brake on, he replied, "With speaking about the necklace and the history that goes with it, I remember placing it onto Tony's grave. Louise arrived later, taking it from the gravestone to give it to John, when I was hoping he would accept it because I did want him to take it. Fear of rejection meant I couldn't offer it to him with me already giving it to Azar many years ago."

Debbie understood what John was saying and closed the subject by saying, "At least it's in the right hands now."

John opened the car door to climb out, making Debbie say, "John. I don't think we can park here because it's an area for loading and unloading only."

John threw the car keys to her saying, "Move the car if you have to."

He closed the door and started to walk over to the same flower shop his son had previously visited. He went inside the shop with a commanding presence, walking towards the woman standing at the counter. He said in a calm way, "Can I have a bunch of yellow and red roses mixed."

The woman replied, "Certainly."

As the woman prepared the bunch of flowers for John, he turned to look outside at Debbie sitting inside the car. Noticing that everything was okay, he turned back to face the shop attendant, noticing a photograph of a young woman placed on a shelf next to the till. The shop attendant could see that John was taking notice of the photograph and said, "That's our daughter, Hayley."

Knowing he had met her at the induction he asked, "What does your daughter do for a living?"

The woman laughed, which made John watch with interest. Looking up at him, she replied, "I wanted my daughter to take over this business where she could have had a comfortable living."

John stood there, moving his eyes slowly, while offering her the money for the flowers and waited for her to carry on speaking. Hayley's mother sighed, and said, "Our daughter has always been the happy go lucky, care free type of girl, where danger doesn't exist."

John, placing the change he had received from the woman back into his pocket spoke in a low voice by saying, "That's interesting."

The woman looked at John after hearing him say something, which made her ask, "Excuse me?"

John stared at her, starting to make her feel uncomfortable and forget the comment she had just made. She decided to carry on speaking to him by saying. "Hayley has been a member of the U.S. Army for many years now and has progressed onto better things."

John already knew who Hayley was and started to smirk, but decided to say nothing and just let Hayley's Mum carry on speaking as she handed the bunch of flowers to him. She changed her facial expression saying, "I do so wish Hayley could have been a bank manager or a doctor. She had the knowledge to go far, but no, what does she do?"

John frowned, but chose to remain silent letting her carry on saying, "She has to become a full blown combat soldier, performing actions to kill the enemy. Can you believe this?"

John gave a casual blink replying, "Amazing."

John turned around holding the bunch of flowers to walk to the door when Hayley's Mum said, "I fear for my daughter!"

John stopped, turned around to face her and asked, "Why?"

Showing a face of concern, she replied, "I can't say too much."

John said, "Then don't!"

She ignored him, saying "Hayley has been transferred into a special unit where she will become an elite Green Beret."

John narrowed his eyes slightly, but chose just as before to remain silent. He watched her pick up the photo of Hayley and then listened to her say, "I hear that the leader of this group of soldiers is a right bastard!"

Smirking once more, John replied, "Is that so?"

Hayley's mother replied, "Absolutely. He made my daughter's hands bleed, and that was just at the induction! What kind of man is he?"

John didn't show any emotion to Hayley's mother; instead he replied, "Maybe, just maybe he would like them to be the best."

John could see the woman was worried for her daughter and walked back to the counter asking, "What's your name?"

Looking up at John with a solemn face, she replied, "Sheila."

John gave a wry grin saying, "Sheila. Your daughter will be fine, where she will make you proud."

Sheila frowned, asking, "How can you be so sure?"

John turned around to walk out of the shop replying, "I have a feeling everything is going to be okay."

John opened the door, making Sheila ask before he walked outside, "Sir. What did you say your name was?"

Turning around to face Sheila with his hair hanging onto his shoulders, he replied, "I didn't. Goodbye!"

Sheila became curious as she walked over to the door to watch him walk to his car, wondering who this man was. She brought her mobile phone from her pocket, wanting to take a photo of John Raven has he walked back to the car.

Debbie saw what the shop attendant had done, making her turn to John as he placed the flowers onto the backseat and ask, "Why did that shop attendant standing at the door take a photo of you using her phone?"

John looked outside Debbie's car window and saw Sheila standing there and replied, "Probably because Hayley Pomfret is her daughter."

John opened the driver's door, climbed in and received the key from Debbie and placed it into the ignition and turned it making the powerful engine turnover and start.

He turned the steering onto the full lock and pulled back out onto the main road and started travelling again. Debbie knew that Hayley was a member of Unit Expendable and asked, "Did Hayley's mother know who you are?"

John, feeling annoyed that Hayley had been in contact with her family, describing him as being a horrible person replied, "I doubt it because she thinks the person training Unit Expendable is a total bastard!"

Debbie started to laugh out aloud, which made John turn his head slightly and just grin, and ask, "So you think I am?"

Still chuckling at what John had just told her, she said, "She does have a point."

Producing a smirk, while watching the traffic in front of him, he said, "Be the best or be expendable. To achieve this I know I will have to be hard, ruthless and respected."

Debbie holding a stern face didn't say anything, she listened to John carry on saying, "Unit Expendable will be my finest achievement, even if it kills me!"

Listening to John speak like this made Debbie narrow her eyes with the thought of John Raven having to die. She didn't interrupt John, instead she decided to watch him placing the signal on has they turned onto the road leading to the cemetery. As he drove down the road John saw her watching him in the corner of her eye and said, "When I have finished training Unit Expendable, they will all be elite soldiers. I suspect one of them will become an extra special soldier, when they will follow in my footsteps. Die for something or live for absolutely nothing!"

Debbie said, "I thought our son John from Unit Invincible, had already become you. After all, he has the scars to prove it."

Pressing the brake to slow down while starting to signal once more, John replied, "You will know when John Weller has become me, when you won't need anybody to warn you."

Waiting for the oncoming traffic to pass by, John held the steering wheel tightly, waiting for a gap to drive into the cemetery. His face appeared stern, which made Debbie ask, "John Weller is an exception, but who, after meeting the soldiers at the induction has the ability to become you from Unit Expendable?"

John revved the engine after judging a gap in the oncoming traffic and drove across the road and through the gates leading into the cemetery. Driving much more slowly he answered Debbie's question by replying, "You can't rule Scott Templeton out, after all I did serve with his brother."

Debbie thinking back to when he took the photograph from Templeton to look at in Colonel Wareing's office said, "A lot has happened since you gave that photograph to Scott Templeton's mother."

Raven sighed as he nodded his head agreeing, with her. He turned briefly to Debbie, reminding her of the dark secret she kept for many years, which made her turn away and cringe. Aware of her guilt, he said, "At that point, the future could have been so different."

Debbie placed her hand below her bottom lip still cringing and replied, "I'm sorry! No matter how many times I say I'm sorry for not letting you know about the kids I can't change what has happened."

John slowed down to stop the 4x4 giving her a menacing stare. They unbuckled their seat belts and climbed out of the car. John opened the rear door to take the bunch of flowers and then walked beside Debbie silently to Tony Hindle's grave. As they came closer, they saw Rachel, who was once Tony's girlfriend had also decided to visit his grave. Debbie hurried on wanting to give Rachel a hug and then ask, "How are you?"

Rachel replied, "Good under the circumstances, with time it does get easier."

Rachel saw Raven walking towards them and said, "I see John has decided to visit Tony's grave too."

Debbie looked back at him replying, "While we were visiting our son John, who is staying with Louise, we thought that it would be a good idea to pay our respects to somebody John always held in high esteem."

Rachel moved away from Debbie, wanting to go to John and place her arms out to give him a hug. In return while looking at Tony's grave, he placed one arm around her to hug her. He asked the same question Debbie had asked moments before, "How are you?"

Rachel looked up to John replying, "I miss Tony. It's hard, especially this time of the year."

John narrowed his eyes showing sorrow on his face, knowing what Tony had been through. He let go of Rachel to walk a little closer to Tony's graveside, where he crouched down and laid the bunch of flowers gracefully onto Tony's graveside. Rachel and Debbie watched John with what he was doing, which made Debbie say, "See, he does have a gentle side."

Rachel's eyes started to glaze over as she was still watching John crouched down at Tony's graveside and replied, "I think we know what he is and what he can do."

Debbie held Rachel's arm tenderly while saying, "Tony was one of his finest soldiers from Unit Invincible."

Rachel chose to ignore Debbie's comment, replying, "John and Louise have visited Tony's graveside because they too have also left a bunch of flowers."

Debbie moved away to stand beside John still crouched down at Tony's graveside. She bent down to read the card that John and Louise had left on the flowers. John noticed her reading the card and said, "John did the right thing while visiting Louise."

After hearing these words, Rachel gave a half-smile, knowing that Raven was right in what he had just said, which made her ask, "Does John still miss Tony?"

Debbie looked up at Rachel showing a face of sadness; John moved his head, then his eyes listening to how Debbie was going to reply. She glimpsed at John, making Rachel think that it was going to be an agreed answer. Slowly, she turned to face Rachel again, replying, "Tony was John's Weller's best mate. They experienced good times, bad times, traumatic times, and even the worst times. Rachel, I'm sure there isn't a day that goes by when John doesn't think of Tony."

John turned away, looking down at the grave where Tony had been laid to rest. Rachel closed her eyes for a few seconds, nodding her head agreeing with her while saying, "You're right."

Tears started to form in Rachel's eyes, which made Debbie move to console her. John saw Rachel becoming upset, which made his eyes narrow slightly. He turned away, looking ahead, in the distance, at the sky for a few seconds thinking about his mentor, Colonel Lewis, who he always felt was looking down watching over him. Debbie let go of Rachel to say in a soft voice, "We ought to go now because we have to visit John and Louise."

Rachel understood and agreed with her. Hearing these words, Raven slowly turned around with his hair resting on his shoulder, watching both women speak about what their next plans were going to be. Knowing that Rachel would be alone this Christmas, he asked her in a polite way, "If you are not doing anything over the Christmas period, you're welcome to stay with us."

Appreciating John's proposition, Rachel placed her hand to her eyes to wipe away the tears. She smiled at John, and then walked over to him, placed her arms around his waist and hugged him. Placing her head on his chest, she replied, "Thank you for the offer, can I let you know?"

Placing his hand tenderly onto Rachel's back, they turned their heads to look at Tony's graveside, which made John reply, "Sure, no problem."

Debbie casually walked over while looking up at John and placed her hand onto Rachel's shoulder. Rachel brought her head away from John's chest saying, "Tony had the utmost respect for you."

John looked down at her, where she for the first time could see all the scars close up on his face from the battles he had previously experienced. Her eyes looked into the menacing stare from John, when he replied, "I should go."

Rachel released her arms from John's waist and watched him walk back to his 4x4 car. Debbie hugged her once more, asking, "Would you like to come and visit Louise and John with us?"

Rachel shook her head from side to side saying no. She gave a prolonged blink, opened her eyelids halfway and replied, "I'll give John's offer some thought."

Debbie wanted to show some more affection towards her, which made Rachel say, "You go now. John is waiting for you in the car."

Turning to walk back to John's car, Debbie said, "If you need anything, let me know."

Rachel held her arm up and waved as she watched Debbie walk back to the car, climb inside and sit next to John. As she pulled the seat belt over her, John started the engine, lowered the window and started to pull slowly away, holding his arm up giving Rachel a wave in return. As he passed by, he said, "Let me know."

Rachel held her hand up again, nodding her head agreeing, and then slowly turned to talk to who was once her partner and best friend.

Visiting John & Louise

$\mathcal{L}$eaving Rachel behind at Tony's graveside left John and Debbie subdued. Both people kept their own thoughts to themselves, until Debbie spoke up deciding to ask, "Do you think we should have left Rachel on her own back there?"

John didn't reply to Debbie's question. He remained quiet amid his own thoughts, which made Debbie, becoming frustrated to ask, "Did you hear what I just said?"

John, while driving on the busy road casually turned his head giving her the thousand yard stare, making her think twice whether to ask him any more questions. Feeling frustrated with how John was still able to bottle up his emotions, she placed her elbow next to the window saying, "You'll never change John!"

Again in the corner of his eye, he gave a menacing stare, watching her turn the volume up on the radio, deciding to remain silent about the rest of the journey to Louise's house.

Louise was in the kitchen making three cups of coffee, when she heard the gravel start to crunch, becoming aware that some visitors had arrived. Walking over to the kitchen window she saw that it was John Raven's car pulling up on the gravel. She shouted to John, who was sitting in the lounge with her father watching the television, "John, your father is here to visit."

Hearing what Louise had just shouted to him, John leaped to his feet and went to the front door, opened it and walked down the steps to greet his father. Louise wasn't so far behind, which meant that her father had to do what was right and welcome them into his house. John shook his father's hand, aware he was glancing at the necklace he was now wearing for a few seconds and said, "It's good to see you."

Raven just replied, "And you."

John saw his mother appear from the back of the BMW X5 carrying a couple of bags, which made John say, "Mother, are you checking on me?"

She laughed at John as she passed him one of the bags to carry. Louise gave John's father a hug and looked up at him saying, "You haven't changed."

Raven turned his head to the left, smirked, and replied, "I hope not."

Louise watched Raven turn his head back to look back down at her, when she spoke in a sincere voice, "Thanks for what you did for me, when I felt I had nobody."

Louise was reminding Raven of *America in Conflict* where he chose to say nothing and remain silent. Debbie had heard what Louise had just said and looked up at Raven's face to see what his reaction was going to be. His face was like stone, after he had heard every word from Louise. He gave a prolonged blink feeling as though he just didn't want to be kept reminding of the previous wars he had been involved in.

He replied to Louise by asking "Is that your father standing on the steps?"

Louise answered back feeling ever so pleased by saying, "Yes."

She gave a quick stride towards her father saying, "Dad. This is John's father, John Raven."

Her father while placing out his hand replied to his daughter, "I know who this is. I saw him at John's presentation when he received his Purple Heart and Medal of Honour from President Berry."

John, in return placed his hand out to shake Louise's father's hand, which made him say to John, "It's an honour sir."

John grinned replying, "Call me John."

Louise's father introduced himself by saying, "Thanks. My name is Kirk."

He then turned to John's mother, asking, "Presumably you're John's mother?"

Debbie gave the remaining bags to Raven to hold and shook Kirk's hand saying, "Hi. I'm Debbie Weller, pleased to meet you."

Kirk shook her hand replying, "You have two people in your life you can be proud of."

As they all walked up the steps, Raven frowned as he listened to Debbie's reply, "That will be four. The other two are my daughter, Sarah Jane and your daughter, Louise, for the way she handled herself during the time when America had been in conflict."

Remembering that time well when Louise had become distraught, Kirk replied, "It was a traumatic time for us all."

Just as before, Raven remained quiet about the subject choosing not to reply about any comment made. Occasionally, Debbie and Louise would watch him just to see what his reaction would be. Raven remained cool and calm, reluctantly listening to them speak highly of him and his son, John Weller-Raven.

They all walked inside the house with Debbie and her son John, placing the bags down. John noticed that Christmas presents were in the bag, which made him ask jokingly, "Are these for us?"

Raven leaned against the kitchen worktop, listening to Kirk ask him if he would like a drink. Raven replied, "After that long drive, I could do with a cold drink."

Debbie watched Kirk walk over to the fridge replying to her son's question by saying, "Actually, they are for you and Louise."

Kirk handed the bottle of lager to John and then asked Debbie if she too would like a cold drink. Debbie remembering what the next day had in store for her, replied, "Just a small white wine will be enough, thank you."

John looked puzzled with his mother's answer about the presents in the bag and reminded her that Christmas was still a few days away. Raven, leaning against the worktop watched everything going on around him, and gave Louise a casual wink, where she just smiled at him. After pouring the wine, Kirk handed it to Debbie, where she thanked him and took a sip of it. After tasting the wine, she said, "That's good."

Raven still watching and listening to everybody speaking in the kitchen took a last sip of his lager, which made Kirk ask, "Would you like another drink John?"

John placed his hand down, holding the bottle of lager, replying, "Thanks."

Debbie turned to him concerned, saying, "Don't forget, you're driving!"

Raven looked at Kirk nodding his head yes, giving him the signal that he was okay to drink another bottle of alcohol. Louise, feeling a little excited asked, "Why don't you stay the night?"

Neither Raven nor Debbie spoke, which made Louise turn to her father and ask, "Is that okay with you?"

Kirk turned away from his daughter to look at John Raven and said, "It would be an honour."

Debbie started to stall with her answer, knowing inwardly what she had to do the following day. She turned to face Louise and John saying, "I have to fly out tomorrow to the Gulf when I'm going to board the aircraft carrier, U.S.S. Abraham Lincoln."

Weller said, "This probably explains why you have brought the Christmas presents."

Debbie gave an acute grin to John replying, "You're sharp, son."

Raven, who had been listening to every word said, "We'll stay the night, and you will be on time for your flight."

Starting to become slightly flustered, Debbie replied, "But what about . . . ?"

Raven interrupted her saying, "You'll make it. Just learn to trust me."

Debbie frowned, staring at John with a hint of worry showing in her face, which made her ask, "How?"

John took another sip of his lager replying with the same answer, "Trust me."

Debbie, feeling worried about her trip, still had her eyes narrowed slightly at Raven. Containing her anxiety, yet still feeling uneasy, she asked again, "You will get me back?"

John always knew how dedicated Debbie was to her job and whilst looking away through the window, he just nodded his head yes as he took another sip of lager. Louise detected Debbie was becoming apprehensive and realised Raven was holding all the cards in how he had become so sure in getting Debbie back to the U.S. military base on time. Trying to break the tension, Louise walked over to her father to ask him for the bottle of wine, and held it out to fill Debbie's glass again. She placed her hand over the glass, which made Weller say, "Don't worry Mum, if Dad says he will get you to the military base. I'm sure he will."

John turned to look at his father, beginning to wonder himself, which made Raven say, "Trust me!"

Debbie, who still wasn't convinced, moved her hand away reluctantly letting Louise fill her glass up once more. She thanked her again and turned to Raven saying, "Let me down, and I will never forgive you!"

John ignored her last comment by taking another sip of his lager, thinking why people doubt him at times. When everybody agreed with the outcome, Kirk asked, "Have we to go into the lounge?"

Everybody moved to make their way into the lounge and sit down, except for Raven, who remained standing next to the door. Debbie noticed all the Christmas decorations and how well presented the lounge had become. Dusk was starting to fall, which made Louise turn on the Christmas lights inside and outside the house. Debbie commented on the way her house looked when all the decorations were on. Kirk turned to Raven saying, "It's not really for us soldier's."

John casually turned his head to Kirk, who was now looking straight ahead. Weller had also heard what Louise's father had just mentioned to his own father, making him turn to Louise to say in a quiet voice, "I never knew your father was in the military. Five minutes with my father and he releases a secret as big as that. How does my father do that?"

Louise glimpsed at Raven and her father, replying, "Your father is a legend, where he is totally unique, with my father, I was aware that he was in the military. I never told you because I'm not committed to you being the full-blown combat soldier."

After telling John her feelings about his occupation, Louise stood up wanting to ask everybody if they would like a takeaway to eat, which almost everybody said yes to. John Weller watched, while dwelling on what Louise had just mentioned to him. He watched her walk into the kitchen wondering whether to confront her about what she had said to him. Not sure of what the outcome would be he listened to her on the phone placing the order for the takeaway for everybody. Feeling despondent, John remained seated watching his own reflection in one of the baubles hanging on the Christmas tree, making him wonder was he now doing the right thing when he decides to propose to Louise. His mother saw him sat in deep thought, making her ask, "Are you okay John?"

Still dwelling on what Louise had just told him, he decided to disguise the truth replying, "Yes."

Debbie wasn't so sure, but with Louise's father standing nearby, she knew she couldn't ask John the question of whether he had proposed to Louise. She did, however, suspect that her son had something on his mind when he like his father would probably bottle it and decide not to tell anybody. Deciding not to dwell on her own assumption, she decided to change the subject asking, "What have you bought Louise for Christmas?"

John grinned, later answering, "Almost everything."

Debbie replied, "That much?"

Kirk, who had been standing close by speaking with John's father, turned wanting to join in the conversation by saying, "He does spoil my daughter."

Raven, who was listening, looked down at his son, and then at Debbie, sitting on the chair beside John. He moved to one side allowing Louise to enter back into the lounge. Noticing that Raven was still standing up, made her stop, turn and ask, "Why don't you take a seat John?"

Then Kirk repeated the same question, "Yes John, take a seat."

John thanked them and said that he would do, but he had to arrange something first, which made Debbie ask, "Like what?"

Deciding to ignore Debbie's question, he turned away to bring out his mobile phone from his pocket. With him wanting to make a private call, he went outside to sit on the steps and ring a member of Unit Invincible, who he had once helped regain his confidence to be able to fly again. After selecting the correct number, he pressed the dial button and held the phone to his ear waiting patiently for his call to be answered. Ricky Stevens answered Raven's call after realising who it was that had called him. They exchanged pleasantries, and then Raven reached the point of the call with him saying sternly, "I need a huge favour Ricky."

Stunned by Raven's request, he replied, "What might this be?"

John explained to Stevens that he would like him to come and collect Captain Weller and him using a U.S. military helicopter confirming that he would take full responsibility if any repercussions were to arrive. Stevens appeared stunned replying, "Sir. Colonel Wareing will go ballistic if he finds out that we have used a U.S. helicopter has some form of taxi."

Raven half expected Stevens' reaction to be just this, fearing that he would receive a Court Marshall. To help ease the worry, Raven assured him by saying, "You will not need to land, and I will fly the craft back to base, leaving you to drive my car home."

Stevens, who still wasn't convinced, asked, "What about Colonel Wareing?"

Raven thinking back to the disagreement they had replied, "Leave the Colonel to me."

Stevens reluctantly agreed, asking, "What time do you want me to come and collect you from Louise's house?"

Raven held out is arm, looked at his watch and said, "Five thirty tomorrow morning."

Stevens, still feeling bewildered by Raven's request replied, "I'll be there."

Raven in a stern voice said, "I don't doubt you!"

He then hung up, placed his phone into his pocket and remained sitting on the steps where he placed both of his hands to his forehead and joined them thinking for a few minutes about his own life.

A van turned in Louise's road with its headlamps shining, which made Raven take his hands away from his forehead to watch the vehicle approaching the steps he was sitting down at. The driver, who was a young lad parked close to Raven, and wound his window down asking, "Would you like to pay for these pizzas?"

Raven, still sitting on the steps, rested his arms onto his legs with his hands clasped together, looked to his side and started to smirk. The driver opened the door, walked to the back of the vehicle, mumbling, "I won't be doing this job forever!"

Raven casually watched, listening to the driver as he collected the pizzas from the back of the vehicle and heard him say in a sincere voice, "One day I may just become recognised."

Raven moved his head slowly, where his hair fell onto his shoulder and asked, "How?"

The driver walked over to John with the pizzas, making him stand up to bring out his wallet from his pocket. Louise, who was in the kitchen pouring Debbie another white wine, had also noticed the pizzas had arrived and saw that John was paying for them. She placed the glass down, picked up some money left on the worktop and trotted outside saying to John, "You don't need to pay for the food."

John and the driver turned to face Louise, with John replying, "It's done, take them inside. I will be with you in a couple of minutes."

Frowning at John's instruction with not being able to pay for the food for her guests, she turned to make her way back inside the house into the kitchen to prepare the food to be served. Debbie was starting to ponder where her glass of wine was. With this, she went into the kitchen to help Louise with the food that was about to be served with the pizzas. Reaching out for her glass and taking a sip of her wine, she saw Raven having a heart-to-heart talk with the young boy who had delivered the pizzas. She opened the door interrupting John by shouting, "John. The food is almost ready to be served."

Still speaking with the young boy, he turned and placed his hand up to her in acknowledgment. The boy walked away, climbed back into his van, and started to reverse slowly, saying to Raven, casually watching, "Thanks for the advice."

Raven while watching him reverse, replied, "Remember. Life is what you make it, and the person you want to impress the most will be aware of your talent and may give you the chance you do so want. Keep working hard, I'm sure it will happen one day. Oh, and if you receive the call . . . ."

The young boy watched Raven's expression knowing he meant every word he spoke, and then watched him widen those menacing eyes, and point his finger to him saying, "Be ready!"

Louise came outside has he watched the pizza van drive away and shouted, "John. The food is ready."

Slowly, he turned around to climb the steps and walk back inside the house. Debbie, who was eating a slice of pizza said, "It looked as though you were having a heart-to-heart talk with that young boy."

Raven, while pulling the top off another bottle of lager, and picking a slice of pizza up just replied, "Hmm."

Realising that she wasn't going to get a proper answer, she asked again, "So what did you talk about?"

Raven taking a sip of his lager glimpsed across at Debbie, then put his bottle down on the kitchen worktop and replied, "This and that."

Louise had cut the pizzas, where Debbie passed a plate to John. Looking up to him, she said, "You will never change!"

John paused, took a bite of his pizza, and then replied, "You mentioned that earlier."

Debbie's face softened when she asked, "John. Why can't you confide in people more?"

Louise was placing more pizzas on plates for her boyfriend and her father, but after hearing Debbie's question, she looked across at Raven wanting to listen to what his answer would be. Raven thought before answering, glancing away from them all wide-eyed. Not sure what to say, he just replied, "Give me time."

Louise shouted to her father, who was in the lounge talking with John Weller. He turned to walk in the kitchen asking, "Would you like me to bring your food into you?"

Louise shouted, "It's okay Dad. I'll take John's food into him."

Louise walked into the lounge to give John the plate of food and then sat next to him. John, who seemed to be dwelling on Louise's feelings that were about the military didn't feel too hungry. He just picked at the food, which made Louise ask, "What's the matter John?"

Before giving his reply to Louise, he paused for a few moments with being aware that his parents had now arrived and that if he said the wrong thing, it could turn a pleasant evening into a disastrous evening. Deciding not to look at her, he put the pizza back down on the plate and gently took her hand, and then slowly turned to face her, looking at the twinkle in her eye. She gave a cheeky grin while saying, "Cheer up. It's almost Christmas."

John leaned forward wanting to kiss her on the lips, making Louise frown, because although he seemed okay, she sensed that something was on his mind. They could hear laughter from the kitchen, making them stand and take their plates away into the kitchen. Kirk asked both men in the kitchen if they would like another drink. Weller accepted, but Raven chose to refuse, which brought a wry smile from Debbie, knowing that he had decided not to drink anymore alcohol.

Everybody remained in the kitchen talking, and laughing, being in high spirits. Debbie helped Louise to wash the pots, and the men, but mainly Kirk, carried on speaking among themselves. Occasionally, Kirk would pat Weller's arm, which was his way of being caring towards him. Raven noticed this, and asked, "Does Louise have any brothers or sisters?"

Louise stopped washing the pots for a few seconds, where she froze on the spot with hearing this question. Kirk showing remorse in his face before answering Raven's question watched Louise turnaround with the water dripping onto the floor from her hands. Reluctantly, he said, "Louise once had an older brother."

Raven placed his head down, but still listened to Kirk carry on saying, "My son wanted to be like me, a Navy Seal, where he achieved his ambition and became what I once was."

Raven slowly lifted his head after listening to Kirk speak about his son. Debbie and John were intrigued knowing the story had similar circumstances. Louise, knowing her father was going to carry on telling the story turned around to carry on washing the pots in the sink, which made Debbie show her some affection by placing her hand on her shoulder stroking it tenderly. Kirk carried on talking about his son in high esteem and then came to the moment where he said, "My son, Gardenzio or Enzio has we liked to call him, was captured in the Gulf by the Iranians."

Debbie asked with concern, "How long ago was it since Enzio had been captured?"

Louise stood still with her hands in the water starting to relive the time she had experienced with losing her brother, not knowing whether he was alive or dead. Raven, who was standing next to the fridge freezer watched each person's reaction, but more so with Louise. Kirk moved his head slowly, facing everybody except Louise, who had her back to him, and answered, "It's been seven long years now, when we always hoped that he would come home by using his military skills to escape. Sadly, we don't yet know to this day, whether Enzio is alive or dead. The shock of it all in the beginning gave Louise's mother a severe heart attack when she died and passed away."

Reliving the nightmare, Louise's eyes started to water, where she couldn't stop the tears from rolling down her cheeks. She turned around saying, "Stop father! We have to accept Enzio has probably been killed, or else he would be home by now!"

Raven moved his eyes, focusing on her, choosing to say nothing. Weller felt sorry for her and was now beginning to understand why she resented the military so much. Debbie remembering what Louise had been like when her son had chosen to do what was right, by protecting the President of the United States also understood more, why she had become such a physical wreck. Debbie didn't want to mention *America in Conflict* and remind her of what had happened, she already knew and had witnessed it all. Instead, she placed her hand on her back, which made Louise look at her with tears rolling down her cheeks and say, "I'm sorry."

John walked across to her and placed his arm around her lovingly and said, "I'm sure your brother will be alive."

Kirk immediately replied in a stern voice, "We have decided to accept that Enzio is dead and move on with our own lives."

Raven listened to every word mentioned, still choosing to say nothing. He moved his head, watching his son turn to Kirk and ask, "How can you be so sure that he is dead?"

Kirk paused for a few seconds replying, "With the Iranians, and what they can do, I have no choice but to believe this."

Raven spoke saying, "There's always hope!"

Louise wiped her eyes, while saying to Raven, "When you went into battle last time, I was hoping inwardly you would also find my brother. I guess my aspirations were just too high."

Raven moved his eyes slowly and caught Debbie watching him with intent. He then replied to them all, "Never say it's over until it's over."

Louise, who held a stern face moved Weller's arm away from her and said to her father, "The perfect Christmas present I could receive this year would be to have my brother back. I can't accept that he has been killed anymore. I have to believe he is alive."

Raven gave a wry smirk and then became stunned when Louise turned to him asking, "John. Will you be able to bring him home?"

Watching intently, Debbie waited for his reply to come to what was an interesting question. Raven just raised his head, gave a sigh, while visualising some of his previous battles, and then the one that almost killed him. He slowly moved his head back to Louise, choosing not to answer her. Louise's father answered her question by saying, "We're too old now! Do you not think we would if we could still perform to the same standard?"

John Weller became deflated, and just as before was once again starting to feel that he was living in the shadow of his father. With this he said, "I need to go outside for some air."

Raven understood why his son had walked outside and decided to follow him where he said to Kirk while passing him, "Believe."

Kirk watched him open the door and walk down the steps to his son and said to Debbie, "I wish I could believe."

Louise immediately replied, "We have to! Perhaps then our relationship will become much better."

Starting to show a face of sadness, Kirk reluctantly agreed by saying, "Possibly."

Debbie gave a smile saying, "Try Kirk. I know it will be hard, but try for the sake of your daughter."

Kirk didn't speak. He just nodded his head agreeing as he walked to Louise wanting to give her a hug and say, "I'm sorry."

Louise started to cry once more while saying, "I can't forget Enzio like you can. I've tried, but I can't do it anymore. I have to believe in my heart that he is still alive. Surely, you must do too?"

Kirk replied, "What sort of father would you think I am if I didn't? Of course I do! It's just that with so much time gone by, I want you and me to have a normal relationship before all this occurred."

Louise placed her arm around his waist and said, "Keep believing for me, and we may still have a chance."

Kirk closed his eyes feeling the pain of losing his wife and son and then replied, "I'll try."

Debbie thought it was about time the subject was changed and decided to collect the bags she had brought into the house earlier. She gave the presents for John and Louise and passed them to her, which made Louise wipe her eyes, and then give her a hug and say, "Thank you."

Debbie brought a Christmas card from the bag and passed it to Kirk, where he said, "Thanks."

He opened the envelope, read the card and said, "I'm sorry about the conversation we had earlier."

Debbie replied, "No problem. At least one good thing may have come from the conversation with you and your daughter possibly becoming much closer."

Kirk nodded his head agreeing, replying, "That's not a bad thing."

Raised voices could be heard outside making the three people in the kitchen turn and look through the window. Louise said, "I should go and stop the friction developing outside."

Debbie gently held her arm saying, "Leave them because it's been a long time in coming."

She let go of her arm to carry on saying, "This is one discussion you don't want to be involved in."

Kirk glanced outside again watching John Weller raising his arm about and pointing his finger to his father. Realising the conversation was becoming heated, he said, "We ought to go into the lounge, I'm sure they will join us once they have sorted their differences out."

Louise reluctantly walked behind them, turning just once more to see that Raven was starting to lose patience. Feeling apprehensive with witnessing the tension outside, she could only hope that he wouldn't lose his temper and perform the wrong actions.

Heart-to-Heart Discussion

*J*ohn Weller kept moving around, shouting and bawling at his father, telling him he was fed up of living in his shadow. Raven listened to every word as he looked straight ahead and said, "You don't live in my shadow and never have."

Weller glared at his father. Raven, who was aware, chose not to look in the face of his son showing anxiety. Instead, he focused on the necklace for a few seconds; he too had once worn many years ago. Containing his anger, he said, "I'm proud of you, especially with the way you performed with *America In Conflict*."

Weller appeared despondent, deciding to disagree by saying, "You're just saying that!"

Raven for a few seconds visualised Colonel Lewis and said, "No, I'm not! You saved the President of the United States and fought against North Korea that is becoming a superpower, and you survived."

He moved his head, staring at his son, where he placed his lip to one side asking, "I taught you everything I know! What is it that you want from me?"

Weller stopped moving around, deciding to stand still. He faced his father, who had been unmoved all the time his son had been shouting and bawling at him and replied, "I want to be you."

Raven swallowed a lump replying, "Trust me; you don't want to be me!"

Weller said, "I would die for you!"

Raven moved his head slightly, and then his eyes giving a menacing stare towards his son. Hearing these words, he replied, "I know you would, it's in your blood!"

Weller, who had calmed down started to speak in a much more methodical civil manner and said, "I wish I could receive the same recognition as you."

Raven looked down at the ground, smirked, replying, "In time you will. Trust me, I'm nothing special."

Weller disagreed saying, "You're everything I want to be."

Raven looked at the ground again becoming despondent as he started to recall his past. He raised his head slowly and said, "Before I was contacted by your mother and Colonel Wareing to take over training Unit Invincible, Colonel Lewis was the only person I could ever trust. I was a person who had been alone for many years. Surely, you don't want to end up like this?"

Weller shook his head saying no, replying, "I just want you to be proud of me."

Raven remained standing there with his hands down by his side, said, "I'm proud of you and Sarah Jane. I just wished you and your sister had taken different paths in life and not followed mine."

Raven watched John walk in frustration, which made him say, "Every single American citizen, if not the world will be proud of what you did when you brought President Berry home safely."

Weller, hearing these words stopped walking in circles, starting to think back to that traumatic time. His father sensed this and carried on saying, "John. You helped me immensely when I was fighting with those savage dogs. If it hadn't been for you, I would have been savaged to death."

Slowly, Weller turned around to face his father, who was pointing to his new wounds from his previous battle and again carried onto say, "I have the scars to prove it."

Weller, listening hard to his father stared at the ground, which made Raven also say, "John."

Weller raised his head to look up at his father, and listened to him say, "War isn't good."

Weller remained silent as he listened to his father speaking sincerely, truthfully and wisely. Raven, who was still standing at the same spot, paused for a few seconds, narrowed his eyes and said, "Keep dwelling like this and one day you will surely die!"

Weller looked down at the ground remembering that Colonel Lewis was his father's mentor. Starting to visualise the short time he had experienced with the Colonel, he lifted his head again to ask his father, "Did you ever want to be better than Colonel Lewis?"

Raven's face mellowed as he too thought back to his mentor, replying, "His expectations of me were so high in the beginning because he made everything difficult for me. No pain, no problem and no whinging would be entertained! Inwardly, he knew I had something, which probably explains why he wanted me to take over training Unit Invincible. I am what I am! I'm no better, no worse and I always believe in fight, survive, and live, and wait for trouble to find you!"

Weller walked forwards to his father saying, "I'm sorry."

Raven immediately replied, "Don't be. You're doing exactly as I once did, only learn to control your thoughts. When you least expect it, you will know when the time has come."

After listening to his father speaking, Weller walked slowly by and placed his hand on his shoulder, with Raven remaining wide-eyed and staring straight ahead. Weller carried on walking to the steps and then heard his father say, "I hear congratulations are in order?"

Weller stopped, turned back to face Raven, who was now slowly turning around to face his son and said, "You've heard about me wanting to propose to Louise?"

Raven nodded his head agreeing, which made Weller say, "With what had been discussed in the kitchen earlier this evening I don't give myself much of a chance of Louise's answer being yes."

Raven frowned with concern. Weller noticed his facial expression and said, "I have to face the truth, Dad. Louise hates me being in the military because of what has happened to her brother."

Raven gave a casual blink, moved his eyes and replied, "Perhaps she is worrying that one day she is going to lose you too."

Weller, while looking down at his father, asked, "What do I do?"

Raven replied. "Life is all about choices! It's your decision where I will stand by you no matter what. Make the right decision!"

Weller listened and said, "Thanks, I will."

Raven watched his son walk to the top of the steps and then brought out his mobile phone wanting to ring Stevens again to be sure that he would arrive at Louise's house at the appointed time previously arranged. Stevens confirmed he wouldn't let Raven down and would be there as planned to hand over the craft to him and drive his 4x4 car back to the U.S. military base.

With John back inside the house with the rest of the family, feeling more at ease with the tension subsiding made Louise come to him and give him a hug. John put his arm around her and kissed her forehead and said, "I'm sorry."

Louise gave him a gentle tap on his arm replying, "John, all of us in this room and probably everybody who lives in this country is proud of you. Never think you're living in your father's shadow because you're not anymore."

Weller didn't reply, he just stroked her back tenderly and kissed her cheek. Debbie, who was sitting down watching television turned to watch Louise and John closely wondering when he would ask her the certain question. Seeing her son being more caring made her produce a wry smile. Kirk stood up, placed his hand on John's shoulder and asked, "Are you and your father still on speaking terms?"

Watching the Christmas decorations flicker, he firstly, looked at Louise and said in a solemn voice, "I love you."

Turning to face Kirk to answer his question, he nodded his head slowly saying yes.

Kirk walked into the kitchen, brought two bottles of lager from the fridge and opened the door to see Raven sitting on the steps with his elbows resting on his knees and his hands clasped together. Kirk closed the door behind him, walked down the steps and offered John a bottle of lager, saying, "I thought you might need one."

Raven took the bottle of lager from him replying, "Thanks."

Kirk sat down next to Raven, taking a sip of his lager and said, "Kids, hey."

Raven turned his head giving a stare at Kirk choosing to say nothing. Kirk, while taking another gulp of his lager asked, "What do you regret the most about being an elite soldier with the military?"

Raven frowned, rotated his thumbs as he held the bottle of lager. He narrowed his eyes thinking back to how he had been cheated of watching his kids grow up; leaving him to fight wars that could have been avoided had he known the truth. In a word, he answered Kirk by saying, "Lies!"

Concerned by Raven's reply, Kirk asked, "Have you been betrayed?"

Raven took a gulp of his lager and placed it on the step next to where he was sitting and replied, "You could say that."

Kirk asked, "Do you want to talk about it soldier to soldier?"

Raven didn't need to think about his reply because he immediately answered by replying, "Not really."

It went quiet for a few minutes where they just remained seated, slowly drinking their beer amid their own thoughts. Raven, later spoke in a solemn voice saying, "I once remember holding my best buddy when he had been blown to smithereens, and I was trying to put him back together. No matter what country you live in, what religion you believe in, war isn't good for anybody because needless lives are lost."

Raven reliving the past picked up his bottle, taking another gulp of his lager. Kirk watching his reactions has he spoke knew that he was still feeling the pain from the past and said in a solemn voice, "No matter how much time goes by, it never does become easier."

Raven, who had rested his elbows back onto his knees while still holding the bottle of lager in one hand thought about Kirk's opinion, but chose to ignore it. He slowly lifted the bottle of lager up to his mouth, taking another gulp and then placed the bottle down on the step beside him. Looking straight ahead and thinking about his own future, he asked Kirk, "Do you ever regret leaving the force?"

Kirk replied, "At first I did, but I blamed the force for losing my son and the disagreements that occurred made me resign and take care of what I have left in my life."

Raven moved his head to face Kirk, asking, "You mean Louise don't you?"

Kirk placed his thumb onto the bottle of lager and rotated it while he thought about how to answer Raven's question. Taking a deep breath, he turned to look at Raven and said, "Louise has never fully forgiven me for turning my back on my son and walking away from the force."

Turning away to look straight ahead, he paused for a few seconds thinking about Enzio. He took a sip of his lager and then carried on saying, "With being a Navy Seal, in the beginning she thought I could just go in there and get Enzio out, which is easier said than done."

Raven listening hard to every word mentioned, made him produce a menacing stare, knowing that he would have died to have saved his kids. He took another sip of his lager, glancing back at Kirk as he carried on saying, "My confidence became low. I couldn't decide anymore, which made me become a liability to my unit. I felt that it was time to go before me or members of the unit I fought with were killed."

Kirk took a last gulp of his lager and then broke the bottle in frustration on the step, which made the glass scatter around. Holding the bottleneck with a firm grip he said, "The Iranians have my son and one day somebody will pay!"

Raven turned away looking straight ahead, while taking another sip of his lager choosing to say nothing.

Debbie, who had been watching the television with John and Louise most of the evening glimpsed at the clock noticing that it was getting late. She stood up, asking Louise, "Which room will John and I be sleeping in tonight?"

Louise stood up and answered her, replying, "Come this way. I'll show you."

Debbie followed Louise as she made her way to the guestroom, and opened the bedroom door, turned on the light and walked inside. Debbie went inside and placed some of her belongings down next to the bed. She turned to Louise, wanting to give her a hug and said, "Be strong for John, because one day he may just need you more than you think."

Feeling confused Louise frowned, asking, "How?"

Debbie refused to reveal any further information to her and just replied, "Trust me."

She then quickly changed the subject knowing she had left Louise feeling mystified and said, "I'm going to see if John's father wants to stop the night with me."

Louise gave a wry grin asking, "Do you think he will want to?"

Debbie smirked replying, "There is only one way to find out because I want to be sure the son of a bitch gets me back to the U.S. military base on time just has he had promised."

She stepped outside the bedroom, walked down the hallway to the kitchen and opened the back door, which made the men sitting on the steps talking and drinking look up at her. Noticing Raven had another bottle of lager in his hand, she asked in a stern voice, "How many more drinks have you had?"

Raven refused to reply. He looked away while listening to Kirk's reply, "He's only had the one bottle, since he came outside, because he's aware that he has to take you back to the U.S. military base tomorrow."

Raven narrowed his eyes while taking another sip of his lager, which made Debbie watch in despair and say, "Come on! He's had more than one! I don't think he's aware because he probably won't be in any fit state!"

Raven glared straight ahead wide-eyed, choosing to say nothing. As Kirk stood up, he patted Raven's shoulder saying, "Come on John, I'll show you to your room."

Raven stood up and followed Kirk, blanking Debbie has he passed her for doubting him once more. She suspected John was annoyed and decided not to push him any further about how she would arrive at the U.S. military base. She closed her eyes with all the unnecessary hassle and then turned around to follow him to their bedroom. Kirk showed John into the same bedroom Louise had brought Debbie to and asked, "Is this okay for you John?"

Raven nodded agreeing, leaving Kirk to say, "I think I will turn in too, goodnight."

Raven closed the door and turned back around watching Debbie seductively unfasten her blouse and take it off. Noticing her black sexy bra, he watched her walk over slowly to him asking, "Do I still look good John?"

John undressed her with his eyes replying, "You always look good."

Debbie placed her arms around John's waist, pushing her soft breasts into John's masculine chest asking, "Would you like to share the bed with me tonight?"

John thinking back to the past replied, "I remember the last time we did this. Many years went by, I fought needless wars, and then I found out that I had a son and a daughter I never knew existed."

Debbie let go of John's waist and looked up to him and said, "No matter what! You're never going to let me forget that! Why can't we just forget the world and everybody that lives in it and be a couple for one more night?"

Raven gave a prolonged blink, looking down at her, choosing to remain silent, which made Debbie carry on saying, "After all, I will be gone for some time after tomorrow."

She came closer to John, placing her arm around his waist and pressed her breasts against his chest once more. John started to fight his emotions because he so wanted to place his arm around her and let the intimate moment Debbie was offering to him be the highlight of his day, possibly his Christmas. Still looking down at her, he watched Debbie look up to him with love in her eyes. Reluctantly, John shook his head from side to side slowly saying no, and then said in a soft voice, "It's over."

Hearing these words made Debbie immediately let go of John and turn her back on him feeling slightly humiliated. John sensed how she would probably feel and said, "I will sleep on the sofa in the lounge."

Debbie didn't answer, which made John turn to open the door and walk outside into the hallway. Debbie turned her head and said in a low voice, "John."

Before he closed the door, John looked back at her to say, "I'm sorry."

With her eyes starting to glaze over, Debbie asked, "Where did it all go wrong?"

John didn't want to get into a debate suspecting the past could be brought up again and answered, "It doesn't matter. You get some sleep because you're up early tomorrow morning."

He gave her a wry smile as he started slowly pulling the door quietly shut, which made Debbie say before he could close it, "John."

Pausing for a few seconds, John waited for Debbie and what she might want to say. Looking at him with love in her eyes, she said, "Somewhere inside me, I will always love you."

John for a few seconds placed his eyes on her dressed in sexy underwear resisting the temptation, replying, "You get some sleep."

He closed the door quietly and walked slowly into the lounge to sit on the sofa thinking about what he had just refused while watching the television. It was well after 1.00am, the house seemed so still and quiet. With being late, John lowered the volume on the television and flicked through the channels. The highlights of American football games were being shown, which he watched for a short time. Starting to feel peckish, he went into the kitchen, took a bag of crisps and then went back into the lounge to watch television. Deciding he had watched enough sport, John picked up the remote control and flicked through the channels once more. When he arrived at the CNN news channel he saw there on the screen, the face of what was once Major Cairns in military uniform. Raven glared with his menacing eyes at the face of Cairns being displayed, remembering how he had betrayed his colleagues and his own American people. This was one of the first reports to arrive in the United States. It was making headlines stating he had escaped and was working with the Iranians. Raven placed his hand to his forehead reflecting on what the Colonel had already told him previously. Aware Cairns had escaped, while travelling to the U.S. he could only stare at the television with hatred showing in his eyes to the man, he despised the most. Knowing Debbie would be travelling close to the region Cairns is now at, made Raven, look down the hallway to the bedroom she was sleeping in. He recalled her words; she had mentioned to him earlier, "After all I will be gone for some time after tomorrow."

Sitting there amid his own thoughts Raven started thinking was it coincidence that Captain Weller was flying to the area nearby to where Cairns was now working with the enemy. Thinking back to when Debbie had mentioned that somewhere inside herself, she did still love him. It made him sigh and move his eyes casually pondering on one thought, would he come back to fight if the unimaginable was to happen.

Raven sat forward on the sofa resting his elbows on his knees and clasped his hands together tightly and looked down at the floor. With the television blurring in the background, he asked himself, "When is it all going to end?"

Military Transportation

$\mathcal{T}$hinking about Cairns, knowing that Debbie will be travelling close to the region where he had been taken, made him feel apprehensive. He walked into the kitchen, deciding to make a cup of black coffee. After turning the kettle on, he glanced at the clock taking notice of the time showing 4.55am. Whilst waiting for the kettle to boil, he placed the coffee and sugar into the cup and then brought from his pocket, his mobile phone. Before scrolling through his list of contacts, he noticed he had received a text while he had been asleep. Realising it was from Stevens, he opened the text confirming that he had left the U.S. military base and was now flying to Louise's house to collect him and Captain Weller. Reading the text made Raven grin knowing that Stevens wouldn't let him down. The kettle boiled producing steam, which made Raven move and turn the switch off and pour the water into the cup and then stir the coffee with a teaspoon. He took a gulp and placed the cup down on the worktop, deciding to go for a shower. After drying his face with the towel, he pulled it away slowly, starting to look at his reflection in the mirror. Starting to stare at his reflection, he could only imagine the face of Cairns and the last time he saw him, when he punched him in the face for performing acts of treason. He placed the towel onto the rack and glanced at his watch again. Aware Stevens wouldn't be too far away; he walked into the kitchen to make a cup of coffee for Debbie and walked to the bedroom she had been sleeping in. He opened the door slowly noticing Debbie was up out of bed and dressed ready to leave. He handed the cup of coffee to her, which made her smile and say, "Thanks."

John then said, "The bathroom is free if you want to take a quick shower."

Debbie, who was just gathering her belongings said, "I don't think I will have the time because we do have a long drive ahead of us."

John smirked, saying, "Take a shower because we will be back at the U.S. military base on time."

Debbie thought for a few seconds sensing that John seemed confident in what he was saying. With this she walked by him deciding to take a shower and said, "John, about last night."

John gave a solemn look, remembering what could have been, and replied, "Forget it. I have."

Debbie chose not to dwell and carried on walking to the bathroom to take a quick shower, still wondering whether John would have her back at the U.S. military base on time. John walked into the kitchen, turned the key in the door and walked outside drinking his cup of coffee, feeling the brisk cold air from the frost that had occurred during the night. Raven walked down the steps listening to the frost crunching beneath his feet as he walked. He looked around at all the coloured lights displayed at Louise's neighbour's houses while waiting anxiously for the sound of Stevens' propellers, in the distance. He lifted his right hand to take another sip of coffee and then glimpsed once more at the time showing on his watch. It was quiet, dark, and cold, but Raven remained standing there waiting for the pilot he had helped regain his confidence back when he felt that he needed it the most. Raven glanced at his watch once more starting to feel anxious. With his face becoming stern, he walked to his 4x4 BMW X5 and unlocked the door. Still holding a stern face, he walked to the rear of the car and opened the tailgate searching inside the boot for the canister of de-icer. It had slipped underneath a picnic blanket where he picked it up, holding it tightly. Thinking about Stevens and when he would arrive, he walked to the front of the car to spray the front and side windows knowing that Stevens would be driving his car home for him.

Debbie walked into the kitchen glimpsing at the clock on the wall showing 5.20AM. She turned to look out of the window to see John outside defrosting the windows on the car. Knowing how long it would take to travel back, she became apprehensive, decided to walk outside to John and ask, "Do you think we should leave now?"

John looked away from her into the distance at the dark black sky hoping that Stevens wouldn't be too far away. Feeling anxiety with not wanting to let Debbie down, he turned back to her replying, "We will leave soon."

Debbie narrowed her eyes starting to worry at how she would arrive back to the U.S. military base and be able to travel to the aircraft carrier, U.S.S. Abraham Lincoln on time. She watched John place de-icer on the door locks and then turned to look, in the distance, when she heard a constant hum. Raven heard the same sound and walked to the rear of the car, throwing the de-icer into the boot. Debbie watched him close the boot and then in a soft voice, asked, "What have you arranged John?"

John glanced at her, and then into the distance, at the bright lights shining from the U.S. helicopter. He walked briskly away from his car, placing his hands up into the air and waved constantly at Stevens to grab his attention.

Stevens saw a figure below on the ground realising it was indeed Raven. Luke Tyler, who had decided to fly with Stevens, also looked down at Raven, asking, "Does the man ever sleep?"

Stevens while watching Captain Weller walk beside Raven replied, "The man is capable of anything and everything!"

Stevens smirked, and then started to worry about what he and Tyler had done, which made him say, "When we get back to base, we will probably receive a Court Marshall for performing these actions, unless they accept, we acted on our own intuition."

Tyler still focusing what was below him replied, "Probably."

He turned to Stevens grinning, starting to enjoy seeing him worry about the consequences when they arrive back at the U.S. military base, which made him say, "Quit worrying and focus on the task in hand."

Debbie grabbed John's arm tenderly, which made him look down gracefully at her. She looked up into John's face to say, "Thanks."

John nodded his head agreeing and turned waiting for the U.S helicopter to descend close by at Louise's house. The noise from the propellers made neighbours living nearby to Louise turn on their lights wanting to know what was happening outside. Louise heard the loud constant humming sound of the propellers and climbed out of bed to watch from the window when she pulled back the curtain. The bright light shined through the window into the house, which woke John, who was sleeping next to her. Louise looked back at him from the window, watching him slowly open his eyes fully and then ask, "What's happening outside?"

Louise turned back around to watch the U.S. helicopter descend lower replying, "I think your father has arranged some special transport for your mother."

Hearing these words made Weller jump out of bed to see what was happening outside. He gave a wry grin as he watched the helicopter hover just above the ground and said, "There is only my father who could have arranged this."

Louise held Weller's hand tenderly saying, "Come on. We should see your mother off, even if it's in different circumstances."

John and Louise put on their dressing gowns wanting to make their way outside to say goodbye to Captain Weller. The sound from the propellers was loud and vast making Louise say to Weller, "They're going to waken the whole neighbourhood up."

Raven, aware Stevens was waiting to jump out of the U.S. helicopter, ran leaping inside the back, where he looked at Stevens, praised him, and said, "Good job!"

Stevens replied, "Sir?"

Raven looked back waving to Debbie, who was giving Louise a hug before leaving. She looked at her son, John, and said, "Good luck."

Louise frowned hearing this remark and became confused. As she watched Debbie walk away, she turned to John asking, "What did your Mum mean when she said good luck?"

Watching his mother trot to the U.S. helicopter, he replied, "I'll explain soon."

Louise turned away watching Debbie climb inside the helicopter that was hovering just above the ground and saw Stevens next to John's parents. She smirked, saying, "It just had to be a member of Unit Invincible."

Weller feeling proud replied, "We're the best."

He raised his hand to Stevens still inside the helicopter, where he returned the same gesture by raising his own hand at Weller. Captain Weller felt proud of what Stevens had done and said, "I won't forget this."

Stevens replied, "You both helped me when I needed it the most. It's the least I can do."

Raven patted his shoulder choosing to say nothing. He turned and saw Kirk standing on the steps where he raised his arm up to him and waved. Kirk, in return held his arm up, which made Louise and John also do the same action.

Weller watched his father telling Captain Weller to take Stevens' position inside the helicopter and take control of the craft alongside Tyler. While watching his father, who just seemed to have a superior presence, he said to Louise, "I can't see my father leaving the military, look at him, he is so at home on that craft."

Louise turned her head slightly glancing at John, and then at the U.S. helicopter once more, replying, "Your father is a special man, who is unique."

Watching his father give his car keys to Stevens, he nodded his head agreeing, hoping that one day he too would become a legend like his father.

Raven thanked Stevens and then turned to Luke Tyler to say, "You travel with Stevens in my car."

Luke climbed out of his seat while asking Captain Weller, "Do you have control of the craft?"

Captain Weller replied, "Don't worry Tyler! I may not be in uniform, but I still know how to perform in my job."

Captain Weller kept the helicopter hovering above the ground waiting patiently for Raven to take his seat. Tyler walked up to Raven and clasped his hand and said "Good luck with Unit Expendable Sir."

Raven moved his head, then his eyes slowly, replying, "Thanks."

Tyler walked to the edge to jump out of the back of the helicopter. Before jumping, he turned back to Raven and said, "When Stevens told me that he was going to collect you and Captain Weller, unknown to him, I had to get clearance."

Captain Weller, sitting in the cockpit turned around watching Raven asking, "You went to Colonel Wareing?"

Tyler replied, "No. I decided to break the rules and ring somebody who holds you in high esteem, the Secretary of State, Sarah Johnson."

Raven felt proud with how Tyler had diversified and handled what could be an awkward situation when he arrived back at the U.S. military base. In appreciation, he asked, "How would you like to become an elite member of Unit Expendable?"

Tyler, feeling pleased at such an offer being made to him, replied, "Do you think I'm capable?"

Raven in a stern voice said, "I wouldn't have asked if I didn't think you were capable!"

Tyler, knowing that time was ticking away replied, "It would be an honour Sir, to serve under you and be in the same unit has your daughter."

Raven accepted his gratitude by saying, "Travel back to the U.S. military base in my car with Stevens. Oh, and if you decide to turn the radio off and listen to the cd, track seventeen is awesome."

Tyler replied "Okay."

Raven said, "Go!"

Tyler jumped off the helicopter, trotting towards Stevens, standing next to Louise and John Weller. Raven briskly walked through into the cockpit to sit next to Captain Weller saying, "I told you I would get you back to the U.S. military base on time."

Captain Weller smirked a little, replying, "Did I ever doubt you?"

John chose not to answer this question. Instead, he rotated his finger to Captain Weller, while saying, "Okay! Let's go!"

Captain Weller made the helicopter climb, where she looked down at the people watching, making her give a casual wave.

John Weller moved away from Louise deciding to walk over to Kirk, to ask, "Are you starting to miss it all?"

Kirk, while watching the helicopter rising, replied, "You could say that son."

Stevens and Tyler watched Raven fly the helicopter away into the distance. Feeling worried, Stevens scratched his forehead reluctantly saying, "That's us on a Court Marshall Luke."

Luke sniggered, replying, "I don't think so because I took care of things when everything should be okay."

Stevens, feeling surprised, turned asking, "How?"

Weller walked over joining the conversation with the two soldiers, replying to Stevens' question by saying, "He probably did what you should have done by contacting the Secretary of State, Sarah Johnson."

Stevens, who still appeared surprised, replied, "Yes! Even so, it wasn't up to us to contact her. It was up to a high ranking officer!"

Weller gave a wry grin replying, "Trust me, after what the U.S. President and Secretary of State have been through, and knowing who had requested the craft, I'm sure a blind eye will have been turned."

Turning to face Luke, he asked, "Isn't that right Luke?"

Luke replied, "Absolutely."

Kirk walked over to the soldiers asking, "Do you guys have to leave, or would you like some breakfast?"

Stevens answered by saying, "Thanks, but we should go because we're officially still on duty."

Louise held Stevens' arm saying, "At least come inside and have a drink of coffee before you leave."

Stevens showed a look of worry on his face, which made Tyler say, "We would love to, in fact, we will visit the café you work at and have breakfast before travelling back."

Everybody walked up the steps and entered the kitchen, with Kirk placing the kettle on to make the soldiers a cup of coffee. Louise said to everybody standing in the room, "I'll go and get showered and dressed so I can take you to the café where I work."

John started to grin, which made Louise ask, "What's funny John?"

John replied, "Nothing at all. I was just thinking back to when I first met you at the same place we're taking Stevens and Tyler to. The only difference is, Tony isn't here to share this moment."

Louise went to John, clasping his hand saying, "We do all miss Tony, and I'm sure I speak for all you soldiers when I say there isn't a day goes by when you don't give Tony a moment's thought."

John released his hand from Louise replying in a solemn voice, "Yes. You're right."

He then walked by Stevens and Tyler, and down the hallway to get washed and dressed. Louise followed thinking about what John's mother had said a few moments ago, which made her ask, "John, what did your mother mean when she said good luck?"

John stopped and stared at Louise for a few seconds wondering whether to propose now. Not sure what John's thoughts were, made Louise say, "Don't look like that because I can see your father in you!"

John softened his look towards her, replying, "Sorry. I'll tell you later."

John walked off, which made Louise, who was still standing there, frown and ask, "Tell me what?"

John carried on walking thinking back to what Louise had mentioned earlier, replying, "Later."

Kirk remained in the kitchen speaking with the two soldiers, telling them stories of when he had once been on the force. It didn't take Stevens long to start speaking about his mentor, Raven; telling Kirk of the missions he had shared with him. Kirk listened hard to every word mentioned and said, "Raven is unreal!"

Tyler smirked saying, "His daughter has his own blood, which makes her a mean machine that will kill if called up on to perform such a task."

Kirk placed his cup down onto the worktop asking, "No doubt his son, John, will also have the same characteristics?"

Stevens knew better than anybody with serving in Unit Invincible alongside him and was about to answer the question, only to be interrupted by Kirk, when he carried on saying, "Don't answer that! I already know because he did bring President Berry home from a difficult situation."

Not feeling too pleased at being interrupted, Stevens thought back to the time when he and Captain Weller flew to South Korea with hostages who were to be exchanged for the President of the United States. He took a sip of his coffee and replied, "You can say that again."

John walked into the kitchen asking, "What are you talking about Ricky?"

Not sure whether John wanted to discuss his last mission, he decided to answer by saying, "Oh just the Christmas break, although Luke and I will have to celebrate it back at the U.S. base because we're not on leave this year."

Louise walked into the kitchen looking radiant. Stevens noticed, and said, "You're looking good Louise."

John smiled, placed his arm around her and kissed her and said, "She has always been the highlight of my day."

Luke joined in the conversation saying, "I wish your sister was the highlight of my day."

John asked, "You like my sister?"

Tyler replied, "I have done, since I first met and walked with her at the U.S. military base when she became inquisitive and went somewhere she shouldn't after I was ordered to attend Colonel Wareing's office."

John gave a wry grin, and said, "I did always wonder how my sister ended up in a warzone in North Korea."

Not sure where this conversation would lead to made Louise interrupt them by saying, "We should go now John."

Tyler and Stevens placed their cups down onto the worktop, thanked Kirk for the cup of coffee and then followed John and Louise outside, walking to Raven's 4x4 car. Stevens pressed the key fob to unlock the doors, so he and Tyler could climb into the car. After the soldiers had placed their seat belts on, Stevens placed the key into the ignition, pressed the start button where the engine immediately turned over and started. Hearing the sound of the powerful V6 engine made Luke say, "You have the power at your feet Ricky."

Ricky turned and said, "Yeah, but it's nothing compared with what we're used to."

Luke, aware that he was speaking about the powerful fighter jets and helicopters they have to fly nodded his head agreeing. He then turned to watch Weller de-icing Louise's Mini Cooper S while she remained sat inside with the engine running. As they waited for John to climb inside the car, Luke asked Ricky, "When Unit Invincible were being trained under John Raven, what was it like?"

Stevens thought back and replied, "Hard, tough, you're taught to feel no pain, and you have to be ready for anything and everything. Why do you ask?"

Luke paused for a few seconds and said, "Raven has asked me to become an elite member of Unit Expendable."

John had demisted the windows and climbed into Louise's car where she slowly started to pull away. Stevens immediately followed her in Raven's 4x4 replying to Luke, "The man is an icon, but trust me, expect no mercy from him!"

Driving down the road behind Louise, Luke asked, "Why would he want me in Unit Expendable?"

Stevens flicked the signal and turned the steering wheel left replying, "Raven has a reason for everything, and if he wants you, it's for a good reason."

Raven, who was travelling to the U.S. military base with Debbie Weller said, "I wish it could be like this when I've had to fly these machines previously."

Debbie looked at the sunrise coming up, in the distance, and said, "It's beautiful."

Raven, noticing the different colours the sun was producing, said, "It's so nice to be able to see various shades of colour that are orange, red, and yellow and be relaxed. Usually when I have seen those colours, they're from huge infernos ignited from warzones I have been involved in when people were killed and badly injured."

Debbie listened to every word John had just spoken and replied, "Please God don't let it happen, but if something were to happen to me while I'm close to the Iranian border, would you come for me?"

Raven stared straight ahead through his visor at the sun and didn't answer. Feeling as though she had been ignored, Debbie slapped his leg and said, "I asked you a question."

Slowly, Raven turned his head, giving her a menacing stare, replying, "No!"

Starting to feel a little rejected, Debbie said, "Is it because it's me?"

Raven had turned his head, staring out of the front glazed panel and replied, "No!"

The same reply was provoking Debbie, which made her ask, "Would you ever fight in a warzone again?"

Raven sat there listening to the sound of the propellers above him, replied, "You already know the answer to the question."

Debbie gave a wry grin and said, "Because it's you, I would like to think that you would say never say never."

Raven moved his eyes stared at her controlling the helicopter, choosing not to reply to her assumption. In the corner of Debbie's eye, she noticed John's reaction, making her think that somewhere inside this man the legendary soldier will never die. She could only hope one day he will return to fight once more. For what and for whom she wasn't sure about. All she was sure about was the warrior she had witnessed before is still inside him lying dormant.

Arrival

*R*aven, aware he was only a few minutes from landing said, "We ought to follow procedure and make radio contact with the U.S. control centre to let them know we will be landing in a few minutes."

Captain Weller laughed, which made John turn and ask, "What's funny?"

Captain Weller still chuckling replied, "You and procedure don't go together."

Raven turned, looking out of the huge front windscreen, smirking and replied, "Maybe not, but on this occasion, I think it would be best to do so."

Raven picked up the radio to contact the control centre telling them he will be landing at the U.S. military base in the next few minutes. The operator understood his request and then picked up the phone to speak with Colonel Wareing. The phone on Colonel Wareing's desk rang a few times before he picked it up to answer it by saying, "Colonel Wareing speaking."

The operator told Colonel that John Raven and Captain Weller were almost at the military base. Colonel Wareing thanked him and placed the receiver down on the hook. He picked up a cigar, lit it and blew the smoke away up to the ceiling. He stood up, walked to the window to watch between the blinds, waiting for Raven and Captain Weller to appear.

The sun shone through the window with Colonel Wareing feeling the heat from the rays reflecting through the glass. Waiting patiently for them to arrive, he observed the frost around the base. Taking another drag on his cigar, he blew the smoke away while looking at the time on his watch. The head of personnel duties, Alison Colquhoun, knocked on the Colonel's door, left open, and walked inside, asking in a polite manner, "Where would you like me to leave this package?"

Colonel Wareing turned around aware of what the package was that Alison had brought into his office. He blew the smoke away, which made Alison pull her face and say, "Sir. You should seriously think about giving up smoking."

Colonel Wareing placed the cigar back into his mouth, walked over to her and took the package from her. He pulled the cigar from his mouth, turned his head away from her and blew out the smoke replying, "Maybe one day I will."

Alison looked away from the Colonel's smoke out of the window, noticing that a U.S. helicopter was approaching. Following Alison's eyes, the Colonel turned to look out of the window to see that Raven and Captain Weller was now inside the military perimeter.

Colonel Wareing looked at his watch again and said, "Son of a bitch! He doesn't know how to fail!"

Alison confused, replied, "Excuse me?"

Colonel Wareing smirked, saying, "That will be all Alison."

Alison turned to walk out of the Colonel's office, leaving him to stand at the window with the cigar in his mouth watching the U.S. helicopter, in the distance, finally land.

Captain Weller turned everything off, climbed out of her seat and said to John, "Thanks for this."

Sitting there taking his helmet off, John replied, "I always said I would get you back."

She gave a wry smile as she leaned forward to kiss John on the cheek. Feeling surprised, John slowly turned his head to look at her asking, "What was that for?"

Debbie, who was starting to show love in her eyes replied, "For just being you."

John listened to her, realising she meant every word she had just mentioned. He stood up and followed her, watching her collect her bags left in the back and then jumped out of the helicopter with her, starting to walk to Colonel Wareing's office. An elite soldier called Bryden Burton shouted, "Captain Weller."

Raven and Captain Weller stopped walking and turned around to face the soldier walking briskly towards them. Raven asked, "What can we do for you Bryden?"

Bryden raised his right hand that was holding a clipboard and asked, "Can one of you sign for the return of this craft?"

Raven took the clipboard from Bryden, signed his name and then gave it back to him, where he thanked them for their co-operation. John liked the attitude of the soldier and asked, "What are your main duties on this military base?"

Bryden replied, "I'm head of logistics."

Raven then asked, "Where in the world have you served using the skills taught to you?"

Bryden answered Raven's question by immediately replying, "Vietnam and Iraq."

Captain Weller, aware that time was ticking by, interrupted the conversation saying, "John. We should go!"

Raven ended his conversation with the soldier saying, "Keep up the good work soldier, I like people that are efficient."

Colonel Wareing left his office deciding to drive to the other side of the U.S. military base to collect Raven and Captain Weller. He saw them, in the distance, speaking with Bryden causing him to beep the horn. Hearing the distraction, they all turned to see Colonel Wareing was driving to meet them all, where he braked sharply and skidded. Bryden saluted the Colonel, where he gave a casual salute back to him. He then said to Raven and Captain Weller, "Get in!"

Captain Weller sat next to the Colonel, while Raven placed the Captain's belongings in the back and went to sit on the seated panel above the wheel arch looking back at the fully armed U.S. helicopter they had just been flying. Colonel Wareing positioned the jeep in first gear, released the handbrake and pulled away quickly and said, "Glad you could make it back on time John."

John sitting in the back with his arms resting on his knees and hands clasped together, replied, "Where there is a will, there is a way."

Colonel Wareing smirked, saying, "You can say that again, but you have a tendency of taking liberties."

John turned his head right, watching the officers sitting in front, and heard Colonel Wareing say, "We don't have much time. You need to collect your belongings, and then you're to fly out to Kuwait, where you will be transported to the aircraft carrier, U.S.S. Abraham Lincoln."

Captain Weller with concern asked, "Why all the rush Sir?"

Colonel Wareing replied, "We have to get you airborne as soon as possible."

Raven asked, "What's the problem Colonel?"

Colonel Wareing replied, "It's classified."

Raven answered, "It usually is."

"Meaning?" Colonel Wareing asked in a stern voice.

Raven replied, "Meaning, it usually is."

Captain Weller already aware of Operation Gulf Warrior said, "It does sound serious, Sir."

Colonel Wareing driving at a speed replied, "Believe me, it is now."

Raven aware of where Captain Weller was being sent to, asked, "Does this have anything to do with the Iranians?"

Colonel Wareing paused for a moment, later replying, "You're on a need to know basis, and you don't need to know!"

Raven turned his head away from the Colonel, staring at the jeep's floor deciding to keep his own thoughts to himself, wondering if the military were using him for his knowledge and fighting skills. What annoyed him, was the fact they couldn't confide in him, knowing that he may just be the one man who could make everything right again.

Colonel Wareing pulled up sharp and jumped out of the jeep. He said to Captain Weller, "Get your belongings and get changed! You need to be in the air in the next thirty minutes."

Raven casually climbed out of the back of the jeep and handed the bags to Captain Weller, where she hugged him while saying, "If things get tricky . . . ."

Raven closed his eyes, which made Captain Weller stop from asking her question. The sudden silence made Raven open his eyes again and say, "I'm sure you will be okay."

Captain Weller showed a loving twinkle in her eye when she looked back at Raven, replying, "I probably will be, but it's always nice if you can rely on somebody like you for backup."

Raven placed his hand out, resting it onto Captain Weller's shoulder and said, "After Unit Expendable, I'm done."

Captain Weller placed her arms around his waist replying, "I wish I could believe you."

Raven gave a casual blink and said, "Trust me, when I say soon it will be over for me."

Captain Weller started to weep, where the tears flowed onto Raven's jacket. Knowing that she had become upset, Raven took his hand away from her shoulder, placing it around her holding her tightly while giving a menacing stare at the Colonel standing close by. Colonel Wareing said, "Debbie?"

She lifted her head choosing to ignore the Colonel and just looked up to Raven, where he said, "Go."

Reluctantly, she let go of Raven's waist looking up to him with love in her eyes. Raven watched her starting to walk away with Colonel Wareing to change her clothing and be ready for her journey to Kuwait, and be transported to the aircraft carrier, U.S.S. Abraham Lincoln when she will have to perform high tech I.T duties. Watching Captain Weller walk in the distance with the Colonel, and knowing how upset she had become made Raven sit down on the bench nearby and look at everything around him. He placed his elbows onto his knees, lowered his forehead onto his thumbs thinking about the possibility of carrying on for just a little longer at least until Captain Weller returns home. Then he recalled the promise, he made to his father when he told him that after he had trained Unit Expendable, he would retire from the military for good. With his emotions becoming mixed up, he looked up to the sky to speak in a low voice to his mentor, Colonel Lewis by asking, "What do I do?"

Captain Weller, who was walking briskly with Colonel Wareing stopped in her stride and said, "I have to do something."

Colonel Wareing frowned replying, "You don't have much time!"

With no time to explain, she turned back starting to trot back down the corridor, shouting, "I'll make it."

Military personnel stopped working to watch her behaving in a strange way, which made some point at her and whisper. The Colonel suspected who she was going to and could only watch her hurry to the man; she is still in love with. Captain Weller dashed through the doors, first looking straight ahead in search of Raven. She placed her head down feeling disappointment, and then in the corner of her eye, she saw him sitting on the bench with his head resting on his thumbs. Quietly, she walked down the steps, making her way to Raven, and said, "John."

Remaining seated in the same position, he moved only his eyes upwards to focus on her. Feeling nervous, Debbie said, "I haven't much time."

John interrupted her, replying, "Then go."

Debbie, crouched down, tenderly holding John's arm and said, "John, after I've finished this mission, I've decided to retire from the military, hoping to share the rest of my life with you."

John frowned. Watching his facial reactions made Debbie carry on saying, "Don't say anything yet because you have plenty of time to think about what I have just told you. I have to go now."

She stood up, turned around and started walking back up the steps. Raven took his hands away from his forehead and said, "Debbie?"

She turned back, looking back at him, where he gave a casual nod agreeing with what she had suggested. Starting to produce a smile of glee she said, "You won't regret it."

Before Raven could reply, Colonel Wareing opened the door and said, "You don't have much time Captain. Go and get ready."

Noticing John sitting on the bench, he decided to walk down the steps to sit beside him, asking, "So what was it that seemed so important that Debbie just had to speak to you about?"

Raven narrowed his eyes because it was no business of the Colonel's. Aware that Raven didn't want to discuss the matter, he stood to his feet jokingly saying, "Captain Weller has probably bribed you to come back into battle if anything should happen to her hasn't she?"

Raven narrowed his eyes slightly, frowning at the Colonel's assumption, after listening to what she had proposed a few moments before. He remained silent, which made the Colonel say, "When you have a moment, will you come to my office?"

Still dwelling on what the Colonel had just asked, John gave a prolonged blink and nodded his head agreeing. Colonel Wareing then said in a stern voice, "Don't be long!"

After listening to the Colonel speak, Raven remained sitting there on the bench with his hands clasped together, just watching everybody performing their duties around the military base on a cold December day. One thought kept coming back to haunt him, which made him question, was Debbie being sincere when she told him that she would retire after her mission and spend the rest of her life with him. The cold breeze blew John's hair has he thought about Debbie's proposal earlier. Unable to come to an honest conclusion, he sighed, while rotating his thumbs thinking about whether she was playing mind games. His hair kept blowing in the breeze, while he imagined Captain Weller, hoping that if the worst did occur, he would be there to help her survive and be able to live to see another day.

He placed his hand into his pocket and pulled out his mobile phone and dialled his son's number. Holding the phone to his ear, he listened to the constant ring waiting patiently for John to answer his call. John Weller noticing he had an incoming call, mentioned to everybody sitting around the table in the café where Louise worked, "My father is ringing me."

Tyler and Stevens were enjoying a cooked breakfast, which made Stevens ask, "Is Raven checking on us?"

Weller answered the phone by saying, "Hi."

Raven replied, "Hi John, have Stevens and Tyler left or are they doing what I would have done, having breakfast at the café where Louise works at?"

Weller glanced across the table at Tyler and Stevens, replying, "They're doing what you would have done."

Raven smirked, asking, "Have you asked Louise the inevitable question?"

With Louise sitting beside John, he gave a methodical reply, "I'm working on it."

Raven sniggered saying, "You haven't asked her then?"

Weller turned to look at Louise, replying, "Not yet, but I'm going too soon."

Changing the subject he asked his father, "What are you doing now?"

Raven stood up, replying, "I'm about to attend a meeting with Colonel Wareing to more than likely discuss Unit Expendable."

Weller gave a half-laugh, saying, "Good luck."

Raven in a stern voice replied, "The good luck has to be for you with what you're about to do. When Tyler and Stevens have finished their breakfast, tell them to proceed back to the U.S. military base."

Weller glanced at the soldiers once more and said, "Will, do, bye."

Raven placed his phone back into his pocket, stood up and started to walk up the steps and make his way once more to Colonel Wareing's office. Some of the military personnel stopped him, wanting to speak with him about the festive season. Others would leave their desk relishing the opportunity in being able to join in the conversation and be surprised to witness a softer side of Raven they didn't usually get to see.

Proposal

At the café where Louise worked, Weller, Stevens and Tyler enjoyed a cooked breakfast, given to them on the house by Louise's boss. Knowing who these men are, occasionally, he would walk across to their table asking them if everything was okay, and if they enjoyed their breakfast. With Tyler and Stevens dressed in military uniform, meant other people sitting nearby to them were watching them. The soldiers knew, but chose to ignore it by carrying on talking to Weller. The boss of the café walked to their table again asking, "Would you men like some more coffee?"

Tyler placed his hand over his cup replying, "No."

Stevens, who had heard the same question held his cup out to be filled with more coffee. Stevens thanked him as he watched Weller ask, "Would it be okay for Louise to join us for a few minutes?"

The owner of the café replied, "I don't see why not."

He then made his way back, passing customers and went into the kitchen and saw Katie and Louise washing the pots. He called over to Louise, which made her look, grab a towel and walk across the kitchen to her boss. Her boss said, "Take your break now. Go and sit with your friends."

Louise thanked her boss as she carried on drying her hands, and then said to Katie, "See you later."

She walked up to the table the soldiers were sitting at remembering it was the same table John sat at when he first asked her out. Standing behind John, sat down drinking his coffee and talking with Tyler and Stevens, she placed her hand on his shoulder, which made John turn and say, "Hi."

Stevens asked, "Have you come to join us? Sit here next to me."

Louise took a few more paces and went to sit next to Stevens where she was now facing John. Tyler looked through the window watching people starting to do their Christmas shopping once more. Louise noticed, asking, "Have you done your Christmas shopping Luke?"

Luke turned from looking out of the window to face her replying, "I've been on duty at the U.S. military base and unable to do any shopping this year."

Louise then asked, "You've sent Christmas cards to your family though?"

Luke replied, "Yes."

Stevens joined the conversation saying, "Christmas is never quite the same when you have to spend it back at the military compound."

Customers sitting close to Stevens and Tyler were occasionally eavesdropping. A couple had finished their breakfast and decided to leave to do some more Christmas shopping. When they turned around the gentleman recognised John Weller and said, "I'm proud of you for bringing President Berry home safely from North Korea."

Stevens placed his cup down on the table waiting for what John's reaction would be. Tyler, aware the sun was now shining after they had been in the café for two hours, glimpsed at the time on his watch knowing they will have to travel back to the U.S. military base.

John modestly replied to the customer, "I'm sure any other soldier would have done the same thing, given the chance."

The gentleman placed his hand out to shake John's hand, which his wife repeated and then said, "Have a Merry Christmas."

The gentleman walked a few paces, stopped, turned around and said to the people sitting at John's table, "Enjoy this Christmas and let's try to forget what the Iranians are threatening to do to the western world. Christmas is about joy and glad tidings."

John watched them walk to the cashier standing at the till to pay for their breakfast while nodding his head agreeing. With other customers watching and listening, they casually raised their hot drinks acknowledging what had just been mentioned to him and for whom he was. Louise sat back saying, "They all know who you are, and haven't forgotten what you did for our country."

John casually glanced around the area he was sitting at and saw some customers gracefully lift their hand towards him. Stevens said, "Quite the hero Weller."

John just moved his eyes to stare at Stevens choosing not to reply. Luke glanced at the time on his watch again and said, "We should go because we have a long journey."

Luke pushed his chair away from the table to stand up, patting John on the shoulder while saying, "Have a good one buddy."

Stevens slid his chair back to stand up and walked behind Louise saying, "You have a good Christmas mate. You know you have a really good looking woman there that if you prefer, I could easily take off your hands free."

Louise stood up, giving Stevens a friendly poke, saying, "Behave you."

She then gave Stevens a hug, with him saying, "Merry Christmas Louise."

John watched and then stood up to give another of his best mates a hug and said, "Enjoy Christmas."

Stevens looked back at John in the face, paused for a few seconds and replied, "Thanks I will try. As you grow older you're slowly becoming Raven, and we know it."

John shook his head disagreeing, replying, "I'm some way off yet, but it would be nice to be a legend like my father."

Louise, standing nearby remained quiet and little frosty faced. Tyler detected her facial expression and said, "Come on Rick. It's time to hit the road!"

They walked to the door, which Louise's boss had noticed. He went to them wanting to shake both of their hands and tell them that they must visit again sometime. John and Louise watched both soldiers place their hand up giving a casual wave to them.

John and Louise sat back down at the table to talk, while watching Tyler and Stevens leave and drive back to the U.S. military base in Raven's car. Louise placed her hand out, tenderly placing it on the top of John's hand saying, "People do know who you are, where I feel you're now free from your father's shadow. You proved that when you brought President Berry home safely and fought alongside your father."

John thought back to the time of *America in Conflict* but chose to say nothing. Louise also thought back for a few seconds saying, "It was a terrible time for us all."

John closed his eyes for a few seconds, sniggered and replied. "Who would have guessed the date, we had arranged to watch the football game between the Arizona Cardinals v New York Giants would have turned out the way it did?"

Louise stroked John's hand gently saying, "I was a mess when you killed those terrorists at the University of Phoenix Stadium."

John looked down at the table and then slowly lifted his head to face Louise, who was now showing a sad face. In a sombre voice he said, "If I hadn't done what I needed to do, you wouldn't be alive today."

Still stroking John's hand, Louise replied, "Your mother told me the same thing too."

John asked, "She did that?"

Louise replied, "Your mother and father were a tower of strength to me when I appeared to be at the most vulnerable point in my life."

John paused, visualising some of the traumatic scenes he had witnessed. Remembering the massacre at the village made him pull his hand away from Louise and say, "Right or wrong I had to do what I had to do."

Louise watched John look out of the window, suspecting he was carrying all the pain he had previously witnessed, which made her ask, "Why don't you leave the U.S. military and just be a normal person?"

John turned to face her with a solemn look, wondering whether to propose to her. Deciding to ignore Louise's question he asked her, "Do you remember that this is the table Tony and I was sitting at when I asked you out for the first time?"

Louise thought back, replying, "Since then it's been an adventure with you Weller!"

John smirked, deciding not to propose at the same table for the fear of bad luck reoccurring. Instead, he asked in a solemn voice, "Do you miss your brother?"

Surprised by the question, Louise replied, "What kind of question is that? You now know that I do!"

John detected a sharp tone in her voice immediately saying, "I'm sorry."

Louise replied, "No. I'm sorry for snapping. Privately, I had to relive the trauma of losing my brother when you were somewhere in the Korean jungle with President Berry. The fear of losing you too was just too much. To be honest, it still is and probably explains why I would prefer if you left the military for good."

John took a sip of his coffee thinking about what Louise had just told him. Choosing to be wise, he decided to remain quiet and say nothing. Louise watched him place the cup back on the table and asked, "John, if it became a choice between the U.S. military and us, which choice would you make?"

Listening to the question put to him made John decide that now wasn't a good time to propose to his girlfriend. Taking too long to answer the question made Louise frown and ask, "Is the question so difficult to answer?"

John lowered his head a little holding a sad face and just moved his eyes to gaze at her. Louise placed her hand back onto John's hand, looking at him for a few seconds, and then in a sombre voice said, "Don't give me the Labrador look."

John raised his head, narrowed his eyes a little and replied, "To be honest I haven't thought about it."

Louise stroked John's hand again saying, "I once told your mother that I just want John Weller the person I first met at the café, because I don't know if I can handle John Weller the elite soldier."

John replied, "I'm not a bad person."

Louise turned her head away, closing her eyes starting to sense that this discussion could become an argument. Slowly, she moved her head back to face John and listened to him say, "It's my job, and it's all I know."

Louise placed her other hand onto the table wanting to hold John's hand with both hands, trying to reassure him, there is life after the military. Although an ultimatum hadn't yet been put to him, John felt it would only be a matter of time before it would be put to him. Churning many thoughts around his mind, he asked Louise, "Why do people try to change people? Why can't people accept other people for whom they are?"

Louise sniggered has she narrowed her eyes slightly suspecting that John was asking her the question about him. Before she could answer him, he stood up saying, "If you love someone enough, you will always accept them for whom they are."

Louise's eyes started to glaze over where she shed a tear that rolled down her cheek. John touched her shoulder tenderly with his left hand. Using his right hand, he placed it into his pocket to bring out the box that had the engagement ring inside. He knelt down on one knee and opened the box and said to Louise, "I know this isn't the perfect place, but it does always have a special place in my heart with meeting you here for the first time."

Louise started to weep knowing now what John was about to ask. She didn't interrupt him. She let him carry on saying. "Louise I love you, and always will no matter what. Will you do the honour of marrying me and become my wife?"

By now, people sitting nearby to John and Louise were watching what John had decided to do, becoming interested in what Louise's answer would be. Louise, still weeping gave a smile at John as she gently rubbed her eyes. John feeling as though she was taking too much time to answer the question said, "I understand you may need time to give me a decision. I'm going to leave and do some Christmas shopping hoping that you may have a decision for me later today."

John placed the opened box showing a stunning engagement ring inside onto the table and then looked down at Louise to say in a solemn voice, "If you love me, you will accept me for who I am."

He then bent down to place his hand onto Louise's shoulder and kissed her forehead. Standing up he squeezed her shoulder tenderly and said, "See you later."

Starting to feel confused, Louise nodded her head agreeing by replying, "See you later John."

As she watched him walk out of the café, Louise picked up the box that John had left on the table wanting to look at the ring. A person sitting at a table close by asked Louise, "What will your answer be?"

Louise placed the box back onto the table replying, "I don't know because it's complicated."

The person that had spoken to Louise said, "It's your decision where only you will know when the time is right what your answer will be."

Louise sat there for a few more minutes reflecting on her good and bad times she had experienced while going out with John. Katie saw her sitting alone and went down to sit down opposite her. She saw the ring inside the box and said, "Wo."

Louise looked across at her, watching her pick up the box to have a closer look at the stunning engagement ring. Katie said, "It's a sparkler."

Noticing that Louise didn't seem happy, she asked with concern, "You have said yes to John haven't you?"

Louise shook her head replying, "I haven't yet given him an answer. All I know is I love John."

Katie, feeling confused asked, "What's the problem then?"

Louise frowned, replying, "The problem will always be the same! I don't want John to remain in the U.S. military if we're to be married."

Feeling concerned for Louise, Katie placed the box on the table, asking, "You've discussed this with John about not being happy with him being in the military?"

Louise looked away feeling guilty about what she wanted, which made her ask, "Am I being selfish?"

Katie started to feel for her friend, replied, "John will always love you. Anybody can see that it's obvious by looking at his eyes when he speaks with you. The guy is totally in love with you."

Louise turned to face Katie listening to her ask, "What is it about the military you don't like?"

Before answering, Louise thought for a few seconds about her brother Enzio and the time John had been in the Korean jungle with President Berry, which made her reply, "I just want a normal life like you and Paul."

Katie stood up, looking down at her good friend feeling concerned for her and said, "Only you know what it is that you want the most."

Louise looked up to her replying, "I know I want John, but I can't share him with the military. What makes matters worse; he always feels he has to impress his father because of whom he is."

Katie said, "It's sounds as though it's going to be a tough decision to make, but only you can make it."

Although Louise already knew this, she reluctantly nodded her head agreeing with her friend. Katie looked back noticing it was getting busy at the other end of the café, and mentioned to Louise, it would be a good idea to get back to work. Louise stood up, picked up the box containing the ring and started to walk behind her towards the kitchens. People sitting down at different tables would make comments to her as she passed them, such as, "Good luck."

"Put the lad out of his misery." and "You do what's right girl?"

Katie stopped walking with noticing a picture of James Cairns being shown on the television hung on the wall. Louise stopped too, to see what Katie was watching on television. Another news flash was being reported confirming that James Cairns had escaped from his military escort and was now working with the Iranians holding a serious grievance against his own country. People who were eating and drinking their coffee or tea mumbled remembering Cairns for being a traitor against the United States. Louise could see people in the café becoming disgruntled, aware that probably most of the United States was feeling angry at this man with what he had previously done to their own soldiers. The report showed Iranian people burning the American flag, which made Louise, think back to the time John had placed a part of it around his head when he had used it has a headband. She opened her hand to look at the engagement ring, and then back at the television with the reporter carrying onto say, "We have live pictures from Iran with President Modarres saying these words a few moments ago."

"We will stand up and fight the United States of America!"

Where there was once light hearted discussions and laughter, suddenly the café had become quiet. Everybody watched the television feeling apprehensive about what else the Iranian president was about to say. Louise and Katie glanced at each other, and then back at the television with President Modarres standing on the balcony, which made the Iranian people cheer with excitement. He placed his hand out to them for calm and then turned to his side to look at Cairns, giving him the signal to come and stand beside him on the balcony. Seeing Cairns in the flesh made people sitting in the café become disruptive, which made Louise say, "Hush a minute, let's see what this weasel has to say!"

One of the customers sitting at a table, who had heard John propose to her earlier said, "Your boyfriend should go in there and kill him!"

Louise without thinking dropped the box containing the ring to the floor. Katie aware of what she had let go of, bent down to pick it up and held it for her. Louise, still watching television said, "It will never just be John and I. It will always be John, the U.S.A, and then me."

Katie replied. "But John only wants you."

With briefly speaking they had missed some of the words Cairns had spoken. When they watched television again the Iranian people were holding their arms aloft cheering, which made Cairns shout, "Revenge to the United States! We will bring you to your knees with the help of Russia."

Everybody sitting in the café seemed dumbfounded and disgusted at how one of their own people could speak out like this against their own nation. Cairns carried on saying, "In my home country it's a time for glad tidings and joy with Christmas being only a few days away."

The Iranian people stopped cheering, suddenly looking up to him in anxiety to listen to what might else he had to say. Cairns looked stern at the people below, making him lean forward, move his head slowly from left to right assessing every single Iranian person standing in the crowd. With a menacing stare, he said, "Christmas is a story that's in the bible! Well here is another story from the same book!"

The Iranian President slowly turned his head and without showing any emotion watched Cairns carry onto say, "If you read the book carefully, it states the next world war will start in the Middle East! They're right because we with the help of our ally, Russia, have nuclear missiles pointing at the United States and other western countries, which we intend to use sooner rather than later!"

Louise and Katie looked at each other in dismay and then at different people's reaction inside the café, which wasn't good. Katie gave Louise the box containing the engagement ring saying, "I'm sure you will make the right decision."

Louise took the box from her replying, "Thanks."

When she turned back to watch television, Cairns was holding a huge picture of John Raven, shouting to everybody, "Soon, all American's will be like this!"

He lit one corner of the huge picture of John Raven and let it burn, which made the Iranian people raise their arms to cheer and rejoice. He placed his hand out to the people of Iran to show calm once more and said, "I promise you the United States will burn and be totally destroyed!"

President Modarres watched Cairns' actions intently, clapped and then placed his arm up and down repeatedly to the Iranian people for support, which the crowd acknowledged. American flags were set alight with black smoke rising up into the air quickly. Cairns, who was still holding the huge picture of Raven watched it burn some more and then threw it down into the crowd. He smirked, as he gave an evil stare, when he said, "Merry Christmas America, this will be your last one!"

He turned to walk back into the Iranian President's quarters, followed by President Modarres. Concerned about what Cairns had just mentioned, the president reminded him that his people don't like false promises. With his hair hanging into his face that made him appear more menacing, he turned to face President Modarres to say, "Atash. Soon the U.S.A. will be history and just a mass of ash!"

The news reporter on television, who was also surprised at Cairns' outburst, composed himself wanting to carry on with his report asking, "How will President Berry react to this threat made by the Iranians? Something has to be done! What I don't know, all I do know is the Spirit of Christmas is now tarnished."

Louise opened her hand once more to look at the box containing the ring and said, "Watching this report has just made my decision so much more difficult."

She placed her hand to her forehead and carried on saying to Katie, "I can't help thinking that John is going to become involved in this mess the Iranians have just announced."

She looked back at the television listening to the reporter finish his report with the camera moving to focus on the face of America's finest soldier burning. Louise focused hard on Raven's face feeling anguish and said, "I feel this is all going to come home and involve the people I love and care for."

Katie placed her hand on Louise's arm replying, "You don't know for sure."

Louise closed her eyes thinking about the traumatic time of *America in Conflict*. She knew this bad experience would never leave her, which made her reopen her eyes to see the picture of Raven's face almost burnt to ash. Watching Raven's face burn made her think what will the future now hold for the person she loves and the people she cares about?

Shock

---

*J*ust like many other American's, Colonel Wareing watched the report broadcasted live on television. Feeling displeased at seeing James Cairns, with what he had become and what he was indeed threatening to do, shocked him. He became concerned with the thought that World War 3 could be beckoning, which may result in the world as we know it, ending. He walked outside his office into the corridor to see John talking with some of the military personnel. Still thinking about what he had just seen on the television, he shouted, "John."

John and the military personnel turned their heads to look at the Colonel, listening to him say, "John, come into my office."

Colonel Wareing walked back into his office, anxiously waiting for Raven. John wished all the military personnel a Merry Christmas and walked toward Colonel Wareing's office, knocking on the door left open and walked inside. Colonel Wareing was standing at the window watching the plane taking Captain Weller to Kuwait take off, when she will then be taken to the aircraft carrier, U.S.S. Abraham Lincoln. Watching the plane climb and aware that Raven was standing behind him, he said, "It's ironic."

John frowned, asking, "What is Sir?"

Colonel Wareing turned around to face John and pointed to the plane rising into the sky and replied, "There you have

Captain Weller travelling to Kuwait, where she will then be escorted to the aircraft carrier U.S.S. Abraham Lincoln, which is in the Gulf and close to Iran."

John interrupted by saying, "Yes, I know."

Colonel Wareing produced an angry face, replying, "I bet you didn't know that weasel Cairns has just threatened the U.S.A with nuclear war!"

Standing there, John became slightly perplexed and asked, "Surely they do realise that if they were to send a nuclear missile and attempt to destroy our country, they too would receive one back?"

Colonel Wareing lit a cigar and then quickly blew the smoke away and replied, "Who is the winner?"

Showing a sombre face, John answered, "Nobody and needless lives will be lost for no apparent reason."

Colonel Wareing placed his cigar down in the ashtray while saying to John, "I was dearly looking forward to this Christmas, when for the first time in years I was going to spend this Christmas with my wife, Michelle and our son, Stuart. With now knowing Cairns is scheming with the Iranians, and the serious threats that have been made, I can't enjoy it no more."

John started to feel sorry for the Colonel, replying, "Let the world and the people in it do what they have to do. Live for today because tomorrow will take care of itself."

Colonel Wareing snatched his cigar, bawling, "This is the whole point Raven, and there may be no fucking tomorrow!"

Listening to the Colonel using harsh words spoken to him made Raven glare back at him and say, "It's Cairns, he isn't capable!"

Colonel Wareing blew some more smoke away from his mouth and said, "You didn't see the report, I watched a few moments ago. He hates America. He despises the people that live in America, and he has a huge vendetta against you!"

John produced a frown, asking, "Who hasn't?"

Colonel Wareing placed his cigar back into the ashtray, walked over to the television and flicked through the channels until he saw the image of John Raven burning. After finally finding a channel he stepped back and said, "Look! This is what the crazy bastard wants to do to us all, and what better way of showing it, but to burn his main enemy, for the world to see!"

John watched the repeated report, seeing the picture of him burning and replied, "It's a pity, he won't get to meet me because my days with the military are almost over."

Colonel Wareing asked, "You can't mean that?"

Watching the image on television, while a reporter spoke, he turned and replied, "It has to end sometime."

Colonel Wareing in a harsh voice asked, "The world or your ego?"

John chose not to answer this question by deciding to turn around and walk out of the Colonel's office, which made him say, "Raven, I haven't finished!"

Still walking toward the door, Raven replied, "I have."

The President of the United States came onto the television, which made the Colonel say in a solemn voice, "John, hold on."

John stopped, turning to face the Colonel and listen to him say, "President Berry is about to speak to the nation."

Giving a sharp glare to the Colonel, John decided to walk back, standing with his arms folded, waiting patiently for what the President of the United States had to say. President Berry, standing on the podium said, "This time of the year should be a time for giving, sharing and being with our families and loved ones."

She paused, feeling sadness for the American people. With people watching her, she knew she had to carry on with her speech. "Although we still can, the happiness is overshadowed by the threat of war. It is with regret I have to tell you our main enemy is Iran. They have an accomplice who was a former U.S. soldier, and highly thought of before performing acts of treason against the United States. We have to take this threat seriously and will indeed retaliate if Iran, with the help of Russia, decides to fire nuclear missiles at the United States. These are tense times! I ask every single American to be strong, prevail and pray for hope that a solution can be reached before the inevitable may happen. The Secretary of State, Sarah Johnson, is to meet with the Iranian foreign secretary to try to resolve what has become a crisis."

Hearing these words made John becoming concerned, say to the Colonel, "It's not a good idea to send the Secretary of State into a crisis meeting, because she has already been a victim when she was held hostage in Iraq."

Colonel Wareing didn't answer. He walked over to his desk and picked up his cigar to take another drag. After blowing the smoke away, he walked back to stand next to Raven, listening to President Berry carry on saying, "I apologise to every single American person, and the world for having to flex our military muscles. We have no choice after being provoked in an uncertain way. We will not tolerate threats from nations that want to destroy our country and our homeland. Any nation that feels they want to attack the U.S.A then be sure we will as a nation become united and defend ourselves with honour and pride!"

People in different parts of the United States and the western world applauded her actions agreeing with every word she had just spoken. Colonel Wareing gave a gentle clap and then looked to his side saying, "She still has the fiery side and the fighting spirit. It's a pity you don't anymore!"

John moved his eyes to look at the floor feeling disappointment with what the Colonel had just said. Hearing his name being mentioned by President Berry made him move his eyes by wanting to focus back on the television. The image of his face burning was shown once more to millions of people, with President Berry carrying onto say, "John Raven is a formidable soldier, the best of the best, and dare I say expendable? To see such an act of insolence performed to a respected soldier can only mean that we remain together and fight like this man would once have done, and I believe still can do."

Colonel Wareing placed the cigar to his mouth, so he could applaud the president and then said, "She believes she is going to need you at some point."

Refusing to look at the Colonel, John carried on watching television, replying, "It has to end sometime."

Colonel Wareing took another drag on his cigar and blew the smoke at Raven's face feeling bitterly disappointed. Raven didn't flinch at the smoke clouding his vision. He chose to listen to President Berry carry on saying in a sombre voice. "Fellow American's, with Christmas almost up on us, I want to wish you a Merry Christmas and hope and pray that we will have a peaceful New Year. It will benefit not only us as a nation, but the world as we know it."

The Colonel and Raven watched the President stand down from her podium and start to walk away with the Secretary of State, Sarah Johnson, who was standing close by. The reporter came on television to speak, which made Raven turn to the Colonel and say, "I ought to go now."

Colonel Wareing frowned at Raven asking, "What about a brief discussion about Unit Expendable?"

John paused for a few seconds, looking out of the window, noticing Danny Armson raising the barrier for Luke Tyler and Ricky Stevens to drive into the U.S. military base with his car. Watching what was happening outside, yet still aware of the Colonel's question, he decided to reply by telling the truth. "They're all elite soldiers in their own right, there is nothing to discuss, only that they get to win, live and survive."

Colonel Wareing slowly moved his eyes to the floor not relishing the prospect that soon Raven will be gone from the military when it will be for good. John walked towards the door, which made Colonel Wareing say, "You will be missed."

John stopped in his stride, turned around looking straight back at the Colonel and listened to him say, "I'm going to miss you John."

John gave a menacing stare at the Colonel and replied, "Maybe."

He walked out of Colonel Wareing's office leaving him to stub out his cigar in the ashtray, reflecting on what the future has in-store for not only himself, but for all the western world.

Emergency Cabinet Meeting

*P*resident Berry while holding a stern face walked with the Secretary of State, Sarah Johnson, to her own office. Both women remained quiet and subdued with the threat of war beckoning during the Christmas period. General Alexander Gee followed the influential women, speaking with the Vice President aware of how serious this crisis had become. When they arrived at President Berry's office, she held the door open for her colleagues to walk inside. Walking inside behind them, she quietly closed the door and turned around to see the Secretary of State, the Vice President and General Gee was looking at her for a solution to the problem Iran had created. She placed her hand to her forehead thinking, which made General Gee ask, "Are you okay Ma'am?"

President Berry slowly took her hand away from her forehead, looking at all her senior colleagues replying, "This Christmas was supposed to be just a quiet Christmas, but now it's going to be a Christmas like no other. I can't allow this threat to happen!"

The Secretary of State, Sarah Johnson, walked over to her asking, "What do you propose to do?"

Susan thought for a few seconds, later replying, "I would like to arrange an emergency cabinet meeting with every member of Congress available. No excuses will be tolerated for their absence. I know it's Christmas, but what is more important the holiday or the future of our nation, threatened with nuclear war?"

The Vice President spoke up saying, "Surely, you don't expect them to go through with such a threat?"

President Berry, who wasn't sure what to expect replied, "We have to discuss our alternatives and decide what we're to do if we're attacked in such a way."

General Gee watched their reaction but chose to remain quiet. President Berry told the Vice President to arrange a cabinet meeting in forty five minutes, when members of the cabinet will be able to voice their opinion about this serious crisis created by Iran and its ally, Russia.

The Vice President agreed and hurried to his own office, where he and his P.A started to make phone calls to several members of the cabinet. They explained that an emergency meeting had been arranged for all members of the cabinet to attend in forty five minutes to discuss choices available that would involve the future of the United States.

Sarah Johnson walked toward the door and then looked back at President Berry, to ask, "Surely you're not thinking of sending me into another hostile situation after what I suffered in Iraq?"

President Berry, aware of what Sarah Johnson had previously experienced, replied, "Everything will be revealed at the meeting."

Sarah turned to walk once more, which made President Berry say, "Sarah?"

She looked back to face Susan, waiting for her to say, "You're a good friend Sarah."

With her Christmas being badly tarnished, she gave a wry grin replying, "See you at the meeting in the boardroom."

General Gee now decided to speak with President Berry, saying, "The Iranians have threatened us before, with nothing too serious coming from it."

Susan sat down at her desk studying the General's comment, while also thinking about Sarah's Christmas; she had so been looking forward to. She picked up the phone to speak with her P.A, giving her new instructions to arrange a meeting with the Iranian president, so she could possibly resolve this crisis peacefully and amicably. She slowly placed the phone down and said to the General, "I will have to go to Iran in a few days where I would like you to come with me."

General Gee was about to answer her, but her phone rang, which she answered quickly. On the other end of the line, it was her P.A, confirming President Modarres would like to speak with her in Iran on the 29th December, and that Air Force One is available to fly. She thanked her P.A, placed the receiver down onto the holder and turned to General Gee standing close by saying, "I was hoping to be able to travel on Christmas Day!"

General Gee replied, "At least they're willing to talk, Susan."

Susan replied, "I know things have to be prepared, and checks have to be made, but with such a threat made, I was hoping for sooner rather than later."

General Gee said, "You've bought us a few extra days, where I'm sure the Iranians with the help of the Russians will not strike now until at least the New Year."

Susan stood up saying, "I can't be sure about that, because they're such a volatile nation, which do hate the U.S.A."

General Gee frowned, replying, "There is good and bad in every nation, when it is usually the good that has to suffer at the expense of a bad person's intentions."

Susan turned to face the General saying, "You're right Alexander about different nations having good and bad people. It's just a pity; we can't all live in harmony."

General Gee sniggered replying, "Then it would be a perfect world."

As Susan signed a few documents on her desk, she replied, "But it's anything but a perfect world!"

General Gee replied, "You ought to know with the experience you suffered in North Korea."

Susan lifted her head and stopped signing some of the papers. She recalled the time when she had been taken captive at the expense of more civilians being killed at the Korean village, when they wanted to help the President of the United States. She dropped her pen on the desk, placing her hand to her forehead thinking, which made General Gee ask once more, "Are you okay Ma'am?"

Susan didn't answer the General because her eyes started to glaze over as she remembered the massacre that General Kwan and Azar Sajadi had performed on innocent people. Then her face became stern, when she thought of the time she had spent with John Weller-Raven. They were together alone in the Korean jungle being hunted by the enemy. She turned back to the General replying, "Yes, I'm okay. I was just thinking back to the last time when big decisions had to be made."

General Gee smirked, replying, "I do also recall that time and can honestly say you handled that situation well, even though you became directly involved in a warzone."

President Berry thought back remembering the two brave soldiers, and said in a solemn way, "If it hadn't been for John Raven and his son, I wouldn't be alive today."

General Gee replied, "They're outstanding soldiers, perhaps you might like one of them to escort you on your trip to Iran?"

Susan opened her eyes wide at having one of those soldiers beside her on what could be a hostile trip. She turned to the General wide-eyed saying, "That's a good idea."

General Gee glimpsed at his watch informing the president it would be a good idea to start making their way to the boardroom and join the meeting with the other members of the cabinet. Susan glanced at her watch, and nodded her head, agreeing with the General, and went to collect her briefcase. General Gee walked to the door, held it open for President Berry to walk through and then followed, walking beside her. They appeared stern, ready for the intense meeting as the sound of their footsteps echoed on the floor as they approached the boardroom. General Gee opened the door and held it for President Berry to walk through, raising her hand to acknowledge all her colleagues. She walked to her position at the table, as members of the cabinet waited in anticipation at what she had to say. General Gee closed the door, and went to stand behind her, where she quietly thanked him. She glimpsed at everyone sitting at the table looking back at her, which made her start to say, "I'm sorry to have to destroy your Christmas plans. As you're now aware, we're in a serious situation with Iran and its ally Russia, with the threat of nuclear war against our nation. As you all previously know, I may have reacted too swiftly in wanting to use nuclear missiles against North Korea. During my time in North Korea, I did learn there are good and bad people in every nation, when it's always the good that seems to suffer for what the bad impose. This is why I am reluctant in releasing nuclear missiles on Iran, unless we are attacked first."

The Vice President casually nodded his head agreeing with her, while listening to her carry onto say, "I've arranged to fly to Iran on Air Force One on the 29th December."

She paused, briefly looking at Sarah Johnson, before carrying on to say, "I would like the Secretary of State, Sarah Johnson, to come with me to see if a diplomatic solution can be reached with the Iranian President."

A member of the cabinet spoke up by saying, "If a diplomatic solution can't be found, and let's not forget, we're speaking about Iran here, what are we to do if we're attacked with nuclear missiles?"

Sarah Johnson turned her head away from the member of the cabinet, to face her good friend, Susan, listening to what her reply was going to be. Susan held a stern face, as she looked at everybody around the table before she spoke starting to make some of them feel uncomfortable. She looked across at Sarah Johnson, and then answered the question, "I'm sure you will all agree that we don't want a nuclear war, because there are no winners! Everybody becomes a loser! If Iran fails to agree with the proposals I have set, which include lifting sanctions, and they're still determined to use these weapons against the United States, then we have to do what I feel is correct. We have to attack with the full force, using nuclear missiles to destroy a nation that may take decades to reappear. I repeat; we attack when it's confirmed the missiles are launched to destroy our nation. If this does occur, which I hope it doesn't, there will be no winners! General Gee has confirmed the Stealth Bombers are fully armed in Kuwait and ready to fly into Iran at a moment's notice. Nuclear missiles positioned on land in different parts of our own country, are now pointing at Iran and Russia. The day these terrible weapons are flying through the air, I can only assume there will be one outcome, Armageddon!"

Another member of the cabinet spoke, asking, "If the worst was to occur, and nuclear missiles are launched, what are we to do with you not being present?"

Susan closed her eyes visualising a huge flame burning, and then reopened them, quietly replying, "You perform the emergency procedure, when you will travel to NORAD with your family."

Members of the cabinet muttered among themselves accepting the prospect of nuclear war becoming a high possibility. One member turned to ask President Berry, "What about you, and the Secretary of State?"

Susan glanced over at her good friend, Sarah, knowing that if the meeting with the Iranian President failed, it would mean their destiny would no longer exist. The Vice President stood up wanting to ask, "Surely you don't want us to fire nuclear missiles while you and Sarah are in Iran?"

Susan replied in a sombre voice, "If the United States is attacked, you now know what you must do. If this means I have to die on foreign soil, so be it."

Sarah Johnson's eyes glazed over, as she looked despondent at the floor, which made Susan ask, "Sarah you are going to fly with me, where I'm asking you as a friend?"

Sarah muttered in a low voice, "I wish John Raven was travelling with us."

Susan frowned asking, "Sorry Sarah, what did you say?"

Sarah lifted her head, repeating in a much louder voice for the rest of her colleagues to hear, "I wish John Raven could travel with us."

Susan looked down on her good friend knowing that she had suffered a terrible time in Iraq, after being held captive, beaten and tortured by the enemy. General Gee glanced at President Berry, while asking Sarah, "Why do you ask for John Raven?"

Susan turned to look at the General with a stern face while waiting for Sarah's reply. Sarah answered the General's question truthfully, saying, "I feel as though I will arrive home at some point, because his view on diplomatic solutions will be so much different from what ours will be."

General Gee had already listened to President Berry speak about John Raven, and his son, which made him reply, "No promises with Raven wanting to retire, but I will see what I can do if it makes you feel better."

President Berry gave a wry smile as she turned back to speak to members of the cabinet by saying, "These are tense times where I will have to tell the nation what I am about to do. The conclusion will be left for the Vice President to give the relevant instructions to the people concerned if and when required."

She looked across at the Vice President, asking, "Are you okay with this David?"

He replied, "Everything will be performed as you have requested."

Susan turned to everybody once more, saying, "It isn't much, but by travelling to Iran on the 29th December, you do at least get time to spend with your family this Christmas. Enjoy it because I don't yet know what the New Year has to offer."

Christmas Day

$\mathcal{I}$n every calendar year, there is one special day for most people to celebrate. Whether you're old, young, rich or poor; Christmas Day always has the magic appeal that makes people want to be gracious to those who are more unfortunate than others. Christmas is a time for sharing, and giving, but with the threat of nuclear war beckoning over the western world, Christmas Day for most people seemed difficult to absorb with having an uncertain future placed in front of them.

It was 7.45 and John Raven was up out of bed early, where he went into the kitchen to smell the turkey cooking slowly during the night. The dogs could smell it, and wasn't too keen on being let outside in the brisk cold air. John went back inside the house into the lounge and turned the television on, only to see the face of Cairns. Seeing Cairns on television, made him glare at him, saying in a low voice, "You're not going to ruin this day."

He grabbed the remote control to switch channels choosing to listen to music being played low while dropping the remote on the sofa before going back into the kitchen. As daylight was starting to break through, he looked outside at the dogs, worrying at how Captain Weller would be spending her Christmas Day. He switched on the kettle and then placed coffee and sugar into a cup. His father, Richard, had woken up and made his way into the kitchen asking, "Are you making me one of those?"

John moved his head slowly replying, "Yeah, can do."

Richard walked over to John, patted his back and said, "Merry Christmas boy."

John watched the kettle boil, raised his head, gave a casual blink and said in a sombre voice, "Yeah, you too, Merry Christmas."

John placed coffee and sugar into his father's cup and then thought that he might as well make Sarah Jane a cup of coffee too with anticipating that she will be up and about reasonably soon. Richard asked John, "What time will John and Louise be arriving today?"

While pouring the hot water into the cups, he replied, "Later today, just in time for dinner if I know John."

Richard chuckled, saying, "That lad can eat like a horse."

John glanced at his father while handing him the cup of coffee, smirked and said, "I remember when you used to say the same thing about me."

Richard took a sip of the coffee and replied, "That's a good cup of coffee son."

He watched him walk to the other side of the kitchen sensing that he was carrying a burden. To ease it, Richard, in a solemn voice said, "You know, time does catch us all up in the end."

John looked through the window at the dogs. For a few seconds he paused, glaring at Sadie, the ferocious dog, he fought with in North Korea and started to think back to his last war, he was involved in. Sarah Jane came into the kitchen interrupting his thoughts by saying, "Merry Christmas Dad."

John turned around and went to her to give her a hug replying, "Merry Christmas Sarah Jane."

Richard stood up wanting to give her a hug and wish her a Merry Christmas too. He said, "Come, look what I have bought you for Christmas."

Sarah Jane followed her grandfather into the lounge, watching him pick a present from under the tree and then give it to her. She tore the wrapping paper away from the box, just as John was walking into the lounge and saw that she was holding a beautiful gold bracelet. John gave a loving smile to his daughter, asking, "Do you like it?"

Sarah Jane placed the bracelet onto her wrist replying, "I'm thrilled with it."

John bent down next to the Christmas tree, searching through the presents to find one he too had bought for his daughter. He picked the one he wanted, and then stood up to give it to her. Sarah Jane thanked him while wondering what her father had bought for her. Sarah Jane, feeling excited, tore the wrapping paper to find that she had been given a music cd and tickets to attend a concert performed by the Black Eyed Peas in the next few days. She asked, "Will you be coming to watch the concert too Dad?"

John smirked, which made Richard say, "Your father is past all that. He prefers what I listen to now, which is Bing Crosby."

John chuckled, replying, "Not quite Dad. You know I've always been a U2 fan and to be honest the Black Eyed Peas are a good group."

John went back into the kitchen leaving Sarah Jane to place the cd into the DVD player with the first track to be played, which was *I Gotta Feeling That Tonight Gonna Be A Good Night*. John listened to those words being sung as he thought about Captain Weller, who was now somewhere in the Gulf on board the aircraft carrier, U.S.S. Abraham Lincoln. Standing alone in the kitchen, he placed his hands to his face wishing if this was to be the last Christmas the United States may ever see, he would have preferred for all the family to be present.

Sarah Jane went into the kitchen to see her father standing there with his hands covering his face, which made her immediately ask, "What's wrong Dad?"

John turned around to face her with a stare, where she said, "Don't look like that, it reminds me of the time when I saw the worst in you."

Again Sarah asked, "Are you okay Dad?"

John's face started mellowing when he replied, "With the possibility of war on the horizon and this Christmas being the last one ever, it's a pity your mother can't visit."

Sarah Jane went to her father to hold his arm tenderly, saying, "It's the call of duty."

John replied, "Yeah."

Sarah Jane looked up concerned to her father, saying, "Mum will be okay."

John narrowed his eyes slightly, replying, "I hope you're right."

Sarah Jane wanted to change the subject, saying, "I'm grateful for the tickets and the cd you gave to me for Christmas."

John asked, "But?"

Sarah Jane said, "Let me finish Dad. When you gave me your knife at the induction that was once owned by Colonel Lewis, it was this item, which means everything to me."

John in a solemn voice, replied, "I hope you never have to use it, but we both know that someday you will."

Sarah Jane looked up to her father once more, pausing for a few seconds, before saying, "Trust me. I won't let you down."

John gave a wry grin, replying, "I know you won't."

Sarah Jane patted her father's arm saying, "Cheer up! It's Christmas, and you're right it could be our last one ever, so let's enjoy it."

She then turned to walk back into the lounge leaving John, who was watching her holding one thought, which was, that's my girl.

Richard and John were preparing the food for the rest of the family when they would arrive later in the day. Sarah Jane, at times came into the kitchen to offer her help, which Richard and John refused. She turned to her father and said, "Take a break, I can finish off here."

Richard agreed and said, "Go and take five minutes John."

John went outside, watching the dogs run up to him to greet him. He patted them, but always found it difficult to make a fuss over Sadie, with fighting with her in North Korea. He threw the ball and watched them all run after it, grinning while walking on the frosty ground to the barn. Arriving at the barn, he went inside, turned on the light and walked over to his bench to sit on it. He looked around the barn, occasionally feeling the cold air from outside, has he thought back to when he was a small boy remembering some of the presents he had received from his mother and father. A wry grin came on his face when he saw himself as a six year old boy dressed as a warrior wearing a headband and holding a huge gun. In a low voice he said, "Some things never change."

As he sat there remembering Christmas past, his mobile phone disturbed him when it rang. He pulled it from his pocket to see that it was his son, John, who was ringing him. He answered the call by saying, "Yo, John, Merry Christmas."

His son replied, "Merry Christmas Dad."

Louise could be heard in the background shouting Merry Christmas, which made John say to his son, "Did Louise like the presents you bought her?"

John sniggered replying, "Yes, she liked every single one of them."

John's father asked, "And you?"

Weller hesitated before answering, which made his father say, "You didn't like what she bought you?"

Weller paused, walked outside to stand on the steps and then answered his father by saying, "I do like what Louise has bought me for Christmas . . ."

His father hearing these words frowned, asking, "But?"

Weller walked down the steps telling his father that he had asked Louise the inevitable question and although a few days had passed by, she still hadn't given him an answer he so dearly wanted to hear. John wanted to reassure his son saying, "You know how she feels about the military, and with us finding out about her brother, Enzio, who's been missing for the last few years. She is going to find it hard to make such a commitment. Give her time."

Weller turned around to look up at the kitchen window and saw Louise, where he gave her a casual wave while asking his father, "What do I do?"

John replied, "You're together! That's what's important. Don't pressure the woman; you may only push her away, which will make things difficult for you. This Christmas could be the last one we ever see in our lives, so why don't we make it one to remember."

Weller saw some of the reports about Cairns making threats at the United States, which made him ask his father, "Do you think they will use nuclear missiles against our country?"

John glanced at his tools around the barn and replied, "You can't rule it out because one day it will happen. It's just a question of who will be crazy enough to do it."

Weller replied, "It does sound serious."

Before answering, John thought about Captain Weller and then replied, "Serious enough for the world to end as we know it. This is why I'm telling you not to pressure Louise, because your proposal may not matter anymore."

Louise opened the door watching John speak on the phone as she walked down the steps closer to him. Placing her hand on his arm she heard him say to her father, "I need to know."

He turned realising Louise was standing there holding his arm, when she asked him, "Know what?"

His father on the other end of the phone heard Louise's voice and replied, "Leave it for now."

Aware that Louise had come outside. He placed his arm around her and decided to end his conversation with his father by saying, "I'll see you later."

John hung up and said to Louise, "You look nice in those new jeans."

Louise ignored John's comment asking, "What did you mean when you mentioned to your father, those words, I need to know?"

Before answering Louise's question, he briefly thought about what his father had just told him to do, when he told him to leave it and don't pressure her. He looked into her eyes and said, "I needed to know for sure if my father was going to retire after he had trained Unit Expendable."

"You're a liar!" Louise shouted.

John replied, "Honestly. I just need to know for sure that my father is going to retire from the U.S. military. He has tried, only to be called back time and again."

Louise shook her head and wagged her finger at him saying, "No way John! You're telling lies and it could be the worst thing you do to me!"

Feeling confused about the advice he had received from his father, and now with Louise detecting, he wasn't telling the truth, he didn't know what to do. He turned away, which made Louise walk up to him, gently place her hand on his arm and say, "I need more time for the proposal you made to me."

John narrowed his eyes, and then moved them to look down at her, wisely choosing to say nothing. Louise placed her other hand around John's back while saying, "I do love you John."

John so wanted to retaliate, with hearing that comment and wanted to bawl, but not enough to marry me. Wisely, he bit his tongue keeping his thoughts inward thinking back to when his father had told him the proposal didn't matter anymore. Remembering those words, he turned to face Louise, where she looked up to him producing a dimple in her cheek as she smiled at him. He looked at her blonde hair that fell down onto her forehead and went to her to give her a kiss on her lips. Louise's father, Kirk, came outside to put some rubbish into the bin and saw that John and Louise were having a kiss. He shouted, "You ought to be travelling to your father's because it is a long journey."

Louise looked up to John and said, "My father is right. We should set off now."

John aware that Kirk would now be alone said, "Come with us Kirk."

Kirk was a proud man and didn't want to burden anybody, and replied, "I'm okay here. You go and enjoy yourselves."

Louise let go of John and walked up to her father to say, "Come with us Dad because you know this Christmas isn't like any other. There may never be another one, so come with us and share it with John's family."

Kirk still thinking that he was going to be a burden asked, "Will your father not mind?"

John smirked replying, "Not at all. Maybe we can all get to listen to some of your war stories around the table after dinner."

Kirk sniggered, reminding them that it was Christmas, and that listening to some of his experiences in war wouldn't be a good idea. John said, "Well at least come and share a beer with my Dad, because who knows, you might just tell each other about the experiences you have faced."

Kirk remembered to when he had been sitting on the steps with John drinking a beer and admitted that he did enjoy it. He looked at John and Louise, which made Louise say, "Come Dad, for me."

Reluctantly, Kirk nodded his head agreeing and replied, "Okay."

Louise replied, "Now that's agreed, let's get our things and begin travelling to your Dad's house."

John watched them walk away to the steps, where he could only stare at Louise's third finger on her left hand wishing that she was indeed wearing the engagement ring he had bought for her. Louise looked back to John asking, "Are you coming?"

John followed Louise and Kirk by stepping inside the house to put on his trainers and jacket and then walk back outside to wait for Kirk and Louise. When they came outside,

Kirk locked the door and walked down the steps beside Louise saying, "This Christmas is going to be special."

John followed that remark by saying, "Let's hope it isn't going to be the last!"

It went quiet as they climbed into the Mini Cooper S to start travelling to John Raven's house for what would be a Christmas never to be forgotten.

Christmas Day is a day that is special for so many people in several parts of the world for different reasons. People spend time with families and friends exchanging gifts. Children are excited at the prospect of being able to play with their new toys and games. The magic you only see in a child's eyes comes but once a year. It's up to the adults to make this Christmas just like any other, even with the threat of war at the back of one's mind, which could make this the last Christmas ever.

Christmas Day in Iran meant President Modarres and James Cairns were planning what the outcome of the visit would be when President Berry and Sarah Johnson arrive on the 29th December.

Cairns was sitting in President Modarres study drinking a large glass of whisky while listening to the hostile crowd outside shouting and jeering against the United States. He stood up, walked over to the French door and looked down at the crowd burning several American flags, which made him grin knowing that sometime soon, his homeland would be annihilated. President Modarres came into the study after having another brief conversation over the phone with President Berry, finalising the details when she and the Secretary of State would be visiting Iran. President Modarres, grinning said, "It's done."

Cairns went to sit in the chair feeling unmoved, rotating his thumb around the glass thinking about what his next move will be. He took a huge gulp of whisky and placed the empty glass down onto the coffee table. He glanced at his reflection in the tinted glass on the coffee table and said, "We should welcome the bitch!"

President Modarres narrowed his eyes, watching Cairns with his scraggy hair hanging down in front of his face looking at himself in the coffee table. With concern he asked, "You really do hate your own nation so much?"

Cairns, slowly turned his head to face the Iranian President, gave an intimidating stare and replied, "Nothing is going to give me greater pleasure than seeing every single American person die in the aftermath of a nuclear war!"

President Modarres replied, "You too will die!"

Cairns stood up to walk across to President Modarres saying, "You think I don't know this, you stupid man!"

President Modarres scowled at Cairns insolence, replying, "Remember, I'm still the President of Iran where a little respect would not go a miss!"

Cairns stared, and then said, "You want this as much as I do, and without me, you're nothing. Remember that!"

Cairns walked over to the cocktail cabinet to pour another drop of whisky into his glass. He held his glass in the air in celebration, with President Modarres watching him take a gulp and listen to him say, "I think we should create a diversion by having pirates using small boats making a nuisance close by to the U.S. Navy."

President Modarres frowned, asking, "Why?"

Cairns stooped forward, walked towards him slowly taking another gulp of his whisky and answered his question by replying, "When that bitch of a President arrives on the 29th December, I want Air Force One to have complications."

Listening hard to Cairns, President Modarres narrowed his eyes at the thought of doing something sinister to Air Force One, but chose not to interrupt him. Cairns walked over to the French door, to look outside watching people jeering and rioting. He turned saying in a stern voice, "Does it matter how the bitch is going to die? Whether it's fried to a frazzle in America, or attacked on her own plane, at least with the latter, we get to see her die!"

President Modarres asked, "What do you propose to do?"

Cairns replied, "I would like you to give the order to the pirates to start being a nuisance nearby to the U.S. war ships. The media will probably show coverage, but they will have missed the much larger picture, when we have sent in a team of terrorists to place explosives in the tunnel."

President Modarres watched Cairns laugh and carry on saying, "A huge part of the runway will explode when Air Force One has landed and is travelling at a speed near to the tunnel below."

President Modarres placed his finger to his mouth thinking about the trains that were travelling below the runway and replied, "This is a good plan, but also stupid for my own people."

Cairns moved his eyes giving an evil stare to the Iranian President and snarled, "I didn't stay in jail just to serve my time! I've schemed up everything to have my revenge on the country that doesn't want to know me anymore!"

He changed his tone asking President Modarres. "Now things are for real, are you scared of following it through?"

President Modarres replied, "Do you want the truth?"

Cairns replied, "You're going to give it me anyway!"

President Modarres paused for a few seconds watching Cairns take another gulp of whisky and then said, "You scare me! You're a dangerous man!"

Cairns replied, "Now we're talking my kind of language!"

He watched President Modarres' reaction while carrying onto say, "Do what I have instructed and soon the United States will no longer exist."

President Modarres hesitated before picking up the phone. He kept his eye on Cairns casually drinking his whisky. Cairns with evil showing in his eyes watched every move the Iranian President was making as he listened to him speaking using his native tongue. President Modarres told his colleagues to do what Cairns had instructed, which made Cairns ask, "What did you just say?"

President Modarres placed the receiver down on the hook replying, "It's done!"

Cairns produced an evil grin and said, "Good. You won't regret this."

Feeling pleased, he went to President Modarres' cocktail cabinet to pour him a drink and hand it to him. President Modarres, while watching every move Cairns had been performing, took the glass from him, which then made Cairns hold out his own glass to make a toast, which made Cairns say, "To America's downfall."

President Modarres repeated those same words, "To America's downfall."

Cairns picked up the remote control, pointed it at the television and flicked through a few channels. He stopped when he saw President Berry speaking on television. Cairns took another sip of his whisky, as he listened to her telling the rest of the world that she and the Secretary of State will be travelling to Iran hoping to prevent World War 3 from taking place. Cairns laughed out aloud. President Modarres raised his glass to President Berry saying, "Soon she will be either dead or will definitely be in our hands."

Cairns produced an evil smirk before moving his head to look at President Modarres and reply, "Absolutely."

When he turned back to watch the television, he saw the picture being shown again of John Raven burning, which made his grin disappear, starting to produce a glare of hatred to the one man, he despised the most.

At John Raven's house, everybody had just eaten a delicious Christmas dinner and was now watching the same report. Raven saw the picture of him again on television and asked his son sitting nearest to the television to change to another channel. He did, only to see the same image of him burning shown on several channels. Louise said, "Turn it off John! This is our day and it's not going to be ruined for anything or anybody!"

John glanced across the table at his father, watching him give the nod to turn the television off. Richard sitting at the table with his head down deciding to look at everybody and say, "Why can't human beings learn to live together? Christ, it's a big enough world for everybody to live in!"

Kirk, listening to Richard's comment replied, "Then it would be too perfect."

Richard leaned forward to take one of the mince pies, which made Sarah Jane say, "Are you not full, with what you have just eaten?"

Richard replied, "I can make room in a corner somewhere."

John grinned, saying, "I think I'll have one of those mince pies."

Holding his hand out, John Weller also said "I'll have one of those too."

Louise chuckled, asking, "Where do all you Raven's put your food?"

John Raven had just finished his mince pie and replied, "It's Christmas, where it may be our last one, so let's enjoy it."

Kirk placed his hand out to take a mince pie replying, "When you put it like that, why not have one?"

Richard asked Sarah Jane, "Would you like one Sarah Jane?"

Sarah Jane replied, "No thanks. I have to watch what I eat, especially with Dad training Unit Expendable in a few days."

Her brother John spoke by saying, "We might not be here in a few days sis, have one, and enjoy today."

Sarah Jane turned away from her brother to glance at her father, when he said, "It's okay. I'm sure you will impress just as your brother has done."

Louise placed her hand out to take a mince pie and then offered Sarah Jane one, which she reluctantly took from her, saying, "Thanks."

Sarah Jane put her mince pie down refusing to eat it, which made her father say, "Enjoy yourself, and don't worry about Unit Expendable."

Raven then picked another mince pie from the plate and carried onto say, "Look, I'm not."

His son, John, replied, "It's a good job Colonel Wareing isn't here because he would be giving you a lecture about how much sugar you're eating."

Raven produced a smirk while eating his second mince pie, and just said, "Possibly."

He then went into the lounge to take from under the Christmas tree, John and Louise's presents, to give them, which they immediately started to unwrap. Raven remained standing there, watching them, feeling proud that most of his family was with him on this special day. The telephone rang, which made Richard say, "I'll get it."

With Raven already standing, he replied, "It's okay Dad. I'll get the phone."

He walked into the lounge, picked the phone up and said, "Yo, John Raven."

Captain Weller replied, "Hi John, Merry Christmas."

John smiled, saying, "Merry Christmas Debbie. We're all missing you."

Debbie could only imagine what it would be like spending Christmas with all her family. Instead, she was walking on the deck of the aircraft carrier, U.S.S. Abraham Lincoln, suspecting she was being watched by Iranian pirates in small boats starting to make a nuisance of themselves by circling the powerful presence of the U.S. warships. She paced the deck passing military aircraft keeping a watchful eye on the Iranians circling close by, saying to John, "I've seen your face on the television a few times."

Suspecting what Debbie had seen on the television, he replied, "Yeah, I can imagine."

Time was starting to pass by, which made Sarah Jane move to see where her father was. When she saw him speaking on the phone, and quickly realised that he was speaking to her mother, she patted his arm, which made him look at her. She then asked, "Can I have a word with Mum?"

John nodded his head agreeing, while telling Debbie that Sarah Jane would like to speak with her. He passed the phone to her, watching her become elated in being able to speak with her mother. John then went to place some music on, by playing a Christmas song performed by the Pogues Feat. Louise started to sing along with the same song and started to try to dance with Raven. John placed his drink down and moved his arm for her, which made him grin. John Weller watched how happy Louise seemed. He just wished that she would give him the answer he so wanted to hear after he had proposed to her. Watching them, he glanced at his father, thinking back to when he had told him not to pressure her. He grinned when he asked his grandfather, Richard, "Are you not getting up to dance?"

Richard laughed replying, "I don't have the energy, but Louise seems to have it."

Kirk watched, feeling hidden glee with watching his daughter being so happy. Richard stood up, asking Kirk and John if they would like a beer, which they accepted. Occasionally, Raven would glance across the room to Sarah Jane to see that she was still speaking on the phone with her mother. Richard came to speak with John and Louise wanting to ask, "Would you both like another drink?"

John closed his eyes while nodding his head yes. Louise replied, "Yes please."

She then went to play more Christmas hits from the past and present, while saying to Sarah Jane, "I've enjoyed today."

Sarah Jane, who was still speaking with her mother, nodded her head to Louise agreeing and gave her a smile. Sarah Jane asked her mother if she would like to speak with her brother, John, which made her reply, "Yes, I would like that."

Sarah Jane went into the dining room listening to the Christmas music being played in the background and said to John, "Mum's on the phone and would like to talk with you."

John took the phone from her saying, "Hi Mum, Merry Christmas."

Debbie said, "Merry Christmas John. I hope you're enjoying this special day."

John frowned, replying, "It would be much better if Louise had given me an answer to my question I asked her a few days ago."

Debbie leaned against one of the military planes feeling for her son, making her say, "She will give you the answer when she is sure. Trust me, with what you are and what you have become, it's a tough decision for her to make."

John starting to feel rather perplexed asked, "What do you mean when you say what I am and what I have become?"

Debbie stood up straight, still holding the phone to her ear after hearing some of her colleagues shouting for her to join them at the party they were attending to celebrate Christmas Day. It was the best they could do, with being thousands of miles away from their families. She gave a casual wave responding to her colleague and then answered her son by replying, "Don't act like the innocent, you know what you are, and you know who you have become."

John looked down at the floor for a few seconds and then at his father, who was enjoying a drink while speaking with Kirk and his grandfather. Although he knew, he asked his mother, "So who have I become?"

Debbie moved her eyes watching the Iranian pirates circling the U.S. warships much closer than before. She waved to a couple of her colleagues to gain their attention pointing to the Iranian's making a nuisance of themselves. She then carried on speaking with John replying, "John. You are your father through and through where you will prevail even more."

John smirked, feeling proud, still dwelling on that one thought about Louise wanting him to leave the force and replied. "I don't know about that, because if Louise is to have her way, and I'm to have the answer I want. I may have to leave the U.S. military."

Debbie listened hard to what John had told her, which made her go quiet for a few seconds. She held her phone down by her side looking out at the huge calm sea wishing she could just be there to reassure him. Slowly, she lifted her arm to place the phone back to her ear and said, "John. My answer is still the same. You will prevail even more."

John feeling confused, decided not to dwell on this subject. With Louise walking into the room to sit beside him, he replied. "Louise has just walked into the room. Would you like to speak with her?"

Debbie replied, "Yes. I would like that."

Before she let John pass Louise the phone, Debbie said, "I'm proud of you John."

John looked at Louise, producing a wry grin and replied, "Thanks."

He passed the phone to Louise, where they wished each other a Merry Christmas and spoke about what their day had involved. One of Captain Weller's colleagues came out onto the flight deck and walked over to her in anticipation wanting her to join the party with the rest of the crew. She said to Louise, "Hold on."

She placed the phone down, replying to the crew member, "I'll be there in a few minutes. Start without me."

She was about to place the phone to her ear once more, but changed her mind, shouting to the crew member, "I'm concerned about these Iranian pirates travelling close to our warships."

He looked at them getting closer to the U.S. warships and shouted, "If they get too close, they will be blasted out of the water!"

Captain Weller asked, "Is there anybody on radar duty?"

The crew member didn't answer; he just carried on walking inside to join the rest of his colleagues, looking forward to the Christmas party they had arranged on the warship. Captain Weller placed her phone back to her ear and listened to Louise say, "It sounds as though it's getting tense where you are?"

Captain Weller gave a half-laugh replying, "The Iranians are circling the fleet of warships, just being a nuisance, but it's nothing we can't handle."

Louise, with concern, asked, "You're going to be okay?"

Captain Weller gave another half-laugh replying, "With all the fire power I'm standing next to. Yes, I'm okay."

Louise watched John drinking his beer and speaking with the other people in the room as she carried on speaking with Captain Weller. Occasionally, they would laugh, which at times made John turn around to watch her being so happy. He went to get another drink and handed it to her, while listening to her asking, "Have you finished your task on H.S.S. Abraham Lincoln?"

Captain Weller replied, "I've been working with another engineer where most of the work is finished on H.S.S. Abraham Lincoln. Tomorrow, I will fly by helicopter to board H.S.S. Blue Ridge, to program the new software so communications can be linked once more with H.S.S. Abraham Lincoln. They wanted me to do it today, but I thought ringing my family was more important."

Louise, who didn't understand computers, asked, "What's the difference, whether you do the job today or tomorrow?"

Captain Weller replied, "I shouldn't tell you, but just for today, H.S.S. Abraham Lincoln is off the grid."

Louise frowned, asking, "What does this mean?"

Captain Weller chuckled, replying, "It means today, which is Christmas Day when it doesn't really matter, we're vulnerable. Any other day and the Captain of this vessel would have given me a direct order to finish the job. With it being Christmas Day and knowing I wanted to speak with my family, you could say he has turned a blind eye."

When John had given Louise her drink, he went to speak with the others again drinking a few more beers in the process. Knowing his sister was a member of Unit Expendable, he stood up, asking, "How about a member from Unit Invincible takes on a member from Unit Expendable?"

Sarah Jane replied, "You've had too much to drink!"

John ignored her by standing in a position ready to use martial arts against his sister. Sarah Jane with having the same blood stood her ground to defend herself. Louise saw what was about to happen, gasped, and said, "Oh my God!"

Debbie asked with concern, "What is it Louise?"

Watching with intent, she saw John Raven stand between them, staring at them with his menacing eyes saying, "You know what you are. You know what you're capable of, with having nothing to prove to each other. Enough!"

Louise, who was still sitting in the dining room shouted in a distressed voice, "John!"

Raven walked into the dining room followed by his son, John Weller, who asked, "What's wrong?"

Louise had become upset, replying, "I was speaking with your Mum . . ."

Raven listened while turning to watch his son ask in a disgruntled way, "And?"

Louise reliving her nightmare when her brother had been captured said, "I think your mother has been taken."

Sarah Jane laughed, saying, "You're joking?"

Louise wiped her eyes, replying, "Do I look as though I'm joking?"

Raven watched, listening with intent. His father, Richard, watched his reaction to the news he had just heard.

John Weller concerned for his mother asked, "Captured by whom? She's on an aircraft carrier for God's sake!"

Louise held her hand out to give Weller the phone, which his father immediately put his hand out to take the phone from him, and place to his ear. Debbie had left her phone switched on where he could hear a scuffle taking place. He heard Debbie shouting while being pulled down some steps, leading to the bulkhead door. The clanging made Raven frown with anger as they carried on dragging her from the warship to their smaller boat. Raven moved his hand tightly around the phone, just like he used to when he held his knife. He gave a prolonged blink of anger when he heard Captain Weller shouting, "The Iranian pirates have me John! The Iranian pirates have me, and I'm scared John!"

One of the pirates snatched the phone and slapped her hard in the face. He put Debbie's phone to his ear and said, "Kidnapping somebody from a U.S. warship is too easy at this time of the year with them all partying. We have a member of the U.S. military and will be in contact about what our demands will be soon!"

Raven's eyes were wide open like daggers with having to accept Debbie had now been captured. Sarah Jane asked with concern, "Dad?"

His son John watched his father's reaction and then asked the same question, "Dad?"

He turned to look at his son, and then at Louise. Remembering what she had been through when her brother Enzio had been taken by the Iranian's made him turn and walk into the lounge to place the phone down on the hook. Sarah Jane shouted again, "Dad?"

He turned around giving everybody in the room the menacing stare of anger. Weller asked him with concern, "How did they board an aircraft carrier that is fifty seven feet high? I'm mystified."

Louise was weeping and replied, "I'm not."

Everybody looked at her, frowning at her reply, which made Raven ask, "Why are you not mystified?"

Louise raised her head to look at Raven and say, "She just told me that H.S.S. Abraham Lincoln is off the grid."

Raven replied, "The aircraft carrier is offline?"

Sarah Jane said, "It still doesn't explain how the Iranian's managed to climb fifty seven feet and board the aircraft carrier without being noticed."

Louise had tears rolling down her cheeks, which made Weller take her hand and hold it tenderly. Raven was standing there with his eyes narrowed thinking about how the Iranian's had boarded the aircraft carrier and replied, "I do!"

Everybody looked at Raven and then listened to Kirk say, "I suspect they gained access using the bulkhead door, which is only twelve feet high. They will have been where the hydraulic flight decks can be raised and lowered with many steel staircases around to take you to the flight deck above. Isn't that right John?"

Louise let go of Weller's hand to wipe her eyes and ask, "How did they get past military personnel?"

Raven moved his eyes to stare at her after listening to her question. Kirk answered by saying, "They've relaxed too much with being Christmas Day."

Sarah Jane said, "The military won't allow that! There's always somebody on duty at some point."

Kirk replied, "You're right there should, but how else can you explain it? They're in the Gulf, thousands of miles away, thinking nothing will happen and it's Christmas Day, when they're missing their families and loved ones. I guarantee they had pressured the Captain of the vessel into letting them have a huge party for just one day when nobody will be any wiser."

Raven looked stern at Kirk sternly as he carried on saying, "How else can you explain it?"

Raven walked away in frustration, with everybody watching him say, "Cairns!"

Sarah Jane moved wanting to follow, but her grandfather spoke up by saying, "Sarah Jane, leave him be!"

She glanced at her grandfather, where he looked at everybody in the room and said in a much softer voice, "Leave him be for now because he has become highly frustrated."

Sarah Jane replied, asking, "And we haven't?"

Louise watched the bickering starting to occur, which made her say, "Today has been badly tarnished, but I do know in my heart either you or your father will find a solution to this problem."

She paused remembering John's proposal at the café from a few days ago and carried onto say, "This is why I can't give you an answer to your proposal."

Sarah Jane appeared perplexed and raised her eyebrows feeling surprised at becoming a sister-in-law to Louise and said, "You kept that quiet John."

Richard and Kirk calmed everybody down while having to accept Captain Weller, Sarah Jane and John's mother, had been taken captive by the Iranians from the aircraft carrier, U.S.S. Abraham Lincoln. For Louise, it was history repeating itself with old wounds now being reopened again.

Raven decided he wanted to be alone for a while by staying outside in the cold brisk air, noticing it was starting to go dark. Standing there feeling frustrated at what to do, he gave a solemn look, aware he was a legendary soldier with a big decision to make sometime soon.

Frustration

$\mathcal{J}$ohn leaned against the fence looking out at the clear sky slowly turning dark. His eyes softened as he thought back to his mentor, commanding officer, and friend, Colonel Lewis. In a low soft voice he said, "Don't expect me to fight this time. It's over!"

With Raven speaking in a low voice, the dogs took notice and walked up to him where he patted each one tenderly. When he patted Sadie, he left his hand on her head starting to recall memories from when he had fought with her in North Korea. He patted her again, which made her lick his hand. He stood up and leaned on the fence recalling some more of Colonel Lewis's words, when he told him he was already this combat fighting machine, they just chipped away the pieces to make him what he is today. Raven felt a sudden shiver when he glimpsed back up at the sky at Colonel Lewis, knowing what he would have expected from him. He patted the dogs taking notice of all the coloured lights around and the music playing, in the distance. Christmas Day, a day when everybody celebrated it their own special way, but all he could think about, was Captain Weller with what has happened to her. He turned with his face becoming stern by showing a scowl and started to walk to the barn with the dogs following him. He opened the door, walked inside, and turned on the light, focusing on just one thought, Captain Weller and her safety. He undid a couple of his buttons on his shirt, rolled up his sleeves and lit the blowtorch. The dogs started slowly walking inside the barn, which Raven had noticed and ordered them outside again. He picked up a garden fork nearby, holding it tightly before throwing it to the other side of the barn in temper while imagining the face of Cairns. The dogs watched outside at the door sensing the dark side of Raven was starting to reappear, and went back to the house. Raven searched for some steel, just wanting to beat it to release the anger and frustration he was now feeling. He found a broken piece of steel, picked it up and placed it into the vice on the workbench. Focusing on what he was about to do, he reached up at the shelf above him and brought down the powerful angle grinder. After turning the mains on, he switched it on with the disc rotating at a high-speed. He placed it against the broken blade, creating plenty of sparks and an almighty screeching sound that could be heard from the blade Raven was starting to shape. Sparks would hit him in the face, on his arm and even on his chest, but Raven remained focused in wanting to release some hypertension. The blade became hot when Raven placed more pressure onto it, eventually breaking away from the large handle. After placing the angle grinder down onto the workbench, he placed on a glove, picked up the blade using the tongues and walked quickly to where he had left the blowtorch burning on a pilot light. Slowly, he placed the blade down in position, and wiped away the sweat on his face with his forearm. His hair hung down into his face, where he flicked it back using both of his hands. Starting to feel hot and clammy, Raven undid his shirt, took it off and threw it onto the workbench next to the vice. Focusing on Captain Weller, he picked up the blowtorch, moved the nozzle with his thumb to make the pilot light become a huge blue flame burning on a jet. Raven glared at the blade as he pointed the blowtorch at it wanting to heat it up further until it was white-hot. Occasionally, he would place down the blowtorch making sure the main jet was back on pilot light and pick up the blade using the tongues and then beat it with a hammer to his own shape. Raven placed his forearm to his forehead wiping away the sweat and then put his hair back once more. Before carrying on to make the blade to his own design, he went to the other side of the barn, picked up the headband given to him by an old wise Korean gentleman and worn by a samurai warrior. He held it with a firm grip while wrapping it around his head and fastened it tightly. He went back to the workbench to carry on heating the blade up, so he could shape it to his own liking. When he picked up the blowtorch and flicked the nozzle with his thumb, the roar from the huge blue flame became vast. Holding the blowtorch with a firm grip, he pointed it at the blade until it was white-hot again, repeating the same procedure as before by beating it with a hammer to the shape he wanted to create. He placed it into the cold liquid with steam immediately rising into the air. He repeated this action several times with more steam occurring each time he dipped the blade into the cold liquid. Feeling as though the blade had cooled enough to hold, he placed a glove on and held it, looking at it, thinking what he could potentially do with it. He moved his arm slowly, knowing he was now holding a lethal weapon that would slice anybody into bits when it had been sharpened. Feeling content with what he had created, he searched the barn for some wood to make a handle for his new knife. He looked at several bits of timber, rejecting them by throwing them on the floor. He kept searching until he found a piece of timber that would be suitable to create a handle for the dangerous weapon he had just made. He held the small piece of hardwood as he looked at the blade aware that this would be suitable to use has a handle. Using a carpenter's plane, he smoothed all four edges, and then machined it to a shape that would be comfortable for him to hold. After holding the handle a few times with a firm grip, he placed it into the vice to start boring out a hole so the blade could be inserted. After boring the hole in the handle, Raven walked across the barn, turned off the pilot light on the blow torch and decided to place a glove on his right hand. He then picked up what was becoming a lethal weapon, realising it had cooled down enough to hold.

The barn door opened with Raven's father, Richard, walking inside. He noticed John had taken off his shirt and was now just wearing his jeans, black tee shirt and his headband. He became concerned displaying a frown causing him to ask, "What are you doing John?"

John could only focus on Captain Weller and chose not to answer his father's question, which made Richard walk up to him and gently grab his hand holding the blade.

Sarah Jane walked into the barn holding the phone to see that her grandfather was holding onto something her father was holding. Already noticing he was dressed as the warrior, she had once witnessed. She then heard him say to her grandfather, "Let it go!"

Sarah Jane interrupted them saying, "Dad, Colonel Wareing is on the phone and would like to speak with you."

Richard moved, reluctantly releasing his hand starting to weep blood from his grip on the blade. John went to his daughter, where she could now see the intimidating side of him once more. She looked up at him, noticing the sweat dripping from his face as she handed the phone to him, which made him say, "Thanks. Go back inside the house. I won't be too long."

Richard frowned, wanting to ask the inevitable question, which John suspected and said, "Go inside the house Dad, I'll explain later."

Richard frowned and walked with Sarah Jane saying, "He is preparing for something."

Sarah Jane looked back at her father where he just stared at them walking back to the house. He placed the blade down onto the bench, leaned against it and said, "Yo."

Colonel Wareing replied, "Hi John. I don't want to ruin your Christmas . . ."

Suspecting what Colonel Wareing was about to tell him, John interrupted him saying, "But you're going to anyway."

Colonel Wareing, who had also heard the news about Captain Weller, captured by Iranian pirates wanted to be the first to tell John. What he didn't know, John already knew feeling frustrated at what to do next. Colonel Wareing paused and then said, "It isn't intentional."

John while leaning against the workbench sighed, replying, "It never is!"

Colonel Wareing ignored John's comment, deciding to focus on the problem replying, "John, the Iranian's have taken Captain Weller."

Although John knew, he went quiet, which made Colonel Wareing say, "John. Are you still there?"

John reluctantly answered by saying, "Yeah. I'm still here."

Colonel Wareing carried on saying, "It has come from the highest authority . . ."

John interrupted replying, "It usually does, and they're never responsible."

Colonel Wareing became frustrated saying, "Please don't interrupt me John, this is hard enough for me to accept as it is!"

John moved his head and gave a casual blink, and let the Colonel carry on saying, "Captain Weller is in the hands of the Iranian's and wait for it?"

John smirked, suspecting Cairns, but chose to say nothing and just listen to the Colonel carry on saying, "James fucking Cairns! What kind of American person is this man?"

As he studied the Colonel's question, John stared outside the barn door noticing a frost was starting to develop outside. He then answered the Colonel by saying, "Cairns is the worst American person you could ever imagine!"

Colonel Wareing asked, "Does this want to make you come back and fight just one more time?"

John gave a huge sigh, picked up the blade he had just created and studied it. Visualising his previous wars from when he had used knives on these missions, he chose not to answer, which made Colonel Wareing ask, "John, did you hear me?"

John placed the blade down back onto the workbench and replied, "I heard you."

Colonel Wareing asked, "So?"

John saw his daughter walk back into the barn where she just wanted her father to share the rest of Christmas

Day with the other members of the family. Just as before, he chose not to answer the Colonel straight away, instead he watched Sarah Jane come closer to him and gently hold his huge muscles on his arm. John turned, looking down to face her with his hair hanging down into his face. Colonel Wareing who was becoming impatient snapped, "John!"

John lifted his head saying, "Tell all members of Unit Expendable to report to the U.S. military base tomorrow."

Colonel Wareing replied, "It's Boxing Day!"

Sarah Jane moved away from her father suspecting he had been inside the barn churning up thoughts in how to save her mother. She walked to the other side of the workbench and picked up the blade Raven had made earlier, which made him say, "Put it down!"

In a stern voice, he then said to Colonel Wareing, "I want all members of Unit Expendable at the U.S. military base tomorrow."

Colonel Wareing, not sure what Raven's intentions were, agreed, telling him that it would be done. John, who wasn't in the mood for a conversation on the phone hung up, and gave the phone back to Sarah Jane. As she took the phone from him, she asked, "What's going to happen tomorrow?"

John sighed, replying, "Wait and see."

Sarah Jane turned away, starting to walk to the barn door. John watched her feeling, as though she may need some extra training, and with this shouted, "Sarah Jane."

John stood up straight after leaning against the workbench and placed himself into a martial art position, which Sarah Jane immediately saw when she turned around. Knowing what her father wanted to do, she said, "I can't fight you!"

Standing there focused, John replied, "I'm not fighting with you! I just want to see what you're capable of so that I'm sure about sending you into the unknown."

Sarah Jane walked back across to the workbench, placed the phone down and faced her father using a martial art position. John told her to attack him, which she did. He told her again to do it using much more force. She placed herself into the same position, attacking him once more, which made

John defend himself to the limit. Sarah Jane was quick in all of her manoeuvres and suspected this, realising she may just be able to beat her old Dad. Raven's reactions were slower, which meant that he couldn't block every punch and kick that Sarah Jane tried. Some connected with Raven's body, and they hurt him. Raven being the man he is, showed no emotion, and no pain defending to the best of his ability with the age he now is.

Sarah Jane knew that although her father still had the skills, it was speed that was lacking and could be his downfall. Detecting this, she said, "I don't want to do this anymore with you."

John understood replying, "Okay. Let me attack you to see what your defensive skills are like."

Sarah Jane asked, "Do we have to?"

John said, "I would prefer not to, but you wanted to become an elite member of Unit Expendable and follow in my footsteps, which I'm not too thrilled about. When a fight is for real, it will be to the death, and I want you to remain alive at all cost."

Sarah Jane went into position to defend herself from her father, waiting for him to attack her. He came at her with such force, she didn't expect it. She adjusted after taking a couple of blows to the body to defend herself as though her life depended on it, which soon it could. Raven, aware that he was training with his daughter didn't use the full impact he could so easily have, but he wasn't gentle either. He turned, picking up the blade and held it, facing his daughter with hatred in his eyes. He asked her, "What do you see?"

Sarah Jane placed her arms down by her side replying, "My father possibly going crazy!"

John smirked, and said, "What if I was James Cairns, or an Iranian soldier wanting to slice off your head. Defend yourself!"

Sarah Jane looked at her father facing her, holding the knife ready to use and his headband resting onto his shoulder. She knew he will always be the supreme warrior and said,

"I'm sorry I can't do this with you. If the time comes when I need to defend myself from this same position, I'll be victorious."

John softened his look understanding why Sarah Jane didn't want to perform to her highest standard and decided to accept it. He placed the blade down, which made Sarah Jane walk over, pick it up and weave it about in the air. She asked him, "Are you planning on returning into battle with this weapon?"

John didn't answer. He watched her as he placed out his hand to take the blade from her and then asked her to pass him the handle. She gave him the handle, as she watched him lean against the workbench pushing the blade that was a tight fit onto the handle and hold it tight. Sarah Jane watching him with respect said, "Mum always said you were the best of the best."

John replied, "She said that?"

Sarah Jane watched her father grip the blade and handle tightly and said, "She's right, you're the best of the best."

John smirked, replying, "The best always die."

Sarah Jane was starting to feel patronised and said, "You know what you are. You know who you are and my Mum needs you, and to be honest so do Unit Expendable."

John now placed the knife onto the workbench. Listening to his daughter's words, he looked at her once, and then down at the floor, feeling pressure at the possibility of having to come back into a warzone one final time and replied, "Let me sleep on it."

With John being away from the house for some time, made the others inside wonder what he was doing. Louise said, "I'll go outside and see what he is doing because he should be here sharing this day with us, his family."

Richard's eyes narrowed because he knew John wouldn't be feeling festive anymore after hearing that Captain Weller had been taken hostage by the Iranians. As Louise stood up wanting to look for John, Richard said, "With what has happened to Debbie, don't you think it would be a good idea to leave him alone?"

Louise became unsure about what to do after listening to Richard's reply. John Weller noticed her reaction and supported her saying, "Come on. Let's see what he's doing."

Louise, feeling happier with the support John had given, started to follow him into the kitchen and watched him take a beer from the fridge for his father. Noticing Louise was watching him, he asked, "Would you like a drink?"

She walked over to him and held his hand tenderly replying, "Yes please."

He poured a glass of wine for Louise, and gave it to her while shouting to Kirk and his grandfather sitting in the lounge to see if they too would like another drink. They replied saying that they did, which made him pour a couple of lagers into two glasses, and Louise say, "I'll take these drinks into the lounge for the guys."

Raven moved his head slowly looking at the knife he had created, and then holding the handle tightly, he picked it up once more, which made Louise become a little apprehensive about him. She placed her hand out to give him the drink, which he received using his other hand and said in a solemn voice, "Thanks."

She watched him take a few much needed gulps to help quench his thirst while turning to face her boyfriend, John Weller. As he watched his father drink the lager, he looked back at Louise starting to read her thoughts, which made him move his eyes to the floor, then turn and say, "I'll see you inside."

Raven placed the knife back onto the workbench and said, "Wait!"

He put his arms around Louise and Sarah Jane, and walked over to his son trying to hide the nightmare he was carrying and said, "Come on. Let's try to enjoy what's left of Christmas Day."

Sarah Jane agreed by saying, "Good idea."

They walked outside feeling the cold frost as they made their way back to the house with the three dogs following. A car drove up the driveway, which made John stop to watch the headlamps shining brightly, coming closer towards him.

As the car slowed down to park, he recognised that it was Colonel Wareing, who had decided to pay him a visit at his home. Colonel Wareing stopped the car, turned off the engine, switched off the lights and started to climb out of the car, where he shouted, "It's getting cold again John."

He walked over to him noticing his warrior appearance, which made him frown at both women standing with him. John Weller was the first to place his hand out to wish the Colonel a Merry Christmas. The Colonel also wished Weller a Happy Christmas and then turned back to face Raven, while wanting to shake his hand. Raven brought his arms away from the women, telling everybody to go inside, which made Louise say, "It's Christmas Day John! Can the military not leave you for just one day?"

Raven looked down at the ground, gave a casual blink, and then watched Louise walk back to the house aware she isn't too keen on the military. Sarah Jane watched her father with concern, which made him say, "I know why he's here. I won't be long."

Sarah Jane asked the Colonel if he would like an alcoholic drink, which he refused with driving. Raven asked her to make the Colonel a hot drink, which she agreed to do and then called the dogs into the house.

As they all walked inside the house, Louise said to John Weller, "This is going to be a Christmas never to forget."

John thought about the proposal, he had made to her and then the possibility of World War 3 replying, "You can say that again."

Richard and Kirk heard voices realising the other members of the family had come back inside the house. Richard asked Sarah Jane if her father had also come inside the house, when she replied, "No. He is outside speaking with Colonel Wareing."

Richard sat up and blurted out in an angry voice, "What!"

Weller repeated what his sister had just told his grandfather, saying, "Colonel Wareing has visited and is speaking with Dad outside."

Richard looked at Kirk shaking his head in disbelief and then said to everybody standing in the lounge, "One day to spend time with your family, one day, and the military has to take this away from us!"

Sarah Jane shouted from the kitchen while making the hot drink for the Colonel, "It may have something to do with our Mum."

Richard thought about what his granddaughter had just mentioned and placed his hand to his cheek stroking it considering what to do. Wisely, he chose to say, "I'd better go and ask them inside."

Richard stood up and went into the kitchen noticing that Sarah Jane had made a hot drink for the Colonel and asked if he could give it to him. Sarah Jane agreed, opening the door for him and watched him walk to both men, who were in a deep conversation. When they noticed Richard coming towards them, they stopped talking about Unit Expendable and Captain Weller and made pleasantries with him. At first he became disgruntled with the military appearing on his doorstep, but chose to accept it with what had happened to Captain Weller. He handed the hot drink to the Colonel while watching the steam rise into the cold air. Colonel Wareing thanked him, which made Richard say, "It's getting chilly outside. Come inside and talk."

Colonel Wareing thanked Richard and followed him inside the house while speaking with John about the serious predicament Captain Weller has now found herself involved in. John held the door open for the Colonel and listened. With the Colonel doing most of the talking, made him become a little frustrated and say, "John, you're not saying too much! We need to discuss this ready for when Unit Expendable reports to the U.S. military base tomorrow."

John glimpsed into the lounge at his family, paused for a few seconds thinking about them and replied, "It can wait until tomorrow."

Colonel Wareing soon realised that John wasn't going to have a serious discussion about Captain Weller's predicament today. Feeling disappointed, he decided to drink the rest of his coffee and wish everybody sitting in the lounge a Merry Christmas and then tell them that he is now leaving. Richard spoke up by saying, "This visit was short and sweet."

As the Colonel placed his scarf back around his neck, he replied, "It can wait until tomorrow."

Richard frowned while glancing at Raven, after hearing the Colonel's comment. Sarah Jane and John Weller stood up to shake the Colonel by the hand again. He assured them that their mother would soon be out of danger, which made them look at Raven standing there showing no emotion.

Louise, watching events unfold beneath her eyes, knowing she had to make a big decision sometime soon started to wonder if indeed her boyfriend, John Weller, would be involved in the rescue of his mother. She watched the Colonel and her father, Kirk, shake hands while thinking if she was to marry John, would it just be her and John, or would it be her, John and the military. Colonel Wareing moved toward Louise to shake her hand and said, "Look after John, because you have a decent bloke there."

Louise thought back to John's proposal and looked across to him choosing not to answer the Colonel back. He let go of Louise's hand saying goodbye to everybody and then turned to Raven and said, "Tomorrow had better be good!"

John replied, "I'll show you to the door."

Both men walked outside to the Colonel's car with the Colonel asking, "What are your plans for tomorrow?"

John looked straight ahead answering, "You'll find out tomorrow."

Colonel Wareing became disgruntled replying, "I'm your superior officer and do have a right to know what it is you're going to do with Unit Expendable."

John moved his head to face the Colonel, and although he had made his mind up what it was he was going to do, he chose to answer him back by saying, "I need to sleep on it."

Colonel Wareing climbed into the car, placed the key into the ignition and turned it to start the engine. He looked back up at Raven and his menacing stare and said, "For several reasons, you seriously need to consider coming back because Unit Expendable will need you. I will need you and our beloved country will need you."

John closed the Colonel's car door dwelling on what the Colonel had just told him. He remained silent choosing not to reply. Instead, he stood there watching the Colonel slowly pull away leaving him, just as before with a big decision to make. His father came outside and walked up to him to place his arm around him. John while watching the Colonel drive away, thought about Captain Weller and what she must now be enduring. It made him recall the promise, he had made to his father when he had told him that he was finally going to retire from the force. Unknown to his father, he was now seriously beginning to consider breaking that promise.

Face to Face

Captain Weller was still suffering from a traumatic time while being at the hands of the Iranian pirates. Her hands had been tied tightly and positioned behind her back, making her feel vulnerable. The pirates spoke among themselves, beginning to laugh, and then turn and stare at her, blowing her kisses from their hands. Fearing she could be raped, she moved her head away to look down at the decking hoping that John Raven would do something to rescue her from what seemed like an impossible position from which to escape. She wept quietly, with tears rolling down her cheeks and onto the decking. The Iranian pirates became aware that she wasn't taking notice of their indecent actions anymore, which made a couple walk over to her. With her head still hanging low, she noticed their boots, which made her slowly lift her head to look at the Iranian pirates. They spoke to each other and laughed, which made Captain Weller become more apprehensive. One of the pirates grabbed her hair and pulled her head back, while the other undid a couple of buttons on her blouse and then ripped the rest of them open exposing her sexy underwear. He produced an evil smirk as he positioned his hand to caress her breast. Captain Weller, feeling frightened, became aware of what the pirate was about to do to her. While glaring at the pirate with hatred showing in her face, she decided to spit into his face. The Iranian pirate wiped his face with his forearm and then slapped her hard across the face. He decided to walk back to his colleagues standing nearby who were laughing, while watching intently. The Iranian pirate who had been holding her hair tightly, released his grip and threw her to the floor, where she decided to remain to protect her dignity. She wept loudly, which made one of the pirates shout, "Shut up bitch!"

One crew member shouted from above. "President Modarres and Cairns will be boarding in a few minutes."

Captain Weller carried on weeping, which enraged one of the pirates. So, he walked up to her, and started kicking her in the ribs with his steel toe capped boots. She wailed in pain, which made the pirate grab her hair and pull her up. His eyes moved from her eyes to focus on her cleavage, she was now displaying, making her shout, "Do what you want to me, but you will be eventually sorry."

The Iranian pirate looked back to call one of his colleagues over to grab her legs tightly, while he undid her belt and then her button on her trousers and began to pull her zip down. He gave an evil grin knowing he was about to slide his hand inside her panties when he heard a voice in the background shout, "Enough!"

The Iranian pirate stood up when he saw Cairns walking over to him. Without hesitation, he moved to one side, letting Cairns take his position to look down at Captain Weller and say, "Well, look at what we have here!"

Captain Weller moved her smudged eyes to look up and saw for the first time, face-to-face that it was James Cairns looking down on her. He crouched down, moved his face closer into hers and said, "It's been a long time, Debbie! The last time you and I saw each other was when the military police was dragging me away, no thanks to you!"

In a quivering voice, Debbie asked, "What happened to you, Cairns?"

Still crouched there, with his hair hanging over his face and looking into Debbie's eyes he said, "You and Raven are the reason I'm here today securing my future!"

Debbie thought back to when she had discovered espionage at the military base in Kuwait and remembered Raven punching him in the face before the military police arrested him. Cairns grabbed Debbie by the throat taking notice of her cleavage and said, "You were too good for Raven!"

He pulled her up by the throat, staring intently at her, and said, "I hope that bastard Raven decides to rescue you because he will get what I have wanted to do for years! Kill the son of a bitch!"

Debbie was in a precarious position and unable to reply with having her throat gripped tightly. She could only hope the man she knew was the best of the best would come back and fight once more to rescue her from this horrific ordeal. Cairns released his grip to look at her menacingly and said, "You look good; you're mine!"

He then threw her to the Iranian pirates where they knocked her about and told them to take her to the military jeep outside. President Modarres, who had witnessed everything watched and said nothing. He turned to the Captain of the boat, placed his hand in his pocket, brought out some money and gave it to him for the capture of a U.S. soldier.

Cairns walked over to them and said "Don't patrol next to U.S. warships because you will be blown out of the water, especially with the actions you have performed."

Watching Captain Weller being dragged up some steps, he turned to the President Modarres and said, "Things are going to become interesting."

President Modarres narrowed his eyes replying, "James, you're one dangerous man."

Cairns turned to face the Iranian President, saying, "You haven't seen anything yet!"

President Modarres then watched Cairns climb the steps, which made him, follow and make his way back to the military jeep. Cairns noticed that Captain Weller still had her hands tied and pondered about whether he should untie them. President Modarres climbed into the passenger seat and waited for Cairns to climb into the driver's seat. He opened the back door and grabbed Captain Weller's arm saying, "Turn around!"

She did as he asked, by turning and placing her back to him. He grabbed her hands and cut the rope using his knife. She brought her arms to the front and stretched out her hands. She turned back to face Cairns and said in a solemn voice, "Thanks for doing that."

Cairns, standing there with his head lowered, still holding the knife, stared at her and said nothing. President Modarres spoke by saying, "James. We ought to go."

Cairns ordered two Iranian soldiers to sit at either side of Captain Weller and then walked to the other side of the jeep to take up the driving position and start travelling to the president's military base. Captain Weller, who was grateful to have her hands free, managed to wriggle and pull her pants up to her waist, fasten her button and pull her zip back up. She wrapped her blouse over the top part of her body, wanting to hide her cleavage, which made her feel more dignified. Sitting in the back of the military jeep as it rumbled along the bumpy dusty road, she could only think of John Raven and her family and wonder how their Christmas day was going. She watched Cairns in front drive the military jeep, aware of the Iranian soldiers sitting next to her holding their guns. She realised that her life was in extreme danger when anything could happen to her before she would be killed. She decided to remain focused hoping just possibly the one man, the one soldier she could rely on the most, may come back and rescue her from what had become a total nightmare for her.

Unit Expendable

$\mathcal{J}$t was Boxing Day, with John Raven up earlier than the rest of the family. He went into the kitchen to let the dogs outside, feeling the cold brisk air hit his face, and then went to make a cup of coffee. He placed his hands down on the worktop, moving his head to the side worrying about what Captain Weller must now be enduring. Sarah Jane, who had also decided to get up early with having to report at the U.S. military base with Unit Expendable walked into the kitchen noticing her father in deep thought, which made her ask, "Are you okay Dad?"

Still thinking about Captain Weller, he slowly turned his head to face his daughter replying, "Not really."

Sarah Jane, who was dressed in military clothing, walked over to him to place her hand on his hand while asking, "What's the matter?"

The kettle started to boil, which made Sarah Jane take her hand away from her father's hand to turn the kettle off. Her father watched the steam rising, while she opened the cupboard to get a cup for her to make two cups of coffee. John watched her, replying, "No matter what I decide to do, it's going to be wrong."

Sarah Jane while pouring milk into the cups asked, "How do you mean?"

John watched her stir the coffee with a teaspoon, and then received the cup from her replying, "If you're honest, you will be more than likely expecting me to embark on this mission with Unit Expendable."

John's father, Richard had just got out of bed and heard Sarah Jane and John talking. Before walking into the kitchen, he remained in the hallway wanting to listen to some more of what seemed like an intriguing conversation. Sarah Jane frowned, saying, "You're the main man!"

John took a sip of his coffee, placed his head down and paused for a few seconds, thinking about the previous battles he had been involved in. He slowly lifted his head replying to Sarah Jane by saying, "Last time when I became involved in a warzone to rescue you and the President of the United States in North Korea, it nearly ended my life. The next time I might not be so fortunate."

Richard, who was listening in the hallway started to frown as he listened to Sarah Jane ask her father, "Do you remember when I asked you to promise me that it won't be one time too many?"

John placed his cup down on the worktop recalling Sarah Jane making him promise that it won't be one time too many. Watching her father's reaction, Sarah Jane carried on saying, "Your reply at the time was I can't promise that."

John nodded his head agreeing with her, which made Sarah Jane say, "With hearing that remark, I always thought the door would be open for one more battle."

John gave a solemn look, shaking his head slowly from side to side replying, "It's over."

Richard, who was still standing in the hallway listening to the conversation between his son and granddaughter, gave a wry smile knowing for sure that his son had now chosen never to go into battle again. His grin deteriorated when he heard Sarah Jane ask in a stern voice, "So why did you make that knife yesterday?"

John gave a menacing stare at his daughter for a few seconds and replied, "Frustration!"

Sarah Jane placed her cup down while asking, "What do you mean frustration?"

John turned his back on Sarah Jane to look outside the window watching the dogs roam around outside. After careful thought, he gave a casual blink, replying, "I'm frustrated because I want to come back and fight, yet know that I can't because I feel as though I'm not guaranteed to arrive back home this time. I'm getting older Sarah Jane."

Sarah Jane gave a half laugh saying, "Dad! You're John Raven. The soldier everybody else wants to be. You'll come back, I know you will."

John turned around to face his daughter reluctantly replying, "Not this time. It's over."

Richard had heard enough, deciding to walk into the kitchen, where he saw Sarah Jane dumbfounded looking at her father. Richard placed his hand on her shoulder saying, "Sarah Jane."

She slowly moved her head to face him and listened to him carry on saying, "It had to end sometime, even for one of our best soldiers."

Sarah Jane didn't respond to her grandfather. Instead, she turned looking at her father while holding a face of disgust. She collected her items and walked outside to her car to start travelling to the U.S. military base and meet with other members from Unit Expendable.

Richard patted John's arm, as he passed him, which made John glance and listen to him say, "Is this the truth boy, you're finished?"

John closed his eyes preferring not to discuss this subject anymore, but reluctantly listened to his father say, "I know your son and your daughter want to be you. The test has now arrived, because you will not be there to guide them."

He turned to look at John concerned, asking, "Will you?"

John held a stern face choosing not to answer his father's question. With this, Richard said in a disgruntled voice, "We both know that you will become involved in the rescue of Captain Weller, which to be honest, part of me doesn't blame you."

John, after hearing those words softened his look, when just as he had done previously to his daughter, he shook his head from side to side replying, "It's over."

Richard stood there staring at his son for a few seconds and then said, "I'm not convinced."

John raised his voice a little by saying, "Maybe you will be convinced when I place Unit Expendable on a plane to Kuwait with me travelling back here, home where I belong!"

Richard narrowed his eyes, choosing to remain silent while watching John collect his keys and start walking to his 4x4 BMW X5. Richard went to stand at the door to watch John climb into the car and start the engine. John revved the engine gradually and pulled away slowly, noticing his father, Richard, was standing at the door. He raised his hand to Richard, who was giving him a stern look wondering what the future did indeed have in store for his son.

As John drove to the U.S. military base, he listened to the radio in the background, while churning things over in his mind about what Captain Weller must now be enduring. Reports were coming through, that Iran with the help of Russia, were preparing to launch nuclear missiles at their main enemy, the United States. Shortly afterwards an attack on Kuwait will take place to take all its wealth and hold the rest of the world that survived the holocaust to ransom.

John flicked the signal on to turn left, murmuring, "You haven't got a hope in hell."

Following the traffic that didn't appear too busy with being Boxing Day, he listened to reports confirming President Berry and the Secretary of State, Sarah Johnson, will be flying to Iran on the 29th December. The world was praying for them to resolve this hostile situation, and be able to look forward to a peaceful New Year. With his elbow resting on the door and holding the steering wheel with his finger and thumb, John while watching the traffic in front of him, started to wonder whether he should fly to Kuwait with Unit Expendable. Holding a stern face, John was churning things over in his mind previously mentioned to him, which no matter how he thought about the crisis, it always left him with that one thought of, should I go? His heart kept telling him that he should go; his head, however, was telling him that he was now past it and should let Unit Expendable do what they have to do. He closed his eyes for a couple of seconds feeling frustrated again, and then banged his hand on the steering wheel. Staring through the front windscreen, he noticed that daylight was now breaking through, making him turn off his lights. He signalled right at the lights, giving way to oncoming traffic before driving across the road. In the distance, he could see the U.S. military base, which made him think once more about whether he should travel with Unit Expendable. A couple of cars overtook him at a speed, which made him think, once over when he was young, he too may have done that manoeuvre knowing danger didn't matter. When you start to think of the danger, you hesitate and thus make mistakes. John narrowed his eyes finally accepting the decision he had made earlier to members of his family about not going into a warzone again.

John placed the signal on to turn left and then turned the steering wheel to drive straight on into the U.S. military base. Looking ahead, he saw inside the cabin, Danny Armson, which made him beep his horn. Danny looked, noticing that it was John Raven's vehicle approaching and opened the window ready to speak with him. John drove up to the barrier, pressing the switch for the window to be lowered, and asked, "Hi Danny. Have they all arrived?"

As he gave John the paperwork to sign, he replied, "Yes Sir."

John signed the paperwork, gave the clipboard back to Danny, where he asked, "Sir, is some serious shit about to happen with what is being reported on television?"

John gave Danny a menacing stare replying, "Raise the barrier Danny."

Danny raised the barrier, watching John start to drive through with him immediately saying, "Good luck."

John drove inside the U.S. military base, parked his vehicle and thought about Captain Weller before climbing out of the car. He looked at the sky visualising his mentor,

Colonel Lewis, and sighed. With thoughts churning around his mind, he climbed out of the car and pressed his key fob to lock it. He glimpsed around the U.S. base as he started to make his way to Colonel Wareing's office greeting different members of military personnel as he passed them. Alison Colquhoun was standing at a filing cabinet, when she saw John Raven walking to the Colonel's office. After seeing members of Unit Expendable enter inside Colonel Wareing's office, and now seeing Raven, she wondered if something more sinister was about to occur with Iran threatening the United States with the possibility of World War 3.

John kept walking until he reached the Colonel's office, when he casually knocked on the door that had been left open for him and members of Unit Expendable to enter. All the members of Unit Expendable had arrived including Radford, which brought a wry smile to John's face when he saw him. He walked over to stand next to the Colonel, noticing the unopened package placed against the wall and greeted Unit Expendable by saying, "Thank you for giving up your Christmas and reporting here at the U.S. military base."

Colonel Wareing remained silent as John spoke, just watching different members of Unit Expendable as they were listening to what Raven had to say. After the pleasantries, Raven decided to tell his latest batch of soldiers what he would like from them. They were standing there focused, listening to what he was saying, but became concerned when he said, "There will be no training programme!"

Before any questions could be directed at him, John carried on saying, "You're already elite soldiers! Training is to brush up on the skills you possess and make you sharper, more alert, and be able to survive. No doubt you will have seen the reports about our country being threatened by Iran and its ally Russia. With what has happened there is no time for training to brush up on the skills you already possess."

Members of Unit Expendable were confused, which John was aware of and said, "The first batch of soldiers I trained were Unit Invincible, then Raven's Nest, followed by Raven's Squad, and now Unit Expendable!"

John paused for a few seconds, and then carried on saying. "Not one of those Units needed further training! They were elite Green Berets who just needed to search inside themselves to become aware of what they actually are and what they have to do to survive."

Different members of Unit Expendable started to frown, but chose to remain silent. John walked away from Colonel Wareing saying, "After studying every members file, including Luke Tyler's, I personally believe you're at the level you should be at to enter a top secret mission."

Williams asked, "Are we being sent on a mission?"

Before John could reply to Williams, Lieutenant Parr asked the inevitable question, "Are you coming with us?"

Sarah Jane grinned, which John noticed. He sighed, replying first to Williams, by saying, "Yes you're all being placed on a mission to rescue Captain Weller, and any other military personnel held captive in Iran."

He turned to face Colonel Wareing, with him watching, waiting in anticipation for the second question to be answered. Turning back to face the members of Unit Expendable, he produced a solemn face and said, "If I were to come, I would probably hinder you now."

Different members of Unit Expendable spoke by saying, "Sir. We need you."

Williams said, "You're our leader. You're the man. We need you!"

John stared straight ahead for a few seconds while listening to these comments made about him and gave a prolonged blink reluctantly accepting that his time had come to stop fighting. He moved his head to look at his daughter, Sarah Jane, and replied to them all, "If I come with you, I'm going to need you more than you need me."

Templeton spoke by saying, "No Sir. You're wrong! We do need you because you're a legend we do all look up to."

Sarah Jane glimpsed at her father and then at the floor, hoping her father would change his mind and become a part of Unit Expendable. John gritted his teeth in frustration, with Unit Expendable watching his cheekbones protruding.

Colonel Wareing understood John was under pressure and said to all the members of Unit Expendable. "John Raven won't be travelling with you on this mission. It's over for him. We have to accept time has caught up with our main man."

Unit Expendable remained standing there, feeling despondent with hearing what Colonel Wareing had just told them. Colonel Wareing, aware of this tried to lift morale by saying; "You will, however, have two mentors travelling with you, Steve Lundgren and me."

Sarah Jane looked across to her father asking, "Is he as good as you?"

Raven, feeling saddened inwardly replied, "Lundgren is a team member who will keep you together and help you to carry out your mission. He is also the brains to help make things happen. Having Colonel Wareing alongside him will only strengthen you as a unit."

Sarah Jane listened to her father's reply, and asked the same question again, "Is Steve Lundgren as good as you?"

John paused for a few seconds studying Sarah Jane's question again. Looking at different members of Unit Expendable, he replied, "You could say he's expendable!"

Starting to feel annoyed, Sarah Jane blurted out, "But he isn't you!"

Other members of Unit Expendable stared at Sarah Jane with her sudden outburst. Colonel Wareing shouted, "Enough!"

It went quiet, with the Colonel carrying on to ask, "What are you, men or mice?"

There was no response from Unit Expendable. Raven watched the Colonel, and then listened to him saying. "Raven is finished! His military days are now behind him. You will have to learn to accept it!"

There was a knock at the door that interrupted Colonel Wareing from speaking, which made him shout, "Enter!"

Alison Colquhoun entered inside the office with Steve Lundgren beside her. When Raven saw Lundgren, he went across to him smirking. Unit Expendable watched them grab each other by the hand, while noticing their muscles protrude to the maximum.

Colonel Wareing thanked Alison for escorting Lundgren to his office and told her to leave. Lundgren went to the front to join the members of Unit Expendable. They saw a carbon copy of John Raven, the same rugged soldier, only he had blonde hair with a few grey hairs starting to show through. Colonel Wareing introduced the members of Unit Expendable to him leaving Raven having to watch.

When the introductions were over, Lundgren went to stand next to Raven, saying, "It's been a long time."

Still watching the Colonel, Raven replied, "Too long."

Colonel Wareing walked back to his desk, taking out a cigar while watching his two elite soldiers leaning on his desk as he slowly started to light it. After blowing the smoke away, he turned to the members of Unit Expendable asking, "After meeting John Raven's replacement, would you like to know the details of what this mission involves?"

Unit Expendable replied in unison saying, "Yes Sir."

When it would normally be John Raven explaining what is expected from each member of Unit Expendable, it was now the Colonel's duty to do so. Between taking drags on his cigar, he explained the mission in detail to the soldiers who were listening to every word the Colonel spoke with great interest. Aware that Raven and Lundgren were speaking in a low voice behind him, the Colonel asked, "Isn't that right Lundgren?"

Lundgren turned away from Raven to reply to the Colonel by saying, "If they die, they die!"

Colonel Wareing stared hard at the rugged appearance of Lundgren while listening to him carry on saying, "No matter what happens, we remain together, and we accomplish this mission!"

John took a few paces forward to stand next to Lundgren and said, "Die for something or live for absolutely nothing!"

Lundgren turned to Raven saying, "You should come with us."

Suspecting that members of Unit Expendable could carry on the conversation from Lundgren's comment, Colonel Wareing while blowing smoke away from his cigar replied, "We've already discussed this Lundgren."

Lundgren stared hard at Raven not feeling convinced, which made him say again, "You should come! I'll watch your back."

Raven replied, "Yeah right! It was always me watching yours."

Unit Expendable watched Lundgren stare at Raven as he looked across to look at his daughter, Sarah Jane. Lundgren aware that Raven would be listening said, "You know who you are. You know what you are. A man who has done it all, achieved it all, and is quite simply the best of the best!"

Raven watched his daughter nodding her head agreeing with Lundgren. He turned to face Lundgren and listened to him say, "You should come!"

Raven moved his head away slowly shaking it from side to side saying no. Unit Expendable watched, feeling aware that standing in front of them were two elite soldiers who were in a class of their own.

Colonel Wareing glanced at his elite warriors and then turned to Unit Expendable saying, "We fly to Kuwait in ninety minutes. Make sure you prepare your kit because there will be no turning back."

Unit Expendable acknowledged the Colonel, where he dismissed them all. One by one they started leaving the Colonel's office to prepare for what could be their war. Raven, with his menacing eyes watched Unit Expendable leaving feeling disappointed at the thought of letting them down. Colonel Wareing placed his hand onto Raven's shoulder as he walked past him and said, "When you're ready, let yourself out John."

Lundgren followed the Colonel deciding to look back at a dejected soldier and said, "Yo Raven. It ain't over until it's over!"

Raven slowly turned his head to look at Lundgren, replying, "Kick ass!"

Lundgren gave a grunt, laughed and said, "I intend to."

Raven, after watching them leave was standing alone in Colonel Wareing's office reflecting on his decision not to go back into the warzone with Unit Expendable. He turned to look at the picture of Colonel Lewis hanging on the wall, imagining he would now be looking down on him as a failure. He placed his hands onto Colonel Wareing's desk feeling the adrenalin flow through his body as he questioned himself whether he should go with Unit Expendable and do what is right? With his head starting to rule his heart, he slowly lifted it to look at the picture of Colonel Lewis hanging on the wall. He felt a shiver go through his body, which made him say, "Not this time. It's over."

Feeling disappointed, he walked towards the door, where he turned to look back at the picture of Colonel Lewis once more. He recalled his words from many years ago, when he told him that they didn't make him the combat fighting machine he is today, they just chipped away at the edges. He produced a wry grin that disappeared when he recalled Lundgren's comment; it ain't over until it's over. Producing a prolonged blink, he closed the door and started to walk down the corridor, he had become familiar with many times before, for what seemed like the final time.

Blessing

*J*ohn walked outside, noticing that it was quiet. He stood there alone looking around at the military base one final time before walking back to his car. Feeling a little disappointed that nobody was around to share a few words with him before he left for good; he pulled the car key from his pocket to unlock the car door. He opened it, climbed inside and placed the key into the ignition to start the engine. Noticing the rear window had become misty, he placed the rear heated screen on to demist the window. Slowly, he reversed placing the steering wheel on full lock and then continued driving forwards while lowering the window to speak with Danny Armson, who was sitting in the cabin. Already aware that Unit Expendable was moving to another part of the base, Danny asked, "Will we see you again Sir?"

John thought about Danny's question before replying, choosing to just look out of the front windscreen. This made Danny ask, "Are you okay Sir?"

John moved his head slowly to face Danny and replied, "Lift the barrier Danny."

Danny pressed the button to raise the barrier with John saying, "Take care Danny."

John drove out of the military base onto the main road listening to music playing on the radio while driving home. Thinking about his burden, it weighed him down all the more, knowing his daughter and latest unit were travelling to Kuwait about to enter a warzone in Iran at some point. Flashbacks from his last battle kept coming back where he began to ask himself where he went wrong to make him begin to think like this. Once over, he wouldn't hesitate fighting in battle, and if it meant losing his life, then so be it.

When John arrived home, the dogs ran towards the car to greet him. Richard was in the kitchen feeling surprised to see his son return home. He went to stand on the step, watching John. John noticed his father and said, "I told you I would be home."

Richard took a few steps, shouting, "I know you did, but for how long?"

John walked by his father and inside the house which made Richard turn and begin to follow him. Again he asked the same question, "John, for how long?"

John turned to face Richard and replied, "To be honest, I don't know anymore."

Richard looked at him with concern as he walked towards him saying, "Somewhere deep down, we both know you will become involved in this mess."

John frowned, eventually replying, "I can't just turn it off, but after what I experienced last time when I fought in North Korea, it is difficult."

Richard gave a smirk and said, "It usually is."

John walked back towards the door wanting to end the conversation by saying, "I'm going to the barn."

Richard replied, "Okay."

As John walked to the barn, he picked up a couple of balls for the dogs to chase. Noticing Roxy wasn't running as fast anymore, made him crouch down, give her a pat and ask, "Is age catching you up, just like me?"

He stood up and carried on walking towards the barn. Arriving inside he walked over to the workbench picking up the knife he had made on Christmas Day. He weaved it about in mid-air while imagining the face of Cairns. With his left hand, he placed his fingers gently onto the blade realising that it now needed sharpening. Walking across to the grinding stone, he flicked the isolator and turned on the machine. After grabbing his goggles, he began to place the blade across the grinding stone until it was sharp. Occasionally after dipping the blade into water to cool down he would place the tips of his fingers onto the edge of the blade. Once he could see blood running down his fingers without sliding them across the blade, he knew then that it was sharp enough to cut a person's throat out. He turned back to face the grindstone to continue sharpening the blade when his father came inside the barn to see what he was doing, choosing not disturb him while he was at work. Richard patiently waited for John to dip the blade into the water to cool it down. While he waited, he picked up the headband John had worn during his last conflict, feeling the texture of the material. John had seen him take the headband in the corner of his eye and decided to place the knife into the water to cool down. He took off his goggles, with his father now asking, "What are you doing John?"

John remained quiet while taking the headband from his father's hand, which made him ask again, "When are you going to come full circle?"

John immediately had flashbacks, replying, "I've heard those words before."

Richard frowned, asking, "Who by?"

John, thinking back to the late Colonel Lewis, replied, "A man who was once a very good friend to me. A man that taught me everything I know. A man that also knew where my limits lie and would even have died for me!"

Richard still frowning, asked, "Who is this man?"

John replied, "You really have to ask? It was Colonel Samuel Lewis, who at times was even like a father to me."

Richard frowned once more as he turned to face his son and said in a solemn voice, "John, I don't know all of your life stories because you choose to keep them private, however I do know that you're not yourself anymore. Hear this boy, you have my blessing to do whatever it is you have to do to make things right again. If this means in you having to go to war again, so be it."

John slowly moved his head to look at his father after receiving his blessing, and replied, "Thanks."

Richard narrowed his eyes at the terrible prospect of having to accept that his son may decide to go back into a warzone, and with this, said, "Just remember to come home."

Richard then walked away leaving John to make up his own mind about what he should or should not do.

Collection of John Raven

$\mathcal{T}$he magic of Christmas had passed by peacefully. Celebrations for the New Year were being prepared worldwide, but would it be worth celebrating with the threat of war on everybody's mind?

It was the 29th December, the day a nation became dependent on President Berry to come up with a diplomatic solution and prevent World War 3 from happening. People around the world became tense, not sure of what the result of this important meeting would entail. Innocent lives were in her hands, where she had to try to salvage what she could to prevent this terrible deed that President Modarres and his accomplice, James Cairns, with the help of the Russians were threatening.

Sarah Johnson was in the president's office making polite conversation with General Gee while waiting for President Berry. With knowing where they were travelling to, she asked the General, "Did you contact John Raven to ask him if he would travel with us on our trip to Iran?"

General Gee stared wide-eyed at the Secretary of State, which made her ask, "You haven't contacted him have you?"

General Gee replied, "Each time I rang Colonel Wareing, or John Raven, they were never available to accept my call."

Becoming distraught, Sarah bawled, "Did you ever think of leaving a message with another officer for at least one of them to ring you back?"

General Gee frowned, which made Sarah answer her own question by saying, "No of course you didn't!"

President Berry stood at the door for a few seconds surprised at Sarah Johnson raising her voice to a well-respected General. With concern, she walked to her desk while looking at her Secretary of State and asked in a solemn voice, "Sarah?"

Sarah remained standing there holding a frosty face and decided to say nothing. President Berry turned to look at General Gee, noticing that he too appeared displeased. Neither of them spoke, which made Susan say, "Today of all days, we should support one another more, especially with whom we have to speak with in the coming hours."

The last thing she wanted at this important time was a difference of opinion. She showed them her stern face, making them aware that she wasn't best pleased. Johnson and Gee glanced at each other as President Berry sat down at her desk. President Berry sighed and then asked, "Now what have you disagreed about?"

Feeling as though her professionalism had disappeared, Sarah frowned, which made Susan look at her and raise her eyebrows waiting for an answer. Reluctantly, Sarah spoke up by saying, "The General didn't contact John Raven to make him aware that we would like him to travel with us."

Susan turned around, asking, "Is this correct Alexander?"

General Gee told the president that he had contacted the military base several times, only to be told that Colonel Wareing and John Raven were unavailable to speak with. Susan turned back around to face Sarah knowing what she had experienced in Iraq, and then thought back to her own ordeal in North Korea. Aware that they were entering a volatile country that hated the American people, she picked up the phone and rang her chauffeur. He answered the phone by saying, "Hello Ma'am, what can I do for you?"

President Berry replied, "Good morning Jackson, can you have the car brought around for us to leave immediately."

Jackson said, "Certainly."

Susan, thinking about what she was going to do replied, "Jackson, bring the Chevrolet 4x4, not the limousine as previously told."

Again Jackson said, "Consider it done Ma'am."

She placed the phone down, which made General Gee ask, "You're taking the 4x4 vehicle rather than the comfort of the limousine?"

Susan closed one of her folders, placed it inside her drawer and replied, "Can you imagine John Raven sitting in a limousine?"

Hearing John Raven's name, made Sarah produce a wry grin, starting to feel more reassured. She stood up, telling General Gee and the Secretary of State to follow because time was of the essence. The Vice President was walking towards her, which made her stop to speak with him. She turned to General Gee and Sarah Johnson, saying, "Carry on walking to my 4x4; I will join you in a few minutes."

Looking up at the Vice President, she asked, "If the worst has to come to the worst, you do know what to do?"

The Vice President gave a solemn look replying, "Everything will happen as planned at the meeting."

Feeling nervous she held David's hand saying, "I hope it won't come to the plan in having to be used."

David replied, "I hope not. Go, our nation is depending on you."

Starting to feel nervous, Susan let go of David's hand, turned around and started to trot down the corridor to the hallway of the Whitehouse. The Vice President watched wondering what the future had in store, and then shouted, "Good luck."

At the hallway, she turned back around feeling nervous about the trip, responding to David by raising her hand, with what he had just shouted. Hiding her fears, she turned to her bodyguards who had been waiting for her in the hallway and said, "Let's go, first to John Raven's house and then onto Air Force One."

Stepping outside the Whitehouse, she made her way to the black Chevrolet 4x4 positioned in the middle for her to climb into and sit next to the Secretary of State. The chauffeur stood at the car door, closed it and then climbed into the driver's seat. Sarah glimpsed at Susan, knowing that now they had reached the point of no return. A bodyguard climbed into the passenger seat and sat next to the driver. He radioed the 4x4 in front to start travelling to John Raven's house. He accepted the instruction by slowly moving the black 4x4 vehicle that had a commanding presence, which made the President's 4x4 Chevrolet and the one behind follow in unison.

The three 4x4 vehicles travelled at a speed with blue and red lights flashing at either side of the front windscreen and on the grille. Other cars moved to one side to let these high priority vehicles through without any hesitation. Occasionally, Sarah Johnson would look through the blacked out window to the outside world. Susan noticed asking, "What are you thinking Sarah?"

General Gee, sitting opposite President Berry moved his head to watch Sarah's reaction. Sarah sat back in the white leather seat, glanced at General Gee and then at Susan replying, "I'm just wondering what the outcome of all this will be."

Watching everything around her, Susan said, "A world, we can still all live in will be a good start."

General Gee joined the conversation by saying, "Usually when fanatics become involved, and they begin flexing their muscles to other nations, it's only a matter of time before they meet their comeuppance."

Sarah, thinking back to her time in Iraq, replied, "I will second that Alexander."

Susan thought back to her ordeal in North Korea, saying "I have to agree with you there. I only hope that this time we get to win again."

General Gee smirked, which made Susan ask, "What's funny?"

General Gee glanced at the Secretary of State sitting opposite him and replied, "We're collecting John Raven, and we doubt that we're going to win?"

Susan lifted her sleeve looking at the imprint of North Korea burnt onto her arm that had scarred her for life. She touched it realising the skin was much softer and had a different texture. She started to have more flashbacks recalling John Raven and his son fighting in North Korea, which made her later say, "John Raven is only going to be standing by our side to ensure that we return."

General Gee laughed replying, "Oh come on!"

Sarah smirked and joined the conversation saying, "I'm glad John Raven is travelling with us. I feel much safer when he is around me."

Susan agreed, replying in a solemn voice, "I understand what you mean Sarah."

They arrived on Raven's road travelling at high-speed, overtaking other motor vehicles in front of them to prevent losing too much time. The entire 4x4 Chevrolet's slowed down when they reached the pillar-box of R Raven, which made them all look out of the blacked out window and listen to the bodyguard in front say, "We've arrived at John Raven's destination."

Each driver in their 4x4 vehicles drove slowly down the long driveway, keeping the red and blue lights flashing continually. Richard saw the three intimidating black Chevrolet 4x4's approaching and mumbled, "If it's not the military, it's probably the mafia."

He opened the door to walk down the steps, and saw at the end of the drive, well-dressed men getting out of their 4x4's. He stopped walking when he saw one of the men open the door of the middle 4x4 Chevrolet and saw the Secretary of State step outside onto the ground. Richard frowned, as he looked over to the barn where John was now working. When he looked back at the black 4x4's, he saw the President of the United States and General Gee had also climbed out of the car. Richard mumbled again, "This is going to be good."

It's not every day the President of the United States and a member of her Cabinet comes to visit an American citizen. Richard became aware of this as he watched President Berry tell her bodyguards to stay inside the vehicles, then turn and walk towards him, where he waited for what was going to be the inevitable question. As the V.I.P's came closer, General Gee holding a stern face asked, "Where is John Raven?"

Richard replied, "It's just like reading a book with you lot."

General Gee glared at Richard's insolence in the presence of President Berry, and asked again, "Where is John Raven?"

Richard didn't take kindly to General Gee's tone replying, "I heard you the first time soldier!"

Susan placed her hand onto General Gee's arm to stop him from speaking, asking in a polite way, "Mr Raven. Where is your son?"

Richard stared at President Berry in the eye, asking, "What does the President of the United States want with my son?"

He took a few paces forward and carried on saying, "I gave him my blessing a few days ago, but I never expected you to turn up on my doorstep."

Sarah spoke by saying, "Will you take us to him?"

Becoming frosty faced, Richard started walking to the barn, telling the V.I.P's to follow, but be careful with the dogs roaming around free with not being too friendly with strangers. Reaching the barn, Richard saw John working. He waited for the V.I.P's to come a little closer and then said, "Wait here, while I go and get him."

The V.I.P's watched Richard walk over to where John was working taking notice of the different items inside the barn. Richard shouted, "John."

He didn't hear him with concentrating on sharpening his knife, so Richard called out again, "John!"

John turned around to his father wearing his headband and holding the knife in his left hand, producing a menacing stare with being disturbed. Sweat dripped from his hair that also showed through his grey t-shirt. With knowing he had his attention, Richard didn't speak. He just slowly turned around to point to the V.I.P's anxiously waiting for him at the barn door. Recognising all three people, he asked his father, "Where are the dogs?"

As they walked over to President Berry, John wiped his hands, as he listened to Richard say, "They're outside somewhere."

Becoming concerned for the safety of these people, he said to his father in a stern voice, "Find the dogs, especially Sarah Jane's and take them inside."

John placed his right hand out to shake General Gee's hand and nodded to President Berry and the Secretary of State. He watched his father walking away while shouting for the dogs. President Berry, noticing John's intimidating presence, thought back to when she had presented him and his son with a Purple Heart and the Medal of Honour. Seeing him standing there holding his new made knife, she spoke, feeling nervous, saying, "John, we would like you to go with us on our trip to Iran."

John gave a prolonged blink of disgust and then with a stern face that made Sarah Johnson look away, he turned to see that his father had his own two dogs. Aware of the dog he was concerned about was still somewhere outside, he replied, "I'll have to clean up first!"

General Gee replied, "There is no time! We have to leave immediately!"

John stared at President Berry, slowly moving his eyes to face General Gee, saying, "Do you expect me to be in President Berry's presence looking like this?"

General Gee and President Berry looked at each other knowing John was right in what he had just mentioned. General Gee looked back to face John and say, "Normally I would say no, but we have to leave, and now!"

The General turned around to face Sadie, Sarah Jane's ferocious Alsatian cowering down and snarling at them. The president's bodyguards climbed out of their 4x4's, pulling out their guns and pointing it at the animal. Raven pushed the Secretary of State to one side and rushed quickly over to her, still gripping his knife tightly. He said in a stern voice, "I never wanted to bring home this dog I fought with in North Korea."

President Berry remembered only too well what it was capable of, replying while watching him walk with a temper towards the dog, "I don't blame you John."

Noticing that she was pulling her nose back and starting to show her sharp teeth, Raven didn't hesitate and wait for her to attack. Instead he gritted his teeth, grabbed her by the throat using his right hand and made her roll on her back where she wriggled her legs, while snarling and growling. With his left hand, he pressed down onto her throat with the knife he had sharpened. Knowing with just a little more pressure he could kill her, he stared into the dog's eyes breathing heavy remembering it was this animal that gave him his new scars on his face from his last battle. It was only a matter of time before John would snap and lose patience with this dog. The V.I.P's glared at John with the position he was now in, gasping in disbelief. General Gee signalled to the bodyguards to lower their weapons, which they did immediately, but chose to remain standing outside their 4x4's feeling close to President Berry.

Richard, who was now in the kitchen, saw what was happening outside, making him hurry outside shouting, "John, leave that dog alone!"

Still holding his knife point on its throat, he turned where his hair hung into his face and saw his father hurrying over to him. Feeling angry, he grabbed John's arm and said, "Take your hands off Sarah Jane's dog!"

Still pressing the knife on its throat, which started to weep blood, Richard again said, "John, take your hands off that dog, now!"

John stared at the snarling dog and pulled away his knife and saw blood running down its neck. Richard scowled when he saw the blood and said, "What are you?"

Releasing his grip slightly on the dog's throat with his right hand he decided to let go and stand up straight with his knife facing outward ready to attack it if it decided to retaliate against him. The dog ran away with the fur on its back standing on edge. John turned his head sharply, asking his father, "Where do you think I received these new scars on my face?"

Richard, feeling angry, paused while staring at John's face thinking of something to say. Feeling angry with the V.I.P's he also stared at them for a few seconds and then turned back to John saying, "If Sarah Jane ever finds out what you did to her dog, she will never speak to you again!"

John, still breathing heavy and holding the knife tightly remained silent. He moved his eyes to stare at his father and then walked by him, back to where President Berry and her colleagues were now standing. General Gee, after witnessing this horrible event said, "I don't think there was any need for that John."

John while walking past all the V.I.P's replied, "She would have ripped you into fucking pieces where your people would then have shot her!"

General Gee, as he watched John walk back to the barn shouted, "Where are you going John?"

President Berry and Sarah Johnson feeling mystified, just watched, listening to General Gee ask again, "Where are you going John?"

John ignored the General and walked back inside the barn, which made the three V.I.P's also follow. John placed a holster around his waist and slammed his knife inside it. Feeling bad tempered he collected his bow and started walking past President Berry, who was now standing at the barn door. Looking at all the V.I.P's he said, "Let's go!"

President Berry raised her eyebrows feeling shock and dismay. Sarah Johnson paused while watching him continue to the black Chevrolet 4x4's asking, "Is Iran prepared for him?"

General Gee frowned, becoming concerned at Raven's volatile behaviour. With this, he asked, "Are you sure you still want John Raven to go with us?"

President Berry watched the back of Raven's huge physique walk to her own 4x4 replying, "This trip isn't going to be straightforward is it?"

Sarah Johnson joined the conversation by saying, "With where we are travelling to, we have to take him."

President Berry sighed, and then listened to General Gee say, "Somewhere inside him is another war just waiting to happen."

President Berry turned away from the General and watched Raven again, replying, "He travels with us. Come on, let's go."

President Berry thanked Richard and wanted to shake his hand, but he chose to ignore her gesture and just watched Johnson and Gee follow Raven to their 4x4. Richard followed, noticing the bodyguards were now climbing back inside their 4x4's. Susan and Sarah climbed inside their own 4x4, followed by the General and John Raven. John closed the door, looked out of the blacked out window and saw his father coming towards the president's 4x4. The chauffeur turned the key, starting the engine, which made John shout, "Wait!"

Everybody sitting in the car stared at him with his sudden outburst, and watched him press the switch to lower the window. His father stood at the door feeling emotionally drained. He placed his hand out, placing it onto the door and said, "Don't kid yourselves! He isn't only going to be a bystander for you lot, so son, remember to COME HOME."

Listening to his father's words, John held his mouth tight, but chose to say nothing, which made, Richard say in a solemn voice, "John?"

At first John didn't turn to face his father. The others sat in the 4x4 watched with intent as Richard said again, "John!"

John moved his eyes to focus on his father, and listened to him say in a solemn voice, "Don't make it *One Time Too Many.*"

General Gee heard those words John's father had just mentioned and recalled a mission John had turned down, hoping one day he would change his mind and decide to accept what seemed like to him as the ultimate mission.

After John had heard those words, he chose to ignore them, by nodding his head once to President Berry, and saying in a stern voice, "Let's go!"

He pressed the switch to raise the blacked out window with his father Richard left standing alone wondering will he ever see his son again as he watched the black Chevrolet 4x4 drive away.

Trip to Iran

$\mathcal{T}$he black Chevrolet 4x4's travelled at high-speed again with the blue and red lights flashing once more, warning other motorists that a commanding presence was travelling, choosing not to stop until they had reached their destination.

John sat next to General Gee with a face of anger showing. President Berry noticed this and asked, "You appear tense John. Are you okay?"

John moved his eyes to stare at President Berry, but chose to remain silent. With not replying to Susan, the General said, "The president has just asked you a question. Answer her!"

John casually moved his head, then his eyes, giving a menacing stare at General Gee still choosing to remain silent. Sarah Johnson, sensing that a bad atmosphere had developed inside the 4x4, placed her hand onto John's knee, wanting to ask him in a gentle voice, "John, what can we do to make things better for you?"

John lowered his eyes a little while thinking about Captain Weller and what she must now be enduring with being held captive by the Iranians. Just as before, John chose to remain silent and say nothing. Susan looked at him with concern, while noticing his huge physique and made a comment about the headband, he was wearing that was resting onto his shoulder. "Didn't you wear that headband when I was with your son in North Korea?"

John moved his mouth, gave a prolonged blink and sighed. He looked at President Berry waiting for a reply and decided to speak, "A wise old Korean gentleman once told me that a samurai had once worn it and he would like me to have it. Had I been born in his country, I would have become a samurai."

General Gee, who had just been watching the traffic they were passing, turned to look at Raven and say, "But not quite the warrior to fulfil the mission, I offered to you sometime after America in conflict. John closed his eyes starting to remember the mission General Gee had offered to Raven. Whilst watching his reaction, President Berry asked, "What mission was this?"

John opened his eyes waiting for General Gee to reply, "It's classified!"

President Berry frowned, asking with concern, "It usually is, but shouldn't I have been informed?"

The Secretary of State, Sarah Johnson spoke by saying, "I took control of this situation working with General Gee discussing the alternatives we have to be rid of the problem."

Susan frowned, holding a face of dismay asking, "What problem?"

Sarah Johnson replied, "It's nothing like what we're going through at this time, but it does need to be dealt with."

Susan replied, "If I don't know about the problem, it can't be that serious!"

John moved his eyes focusing on Susan, knowing the problem was serious. General Gee sensed the president wasn't too happy about something untoward involving the military that hadn't been discussed with her. Deciding not to let the subject drop she asked John, "What are they talking about?"

John stared at President Berry, refusing to speak and then slowly moved his head to look at the General. General Gee said to John, "The way you held that ferocious dog earlier,

I know you would succeed with the mission in the Arctic Circle, with what you had to come to terms with."

Susan, feeling left out of this conversation asked in a stern voice, "Will somebody please tell me what we're talking about?"

Sarah Johnson glimpsed at the General and John watching for a reaction, and replied, "We have a situation in the Arctic Circle that needs the best of the best to deal with it."

John moved his eyes, focusing on Johnson, and then heard General Gee say, "The other members of Unit Extreme are still up for this mission, stating that you're the only man they would prefer to work under. You know what I'm talking about don't you John?"

President Berry interrupted saying, "I wish I did."

John replied, "The savage hunt."

President Berry frowned again, and then listened to General Gee ask, "Why don't you reconsider John?"

Sarah waited anxiously for John's reply after planning the mission so meticulously with General Gee, and listened to him say, "I read the file."

Sarah asked in a concerned manner, "All the other members of Unit Extreme are willing to fight this beast, why won't you when you're the main man?"

John visualising the danger replied, "You're right I am the main man! Especially where this mission is concerned, it will be up to me if and when this does ever occur!"

President Berry not sure what her colleagues were talking about asked John in a concerned voice, "What made you decline being involved with this mission?"

Before John could reply, General Gee also commented by saying, "That's an interesting question because you have never told us."

John tilted his head to one side producing a graceful look on his face thinking about the proposal put to him previously. Speaking to everybody he replied, "Reasons."

President Berry, aware that John Raven was the legendary soldier everybody else looked up to and just wanted to be, narrowed her eyes asking, "Which are?"

John immediately replied, "No matter, which warzone I have been involved in, I've always had a reason to fight. You've heard the saying, die for something, live for nothing, what is it, I'm going to be dying for in the Arctic Circle, apart from covering somebody's political ass?"

The 4x4's had arrived at the airport with the crew of Air Force One waiting for President Berry and her colleagues to board. She noticed a podium close by to her plane and said, "We discuss this again later when we're aboard Air Force One, because I'm going to have to give a brief press conference."

John looked out of the blacked out window, noticing the television cameras and newspaper reporters were waiting for the U.S. President. With this he said, "I can't be seen!"

General Gee became startled, but feeling concerned for John, he asked, "Why can't you be seen?"

John turned to face them all replying, "I need to finish something in Iran and can't give Cairns the satisfaction of knowing that I'm travelling with you."

President Berry replied, "Okay, stay here in the car with Sarah until the press conference is finished, and then board Air Force One with her."

John watched President Berry and General Gee climb out of the Chevrolet 4x4, which made Sarah ask, "What do you plan to do in Iran?"

John turned back and replied, "What's right and what the United States would prefer to see."

Sarah asked, "How?"

John smirked, replying, "Don't worry, you will arrive home!"

Sarah asked, "Will you?"

John replied, "I don't intend to stay longer than I have to!"

Sarah gave a wry smile saying, "Don't answer this now because I do know what you've been through. If we do come through this situation with Iran, will you seriously consider the savage hunt?"

John went quiet, moved his eyes that cut through the Secretary of State and just nodded his head reluctantly saying yes.

President Berry and General Gee were surrounded by reporters and photographers. Questions were being asked to her from all directions, making General Gee and her bodyguards shout, "Get back!"

The world was watching hoping that a solution could be found from the meeting she was going to attend with President Modarres. Climbing onto her podium, she waited for General Gee to stand beside her, and then watched her bodyguards trying to keep control of the impatient reporters. Placing her arm up, the sound of the media slowly started to dwindle, waiting eagerly for her to speak.

John Raven and Sarah Johnson, still sitting in the Chevrolet 4x4 watched with interest at what the President was about to say.

President Modarres and James Cairns were also watching the television report that was being broadcasted around the world. They were pleased with how things were progressing, which made Cairns ask, "Has everything been set at the tunnel for when Air Force One has landed?"

President Modarres gave an evil grin replying, "With the catastrophe that will occur, it will also kill some of my own people!"

Cairns moved his head away from the television to face President Modarres and say, "See, there you go again! Learn to see what the bigger picture has to offer, and I'm sure you will be rewarded greatly."

President Modarres wasn't too happy suspecting that some of his own people will be killed when Air Force One lands and replied, "When you die, you will go to hell!"

Cairns turned back to watch the television laughing, replying with a question, "Is there anywhere else to go?"

President Berry started to speak, knowing that she was going to be heard in every part of the world. Feeling drained from the pressure, she gave a sigh and said, "Fellow American's, I know the world is depending on me to come up with a solution that can be agreed between the United States and Iran. I hope it can be reached if President Modarres, can search inside his soul and start to see the evil in a man that was once a U.S. soldier. James Cairns is the instigator for diverting him away from what I'm sure he knows is right."

Cairns turned to look at President Modarres, where he remained unmoved, choosing not to respond to Cairns. Instead, he carried on listening to President Berry saying, "I'm sure you would agree with me if I was to say that you would prefer to keep our world as we know it just the way it is."

Cairns smirked, saying to President Modarres, "The American's always want their own way!"

President Modarres as he listened to President Berry on television glanced at Cairns wondering how a man could hate his own country so much. There was a knock at the door, making both men turn to see Colonel Vladimir Mihailov enter the room. Dressed in a smart Russian uniform, he went to President Modarres' desk, while noticing President Berry on the television. He took off his gloves, placed them onto President Modarres' desk, asking, "Is America's First Lady still travelling to visit us all in Iran today?"

Cairns answered, "As you can see, she is standing close to Air Force One where I expect she will be taking off after her charade of a speech."

Colonel Mihailov replied, "Good."

President Modarres asked Colonel Mihailov, "Have your troops been briefed about working with the Iranian soldiers in making President Berry welcome in our country?"

Cairns sniggered, which the Colonel noticed, but chose to ignore and reply to the Iranian President saying. "They're all briefed where they are ready to work alongside the Iranian soldiers to ensure that we get what we have tried to achieve before."

President Modarres replied, "If we survive the possibility of World War 3, we will take Kuwait and be the supreme power of the world!"

Colonel Mihailov grinned at the thought of ruling the world with President Modarres and said, "Now it begins!"

Cairns feeling disgruntled, carried on watching television watching the President of the U.S. stand down from her podium and board Air Force One beside General Gee, who were followed by her bodyguards.

Some of the media started to leave, but other reporters decided to remain and film Air Force One take off and use the footage in their televised reports. President Berry looked across to the black Chevrolet 4x4 feeling anxious at the prospect that her colleague and good friend, Sarah Johnson, would now follow with whom she was sat next to.

Sarah Johnson said to John, "We have to go now."

John looked outside and saw that some of the media had remained to probably record the take-off of Air Force One. Not wanting to be seen, he said, "If I'm filmed it could be to the advantage of Cairns."

Sarah opened the door replying, "You're John Raven! Surely, you're not going to let a weasel like James Cairns have to make you hide behind a screen? If the world saw that you were travelling with the President of the U.S. to Iran, it can only be a morale boost for the world."

John clasped his hands together, closed his eyes, asking Sarah, "I agree, but what if the safety of Captain Weller is put at risk?"

Sarah started to climb out of the car, which made Cairns say to the Russian Colonel and Iranian President, "It looks as though we're going to be joined with the U.S. Secretary of State too. This is going better than I had expected!"

Before Sarah turned around to make her way to Air Force One, she replied to John still sitting inside the 4x4, "Like many others, she is already in danger. We have to go and now."

Sarah turned, making her way walking towards Air Force One, casually looking back to see if John would climb out of the 4x4. With his hands still clasped together he moved his head to watch Sarah, and then Susan standing at the door of Air Force One. Knowing he had to go, he climbed out of the 4x4, which made the media move their cameras and zoom in on him. When they realised it was John Raven, shouts could be heard such as, "One of the United States legendary soldiers will fly to support President Berry." and "Raven returns but will he fight?"

President Modarres saw John Raven on television and replied to Cairns, "Do you still think it's going better than expected?"

Cairns watched John Raven walking to board Air Force One. His arrogant smile slowly disappeared, which made him walk out of the room quickly feeling rather angry and wanting to speak with Captain Weller while visualising the picture, he had set alight of him.

John Weller and Louise saw Raven boarding Air Force One, with his son saying, "He looks as though he's prepared for a battle."

Louise, who was still aware that she had to give John an answer to his proposal replied, "He wanted a battle on Christmas Day when we visited him."

John Weller said, "Look at him with the determination showing on his face, he isn't there for just President Berry."

Louise looked down feeling saddened at the prospect; she may also lose her boyfriend to this conflict, which made her ask, "When do you become involved?"

John looked away from the television to face Louise feeling worried. Before answering her, he decided to study the question, knowing that he still hadn't received an answer to his proposal. Wisely, just as his father would have done, he turned away remaining silent, leaving Louise with a big decision to make, sooner rather than later.

Unit Expendable had arrived at the military base in Kuwait also watched the television report that was being broadcasted, which made Colonel Wareing say, "The son of a bitch!"

Lundgren said in a stern voice, "I told him he would become involved. You just can't keep a good man down."

Colonel Wareing and General Hardaker listened to different comments being made about the leader of Unit Expendable.

He felt proud when they praised him for wanting to come back to fight for his country and help make things right again for the world as we know it. The morale of Unit Expendable lifted when they saw John Raven climbing the steps to board Air Force One. The officers in the room noticed this, which made Colonel Wareing say, "When Air Force One has landed, we, including me, all begin our mission. You know what we have to do! It will only be a matter of time before you're reunited with John Raven. Trust me when I say he isn't just here for President Berry."

Sarah Jane saw him, immediately thinking of the times she had provoked him to embark on this mission. Not sure how, but there on the screen was her father who had contradicted everything he said to her. It made her think back to the time she had tried to make him promise, don't make it one time too many. Hayley saw her in deep thought, making her ask, "Are you okay Sarah Jane?"

Sarah Jane while watching the television replied, "I was just starting to get used to not having him around."

She paused, thinking about her father and then carried onto say, "We will probably become involved in a warzone like no other."

John Raven reached the top of the steps to stand next to President Berry, looking back at the media, who were recording for the world. His headband blew in the wind as he looked down at the people filming, where they started to feel encouraged with his huge presence. Susan gave a casual wave and said, "Come John, let's go to our seats."

President Berry went inside leaving John standing at the door on his own where he raised his arm and then point his finger in a shrewd way. The media positioned their huge microphones anticipating that he was about to say something. They were right because he scowled and said in a stern voice, "Cairns, I'm coming to get you!"

He turned around and heard one of the reporters below shout, "America loves you, John."

John moved his eyes to stare at the person who had shouted to him, and then responded to him by slowly nodding his head once agreeing. He walked inside Air Force One leaving a member of the President's crew to close the door securely so they could start to taxi around to the runway.

Everybody on board Air Force One took their seat, waiting for authorisation from the control tower to be able to take off and start travelling to Iran. President Berry, Sarah Johnson and General Gee watched Raven while he held his head low thinking about the extreme danger Captain Weller was now placed in with the enemy now knowing that he was travelling with President Berry.

The pilots of Air Force One had received clearance for take-off. They relayed the message to the U.S. President and taxied a little further, turning the huge 747 plane right to position it on the runway. The powerful engines revved hard as it started slowly rumbling down the runway, while gathering momentum at the same time. Travelling at high-speed, Air Force One eventually lowered its rear end and began to rise into the sky. General Gee spoke by saying, "Next stop Iran."

John lifted his head and gave him a stare, which made President Berry say, "I would like to continue with the conversation about the mission in the Arctic Circle because it does have me intrigued."

John clasped his hands together and lowered his head again not wanting to discuss this mission. President Berry did and wanted to know all the details, which made General Gee and Sarah Johnson reveal information about what the savage hunt involved. Hearing details being mentioned that John had already seen in the file, made him raise his head slowly and look across to General Gee and say in a disgruntled manner, "This is not the right time to discuss this!"

General Gee replied, "There is never going to be a right time!"

President Berry, now aware of what the savage hunt involved watched with interest expecting General Gee and John Raven to have a heated debate. Sensing this could happen, she interrupted them by saying, "Although I would like to discuss this matter, I feel we should leave this subject alone, at least, for the time being."

John moved his eyes to focus on her where she looked straight at back at him. He softened his stare, which made her carry onto say, "Now that we're in the air and travelling to Iran, we should discuss what our alternatives are if Iran refuses to co-operate?"

Sarah Johnson asked, "All of our contingency plans are in place, what else is there to discuss?"

John sat there listening to them discussing the prospect of a nuclear war when there are no winners. Sarah, with concern asked President Berry, "I know Iranians can be irrational, but surely you don't think they will use nuclear missiles against us?"

President Berry sighed at the thought of Armageddon being created and the world ending as we know it. Trying to imagine what the effects would be, she replied, "You never know what to fully expect with the Iranians."

John listened to every word being spoken, choosing not to interrupt their conversation. Susan, watching John's reaction, carried on saying, "Let's not forget that Iran does have a powerful ally in Russia, where they have always wanted to attack Kuwait for its oil and wealth."

John stood up, which made bodyguards sitting nearby watch his movements. Glancing at them and then back at Susan, he said, "Iran isn't the problem . . ."

General Gee interrupted him before he could complete what he had to say, asking, "What is then?"

John moved his eyes, giving a menacing stare at General Gee, replying, "You already know. It's Cairns!"

They all looked up at him, listening to him say, "Take him away and you have a chance of achieving a diplomatic solution."

He then walked away from them all with President Berry and Sarah Johnson watching him, choosing to keep their own thoughts to themselves. General Gee, who also watched Raven walk down the plane saw his headband hanging onto his back and said, "I don't care what you say Ma'am but John Raven is here for more than just you and Sarah."

President Berry and Johnson listened to General Gee giving his opinion and then looked back taking notice of Raven further down the plane drinking a cup of coffee and casually speaking with one of the President's bodyguards. Susan replied, "Maybe, maybe not. We shall have to wait and see."

She glanced at Sarah starting to feel apprehension where they knew what the other person was thinking after experiencing being in a warzone with this legendary soldier.

Weak & Vulnerable

$\mathcal{T}$ he pilots taking Air Force One to Iran were well on their way into their journey, confirming that they will be landing at Imam Khomeini International Airport inside the next two hours.

John Raven decided to walk to another part of the plane choosing to be alone to reflect in his own thoughts about how Captain Weller must be feeling. He closed his eyes, remembering her words that she was going to leave the force and spend the rest of her time with him, and finally enjoy life without the pressures of war being placed on them. The memories of Captain Weller that came flooding back to him made his face turn to anger when the life he so wanted conflicted with what General Gee had mentioned earlier about the savage hunt. He placed his hand onto the handle of his knife, holding it tightly. Sarah saw him holding the handle of his knife and walked up slowly not wanting to startle him. She placed her hand onto his back tenderly and asked, "Are you having flashbacks from last time?"

John moved his menacing eyes to look at her, as he started releasing the grip on his knife, replied, "You could say that."

Standing there smartly dressed, Sarah took her hand away from John and said, "You can get showered and changed into something much smarter if you prefer."

John shook his head slowly from side to side saying no, which made Sarah say, "Admit it, you're eventually going to become involved in a warzone, aren't you?"

John moved his eyes to look into Sarah's eyes with a menacing stare. She felt intimidated, wanting to look down and away from his stare. Casually, she looked back into his eyes with John replying, "I will do what I have to do."

Sarah, feeling concerned for her life asked, "Are we going to make it?"

John moved his eyebrows slightly and replied, "I promised that you will arrive home."

Sarah grabbed John's arm, asking, "But will you?"

John moved his head to look at Sarah's hand touching his arm, which made her, pull it away sharply and John reply, "Like I said, I will do what I have to do."

With seeing John as the warrior and the well-dressed soldier, she wanted to discuss so much with him. With John being a man of few words, he didn't, so in a stern voice he said, "Leave me, go back and join the others!"

He turned his back on her, making Sarah reply, "There could only be you who could speak to the Secretary of State like that and get away with it."

John turned around to face her choosing to ignore her comment and said sternly, "Go!"

He turned back around listening to Sarah walk away from him, leaving him to think about what Captain Weller must be feeling; now she is in the hands of the Iranians and worst of all, Cairns!

Captain Weller had been placed in a cell on her own. She was sitting in a corner with her head resting on her arms hoping that her colleagues, possibly Raven would come to free her from this nightmare she was now living. Looking untidy with not being able to wash for a few days she became nervous when soldiers walked by her cell. With most of her buttons ripped off her blouse, she kept pulling either side of the blouse tight, stopping soldiers from seeing her flesh. It went quiet where she rested her head down back onto her arms wondering what the rest of her family was now doing and how they had spent their Christmas. With missing them all so much, tears started to fall down her cheeks. Her sobbing became louder because now she was starting to feel as though her heart was broken. She lifted her head again when she heard soldiers once more and looked at the cell door listening to the jangle of keys placed into the lock. Feeling frightened, she pulled her legs in closer while placing her arms around her legs and clasped her hands together tightly, while still waiting for the door to open. The Iranian guard took the keys out and pushed the huge wooden door open to let Cairns and three soldiers walk inside the cell. They stood there looking down at Captain Weller, who was feeling frightened at what they might do to her. Cairns walked away from the Iranian soldiers and said "Stand up!"

Showing a saddened face, Debbie looked up to Cairns, asking, "Why?"

Cairns, already provoked, with now knowing that Raven was travelling to Iran and wasn't in the mood for having questions directed to him. He walked over to where Debbie was sitting and grabbed her hair, pulling it hard, making her yelp and have to stand. She kept one hand held on her blouse, which Cairns had noticed. He looked into her sad eyes with his evil eyes and grabbed her hand, forcing it away from her blouse, which made it become loose, exposing her sexy underwear and her cleavage. He took off his shirt, where she became scared with the thought of being raped. The Iranian soldiers laughed as Cairns went and placed his hand inside Debbie's blouse onto her waist and started to kiss her neck. She pulled a horrible face at the thought of him touching her body and decided to kick him on the shin. He immediately pulled his hand away from inside her blouse, created a fist and punched her hard in the face, knocking her down onto the floor. He bent down, grabbed her hair and pulled her head back, saying, "I can do you anytime I want!"

With the position Debbie was in, she chose to say nothing and remain silent. By doing this, it angered Cairns more, making him pull her hair harder and say, "Anytime, you're mine!"

President Modarres and Colonel Mihailov walked into the cell to see Cairns holding Captain Weller by the hair with a tight grip, which made them smirk. Cairns looked back at them and listened to the Iranian president say, "It's time!"

He threw Debbie back down to the floor, stood up straight and said, "Okay, prepare the soldiers to travel and welcome our guests. I'll be with you in a few minutes!"

The Iranian President nodded his head agreeing while looking down at Debbie lying on the floor, before turning around to gather his troops and travel to meet the President of the United States.

Colonel Mihailov watched Cairns place his shirt back on, looked down at Debbie and said, "You disgust me!"

Cairns closed his eyes for a few seconds while he buttoned his shirt. He glimpsed at Colonel Mihailov, and then placed his hands through his hair tightly. Feeling annoyed at the comment the Colonel had made, he walked briskly across the cell, grabbed Colonel Mihailov by the throat and pushed him against the wall, where he was finding it hard to breathe. Cairns put his face close to the Colonel's face, saying, "You and I don't seem to be getting along too well!"

Gripping his throat much tighter, he asked, "Do we?"

Debbie watched what Cairns were doing and looked bemused with him attacking an ally of Iran.

Cairns laughed when the Colonel was fighting for breath. The three Iranian soldiers standing inside the cell that had been laughing at Debbie's misfortune moments before had suddenly stopped with now seeing Cairns attack Colonel Mihailov. Cairns, still glaring in the face of the Colonel said, "You don't want to cross me, do it again, and I will personally kill you!"

He released his grip on the Colonel's throat, which made Colonel Mihailov, who was still glaring at Cairns, place his own hand to his throat and gently massage it. Cairns shook his head, making his hair swiftly move to the back of his shirt and say, "Go with Modarres. I'll be with you in a few minutes!"

Feeling humiliated, Colonel Mihailov walked past him saying, "This is not over!"

Cairns stared at the Colonel as he watched him walk out of the cell and then turned around to Debbie still lying on the floor to say, "You see. I get no thanks when I let him live!"

Debbie turned her face away frowning at Cairns' behaviour. Cairns carried onto say, "When are they going to realise that it's me that's responsible for this country now. I'm the brains of this outfit, when soon it will be official!"

Hearing these words made Debbie, who was still looking away from Cairns raise her eyebrows in total disbelief at what he had just told her. Cairns took a few more paces forward, looked down at her body and said, "It's time to welcome the President of the United States, only when Air Force One has landed, I guarantee it will also crash!"

Debbie turned around in shock with hearing those words. Cairns laughed, saying, "Have I got your attention now sweetheart?"

Cairns walked to the cell door, turned back around and said, "If they die, they die, if they live, we throw them in a cell like a piece of meat!"

Cairns ordered the Iranian guards out of the cell, placed his hand onto the door and started pulling it. He stopped, wanting to say to Debbie, "Oh yes, I now know that John Raven is aboard Air Force One, and I'm personally going to see to it that he is killed!"

Debbie watched in dismay has he slammed the cell door shut. Feeling perplexed, she heard the guard jangle the keys to lock the cell door. After the horrific experience, she had just endured; she sat up, pulled her blouse around the front of her body tightly managing to bring a wry smile to her battered face. Knowing John Raven has travelled to Iran to try and rescue her gave her renewed hope. What follows, she doesn't yet know, all she does know is that if John Raven was involved, and Cairns is the prime enemy, it is only a matter of time before another huge warzone occurs. Her wry smile became bigger with starting to feel pleased at the prospect the one man she relied on the most came back to fight for her. She could only hope and pray this time it isn't *one time too many*.

Devastation

Cairns went outside aware the Russian and Iranian soldiers were now assembled waiting for him. Before he went to join President Modarres, he pulled out his sunglasses, placed them onto his face, while feeling proud with what he had achieved. The hostile Iranian crowd outside, who were also waiting for President Berry to arrive were shouting and jeering against her visit. More American flags were set alight, which made Cairns smirk as he walked to the jeep to join President Modarres, who was patiently waiting. Colonel Mihailov, who was sitting in the vehicle behind President Modarres, glared at Cairns as he watched him walk past his vehicle. Sensing it, Cairns looked back, giving a hard stare at Colonel Mihailov while still walking to President Modarres' vehicle. Colonel Mihailov watched him, saying to his driver, "This man Cairns has serious issue problems!"

The driver while listening to Colonel Mihailov speaking glimpsed across at Cairns, watching him turn and swagger to his own vehicle. He climbed inside the jeep to join President Modarres, saying, "I've waited for a long time for this, where I'm going to enjoy watching Air Force One crash."

President Modarres grit his teeth asking with concern, "What about my people?"

Cairns turned to face him, patted his arm gently and replied, "Look at them rejoicing at President Berry's visit."

President Modarres looked around, watching youths turning cars over and setting them alight. Some exploded which made the crowd move back and cheer. He turned to Cairns saying, "This is not right. It's gone too far!"

Cairns became stunned after hearing this comment, which made him tilt his head slightly in disbelief. Slowly, starting to absorb what the Iranian President had just said, he turned his head to place his evil eyes into his face asking, "You're not starting to go soft on me, are you?"

President Modarres moved his eyes to see the evil face of Cairns still staring back at him and replied, "We see this through until the end!"

Cairns leaned back, turned away feeling calm, replying, "For a moment there, I thought that you were going to give up the fight!"

He turned his head to face the Iranian President again while carrying onto say, "Do that, and I'll kill you!"

President Modarres remained looking straight ahead narrowing his eyes in anger, choosing to ignore Cairns' last comment. Instead, he said calmly, "Let's go and welcome President Berry our way."

He turned to look at Cairns, watching him, starting to produce an evil grin and said, "I'm still the man at the top!"

Cairns smirked, replying, "Of course you are. I wouldn't have it any other way. Now tell the driver to start travelling, so we can welcome this bitch to Iran!"

The driver didn't need telling. Hearing Cairns' voice was enough for him to start the engine to begin their journey.

As the enemy had just begun their journey, President Berry and her colleagues had almost reached the end of their trip to Iran. The pilots had already been in contact with the control tower at the Imam Khomeini International Airport, with the tower confirming they would be landing in twenty minutes. The pilots turned on the loud speaker relaying the message confirming they would be landing soon, and it would be advisable to be seated with seat belts fastened ready for their landing.

President Berry was now in her own office speaking with Sarah Johnson, saying, "We ought to go and buckle up for our landing."

They went to the door with Sarah asking, "Do you feel apprehensive?"

Susan closed the door behind her replying, "I would be a liar if I said no."

They started to feel the plane descend, which made Susan say, "Come, we had better go back to our seats until we land."

They saw General Gee passing, making his way to take his seat, which made Susan stop him to ask, "Where's John?"

General Gee replied, "I haven't seen him for a while, but he can't be faraway."

Susan frowned, wondering where he might be and said, "Okay General, lead the way."

They all made their way to their seats and sat down, placing their seat belts on ready for Air Force One to land. Nobody wanted to say anything, although at times they kept glimpsing at Raven's empty seat wondering where he was.

John was at another part of the plane on another level speaking with a couple of bodyguards about weapons allowed on this plane to help protect the U.S. President whenever they had to be used. They knew who John Raven was, respecting him as an elite soldier and a person. As he spoke to the bodyguard, occasionally he would pick a weapon up and hold it remembering how he had used the same weapon on previous missions. When he saw the sub machine gun, he placed down the gun and went to hold it, turning back to the bodyguard asking, "You have these on Air Force One?"

The bodyguard replied, "We have everything because we have to be ready for anything and everything."

Raven grinned while lifting his head replying, "That's my line."

As they spoke together, at frequent intervals, they could feel the huge 747 plane descending, which made the bodyguard say, "I should go and take my seat."

Raven replied, "You go."

The bodyguard asked, "What about you, are you going to take your seat?"

John smirked at the question being asked, and replied, "Me rushing back to place a seat belt on?"

The bodyguard feeling concerned about how things are done on Air Force One said, "It's procedure."

John still looking down at the gun moved his eyes upwards, replying, "You go."

The bodyguard still feeling concerned about the procedure involved on Air Force One asked, "But?"

John interrupted him before he could finish what he was saying, replying, "You go!"

The bodyguard looked at John sternly, reluctantly deciding to turn around to go back to his seat. John watched him for a few seconds, and then turned back to look at all the weaponry that was aboard Air Force One. He picked up weapons visualising what he had once used when he had been at war. He also thought back to when his son, John Weller was aboard Air Force One, suspecting he must have visited the same room to gather weapons to help protect the President of the United States. He placed the weapon down, while thinking of his son and said in a low voice, "You did good John when America was in conflict."

Air Force One had received permission from the Iranian control tower to begin their approach and land on to the designated runway. The pilot repeated the message to President Berry and her colleagues, who made General Gee ask, "Shouldn't Raven be back sitting with us by now?"

Sarah grinned replying, "Be patient General. He will be here soon."

President Modarres, James Cairns, Colonel Mihailov with soldiers from Iran and Russia had arrived nearby to the airport. Cairns sat there amid his own thoughts while watching planes coming into land at Imam Khomeini International Airport. President Modarres feeling concerned about his own people asked Cairns, "Why do . . ."

Cairns suspecting what he was about to ask, interrupted him replying, "You know why!"

He pointed into the sky at Air Force One coming into land, which made President Modarres look up at it and then turn to Cairns to watch him take out of his pocket a remote detonator. Cairns brought an evil grin to his face as he watched Air Force One approach the runway. He held the detonator tightly while focusing on the plane. President Modarres knowing that he would be responsible for this disaster watched closely at what was about to happen. Cairns looked at Colonel Mihailov parked at the side of his jeep and nodded to him to have the soldiers placed in position once Air Force One had been severely damaged.

Everybody watched in anticipation waiting for Air Force One to make contact with the runway and for Cairns to do what he had to do. Cairns noticing how low Air Force One now was, stood up to watch its wheels hit the runway, screech a little and land while still travelling at a speed. The flaps on both wings rose helping the plane to slow down. With still moving at a speed, before arriving at the point of the tunnel directly below, Cairns pressed the button. He grinned when he heard an almighty explosion in the tunnel, making the runway above break up and separate. The pilots struggled to keep control of Air Force One, but couldn't. The plane tilted with one of the wings scraping the runway making a mass of sparks.

On the plane automatic procedures occurred with everybody on board being told by the Captain to take crash positions. Feeling shocked, but without any hesitation, all crew members and the president's staff did so, which made General Gee ask, "Where's Raven?"

John was still in the room where all the weapons were stored and became concerned when the plane tilted onto its wing. Sensing that this could be a terrorist attack, he armed himself with some of the weapons, immediately starting to make his way back to see if President Berry and her colleagues were safe.

Cairns, who had remained standing wanting to watch Air Force One travel and fall through the huge hole created by the explosion moments before produced an evil grin. He saw the emergency services with the sirens blurring speeding down the runway after Air Force One. President Modarres watched in total disbelief wondering how many people had been killed on the metro line below the runway. He asked Cairns, "Shouldn't we send the soldiers in now?"

Cairns, while still watching Air Force One career towards the huge hole created by the blast, placed his hand up replying, "Wait!"

The pilot tried to keep control of Air Force One the best way he could. The loud speaker had been left on when everybody heard the co-pilot shout, "The wing has caught fire!"

Raven, who was rushing back to be at President Berry's side stopped briefly to look outside one of the windows to see the wing was in flames. Aware that fuel would still be in the plane he knew he had to do something and fast.

Staff in the control tower stopped all flights from entering Imam Khomeini International Airport as they looked down in disbelief at the position Air Force One was now in. People were going frantic on the telephone knowing the safety of the U.S. President was in jeopardy. Although the plane had slowed down, it couldn't stop travelling towards the huge hole created by the explosion that occurred a few moments earlier. The pilots were the first to witness what was about to happen, which made one of them say, "We're heading for the Iranian metro with trains beneath us!"

President Berry raised her head slightly, holding a stern face, aware the Secretary of State was sobbing quietly. She said nothing. All she could do was patiently wait until Air Force One stopped and hope they would all live through what has become a nightmare of a visit to Iran.

The pilots of Air Force One could hear the sirens from the emergency services in the background hoping they will be able to help once the unavoidable has happened.

Airport personnel that were working in the tunnel were shouting frantically at people to move away from this area quickly knowing that Air Force One had landed above. Some looked back to see Air Force One starting to fall through the huge hole, which broke the wing that was on fire away from the main fuselage. The fuselage nosed dived, heading for the moving train below, hitting it with such velocity that a huge fireball erupted. It kept travelling through several carriages killing everybody instantly on board and standing on the platforms close by. Carriages derailed and lifted sliding on their side down the platform crashing into concrete pillars that cracked and started to crumble. Some people couldn't move because they were in shock. Others that wanted to live pulled them to safety before the runway above or the carriages from the metro train crushed them.

With the impact, President Berry was knocked out of her seat lying on the floor unconscious. General Gee, who was badly cut and bruised, struggled to stand up feeling concern about the welfare of President Berry's life. As he stood there about to crouch down to the U.S. President, another huge explosion occurred, which made part of the roof of the plane break up and fall on him, making him fall to the floor unconscious.

Sarah Johnson feeling distressed had already unfastened her seatbelt and tried to manoeuvre around the wreckage the best way she could to search for Raven.

When Air Force One had finally stopped after killing many Iranian people, Cairns gave the signal to Colonel Mihailov to send the soldiers in and collect people from the plane that were still alive. Aware that Raven was also on board, he said, "Let's go and view the devastation the American's have caused!"

President Modarres glanced at Cairns with the remark he had just made and then told the driver to continue to where the soldiers were now approaching. The driver, who couldn't believe what he had witnessed, started the engine to drive closer to the scene of devastation.

Huge flames rose from the tunnel below the runway, which created black smoke all around. When they arrived at the metro railway station, Cairns and President Modarres climbed out of their jeep and went down the steps trampling over dead bodies with allied enemy soldiers following. They pushed frightened people, who had survived, away from the catastrophe they had just witnessed, when all they wanted, was help.

Cairns and President Modarres saw Air Force One, and the train it had crashed into, in the distance. President Modarres looked around to first all the dead people, then the injured. He turned to look in despair at Air Force One and the Iranian train it had crashed with and the destruction caused by the instigator, Cairns. He closed his eyes wishing this had never happened and then re-opened them to look back at Cairns, seriously wondering if he had done the right thing in working alongside what seemed to be a dangerous man.

They walked cautiously to the wreckage of Air Force One that still had small fires burning around it, with Cairns saying, "This is the happiest day of my life."

Colonel Mihailov narrowed his eyes thinking about what world opinion would be when this atrocity is broadcasted through different sources of the media. Cairns told Colonel Mihailov to follow him and bring a group of soldiers to search the plane for the U.S. President, and more so John Raven. Dead or alive, he wanted them!

Cairns, Colonel Mihailov, and the allied enemy soldiers climbed up some rubble and scrambled into Air Force One to see the devastation they had created. Cairns scanned the plane with his eyes hoping to see President Berry and John Raven, and with this, told the soldiers to search the plane for anybody that may still be alive.

Cairns walked around the plane noticing bodyguards were unconscious or killed in the aftermath of the explosion. He grinned when he found President Berry lying on the floor. Looking down at her through his scraggy hair, he said, "Well, look at what we have here! Welcome to Iran Ma'am!"

He crouched down, immediately gripping her wrist to see if she still had a pulse. Realising that she had, he looked up to Colonel Mihailov and said, "She's still alive. Take her!"

Colonel Mihailov thinking back to what Cairns had been doing with Captain Weller in her cell asked, "Just another woman for you to rape eh?"

Cairns stood up choosing to ignore the Colonel's snide remark by saying, "Take her!"

Colonel Mihailov passed a frail President Berry to his soldiers, telling them to take her back to their military vehicles. As she was being taken, she at times would open her weary eyes taking notice of the devastation all around. She stopped moving, which made the enemy soldier holding her shout, "Move it bitch!"

With being spoken to in such a way, she turned staring at the soldier who had no respect for her. He glared at her, shouting, "Move!"

President Berry briefly turned around to look at the damage Air Force One and the remains of the train had created, where a tear started to roll down her cheek. With not moving the enemy soldier hit her hard in the face, making her fall to the floor. She cried, with not wanting to go through more torture. The enemy soldier asked one of his colleagues to help him pick her up. They dragged her up, with one of them saying, "Walk lady or die!"

She didn't hesitate in walking with them, deciding to look back at Air Force One again hoping that John Raven survived and would help her to escape from what had become her worst nightmare.

Inside Air Force One, Cairns kept searching for more people, eventually finding a badly wounded General Gee lying unconscious, which made him grab him by the neck and pick him up. A weak General Gee opened his eyes to see a blurred vision of Cairns standing in front of him. Cairns asked, "Remember me?"

General Gee didn't have the strength to reply to Cairns' question, feeling weak he closed his eyes again. Colonel Mihailov watched Cairns' actions closely and wasn't impressed when he brought out his gun to shoot him in the head. Cairns let go of Gee, watching him fall to the floor and said, "The same action will apply to Raven when I find him!"

One of the enemy soldiers brought the co-pilot to Cairns asking, "What have I to do with him?"

Cairns brought his gun out again and replied, "He isn't needed!"

He aimed the gun at the co-pilot shooting him twice in the heart, killing him instantly. The soldier let go of him and watched him fall to the floor. Cairns asked the soldier, "Where is the Captain?"

The soldier replied, "He's dead from the impact with the train."

Cairns laughed, saying, "Good! Now search the plane and find John Raven and bring him to me."

The soldiers carried out Cairns' instructions with him also walking casually around the wreckage hoping to find John Raven himself.

Sarah Johnson was also looking for Raven, and kept calling his name quietly in anticipation, "John! John Raven!"

John heard her, watching her wide eyed. He waited for her to come closer so he could place his arm out and put his hand over her mouth and drag her to where he had been hiding. He said, "Don't talk!"

She saw that he was armed with weapons and was going to fight for his country. After Raven had taken his hand away from her mouth, feeling concerned for her own life, she couldn't resist from asking, "What do we do?"

Raven replied, "Stay with me!"

Sarah, feeling scared and apprehensive, looked down the plane, and then back at Raven asking, "What about President Berry?"

Raven stared at her, replying, "If she isn't already dead, I'll get her out!"

Sarah, feeling a sense of relief after hearing those words, moved a little closer to John, noticing that he had a bad cut on his chest. Concerned for him, she said, "This cut looks deep."

John looked down at the blood starting to soak through his t-shirt, and then at Sarah, replying, "It's just shrapnel from the impact of Air Force One and the train."

Sarah said, "Let me have a look."

Raven refused, replying, "I don't have the time right now, but I'm trained to survive!"

Russian and Iranian soldiers heard voices, which made them shout back to Cairns. He ran over shouting, "You there!"

Sarah, feeling despondent looked at Raven, who couldn't yet be seen, and asked in a low voice, "I'm about to be captured, will you get me out and take me home?"

Raven didn't answer Sarah; he nodded his head once agreeing with her. How he wasn't sure.

The soldiers came closer to her, grabbing her arms to take her hostage. They turned around to take her back to Cairns approaching, wanting to see who this person alive was. Raven showed himself, immediately starting to shoot at the soldiers holding Sarah, killing them instantly. Sarah dived to the floor for cover. More enemy soldiers came to retaliate, which Raven fired at and killed. Cairns had been taken by surprise. He used his gun, starting to fire bullets. Raven hid to take cover, knowing that he would probably be bombarded with gunfire from many allied enemy soldiers. Cairns muttered, "You lot! Kill him!"

He turned to Colonel Mihailov, saying, "Go and bring the Secretary of State to me."

Colonel Mihailov relayed the order to the soldiers, and watched them go to collect the Secretary of State, Sarah Johnson, who was lying frightened on the floor. Other soldiers kept firing, which stopped Raven from revealing himself again. One of the soldiers grabbed Sarah Johnson by the arm and pulled her up. Cairns walked across to Sarah Johnson staring at her wide eyed in her face. Before speaking with her, he asked the soldiers in a stern voice, "Have you found him? If you haven't, keep on searching!"

Two soldiers held Sarah Johnson by her arms with a tight grip. Cairns asked, "Who were you speaking with?"

Sarah Johnson replied with a little impudence, "To the man you most fear!"

Cairns produced a stern face, took a couple of more paces forward to her and slapped her face hard replying, "I fear no man alive!"

Looking at the Secretary of State with hatred in his eyes, he said in a stern voice, "Take her, and place her with Berry!"

Sarah closed her eyes feeling relief, now knowing that Susan was still alive. Cairns stood there shouting, "Raven! Can you hear me?"

Soldiers were searching as Raven started to use his homemade knife to perform silent elite kills one by one. Cairns shouted again, "Raven!"

There was no answer, which made Cairns say, "Let's blow the plane and him up with it!"

Raven, watching, glared wide-eyed with hearing about the remains of Air Force One being blown up with him still on it. He waited for Cairns to turn and leave with the enemy allied soldiers and started to hurry down the lower decks to the rear part of the plane, hoping to escape.

Cairns started running with the soldiers and climbed out of Air Force One to stand next to President Modarres again. Noticing that Cairns had taken the pin out of a hand grenade, President Modarres asked, "Did you find John Raven?"

Cairns looked at President Modarres in disgust as he raised his arm to throw the hand grenade into the plane, which he repeated several times. President Modarres looked with concern. Knowing they hadn't too much time, they quickly moved by running to make their way out of the tunnel before the huge explosion occurred.

Raven ran as fast as he could knowing there was about to be a massive explosion. His aim was to reach the cargo bay. He didn't make it there, with the first hand grenade exploding, which blew the side of the plane out creating a huge fire. He saw the damage, realising it was a way out for him. He turned back, when another hand grenade exploded. He placed his arms to his face, as he kept running by the inferno. More explosions were heard, but undeterred; Raven kept running for the opening for his life, wanting to leap out as the plane erupted from larger explosions. He landed on to the buckled railway line with his back on fire. He rolled around on the railway lines to smother the flames and then cowered from all the remaining shrapnel flying around from the plane. Another huge fire was burning on the train and Air Force One, which would now make them become a burnt out shell.

Cairns arrived outside and heard the explosions, which brought an evil grin to his face. Remembering President Modarres's question he had asked earlier, he replied, "I've sent Raven to hell!"

President Berry, who was now conscious and sitting next to Sarah Johnson, wanted to believe that John Raven was still alive as she glimpsed at Sarah, where they both said nothing. All they could do has they travelled with Cairns, was watch the hostile Iranian people they passed, laugh and jeer at her and sadly see the American flag burn once more.

Raven, who was still in the underground tunnel, crawled along the buckled railway line to the badly damaged platform? He placed his hand on the platform to pull himself up slowly, and then stand alone on what was once a busy station. Looking badly burnt, with blood dripping from a serious wound, he stood there holding his knife handle tightly, annoyed at the devastation Cairns had created, and he had just escaped from. With smoke rising from the devastation he had become involved in, he now knew for sure he was involved in yet another warzone.

Patriotism

Standing alone on the platform, Raven moved his head slowly looking hard at the devastation Cairns was to blame for and had now created. He looked back at the burnt-out wreckage of the train and Air Force One; giving a solemn look to the Iranian people he saw killed lying on the ground. He could hear the emergency services with people making their way down to the platform wanting to see the disaster for themselves for the first time. Not wanting to be seen, he decided to move, climbing over some rubble. He heard shouting outside, becoming aware there wouldn't be much time to escape from something he would probably be blamed for. Deciding to keep moving, he climbed into one of the carriages blocking part of the platform, looking at some of the Iranian people that sadly had their lives taken away from them. At first he chose to ignore it, focusing on what he had to do, but when he saw the injured innocent Iranian people that were placing their arms out to him for help, he stopped in his stride. Aware the emergency services were not too far behind; he looked back, then at a girl crying. Noticing the young girl was frightened, he let the adrenalin flowing through his body subside making the warrior mode disappear, and become the loving father once more by looking down sincere at the young girl. She looked up to Raven's huge presence feeling scared. John's eyes were wide open as he crouched down to her feeling concern about her safety. Deciding to move rubble away from her, he asked, "Does your leg hurt?"

The girl feeling apprehensive about Raven's presence just stared, choosing not to reply. Raven looked back and could see that several emergency people were now in the tunnel searching for survivors. He stopped moving the rubble for a few seconds aware that these people would find this young girl. He glimpsed back at her feeling as though it didn't feel right to have to leave her. He started to move more rubble from her leg and saw that she had a badly sprained ankle. Knowing the Iranian authorities were close by, he placed his finger to his lips to say hush to the girl. She watched closely as he picked her up and started walking with her. The young girl looked behind as Raven walked forward. She spotted her mother lying on the floor, which made her say, "Mum."

Raven stopped and could hear an Iranian woman lying down on the floor sobbing her heart out. John frowned, feeling sorry for the lady and said, "Ma'am."

She didn't respond at first, which made John say once more in a solemn voice, "Ma'am."

She slowly lifted her head and saw the intimidating presence of Raven standing there holding a young girl in his arms. Realising that it was her daughter, she stood up and placed her hands up in the air, starting to shout aloud, "Delroba, Delroba!"

John watched her, asking, "Is this girl your daughter?"

The ecstatic lady crying tears of joy that her daughter was still alive replied, "Yes, yes."

She then looked up to her daughter asking John, "Will you give her to me?"

John replied, "We have to keep moving."

The lady repeated herself by saying, "Please, give her to me."

John looked at the young girl and in a calm voice, asked her, "Is this person your Mum?"

Delroba grinned at John, nodding her head yes. He graciously handed her to her mother, where she immediately closed her eyes wanting to give her daughter a loving hug feeling grateful that she was still alive. When she opened them, she saw John looking down on them, where she wiped her eyes, saying, "Thank you."

John looked back, after hearing voices, suspecting it could be from the Iranian emergency services with some of the allied enemy soldiers Cairns had left behind. Aware of the woman's gratitude, John nodded his head once agreeing with her. She walked forward carrying her daughter towards John and placed her hand onto his wound. John moved his head slowly and watched as she said, "You're bleeding badly, come with me."

John placed his hand out, wanting to carry the young girl and started walking with her, feeling anguish at witnessing the deaths of so many innocent people that had been standing on this platform. Bloodstains were all around that made him produce a casual blink, thinking only of Cairns, as he walked well away from the atrocity they had witnessed towards another exit. John and Delroba's mother briefly spoke about what had happened in the tunnel. Delroba, who was also listening to the conversation while resting her head on John's shoulder asked, "What's your name?"

Still walking beside her mother, he replied, "John."

Delroba lifted her head from John's shoulder to say, "You look sore John."

John moved his eyes, looking at her, but soon softened the stare replying, "I'm trying not to think about it."

Delroba's mother placed her hand out to hold John's arm, which made him stop walking. He looked down at her concerned, listening to her say, "You're losing blood. I need to help you, as soon as I can."

John could already feel the blood running down his chest, which made his t-shirt become soaked in blood. Knowing this, he glimpsed down at his t-shirt at the blood, and slowly shook his head from side to side replying, "There isn't time."

John turned from Delroba's mother and started walking once more, making her watch and become concerned for his life. John was aware Delroba's mother wasn't following and decided to ask Delroba, "What's your mother's name?"

Delroba moved her head, looking back with concern, shouting, "Mum."

John asked again, "What's your mother's name?"

Delroba looked at him, taking notice of the scars on his face replying, "Farrin."

John stopped, shouting in a stern voice, "Farrin!"

She looked, in the distance, at a warrior, with his headband resting onto his shoulder. Noticing his menacing stare, she decided to walk up to him and listen to him say, "We keep moving!"

Farrin asked, "What about the serious wound you have?"

Still walking, John looked straight ahead focusing on what he had to do, replying, "No pain!"

In the distance, there were steps leading them to the outside world. They made their way starting to climb up them noticing large groups of Iranian people shouting at the television when they saw reporters talking about the disaster they had just walked away from. Raven scanned the area with his menacing eyes, feeling vulnerable with being an American. Starting to feel intimidated, but not wanting any trouble, he walked on by with the Iranian people not questioning him with holding Delroba.

Farrin's husband had heard the news that Air Force One had been involved in a terrorist attack and rushed to the next nearest metro rail station to where the disaster had occurred. He saw Farrin walking with Raven and shouted, "Farrin!"

Farrin stopped walking, which made Raven look with concern. With hearing her father's voice, Delroba placed her head up, shouting, "Daddy."

Afshin rushed over frowning at the intimidating presence Raven had. He kissed his wife, while noticing Delroba was still in Raven's arms. He asked in a sharp way, "Who is this man?"

John put Delroba down gently, ignoring Afshin's question put to his wife and said, "She has a badly sprained ankle."

Noticing how much blood was on John's clothes, and then recalling his headband from pictures he had previously seen while looking at his burnt face, Afshin said, "I know you!"

John just stood there in silence, narrowing his eyes slightly. Afshin turned to his wife and said, "He's American! He's the man we've been burning when our president and his accomplice promised us that we will destroy America."

Listening to Afshin speak, John chose to remain silent, just moving his eyes slightly at the man who kept talking to his wife about Raven. Emergency services hurtled passed with sirens blurring, heading for the disaster at the airport, which made Raven look and then say, "I don't have much time."

Afshin stopped talking to his wife to look in dismay at Raven asking, "Don't have much time for what?"

Feeling hatred for Cairns and wanting Iran to respect the United States and its people for what it is, he replied, "To put things right!"

Afshin turned wide-eyed, staring at his wife, where she said, "Afshin! He saved our daughter's life, and has helped me."

Afshin went quiet and turned back to look at Raven, who was just watching every move he was making. Convinced Raven was the enemy, he bawled, "This man is an American and would not choose to help an Iranian person!"

Inwardly, John felt saddened at what the human race had become. Farrin screamed, "We're going to help him!"

Her loud voice made passers-by look and take notice of them all as a group that had been involved in the disaster being reported. Aware of this John said, "I have to go."

Farrin turned, glimpsing once more at John's t-shirt dripping in blood and said to her husband, "He comes with us!"

Hearing his wife speak like this, Afshin knocked Delroba to the floor, which made her start to cry and hold her ankle. Not bothered about Delroba, he slapped his wife hard in the face, which made John move and say, "Hey, hey, hey!"

John lunged forward, grabbing Afshin by his gown and pulled him away from Farrin using a strong voice saying, "There is good and bad in every nation!"

Delroba, looked up crying and said, "Mum."

Farrin held John's arm tenderly, saying, "Please."

John broke his stare with Afshin, by looking to his side at Farrin, while releasing his grip on his gown. Afshin asked in an arrogant way, "What are you, good or bad?"

As he turned his head slowly away from Farrin, he thought back to the previous times he had been asked the same question. Facing Afshin with a stern look showing on his face, he replied, "Somewhere in the middle!"

Afshin said to his wife, "See, see, just like any other American!"

Still glaring at Afshin, Raven using a stern voice, replied, "I'm not like any other American!"

He bent down to pick up Delroba, which made Afshin say, "Leave my daughter alone!"

Raven was getting tired of the bickering and replied, "Why don't you live up to what your name actually means, General, and let me do what I have to do by putting things right for both our nations!"

Afshin became stunned at Raven, with him knowing what his name stood for. Farrin walked by him to climb into their old van, which made Raven, who was now carrying Delroba in his arms follow. Afshin watched and could only visualise pictures of Raven burning and found it hard to see his wife walking with the same man holding his child.

Farrin opened the doors at the back of the van for Raven to climb into. He placed Delroba down noticing a black strap. He picked it up, looking at it closely noticing how the handle had been shaped for a hand to have a good grip. He turned, watching Afshin walk to the van, and then looked at the width of the strap, glaring at the brass stud at the top. He asked Farrin, "Does he beat you with this?"

She opened part of her gown showing red marks from what the stud had made on her skin, which made Raven while gritting his teeth roll the strap up and grip it tightly.

Farrin moved her gown back while saying, "Please get inside the van."

John climbed inside, sitting opposite Delroba, looking at her wondering if Afshin does the same thing to her. Afshin pulled the driver's door, sliding it open, still deciding to have a few words with Farrin about this situation, he wasn't happy with. Farrin didn't want to sit next to Afshin at the front of the van. She chose to climb into the back and sit next to her daughter. She noticed again how badly soaked John's t-shirt had become and leaned forward, which made Afshin turn and stare before starting the engine. John, suspecting how cruel he must be to his wife and possibly his daughter, said in a stern voice, "Drive!"

Afshin feeling a little humiliated turned, starting to drive. Farrin looked into John's eyes and said, "Thank you."

Afshin turned his head slightly, which made John notice and watch him look back to concentrate on his driving. Raven placed his hand on to his chest filling it with his own blood. He took his hand away and opened it to reveal his hand was covered in blood. Farrin knowing the wound was serious tore some of her gown, which made Afshin, look back once more to see what his wife was now doing. Seeing Raven's eyes staring back at him, made him look back, say nothing and carry on driving.

Delroba watching, asked, "What are you doing Mum?"

Farrin replied, "Hush little girl."

Farrin, feeling concerned about the wound, asked John to lift his t-shirt up. Reluctantly, John did as he was asked by lifting his t-shirt up, displaying his masculine chest that had a deep cut about five inches long. The blood pouring out was dark red, which made Farrin look at him in the eyes with concern. She placed part of her gown; she had torn on to the wound and wrapped it around his huge muscular frame. With the gown being white, it didn't take long for the blood to begin seeping through. Farrin noticed this and wrapped it around his body again, pulling it tight, which made John grunt in pain. Farrin moved her eyes and saw the face of pain in front of her and said, "It isn't perfect, but it may clot the wound again."

John opened his eyes, nodded his head once agreeing, and then slowly pulled his blood-stained t-shirt down while holding his hand on the wound hoping that it would start to clot.

Afshin, who was in front driving, put the radio on and could hear shouting and jeering from what was presumably a hostile Iranian crowd. Cairns came onto the radio saying, "Today we have the President of the United States and one of her influential colleagues."

Afshin laughed out aloud, which made John stare at him. He then listened to President Modarres say, "With the help of my good friend, James Cairns, soon the United States will be annihilated!"

Afshin took his hands-off the steering wheel and clapped a couple of times in excitement. Raven glared, as he watched him place them straight back onto the steering wheel, so he wouldn't lose control. Raven looked down feeling disappointed. With his head still lowered, he listened to Cairns on the radio carry on saying, "If we survive their onslaught, because let's not forget we now have the President of the United States. I doubt no American person will want to kill their own President, unless you're me!"

He laughed a little and carried on saying, "Kuwait will be ours for the taking, and then it will be a whole new world."

The crowd cheered, shouting for Cairns and President Modarres knowing that they could with the help of Russia bring a superpower down to its knees. American flags were set alight once more, which brought a wry smile to Cairns' face. Placing his hand up responding to the Iranian crowd, Cairns said to President Modarres, "All you had to do was place just a little trust in me, and the rewards would be huge."

He turned away from the crowd, carrying onto say to the Iranian President in private, "You doubted me."

Afshin, still driving the van laughed again and said, "Soon Farrin, it will be a whole new world, when we will not be dictated to anymore by super powers trying to police the world."

Farrin watched John place his head in his hands in disgust and then pacified Afshin by saying, "Yes Afshin."

Feeling as though he had heard enough, John took his hands away from his face and said, "Stop the van Afshin!"

Afshin slowed down bringing the van to a stop and turned to face all the people in the back. John stood up saying, "I have to go and finish this my own way. I can't do this listening to your husband who is totally against the U.S. and is united with somebody that wants to help bring the United States to her knees!"

He opened the back doors, saying to Delroba, "You take care."

Farrin climbed out of the van, shouting, "John."

John turned back around to face Farrin, noticing Afshin clasp his hands together showing John that he wanted his strap back that he had rolled up and was still holding. John ignored Afshin, deciding to give a sincere look to Delroba and then Farrin. He paused for a few seconds thinking about the human race and decided to say, "It's time to go after the bad!"

Farrin held his arm tenderly, asking, "Does this make you good?"

John moved her hand away from his arm and slowly walked away holding Afshin's strap and replied, "Only you know for sure."

Starting to walk further away, Farrin shouted, "John!"

John turned around to face Farrin where the breeze of the air blew his hair back. She gazed at him shouting, "Thank you."

John closed his eyes and nodded his head once agreeing, and then watched Farrin climb back into the van. He raised his arm to look at the strap, and then back at Farrin where he said in a low voice, "Take care Farrin. You take care."

After watching the van drive away, he turned around walking in the opposite direction thinking what his next move would now be in this new war he had now become involved in.

One Man Alone

John walked down the road showing a face of anger. He felt personally responsible for President Berry and would try to do anything to prevent her from being killed. He glanced at the traffic passing by him, occasionally placing his thumb up for a lift. The Iranian people would look back at him and laugh when they realised he was an American. Watching vehicles pass him, made him start to think back to the promise, he had made to the Secretary of State, Sarah Johnson, when he told her he would get her home. He closed his eyes for a few seconds, listening to obscene messages shouted from people in cars. Containing the anger inwardly, John reopened his eyes gripping the strap tightly he had taken from Afshin's van. Glancing at the sky visualising the late Colonel Lewis, he said in a low voice, "What would you have done in my position?"

He felt a shiver go through his body, when he knew he had to improvise. In the far distance, he saw what he suspected as large military vehicles travelling, presumably to where Cairns now had Captain Weller, President Berry and Sarah Johnson. He stopped walking, deciding to turn and look at the oncoming traffic travelling in his direction. He gripped the strap tightly, almost creating a fist, knowing he had to do something extreme to carry on with what had now become his personal war with Iran. In frustration, he glared at the traffic driving in the opposite direction, and then immediately back to the traffic travelling in front of him. In the distance, he saw a group of Iranians on motorbikes, which made him slowly unwind the strap he was holding. As they approached at speed, Raven placed the strap into his right hand and pulled back his arm to throw it at one of the rider's wheels. The rider's, aware something sinister was about to occur, tried to manoeuvre from the strap Raven had thrown at their motorbikes. It went into the front wheel of one of the motorbikes, causing the rider to lose control and crash to the floor, where he kept rolling with the motorbike following him. Cars on the opposite side of the road would steer away changing direction trying not to hit the biker and cause serious harm to him.

With the three bikers witnessing what happened to one of their friends, they stopped, placed their visors up while staring at Raven, who was making his way to the motorbike now lying on the road. Feeling angry that their friend could be injured, or even killed, they decided Raven should now pay for his actions. The entire rider's placed their motorbikes onto their stands and climbed off leaving their helmets on their seats and walked over to Raven, who was rushing to take the damaged motorbike lying in the middle of the road. Raven, sensing more trouble was about to occur, placed his hand tightly on his knife handle. He passed the rider's with one of them asking in an arrogant voice, "You! What are you doing?"

Raven moved his eyes focusing on all the bikers, knowing that if he had to, he could kill them all. Holding a stern face, he passed them by, choosing to say nothing, which made one of the bikers say, "Let's kill this American piece of trash!"

Raven sensed that they were briskly coming up behind him to attack him. He pulled out his knife, holding it tightly, but not wanting to use it, but would if needed, defend himself. One of the bikers pointed at him, which made Raven say in a stern voice, "Live to see another day!"

The three bikers laughed in disgust, as they clenched their fists, wanting to make Raven suffer for what he had done to one of their friends who was still lying injured in the road. They approached Raven aggressively, where he used his knife by slicing one of them on the chest, drawing blood instantly. The other two paused, glancing at the wound Raven had just created. Raven again said, "Choose to live or choose to die!"

They looked at one another, starting to have second thoughts. Raven said in a stern voice, "Go home!"

Realising the bikers was getting the message; he turned around while still holding his knife and walked to the damaged motorbike. One of the bikers said, "That guy has serious issues!"

Another biker standing next to him, asked, "Do you think he would have killed us?"

They watched Raven put his knife away into his holster, which made one of them reply, "No! Who is that guy anyway?"

One of the bikers brought from his pocket a folded piece of paper. Slowly, he unfolded it, showing a picture of John Raven, which he recalled burning a few days ago, when Cairns had set a huge picture of him on fire. The bikers now aware of whom he was after seeing that picture, and then seeing Raven climb on the motorbike, made one of them say, "This guy is on a suicide mission!"

The others stood next to him watching Raven ride into the distance saying, "We have to tell President Modarres of what has happened or else the new future we're living for will never happen."

Concerned for their friend lying injured on the floor, one of them asked, "What about him?"

They agreed among themselves that one of them should stay with him and wait for the ambulance to arrive. The other two bikers decided to travel, wanting to tell President Modarres of what just happened, and who it involved.

Raven was riding fast on a sports motorbike with his hair blowing back from the draught of the wind. He was one man with one mission, seeking one purpose. He weaved in and out of traffic causing them to beep their horn and wave their fists at him. Thinking about what he had to do, he said in a strong voice, "Fuck off!"

In the far distance, just as before, but much clearer, he saw military vehicles transporting tanks, but the one that became of concern, was the one carrying nuclear missiles. Travelling at a speed, he knew he had to chase these military vehicles, hoping they would lead him to where Cairns would now be staying.

The traffic lights changed to red making Raven brake and screech to a halt. Iranian police sitting in a police car at the traffic lights changing to green saw Raven not wearing a crash helmet and noted his erratic riding. His appearance didn't go unnoticed either, especially with bloodstains being on his t-shirt. They noticed the damaged motorbike, which made one of the Iranian police officers say without any hesitation, "Let's pull him!"

They put on the siren and flashing lights, which made Raven look sharply across at them. Sensing they were going to stop him, he glimpsed at the traffic coming the other way, and then stared with his menacing eyes, at the military vehicles disappearing into the distance. He turned the throttle with his hand revving the engine several times. He edged the motorbike out, while the lights were still showing red. The Iranian police stopped in the middle-of-the-road deciding to block all the traffic with just one intention, to speak with John Raven. Aware of this, Raven revved the engine as he watched the police climbing out of their car. People shouted at the police for parking their car in a hideous position. Some stared at Raven suspecting that he was trouble waiting to happen. Approaching John, he revved the engine again and started to move and weave through the traffic. One of the police officers brought out his batten and beat his arm once knowing he was about to escape from him. The police officer rushed back to his car, and radioed for immediate backup, reporting the registration plate of the motorbike John was now riding.

John sped down the road listening to the siren of the police car behind him. He glanced behind at them and opened the throttle more to go even faster.

The police chasing him were frantic and radioed for more backup immediately while watching him pull further away from them. Raven went through traffic signals that were showing red to escape the police. Innocent Iranian people driving in traffic became aware the police were following with a large presence, wisely chose to wait until they too had passed by. Blurring sirens could be heard, which made Raven look back quickly at the police, noticing several police cars were now chasing him. He gritted his teeth, pulled his hand forward on the throttle to slow down and placed his hand into his pocket on the side of his trouser leg and brought out one hand grenade. Aware the police were now catching up with him; he placed the grenade to his mouth, pulled out the pin using his teeth and slowed the motorbike right down creating a skid. He stared at the oncoming police, waiting a few more seconds before throwing the hand grenade through the air at the Iranian police. When it hit the ground, a huge explosion occurred causing several police cars to crash into one another. Raven wasn't sure whether he had killed anybody; he had to remain focused in what he had to do. He carried on speeding to catch up with the enemy travelling in front of him, and then noticed in the sky, two U.S. helicopters flying in the same direction as the military vehicles. Lee Seager, who was piloting one of the U.S. helicopters with Luke Tyler, noticed the biker riding erratically, in the distance. Watching the headband blow into the breeze, Seager shouted to Colonel Wareing, "Sir. Look at this."

Colonel Wareing stood up and went to stand at the edge of the opened door, looking down at the biker riding erratically. When he saw the headband blowing in the breeze, he said, "Christ!"

Hearing the Colonel blaspheme made other members of Unit Expendable move to see what had taken the Colonel's eye. Sarah Jane saw the biker, immediately realising that it was her father. Feeling proud, she watched him riding the motorbike, where nothing and nobody was going to be able to stop him from achieving his main objective. Sarah Jane looked to her left at the Colonel, when he could only say, "One man alone on a mission."

He placed his hand onto Sarah Jane's shoulder and went back to take his seat, leaving her to look down at her father hoping that this time, it wouldn't be one time too many.

Pre-Warning

$\mathcal{T}$ he two bikers decided to travel to President Modarres military base wanting to tell him and Cairns that Raven had taken one of their friend's motorbikes and was heading in his direction. Cairns laughed, but stopped when one of the bikers showed President Modarres a picture of Raven, confirming that he was the man. Cairns took the picture and looked at it holding a stern face. Slowly, he looked back at the bikers while starting to tear the picture of Raven, saying to the bikers, "Thank you for your loyalty. This will be dealt with immediately won't it Colonel Mihailov?"

President Modarres watched Cairns closely, and then turned to see what Colonel Mihailov's reaction would be. He picked up the phone giving the order for all his soldiers to be on red alert. Cairns, and the bikers watched in anticipation, which made Cairns say to them, "You can go now."

Colonel Mihailov was still on the phone when Cairns said, "You do not kill Raven because this will be my task and my task alone!"

Colonel Mihailov, still speaking on the phone to some of his soldiers repeated what Cairns had just told him, but became concerned when the Russian soldiers in the Iranian control centre detected two U.S. helicopters approaching their military headquarters. He thanked the operator for the information and held the phone to his chest, so he could pass the same information onto President Modarres and Cairns.

With concern, he said, "The U.S. is sending two military helicopters, presumably to attack us!"

Cairns stared at Colonel Mihailov replying, "Are they now."

Cairns turned away gathering his thoughts, which made President Modarres become slightly worried and ask, "What are we to do James?"

Cairns turned around to face President Modarres, replying, "If it hadn't been for those two bikers, we could have been taken by surprise! We now know what is about to happen, so I think we should surprise the American's with an attack of our own. Let's make it like dogs chasing cars with no mercy involved!"

President Modarres watched Cairns closely with what he was about to order. Cairns, feeling angry paused looking at the floor thinking about John Raven. Still thinking about Raven, he raised his head saying, "Launch a couple of Russian Mig fighter planes to blow the U.S. helicopters out of the sky."

President Modarres frowned slightly at the thought; he could do this to his own people. Colonel Mihailov looked at President Modarres for reassurance, and watched him nod his head agreeing. Colonel Mihailov placed the phone back to his ear ordering for the launch of a squadron of Russian Mig's to attack the U.S. helicopters immediately. Cairns lowered his head again thinking only of Raven.

Cairns produced an evil grin while saying, "They're about to send the cavalry in order to try to save their President. How touching! I think we should go and break this exciting news to her!"

President Modarres laughed, replying, "I will come with you."

They walked past Colonel Mihailov, when Cairns stopped, saying to the Colonel, "You make sure all the soldiers are ready for Raven's arrival."

Colonel Mihailov replied by asking a question, "This man Raven, is only one man, are you scared of him?"

Cairns took a few paces forwards towards him replying, "I'm scared of nobody! Just be ready, because I can assure you he will be a loose cannon when he has to be, making him the ultimate opponent for somebody that wants a challenge!"

Colonel Mihailov listened hard, and then asked Cairns, "Will this be your challenge?"

Cairns produced an evil grin visualising how he would kill John Raven, replying; "Now you're beginning to see things my way."

He turned to look at President Modarres and said, "Let's go and pay President Berry a visit. Like Weller, she should have had a nice welcome reception by now."

They walked out of the office, starting to make their way to the cells where the U.S. prisoners were being held. The Iranian guards saw the influential people coming in their direction, and stood to attention as they passed by. With the news, the U.S. was sending in soldiers to try and rescue President Berry, made Cairns clench his fist in anger, which made the adrenalin flow through his body much more rapidly.

Arriving at the cell where the American women were being held, the guard placed the key into the large wooden door, which made all the women turn feeling apprehensive about who was entering their cell. The Iranian guard took the keys out of the lock and opened the door to let President Modarres and Cairns walk inside. Cairns looked at all the women, relishing the thought of being able to rape Weller sometime soon. Turning away from her, he looked down at President Berry sitting on the floor feeling frightened, and scared for her life. With knowing Raven was coming, he walked over and kicked her hard on her thigh in frustration. Captain Weller watched her scream, fighting back the tears and shouted in anguish, "That is the President of the United States you have just abused!"

Cairns took a deep breath, turned to President Modarres asking, "Did I ask for her opinion?"

President Modarres turned around to look at Captain Weller sitting on the dirty floor and replied, "No! I can't say you did."

Cairns held his head high, nodding it agreeing, while replying, "I thought not."

He briskly walked across to where Captain Weller was now sat and bent down placing his face in hers. Feeling scared that he was going to touch her again; she clasped her hands to her clothes tightly and kept her head low, so she didn't need to look at Cairns' evil face. Cairns gripped her hair, pulling it tightly, which made Captain Weller have to look up at him. Using an evil tone he said, "You speak when you're spoken to, whore!"

Captain Weller's face started to change to a face of anger when she heard the word whore being called at her. It brought back memories from when she had a conflict with the terrorist, they called 'the blade' when he too had told her that her kids had come from a whore. In her defence she glared at Cairns replying, "I'm no fucking whore!"

Cairns laughed out aloud while turning to President Modarres saying, "This one can be a feisty bitch when she wants to be!"

President Berry and Sarah Johnson watched Cairns feeling scared at what he might do to them next.

Cairns threw her head back hard, grinning after it had hit the stone wall causing her forehead to bleed ferociously. Susan, sitting there feeling scared chose to say nothing. She had been through something similar before learning that it's always wise to remain quiet in these situations, but it didn't stop her from becoming sad and concerned with what she was now witnessing for herself.

Sarah Johnson watched feeling anxiety after having a traumatic time in a similar situation, when she had been held captive with Richard Gerrard in Iraq. This resulted in John Raven rescuing her after he found out that John Weller-Raven, which was always the primary reason for having to come back to war, was his son and his own blood.

Cairns turned around laughing, while Captain Weller held her head after the bang she had just received. Sarah asked, "Look inside yourself Cairns. You have the blood of an American, remember who you really are."

Listening to the Secretary of State speak made Cairns produce a prolonged blink and look at her with a face of disgust. Feeling anger rush through his body he shouted, "The person I once was will be never again, especially with her sat there and Raven, who had me arrested for espionage I performed in Kuwait. I had everything planned and they took everything away from me, my family, my pension, my job, everything!"

He turned in temper to walk over to Captain Weller and kicked her twice on her thigh with his steel toe capped boots, which made her scream in pain and start to hold her thigh. He gripped her hair tightly again, while saying, "Tell them that it was your fault, I'm in this position today. Tell them!"

Susan looked across at Debbie feeling concern for her safety, and then gave a stern look at Cairns, where she couldn't refrain from having to say, "You performed the highest acts of treason knowing what you were doing was wrong! You have nobody to blame except yourself. Captain Weller and John Raven performed their duties correctly, which you're annoyed with because your plan didn't work! The U.S. can do without soldiers like you because we have soldiers like John Raven, who will fight for their country and give their lives if they have to do so to carry out what is right. You're in the wrong Cairns, then and now with what you're conspiring with Iran!"

Cairns stared hard after listening to the outburst performed by President Berry. Feeling anger, he moved his cheekbone staring at Captain Weller deciding to throw her to the ground again after listening to some home truths being mentioned from the U.S. President. He walked over to President Berry, with President Modarres immediately saying, "Take it easy James!"

He stared at her hard and said, "Stand up!"

Susan stood up straight away to help prevent Cairns from dragging her up by her hair, which she had previously suffered from with Azar Sajadi and General Kwan after being held captive in North Korea. She looked into Cairns' eyes saying, "You haven't got the guts to see this through!"

President Modarres moved his head slowly admiring President Berry's bravery. He then watched what Cairns' reaction would be, as he just stood there still, looking back at President Berry, nodding his head agreeing to disagree. He turned around to walk a short distance away from her and lashed out his hand giving her a backhanded slap across her face, which knocked her to the ground. Captain Weller couldn't believe what she had just seen, which made her say, "John Raven will destroy you!"

Cairns nodded his head agreeing again feeling angry with the thought of John Raven's name being mentioned. He shouted for the guards standing outside to bring the oil and acid into the cell. Holding both substances, they rushed into the cell awaiting further instructions. Cairns said, "Grab her sat there and rip off her blouse!"

Sarah Johnson feeling apprehensive glimpsed at President Berry stroking her face, feeling concern for Debbie, fearing the same thing happening to them. After placing the acid and oil down onto the ground the Iranian soldiers grabbed Captain Weller and pulled her up, where she tried to fight, but the soldiers were too strong for her. They tore off her blouse, making her weep and cross her arms over her breasts that were now hanging out of her bra. Cairns watched, laughed, and then took a sneaky stare at President Berry and Sarah Johnson to see what they were doing. President Berry had her head held low feeling despair for Captain Weller. Sarah Johnson had a sad face, and couldn't refrain from saying, "You're a coward Cairns!"

Cairns watched the soldiers hold Captain Weller with her arms and legs stretched out. She struggled to break free as they ogled her beautiful body. Cairns laughed while deciding to walk over to Captain Weller, giving an evil glare to Sarah Johnson, after hearing what she had called him. Watching

Captain Weller wriggle, he said, "You look good! Maybe I should see some more of you!"

With his smile disappearing, he said in a stern voice, "Take off her trousers!"

President Berry squirmed at the possibility that Cairns was about to rape Captain Weller and said, "Don't do this!"

The Iranian soldiers stopped before taking Captain Weller's trousers off to watch Cairns turn his head slowly to his right feeling surprised at President Berry's outburst and ask, "Maybe I should rape you eh?"

The Iranian soldiers chuckled, speaking among themselves. Susan became wide-eyed and reminded Cairns that she was the President of the United States, which made him walk over to President Modarres, laugh, and repeat what she had just said, "She is the President of the United States."

President Modarres produced an evil grin at Cairns' actions. Cairns held his hand to his mouth appearing that he was in shock and horror mode. The Iranian soldiers grinned once more while still holding Captain Weller with a tight grip. Again he moved around the cell making his way back to Captain Weller, who was lying in a precarious position. Noticing the acid and the oil on the floor close by to him, he picked both bottles up and went to stand next to Captain Weller. Looking down at her, he said, "You have a beautiful body."

Captain Weller shouted in a strong voice, "Screw you!"

President Berry tightened her lips knowing what the result of her outburst would be. Cairns gave an evil stare at her and then at both soldiers one by one. In a stern voice he asked, "Why is she still wearing her trousers?"

The Iranian soldier holding Captain Weller's legs released his grip, which made Captain Weller kick out in defence at him. Cairns looked back at President Modarres while unscrewing the top off the acid bottle and said, "She's a feisty bitch, this one! Maybe I should tame her!"

He threw the top of the bottle onto the ground as he watched her wriggle while the Iranian soldier undid her button on her trousers and tried to pull her zip down, almost breaking it. Aware that she was still wriggling and probably fighting to contain her dignity, Cairns held the bottle aloft and poured some of the acid onto her stomach, which made her scream and immediately stop wriggling. The soldier found it much easier to pull down her trousers, which the men couldn't resist but to look at her now just wearing her underwear. Captain Weller was in great pain and was giving up the will to fight on and live. Aware that she was about to be raped, she cried holding one thought, which was John Raven, and that he would free her from this callous cruel sadistic man.

President Berry remained sat there tight-lipped feeling helpless with Sarah Johnson, disgusted at the whole scenario about to occur. President Modarres watched, choosing not to interfere with Cairns' antics. Cairns knelt down, placed his hand onto Captain Weller's stomach close to where he had burned her skin. She cringed at the thought of him touching her, using her muscles to pull her stomach in. Cairns looked at her in the face noticing she had stopped crying and said, "Anybody would think that you don't like me."

Captain Weller replied, "No shit Sherlock!"

Cairns placed his hand on her leg feeling the texture of her skin as he looked into Captain Weller's eyes. Tears rolled down her cheeks as Cairns started slowly moving his hand up to her knickers, which made him reply, "There is still a little attitude there with your mouth, maybe I should fix that!"

With his other hand, he placed the bottle of oil to his mouth and screwed the top off with his teeth and spat it out onto the ground. He let go of the top of her leg and moved forward producing an evil face. He nodded to the soldier to hold her head, making her use her arms to defend herself. Cairns tutted twice as he poured oil onto her face and into her mouth, making her start to choke. Briefly, he stopped pouring the oil, moving his face into her face and said, "You're not ready for me yet, there's still a bit of fight left in you!"

Susan shook her head in total disbelief at Sarah Johnson after witnessing what Captain Weller was going through. She saw Colonel Mihailov walk into the cell, where he saw Cairns beside Captain Weller, almost undressed. He couldn't resist from looking at Captain Weller's body and then a little more sternly at Cairns. He said in a stern voice, "Cairns!"

Cairns turned around with his head held low, and moved his eyes to stare at Colonel Mihailov and shouted, "What!"

Colonel Mihailov had already faced one disagreement in the same cell when he thought now was not the time to have another one. President Modarres turned to listen to what the Russian Colonel had to say. Cairns became impatient saying, "What do you want? Can't you see I have this whore to rape?"

Captain Weller moved her head to one side to look away in despair from the enemy and then heard Colonel Mihailov say, "The American's are close!"

Cairns closed his eyes asking, "What's happening with the Russian Migs?"

Colonel Mihailov raised his eyebrows replying, "With one of the planes being shot down, I told the other pilot to return to base."

Captain Weller, hiding her face, produced a wry grin knowing that this would probably enrage Cairns. Still knelt beside Captain Weller, he turned his head with his eyes remaining closed. With his head held low and his scraggy hair hanging over his face, he tried to contain his anger before opening his eyes to see Captain Weller's body disfigured from the acid he had used earlier. He glanced at her hiding her face, deciding to climb to his feet still containing his anger. When he stood up, he mumbled, "Problems, problems!"

He turned around to face Colonel Mihailov and said, "You see! This is what happens when there are too many chiefs and not enough Indians!"

President Berry smirked, which Cairns noticed. Colonel Mihailov appeared uneasy, which made him say, "I thought . . ."

Cairns starting to breathe heavy in anger interrupted Colonel Mihailov by picking up the bottle of acid once more and replied, "You know what thought did? He pissed his pants and thought he was sweating!"

He then threw some of the acid onto the Colonel's trousers which made him leap in pain. Cairns stood there annoyed, and said, "Get those fighter planes into the sky and blow those American assholes to smithereens!"

The Colonel turned around to do as he was asked, leaving President Modarres to ask, "What about John Raven, who is also heading in this direction?"

Cairns turned to look back at Captain Weller for a reaction, but she remained stony faced, relieved to hear again that he was somewhere nearby. Feeling angry, he shouted, "Can nobody think for their self-around here. Interruptions, that's all I get! Well, if you want a job doing, you might as well do it yourself!"

Captain Weller moved her head slowly, to look at Cairns and saw him looking back at her. He gripped the bottle of acid tightly while looking down at her with hatred knowing that she was once his lover. He tilted the bottle and poured the remaining acid onto her breasts and stomach and then onto her knickers, where it soaked through to sting and burn her vagina. She screamed in pain, still spitting slabs of oil out of her mouth and shouted, "You bastard!"

Cairns laughed, saying, "I wanted to rape you and then pre-warn you that Raven was coming to try and save you. I guess I'm just going to have to deal with him first, and then rape you when I get back."

He turned back to walk towards President Modarres saying, "Prepare the troops; I have other things to consider without these minor issues that do seem to be annoying me lately. Annihilating the United States and taking Kuwait are my primary objectives! He gave a snide stare at President Berry and carried on saying, "This will be done when you two will eventually be killed."

He told the Iranian soldiers to leave the cell and follow President Modarres, who for once gave a sincere look at President Berry.

When they had left the cell the Iranian soldiers banged the huge wooden door closed and locked it. Sarah and Susan made their way across to Debbie, who had suffered a traumatic time. Looking at the burns on her skin starting to blister badly, Susan said, "President Modarres doesn't want to go through with this, I saw it in his eyes."

Debbie replied, "No matter what, we're still in this Iranian cell where we don't know what the future holds anymore."

Sarah went to collect Debbie's trousers and handed them to her, where she thanked her. Slowly, she placed them back on, cringing in pain as the trousers pressed against the skin that had been burned. After fastening the button and pulling the zip up, she looked down at her breasts, noticing they were blistered and slightly disfigured. Susan took off her jacket, wanting to give it her to restore some of her dignity. Debbie thanked her as she placed on the jacket and fastened the buttons. Debbie, even though she was feeling incredible pain, gave a chuckle, which made Susan ask, "What's funny?"

Debbie immediately stopped chuckling remembering to the reason she had bought the underwear and who it was for. She coughed a little spitting the taste of some more oil out of her mouth. With Susan being the President of the U.S. she ignored her question and apologised for her behaviour, which was un-ladylike. Susan smirked, as she held her arm tenderly replying, "Well, we're hardly at the Whitehouse."

Debbie walked away to sit down in the corner feeling intrigued and asked Susan, "How did John become involved?"

Sarah sat down on the ground replying, "It's my fault."

Susan stopped her colleague and good friend, Sarah, from saying anything further and said, "It wasn't your fault, if you have to blame anybody, blame me because I sanctioned it."

Debbie placed her arms around her legs, clasped her hands together and asked, "How did you do it? He was so determined that last time was the final time."

Sarah replied, "We went to collect him at his home, when we noticed he appeared frustrated and tense. We asked him would he come, when to be honest it wasn't just to be with us, he wanted to help you."

Debbie, although she knew, asked, "You think so?"

Susan, sitting down on the ground replied, "You know so."

She paused for a few seconds and then carried on saying, "We know who he is, what he can do, and what will probably have to happen. It's the one positive thing that must give us all hope that he will help us escape from this hellhole."

Sarah joined in the conversation again by saying, "He promised me that he would get me home."

Still feeling battered, bruised and humiliated, she managed to produce a grin while thinking about John. She started to cough, choking up some more oil, which she again spat out. Susan raised her eyebrows saying, "Better out than in."

Debbie replied as she held her throat, "You can say that again."

After clearing her throat once more, she went back to the conversation saying to Sarah, "So John promised he would get you home?"

Sarah replied, "I've been in a warzone with him before."

Debbie placed her head back onto the stone wall replying, "I know, that was the time I told him about the son he never knew existed, which made him have to come back and fight again."

Susan spoke by saying, "His son, John, is also a brave soldier because he helped me immensely during my time in North Korea. When his father finally arrived at the warzone, I knew then I would get home. How? I didn't know but between them, they saved my life where I'm still the President of the United States."

Debbie still had her head resting on the stone wall feeling proud of her son and his father, John Raven, and replied, "I'm glad you brought him with you because I have more chances of living now."

Sarah said, "I agree."

Susan looked at them replying, "But will he live after what he went through last time?"

Debbie moved her head away from the stone wall defending him, replying. "John Raven is expendable and will do what he has to do to accomplish his mission."

She placed her arms around her knees again and clasped her hands together as she looked at them with hope in her eyes and carried on saying, "Raven is coming and Cairns is scared!"

Susan placed her hand onto Debbie's arm saying, "It's a good reason to live."

Debbie brought a wry smile to her face replying, "I've heard those words before, only it was me saying them to John."

Susan replied, "We'll make it. We have to."

Debbie nodded her head agreeing with Susan, visualising John as the caring father with their daughter, Sarah Jane and their son, John. She gave a wry smile, which slowly disappeared when she visualised him as the legendary soldier we do all know. She recalled images of him as the warrior on a mission in dangerous warzones when nothing and nobody was going to stop him from achieving his main objective. Knowing he was coming into battle once more, she turned to President Berry to say, "Raven is coming with a vengeance!"

Warzone

$\mathcal{J}$ohn Raven was moving at a high-speed on the motorbike he had taken from one of the Iranian biker's earlier. He was in pursuit of the Russian military trucks, he could now see clearly, in the distance. Noticing one of the trucks was carrying missiles, and others were transporting tanks, used to invade Kuwait, he knew he had to do something drastic before it was too late. He opened the throttle up more, weaving in and out of traffic, making his hair and headband blow in the breeze. Focused on what he had to do, his face remained stern as he started to catch up with the Russian trucks preparing for war.

Cairns and President Modarres were also travelling in the opposite direction to meet their own military vehicles. Cairns and Colonel Mihailov had already told their soldiers approaching the Iranian base that Raven is on a suicide mission and should be extra vigilant about anybody riding a motorbike erratically. In the distance, Cairns saw the U.S. helicopters, which made him snatch the radio from the dash to ask Colonel Mihailov, who was travelling in a different truck, "Where are those Russian Mig fighter planes?"

Colonel Mihailov looked up at the U.S. helicopters, replying, "They will be here soon!"

Cairns paused while watching the U.S helicopters and then said, "Make sure it's in the next three minutes!"

He placed the radio on the dash, looked up again concerned at the U.S. helicopters, which made him ask President

Modarres who was sitting beside him, "Are all the soldiers back at the base ready for what is about to occur?"

President Modarres, while also watching the presence of the U.S. helicopters replied, "They're in position and will defend with honour."

Unit Expendable, on board the U.S. helicopters had already had one encounter with a Russian Mig, successfully blowing it out of the sky. Colonel Wareing looked down to see all the military activity sensing that conflict was now near. He ordered Williams and Sarah Jane Weller-Raven aboard his own craft and Steve Lundgren and Scott Templeton travelling in the craft beside them onto the huge machine guns positioned next to the doors. Lieutenant Parr, anxiously watching asked Colonel Wareing, "Do you think we should radio for backup because they're aware we're coming?"

Colonel Wareing glanced outside the door once more at the military presence below, replying, "Give me the radio."

Colonel Wareing held the radio tightly wanting to contact General Hardaker at the Kuwaiti military control centre requesting if Des O'Brien, Dave Aindow and Gary Simpson were available. At first, General Hardaker seemed bemused asking, "Why?"

Colonel Wareing immediately replied, "Because the Iranians and the Russians know we're coming!"

General Hardaker, while thinking, looked at his staff in the control centre, and then said, "This is not good."

Colonel Wareing replied, "With your permission Sir, launch the Stealth Bombers."

General Hardaker, just like every American person, and probably the rest of the world had seen the reports on television that Air Force One had been the subject of a terrorist attack. President Berry and the Secretary of State, Sarah Johnson, were kidnapped and now held captive in a foreign country. Aware of this, he said, "Consider it done."

Colonel Wareing thanked the General, and then went onto ask, "Did you know John Raven is here too?"

General Hardaker looked straight ahead after hearing Raven's name, replying, "I guess he had to become involved somewhere."

He paused suspecting a huge aftermath, with Raven being on the scene, remembering how he had finished his last mission. He then carried onto say to the Colonel, "I'm sending a squadron of F35 fighter planes in too."

He turned the radio off immediately signalling a red alert for the Stealth pilots O'Brien, Aindow and Simpson to be airborne in the next fifteen minutes, when they will be briefed in the air. He thought of the consequences about to happen, suspecting Colonel Armstrong was reading his thoughts, which made him say, "We have no choice."

Colonel Armstrong replied, "There is always a choice."

Feeling hidden apprehension he said to Colonel Armstrong, "Have Stuart Wareing and Kevin Burton up in the air immediately. Things are about to become ugly."

Colonel Armstrong agreed to the General's order, picking up the phone to relay the message through to the pilots. General Hardaker started to walk away, and then turned to the Colonel still on the phone to say, "Have Martin Womack and Bruce Jackson on standby."

Colonel Armstrong, while still speaking on the phone nodded his head agreeing to General Hardaker. He turned to carry on walking away saying to several military operatives working nearby, "It's time to get tough!"

The military operative replied, "It's going to be total carnage Sir."

Before answering the operative, General Hardaker thought of John Raven and what he must now be doing. No man or military machine would stop him from reaching his main purpose. General Hardaker looked at the operative replying in a low voice, "Total carnage? Keep your eyes peeled on the screen for the enemy who could prepare for a possible attack of retaliation."

He left the operative to attend to his duties again, deciding to walk away from the control centre, outside to watch the Stealth Bombers take off and the F35 fighter plane's taxi around to the runway. In a low voice, he said, "Hang in there John; we're coming to help you and Unit Expendable."

Raven, who was still travelling at high-speed on the motorbike, was now behind the last military truck carrying weapons. The Russian soldier driving the vehicle could see Raven weaving about behind him in his mirror. Remembering what he had been told by Cairns, he tried to make it difficult for Raven to pass by. Raven kept accelerating and then braking, sensing the huge truck would run him off the road. He tried repeatedly, when each time he had to back down, which made him grunt in anger. He heard the sound of gunfire in the sky, making him briefly look up to see members of Unit Expendable constantly shooting at the Russian Mig fighter planes that seemed to be toying with the U.S. helicopters. Knowing they were in a precarious position, he accelerated, travelling beside the huge military truck. The Russian soldier driving the truck saw Raven in his mirror and manoeuvred to hit him. Aware of this, Raven quickly let go of the handle bars to leap onto the side of the truck, leaving the wheels of the truck to ride over his motorbike. He held on to the curtain tightly, as it dragged him along the road. The driver laughed at the thoughts of the motorbike and possibly Raven being squashed under his wheels as he carried on travelling in convoy behind the might and power of the Russian military vehicles.

Raven moved his foot scraping along the road onto the rear wheel arch, using all his strength to pull himself up. At first, he struggled to pull out his knife. With perseverance and without falling off the side of the truck, he sliced the curtain and fell through into the back of the truck. Still hearing the sounds of gunfire and the Russian Mig fighter planes flying by at a speed, he scanned with his menacing eyes what he could use to help Unit Expendable aboard the U.S. helicopters. He noticed a crate with weapons placed on top of it. Suspecting what it could be, he hurried, throwing weapons placed on top of the crate to the other side of the truck. After placing a bow over his shoulder, he quickly opened the crate to show a Russian rocket launcher. Keeping one eye on the enemy, while the adrenalin pumped through his body, he placed it on his shoulder and rushed to the back of the truck. To his despair, he saw one of the U.S. helicopters rotating out of control with smoke rising as the pilot tried to perform a crash landing, after it had been hit by the enemy. Feeling angry and unsure whether his daughter was with other members of Unit Expendable inside the helicopter, he focused on the Russian Mig fighter planes circling to attack the second U.S. helicopter. Holding the trigger tightly, he waited for the right moment to aim and fire at them. He saw Sarah Jane on the huge machine gun firing at the enemy, feeling relieved, she was still in the air. With his menacing eyes, he quickly focused on the Russian Mig coming in order to attack the remaining U.S. helicopter. Knowing they were in a precarious position, he pulled the trigger, releasing the rocket that travelled at a speed in pursuit of its target. It collided with one of the Russian fighter planes in seconds, creating a loud explosion, resulting in a huge inferno burning in the sky. The fireball Raven had created made Tyler have to react swiftly by banking hard to avoid the inferno and debris directly in front of them. Sarah Jane fell back inside the helicopter with the sudden movement Tyler had performed. Colonel Wareing looked out to see Raven holding the rocket launcher in the back of the Russian truck, aware he had just saved their lives. Not sure about whether other members of Unit Expendable were alive, he ordered Tyler and Seager to take the helicopter down to search for members of Unit Expendable, who were fleeing for their lives.

Two more explosions were heard, resulting in the U.S. helicopter burning to a shell. Colonel Wareing saw the Russian and Iranian soldiers, in the distance, where they were starting to fire their guns at members of Unit Expendable.

Raven picked up a submachine gun, quickly placed the bullets over his shoulder, while watching members of Unit Expendable running for their lives. He tore the opposite curtain using his knife, positioned the machine gun and fired bullets frequently at the Russian soldiers, refusing to stop. Sarah Jane in the helicopter fired the huge machine gun at the allied enemy, killing many soldiers. Tyler released a couple of missiles, which travelled at a speed, hitting a military truck carrying enemy soldiers who were ready to fight for Iran. Lieutenant Parr held his gun and kept firing at the enemy from the opposite side of the helicopter, while they tried to rescue their colleagues who were in a vulnerable position.

Tyler and Seager flew low, with plenty of gunfire occurring around them. Radford and Templeton ran to the helicopter, leaping to grab the legs.

Raven was scrambling down the side of the military truck noticing the soldiers hanging in a precarious position.

Sarah Jane glanced down at Radford and Templeton, still firing at the enemy hidden in the smoke. She shouted to Lieutenant Parr and Colonel Wareing to help these soldiers inside the craft. Lieutenant Parr threw his gun down, hurried across and placed his hand out to Templeton. Colonel Wareing and Lieutenant Parr pulled him inside, with Templeton glancing back at the warzone behind him saying, "Thanks for that."

Colonel Wareing nodded his head quickly agreeing, and hurried back to help Lieutenant Parr drag Radford into the helicopter. As they were pulling Radford inside, he was shot in the back several times, leaving him to look up at his officers, shaking his head from side to side letting them know he had accepted the unavoidable, his death! Colonel Wareing and Lieutenant Parr pulled him inside as fast as they could, but he had been killed. The Colonel ordered Tyler to climb, knowing he couldn't save the remaining members of Unit Expendable. Seager released another couple of missiles blowing some of the enemy to smithereens and creating mass fires. Colonel Wareing shouted again, "Climb Tyler, before we're blown out of the sky!"

Raven still holding the machine gun had almost reached the driver's cab. He glanced relieved to see the U.S. helicopter was starting to climb. Knowing that some of his unit were still in a vulnerable position, he edged his way forward, pulling out his knife when he was close to the driver's cab. He opened the passenger door of the truck and quickly climbed inside, startling the enemy soldier. Without hesitation, he threw the knife stabbing the Russian soldier in his heart, killing him instantly. Raven threw the machine gun inside the truck and climbed in quickly to try to regain control of it. The truck was starting to weave out of control, which made Raven retract the knife, from the Russian soldier's heart, lean across to open the door and kick him out of the cab. Holding a stern face, he moved across into the driver seat to gain control of the truck. He accelerated, starting to pass another military truck in front of him. The Russian soldier with not knowing that Raven had taken the vehicle felt surprised, but soon became aware of what was happening when Raven tried to ram him and steer him off the road. In retaliation, the Russian soldier performed the same manoeuvre back, which made Raven even angrier. He picked up the machine gun with one hand he had left on the passenger seat and pointed it constantly shooting at the Russian soldier in the vehicle beside him until he had hit him. He didn't care where. He just had to die! Bullets hit him at the side of the head and in his chest, which killed him outright. The vehicle he was driving became out of control, crashing, creating another huge inferno with all the weapons on board.

Some of Unit Expendable was running towards the enemy truck Raven was now driving, which made him slow down to let Steve Lundgren inside the cab. Lundgren picked up the gun on the passenger seat, and then waved his arms shouting to Williams and Lerner, "Get in the back and take what weapons you can!"

Raven waited for a few seconds, shouting, "Come on! Come On!"

Lundgren turned to look at Raven sitting there with a stern face in warrior mode and replied, "They're in!"

Raven stared through the front windscreen focused in what he had to do as he started to accelerate after the remaining Russian military vehicles. Raven asked Lundgren, "Where's Pomfret and Ashworth?"

Lundgren moved his eyes noticing Raven's headband resting on his shoulder, then at the huge machine gun he had just been firing and replied, "I hope they've diversified."

Raven turned the steering wheel sharply saying, "Yeah, I hope so!"

He looked up to see the U.S. helicopter heading inside the Iranian military base. He said to Lundgren, "We're close to the enemy base."

Lundgren turned his head to look at him, and then listened to Raven say, "Take the wheel!"

Raven opened the door, deciding to climb out, which made Lundgren move across quickly to take the steering wheel, while asking, "What are you doing?"

Raven turned, replying, "Watching your back!"

Lundgren asked, "Who's watching yours?"

Raven stared for a few seconds, and then jumped off the truck onto the military transporter carrying the Russian tanks. He pulled out his knife once more, as he made his way up the trailer to the driver's cab. The Russian soldier saw him in his mirror and wound his window down to fire his gun, which made Raven hide for cover behind the drivers cab. Using his knife he cut the brake cables connected to the trailer, and then climbed up the back of the cab onto the roof.

Lundgren, following behind watched what Raven was doing, and said to himself, "You're still the man!"

Raven, who was now on the roof, scanned the area with his menacing eyes and saw, in the distance, more Russian military vehicles travelling towards him. The soldier's sitting on the back of the truck stood up, starting to fire bullets at him, which made Raven lie down on the roof to take cover.

Colonel Wareing looked out of the helicopter at Raven, lying down on the roof of the truck and said, "Christ!"

Sarah Jane came to the opposite side to see her father lying in a vulnerable position on top of the truck's roof and didn't hesitate in firing more bullets constantly from the huge machine gun positioned at the door.

Raven glanced up and could see Sarah Jane pumping bullets to protect him from being shot. Tyler released a couple of missiles from the wings of the helicopter, where they blew Russian vehicles from the ground, up into the air, creating huge fireballs. Colonel Wareing could see all the Russian firepower appearing, and said, "Get us out of here Tyler!"

Cairns could see the devastation happening in front of his eyes. He became wide-eyed when he saw Raven lying on the roof of a Russian truck. Feeling annoyed, he placed his hands through his scraggy hair, put his head back and said, "Pass me the rocket launcher!"

President Modarres was horrified feeling shock with being involved in a warzone. He watched Cairns assemble the rocket launcher, deciding to warn him by saying, "Don't hit the missiles on the vehicle in front of Raven!"

Cairns had his head lowered, frantically assembling the rocket launcher. With being distracted, he stopped, turned with his hair hanging back into his face, replying to President Modarres, "I intend to kill John Raven!"

He carried on assembling the rocket launcher and then quickly stood up to aim it at the vehicle Raven was now lying on.

Sarah Jane saw Cairns aiming the rocket launcher at her father, making her want to defend him by starting to fire repeatedly at his vehicle, causing Cairns to take cover and order some of the soldiers by saying, "Kill that bitch on the helicopter!"

Sarah Jane had to take cover, which meant that Cairns could stand and aim the rocket launcher in Raven's direction. Raven moved his head to his right and saw Cairns holding the rocket launcher aiming straight at him. Aware of Cairns' actions, in a split second he jumped off the roof and went behind the cab. Cairns had released the rocket when within a few seconds it collided with the main unit pulling the trailer, creating a huge fireball. Raven immediately jumped from the trailer suspecting what Cairns was about to do, but was burned from the huge fireball behind him. The trailer buckled, crashing onto its side, with the tanks left leaning against it upright.

Sarah Jane looked down in total disbelief, which made Colonel Wareing say, "Sarah Jane!"

Sarah Jane didn't take any notice of Colonel Wareing, which made him get up and pull her inside the helicopter shouting, "Weller-Raven!"

Sarah Jane was in shock. Colonel Wareing ordered Lieutenant Parr to take her position on the machine gun and carry on firing at the enemy. Lieutenant Parr took her position looking down at the smoke and flames. It didn't take long for the Russian's to fire at him once more, where he retaliated with a vengeance. Colonel Wareing shouted to Seager and Tyler, "Get us out of here!"

Colonel Wareing patted Sarah Jane's face gently, saying, "Sarah Jane."

She moved her eyes to face the Colonel, listening to him say, "I know that stare!"

Sarah Jane's eyes started to glaze when she replied, "My father can't have lived through that explosion."

Colonel Wareing said, "Trust me, with John Raven, where there is a will, there is a way!"

He looked out of the door and saw a badly burned Raven scrambling to his feet and starting to hurry to the tanks resting against the transporter trailer. Raven climbed onto the tank, used his strength to open the top and crawled until he fell inside. He held his body, feeling the pain from head to toe, but just as he had been taught by his predecessor, Colonel Lewis, he chose to ignore it by standing up and taking the driving position inside the tank. He started the powerful engine, placed the tank in gear and started to climb at an angle on the trailer, which gave way with the weight of the tank now moving on it. The trailer moved causing it to crash down out of the flames onto the ground with the tank Raven was driving bouncing hard, once from the trailer and onto the ground. The second tank fell on its side leaving it indisposed and couldn't be moved. Raven held his face stern travelling in pursuit of the enemy, constantly shooting bullets from the gun. He killed many Russian and Iranian soldiers as they tried to protect themselves from a massacre. Occasionally, he would fire shells at the Russian military vehicles with loud explosions and large fireballs occurring.

Lundgren was still following some distance behind in the Russian truck carrying weapons, knowing that when he and the two soldiers in the back were called up on. They had to be ready.

Raven stopped the tank to watch the articulated truck that had broken away from the convoy carrying the missiles, in the distance. He glared at it. Not knowing whether the missiles were live or not, it didn't seem to matter. He rotated the huge gun, wanting to aim it at the Russian vehicle transporting the missiles. He glared at it again, wiped his hair on his shoulder and fired a shell at it. Watching it in anticipation has it travelled at a speed to its intended target, he started to rotate the gun back into its original position and move the tank once more. Waiting for the explosion, he picked up speed knowing he just had one incentive, which was to free Captain Weller, President Berry and Sarah Johnson. He heard the loud explosion, managing to give a casual grin, suspecting they were the nuclear missiles to be used against the U.S. once they had the live chips inserted, were now destroyed.

Cairns stood up and saw the Russian tank creating all the carnage in front of him. Colonel Mihailov was on the radio, when President Modarres picked it up and heard a furious Colonel Mihailov speaking to him. Not sure what to do, he handed the radio to Cairns, who refused to take it. Instead, he picked up the rocket launcher again, aiming it at Raven, who was driving the tank in his direction. Raven fired his gun a few times, making Cairns duck for cover and say, "The bastard!"

Sarah Jane moved, suspecting her father was driving the Russian tank towards Cairns, which made her watch with concern. She looked up at Lieutenant Parr firing the gun where he caught Cairns on the arm, which knocked him off balance and fall onto President Modarres. Raven kept driving the tank, not wanting to stop, making the caterpillar wheels climb onto Cairns' wing, crushing it. He wouldn't stop, he carried on by crushing the bonnet, and then the other wing, demobilising the vehicle.

Raven was on a mission where he was travelling to the Iranian military base with one sole objective, seek and destroy. Lundgren followed in the Russian truck, ready for whatever Raven needed him to do. Colonel Wareing noticed the U.S. F35 fighter planes and Stealth Bombers were now approaching, in the distance. Tyler and Seager saw them too, and then heard Colonel Wareing give the order to follow them into the Iranian military base. They suspected more conflict, but felt at ease knowing that more U.S. firepower was coming up in support behind them. Then below travelling in a Russian tank, John Raven, one man on a mission, when nothing was going to stop him from doing what he had to do.

Destruction

Cairns crawled out of his wrecked jeep onto the ground, slowly standing up to see the American's travelling to the Iranian military base. He rushed around wanting to help President Modarres out of the jeep while holding his arm that had been shot. He let go of it deciding to ignore the pain, to place his hand in the air, signalling to the soldiers, who were following to stop. Colonel Mihailov opened the door, climbed out of the vehicle and hurried towards Cairns shouting, "You didn't see this coming did you?"

Cairns was feeling annoyed, refusing to answer the Russian officer. Colonel Mihailov was furious, when he looked stern at President Modarres asking him, "Why did you bring an outsider into our plans?"

Cairns placed his hand into his pocket, resting it on his gun considering whether to point it at the Russian Colonel. Staring at him, Cairns answered, "They need me because I'm the brains of this outfit!"

Colonel Mihailov turned away to look at the destruction replying, "It isn't going too well, is it?"

Cairns, feeling angry, held the gun in his pocket tightly. President Modarres intervened saying, "We go back to the military base to try to stop a mass destruction!"

Cairns, standing there watching the American's travel in the distance, said, "Launch everything you have Colonel!"

Colonel Mihailov looked at Cairns, narrowing his eyes in anger. He hurried back to the truck to contact the Iranian military base, ordering them to be on red alert for fear that they will soon be under attack from the U.S. military. President Modarres turned to look, in the distance, and said, "The American's have become a real problem!"

Colonel Mihailov walked back listening to Cairns' reply, "No! It's not the American's. It's just one man, John Raven! I'm going to kill the son of a bitch!"

He started to make his way to Colonel Mihailov's truck, which made President Modarres and the Colonel follow. Cairns pointed at the American's saying, "It may seem that they have won this battle, but they have not won the war!"

He climbed inside the truck with President Modarres and Colonel Mihailov sitting in the cab behind the driver and Cairns. Cairns, showing anger on his face when he turned to the driver, said, "I suggest you take me to see all this carnage!"

The driver placed the gearstick into gear, slowly steering the vehicle around the opposite way to start travelling back to the Iranian military base. The soldier's behind in their vehicles also repeated the same manoeuvre by following Cairns. All Cairns could do as they travelled back to the Iranian military base, was to keep muttering to himself, "I'm going to kill John Raven!" has he stroked his arm trying to ease the pain.

Raven was travelling as fast as the tank would go. It rumbled along when he saw the U.S. helicopter above flying in the direction of the Iranian military base. The red alert sirens had already been sounded with Russian Mig fighter planes starting to take off. The Stealth Bombers banked, flying over the base, starting to drop bombs on the runway destroying Russian Mig fighter planes about to take off and prevent no more from being able to take off.

Three Russian Mig fighter planes did manage to take off before the Stealth Bombers had arrived on the scene and were now in a dogfight with the U.S. F35 fighter planes. Colonel Wareing appeared stern, while watching members of Unit Expendable take their positions to try to protect their own people. He shouted to Tyler and Seager sitting in front of the helicopter, "Do we have any missiles left?"

Seager replied, "Not many Sir. We have used most of them."

Colonel Wareing looked outside the helicopter noticing the Russians had the advantage in the ariel dogfight, asking again in stern voice, "How many?"

Tyler replied, "We're down to our last three Sir!"

Colonel Wareing looked anxious at the F35's and then down at Raven, in the distance, who was now firing at the enemy on patrol in the watchtowers. He asked Luke for the radio, immediately ordering, O'Brien flying in the Stealth Bomber to break formation and help the F35 fighter planes. O'Brien responded to the order by breaking formation with his colleagues, flying at an enormous speed to help Kevin Burton and Stuart Wareing, who were in a vulnerable position with being outnumbered. He soon joined them when without hesitation, started to fire his guns at will while rotating the black plane into defensive manoeuvres from shots fired in retaliation from the Russian Mig's.

Allied enemy soldiers fired at the vulnerable U.S. helicopter, with Lieutenant Parr and Sarah Jane firing back using the huge machine guns positioned next to the doors. Templeton, also standing at the door was firing his own weapon at the enemy. Sarah Jane shouted, "Sir! We're getting low on ammunition!"

Templeton glimpsed at Sarah Jane in anguish and then turned to see Colonel Wareing give a stern look, deciding to radio the U.S. military base in Kuwait. Colonel Armstrong picked up the radio listening to him frantically seeking an immediate backup. General Hardaker had arrived back in the main control centre suspecting what Colonel Wareing wanted. He nodded his head agreeing to Colonel Armstrong, with him now answering Colonel Wareing by giving the order for Womack and Jackson to be airborne in their F35 fighter planes.

General Hardaker watched the operators perform their duties and then turned to see Womack and Jackson taxiing to the runway to take off and support their colleagues in action. Colonel Armstrong went to stand next to the General asking, "Have things just got better or worse?"

General Hardaker watched the two pilots take off and then turned to Colonel Armstrong, while thinking of John Raven and chose not to reply to the Colonel.

John Raven was heading for the enemy military base, where he was pumping the gun constantly firing shells at the base. Iranian soldiers on patrol in watchtowers placed around the base were firing back. Raven stopped firing shells, switched guns and started to fire bullets constantly at the soldiers who were now firing back at him in retaliation. Raven rumbled forward in the huge tank, killing many soldiers while creating destruction with one sole purpose, to free Captain Weller, President Berry and Sarah Johnson.

Colonel Wareing saw one of the Iranian's aiming a rocket launcher at Raven's tank, which made him shout to the pilots at the front. "Do something now!"

Tyler and Seager had also seen the same thing and didn't hesitate in releasing a missile, which left at a speed, watching it collide with the watchtower, creating a huge inferno, killing the Iranian soldiers outright.

One of the Russian Mig fighter planes had been severely hit with the pilot deciding to point the damaged jet at the U.S. helicopter. The pilot ejected leaving the fighter plane to free fall hoping it would collide with the U.S. helicopter and kill everybody on board.

Sarah Jane saw the fighter plane free falling towards them all with the pilot parachuting away. She shouted at the top of her voice, "Sir!"

Then she opened fire at the pilot trying to parachute to safety.

Colonel Wareing saw the huge Russian Mig fighter plane coming straight for them and shouted, "Get us out of here Tyler and fast!"

Seager looked astonished at the huge fighter plane heading straight for them. Tyler took evasive action deciding to place the helicopter into a dive. Lieutenant Parr and Sarah Jane held onto their fixed weapons tightly as the fighter plane just narrowly missed them by going over the top of the rotating blades, still free falling in the direction of Raven's tank. Colonel Wareing said, "That was too close for comfort! You two at the front, that was excellent flying."

Tyler and Seager were pre-occupied to respond to the Colonel's praise. They carried on flying into the warzone Raven was now creating on the ground. Still keeping an eye out for the enemy, they watched anxiously at the Russian Mig fighter plane free falling straight for Raven's tank, with him not yet knowing. Sarah Jane and Colonel Wareing looked down waiting for the unavoidable to happen wondering if John Raven would come out of the huge collision alive. As the Russian Mig fighter plane got closer and closer to Raven's tank, Sarah Jane shouted at the top of her voice in anguish, "Dad!"

The Russian fighter plane carried on falling at high speed ploughing through a perimeter wall, hitting a military truck while heading straight in line with the side of Raven's tank. It eventually crashed with it causing a loud explosion, creating a huge inferno, moving the badly damaged tank sideways and through a sidewall of a building. Another explosion occurred, which created a fireball that rose up into the air, followed by burning flames and black smoke.

Tyler and Seager were stunned at what they had just witnessed suspecting Raven couldn't be alive after such a crash. Tyler looked back to see the Colonel, Sarah Jane and Lieutenant Parr looking down at the mass destruction, the Russian fighter plane and the tank had created when they collided with each other. Colonel Wareing ordered Tyler to take the helicopter down and be extra vigilant with the enemy. He placed his hand tenderly on Sarah Jane's shoulder, as she just looked down at the burning flames, the black smoke and the devastation not sure whether her father was still alive.

Steve Lundgren, who was driving the Iranian military truck, saw the huge Russian Mig fighter plane crash into the side of Raven's tank, hoping that his good friend would be still alive after such a horrific crash.

President Berry, Sarah Johnson and Captain Weller also heard the huge explosion nearby, which made Sarah Johnson ask, "What in God's name was that?"

Captain Weller lifted her head from resting on her arms and asked, "You have to ask?"

President Berry narrowed her eyes a little replying, "John Raven?"

Captain Weller nodded her head agreeing and then said, "He's here! How? I don't know, but he's here."

John Raven had arrived but unknown to them; he was lying down in a demolished tank with debris all around him. Feeling battered, wounded and still lying down he felt the heat of the flames close by, which made him open his eyes to stare at the small fires burning beside him. Starting to feel the heat from the Russian fighter plane that had been destroyed made him look back in anguish, especially with fuel leaking from the tank and flowing steadily to the small fires. Raven, although he was badly burned, turned his head back, produced a prolonged blink, then a grunt, and started slowly climbing to his feet moving rubble. The hatch he had to open was burning when he placed his hand out trying to open it. The heat from the flames made him pull his hand away. He gave a menacing stare at the fuel gradually making its way to the closest fire in its path. Realising he had to do something, he ignored the pain by placing his hand and arm through the flames, starting to release the hatch and push it open. The pain was too much for him, because he fell down clutching his arm and then opened the palm of his hand to look at his badly burned hand. Placing his arm down, he took notice of the fuel still travelling to the small fires. Knowing the remainder of the tank could blow at any moment he had to act fast. He scrambled to his feet, placed both of his hands on to the hatch, screaming in pain as he pulled himself up and rolled out of the hatch to look at the tank now lying on its side. Ignoring the pain he scrambled to his feet once more rushing to the door left open wanting to be as far away as possible from what he suspected could be another huge explosion.

Tyler landed the helicopter aware that angry Iranian people were waving their arms at him and running inside the military base. Colonel Wareing told Seager and Tyler to remain inside the helicopter while they went to search for John Raven. Seager asked, "What about them coming running towards us?"

As Colonel Wareing collected more weapons, he replied, "You improvise!"

Sarah Jane and Lieutenant Parr collected their weapons and quickly jumped from the U.S. helicopter witnessing all the damage and destruction Raven had created. Soldiers were lying dead, others were mutilated, which made the Colonel say, "We haven't much time! Come on!"

Steve Lundgren arrived at the Iranian military base in the truck he was driving where he pulled up sharply, opened the door quickly and climbed out. Williams and Lerner climbed out of the back of the truck collecting as many weapons as they could carry. Colonel Wareing saw the three members of Unit Expendable, and waved his arms, shouting, "You lot!"

Holding a stern face, he waved his arm at them, as they hurried to him. The fuel travelling inside the tank had reached the small fires creating a vast explosion, which blew stones and bricks at the U.S. helicopter. Tyler, holding a face of concern didn't hesitate. He started to take off once more, as Colonel Wareing and the rest of Unit Expendable dived for cover.

Raven was thrown to the floor once more with ceilings from above falling down onto him. He didn't wait to see what else was going to happen, he scrambled to his feet to carry on searching for his own people. Occasionally, he would see individual enemy soldiers, where he would kill them by using his knife and then take their weapons. He scanned the area with his menacing eyes noticing more soldiers coming towards him. He held the gun he had just taken tightly and started firing constantly at the enemy, killing them all instantly.

Captain Weller heard the firing immediately shouting, "John!"

With John firing bullets from his gun at the enemy, he couldn't hear the shouting from Captain Weller. President Berry and Sarah Johnson joined in with Captain Weller making the shout become much louder. John stopped firing after hearing something, in the distance, and decided to head in the direction of the sound.

Outside after the huge explosion and eruption of more flames from the remainder of the military tank, Colonel Wareing and the members of Unit Expendable that were with him stood up quickly assessing the damage once more. They all knew they couldn't take Raven's path, so they searched outside for an opening while remaining vigilant for any further enemy soldiers wanting to kill them.

Iranian civilian people arrived at the military base shouting in anger while throwing stones in protest at what the U.S. soldiers had done to their military base. They set the American flag alight once more and let it burn. Slowly, the crowd started to become much larger, with one sole purpose, death to the Americans!

Cairns could hear the shouting with almost arriving back at the Iranian military base. He could now see the damage and destruction Raven and Unit Expendable had created and was not too pleased. Looking straight ahead at the carnage he said, "Somebody is going to pay dearly for this!"

President Modarres, who was sitting in the back of the military vehicle, stared hard at Cairns and then at the destruction replying, "John Raven is a dead man!"

Cairns turned to look back at the Iranian President saying, "Mark my words! I'm going to be the man who kills this bastard!"

Colonel Mihailov, who was also travelling to the Iranian military base in the same vehicle said, "This is not good for both of our nations!"

Cairns replied, "Trust me. It's nothing that can't be fixed!"

He then turned to the driver, telling him to drive faster because he had every intention of catching elite soldiers from Unit Expendable and most of all, John Raven.

Raven carried on moving up the dark corridor always watching out for the enemy. As he drew closer to Captain Weller's cell, the shouting became much louder. Still moving, he stared at all the huge cell doors wondering which cell the American's would be placed in. He scanned the area with his menacing eyes once more, while listening to the three women shout his name again. He shouted back, "I hear you!"

Captain Weller heard his voice, closing her eyes feeling relief. All three women shouted much louder, which made him come to the door and say in a stern voice, "Get back!"

Captain Weller immediately told President Berry and Sarah Johnson the same thing suspecting that John was about to blow the door from its hinges. They went to the back of the cell waiting in anticipation for the explosion to occur and blow the door from its hinges. It didn't take long for a loud bang to happen, leaving John to hurry inside the cell to see that all three women were still alive. They saw how badly burned he was, which President Berry realised he must have gone through so much to help them to escape from what had become a nightmare for them all. John saw Debbie wearing President Berry's jacket becoming aware that she didn't have much else on underneath. He took his blood stained t-shirt off with Debbie noticing a blood stained gown wrapped around his chest and then his wounds from his latest battle. She walked to him with tears starting to form in her eyes knowing for sure that he must be in real pain. Raven didn't have any time for emotion and told her to put the t-shirt on. She took off President Berry's jacket, dropped it on the floor and quickly put on Raven's blood stained t-shirt with him shouting, "Come on! Come on!"

They were coming out of the cell when Susan was going to pick her jacket up from the floor. Raven shouted, "Leave it!"

Debbie hurried by John, stroking his arm tenderly, which he took notice of by looking back at her. President Berry and Sarah Johnson hurried by him where they looked at Raven in warrior mode once more. He ignored them saying, "Come on! Let's move. We don't have much time!"

Raven knew he had to find a different way out of the building. He glimpsed at the burns on Captain Weller's skin as he threw his gun to her asking, "Do you still have what it takes?"

Captain Weller gave a sincere look back at John taking notice of all his wounds asking, "Have you?"

John ignored the question, quickly assessed the area and said in a stern voice, "Come on! Keep moving!"

President Berry remembered those words only too well, which brought back more memories of her horrific time in North Korea when she was with John Weller. At the time she mimicked John's son by repeatedly saying, keep moving, keep moving. Seeing the huge presence of John's father, she chose to say nothing and just do as she was told.

Gunfire could be heard outside, followed by more explosions. John turned quickly to the three women saying, "We have to get out of here!"

President Berry replied, "We're right with you soldier."

As they made their way through rubble and stone, voices could be heard around a corner of a corridor, which made Raven say to President Berry and Sarah Johnson, "Get back!"

He looked at Captain Weller, listening to her reply, "I'm with you!"

He then placed his hand onto his knife handle, quickly pulling it out of its holster, while gripping it tightly. Sarah Johnson and President Berry were speaking, which made Raven say in a quiet stern voice, "Don't talk!"

President Berry and Johnson watched him as he edged his way forward. He pointed to Captain Weller, signalling for her to manoeuvre still pointing the gun directly in front of her and would not hesitate in using it against the enemy. More explosions occurred outside, which made dust fall from the ceiling and walls land onto the floor. Raven still gripping his knife tightly, said, "We have to get out of here fast! The building could collapse at any time!"

President Berry looked anxiously at Sarah Johnson and then at the dust above that kept falling on them and the ground. Raven could hear the voices becoming louder, where he nodded to Captain Weller, giving her the signal to shoot when he attacks the first person with his knife.

Holding a stern face he lunged out grabbing one of the men, which made the others place their guns up to point them at Raven. Captain Weller had her gun positioned at the people placing their guns at Raven and soon realised that they were members of Unit Expendable. She turned to see Raven with adrenalin flowing through his body, holding his knife tightly onto Steve Lundgren's throat. He too quickly realised that it was Steve Lundgren and slowly started to take the knife away from his throat. Lundgren feeling relieved said, "Now that is why he is the best of the best! The first sign of me being the enemy, I would have had my throat cut from end to end."

Templeton, who was standing nearby to Lerner nodded his head agreeing. Captain Weller looked across at John with hearing such praise. Colonel Wareing saw Captain Weller and hurried across to her feeling thankful that she was still alive. Raven turned back, waving once for President Berry and Sarah Johnson to join them.

Watching anxiously, Sarah Jane felt relieved that her mother and father were still alive and then warned everybody by saying, "We have to move and fast!"

John feeling battered and bruised placed his knife away as he walked over to his daughter, where he looked at her and placed one arm around her to give her a brief hug. He let go of her saying to everybody, "Let's go!"

They were all about to make an exit from where Unit Expendable had made their entrance. With explosions that could still be heard outside, they paused, which made Raven ask Colonel Wareing, "Where's Tyler?"

Colonel Wareing replied, "He is probably circling the warzone, whilst waiting for us."

A voice was heard, which made President Berry look and ask them all, "Did you hear that?"

Raven turned his head sideways, giving a menacing look back down the corridor. Colonel Wareing asked, "What did you hear Ma'am?"

Raven stood still anxiously waiting to hear what President Berry had just heard. Sarah Jane moved closer to her father asking, "I heard something too."

President Berry replied, "See, I told you!"

Raven frowned saying, "I heard nothing!"

Sarah Jane turned around sharply, when she was about to unleash her tongue to her father and then remembered that he was her superior officer and the Commanding Officer of Unit Expendable. John knew what she was about to do, which made him glare at her. He let the moment pass asking, "What did you hear?"

President Berry heard it again and looked at John, causing him to frown, suspecting that he had now heard something in the distance. Sarah Jane placed her gun in position saying, "We should go and check it out."

John glanced at President Berry and Sarah Johnson knowing the safety of these two people was paramount. He replied to Sarah Jane, "Lundgren and I will check it out."

He turned to Colonel Wareing and carried on saying, "Take President Berry and the Secretary of State. We will join you somehow later."

Sarah Jane had forgotten about military orders with saying in a stern voice, "I'm coming with you!"

Raven turned producing an evil stare at her, replying, "No! You're not! Your mother needs you. Watch and protect her!"

Sarah Jane looked back at her mother, Captain Weller, where she just nodded at her in a way like to say, don't provoke him. When she turned and went to stand with her mother, Raven softened his look towards her, and then turned to Lundgren to say, "Let's go and check it out."

As they walked in the opposite direction, he looked back for a few seconds to watch other members of Unit Expendable perform their duties, while taking care of President Berry and Sarah Johnson. He produced a wry grin when Sarah Jane placed her arm around her mother, but soon disappeared when he heard gunfire being fired at them all. Lieutenant Parr, Lerner and Williams reacted quickly, starting to spray bullets back at the enemy soldiers. One of the Russian soldiers threw a hand grenade, which made Raven turn to Lundgren wide-eyed and say, "Protect and serve!"

Colonel Wareing ushered Unit Expendable away as fast as he could, still firing bullets at the enemy.

Raven and Lundgren sprinted as fast as they could, wanting to protect President Berry and Sarah Johnson. Raven leaped through the air lunging for President Berry, instantly knocking her to the floor, with him lying on top of her to protect her from the blast. Lundgren ran past Sarah Johnson, reaching out for the hand grenade, which he threw to where he and Raven were about to walk to. A huge explosion creating a fireball travelled throughout the eerie corridor, which made Lundgren jump and land onto Sarah Johnson to protect her from the flames travelling to where Unit Expendable was at. The flames passed with members of Unit Expendable scorched from the heat of the flames after they had taken cover. When the flames had passed, Russian and Iranian soldiers came down to see if they had killed the American's. All the members of Unit Expendable stood up, starting to fire at the enemy by pumping bullets into their bodies, killing them instantly. Raven slowly climbed off President Berry, looked down at her and placed his hand out to her to pull her up. She looked up at him, saying, "I think you've broken one of my ribs!"

Raven stared at her replying, "You're alive!"

Lundgren was already at his feet with Sarah Johnson thanking him for his bravery. Raven turned to see if the way out was clear, it was. He turned to Colonel Wareing and said, "Get Tyler here and get the fuck out of here!"

Sarah Johnson touched Lundgren's arm as she passed him, where he noticed a figure in the smoke crawling. Lundgren turned to Raven and said, "John! Over there!"

John was still waving members of Unit Expendable out, shouting, "Go!"

He turned to Lundgren replying, "What!"

Lundgren pointed, immediately starting to run to the figure that was crawling. Raven, now also saw something and ran to catch up with Lundgren. They ran side by side suspecting the person they could see could be a U.S. soldier. They crouched down to him noticing the burns he had received and how thin he had become. He couldn't move anymore. He looked at Raven's eyes, which made Lundgren say, "He's dying!"

Raven asked the person he suspected was a U.S. soldier, "Are there others?"

The soldier slowly lifted his arm up pointing to one of the cells. Raven concerned for the U.S. soldier said, "We can't leave him here."

Lundgren looked back across to Raven feeling anguish asking, "What do we do with him?"

Raven turned to look at the soldier, who was almost at death's door and replied, "Take him! I'll join you in five minutes!"

Lundgren placed the U.S. soldier onto his shoulders and held him with one hand while holding his gun in position with his other hand ready to use against the enemy. He turned when Raven called out, "Lundgren!"

Lundgren turned around with his gun facing Raven waiting for him to speak. Raven carried onto say, "Now you know why they chose you."

Lundgren produced a smirk replying, "I have the same blood as you! You make it out Raven!"

Lost Seal

$\mathcal{L}$undgren nodded his head agreeing, and turned to make his way out, leaving Raven to watch for a few seconds. He turned around the opposite way, hurrying in the direction the U.S. soldier had pointed to moments before. With everything going on around him, the gown Farrin had used to dress his wound on his chest had fallen to his waist. He brought out his knife to cut it and let it fall to the floor while visualising Farrin, realising that not all people in Iran were bad. At times he placed his right hand onto the wound, starting to clot, still feeling great pain from it. He noticed some cell doors had been blown off their hinges, making him want to search. He entered prisoner's cells seeing to his disappointment, they were empty, but knew he had to carry on in search of the U.S. soldier. He climbed over rubble constantly scanning the area for the enemy. He picked a gun up from a dead Iranian soldier lying on the floor and pointed it in front of him. He moved his head in all directions hoping that he would find the U.S. soldier in question. He came to a cell where he entered and saw what he suspected a U.S. soldier. He looked down at him with his menacing eyes, noticing that he seemed weak and fragile, but could move. Aware that he didn't have too much time, he said, "You! Come on!"

The U.S. soldier sitting on the floor looking at the ground assuming it was Cairns, mumbled, "Fuck off!"

Raven glared, bit his teeth and replied, "I'm here to get you out of this five star shithole, now move!"

The person sitting on the floor slowly moved his head to look up at Raven, displaying his cuts, wounds and bruises that he had received from the Russian and Iranian soldiers. Raven stared down at him saying, "We don't have much time! We have to go and now!"

Raven held out his hand to pull the soldier to his feet, which made him ask, "How long have you been here?"

They hurried to the cell door, with the U.S. soldier replying, "About seven years. I've lost track of time."

Raven grabbed his arm, starting to move quickly knowing the U.S. helicopter should have picked up the other members of Unit Expendable. The U.S. soldier grateful that Raven had come to rescue him asked, "What's your name?"

Still moving quickly, he replied, "Raven. What's yours?"

The U.S. soldier replied, "Gardenzio."

Raven still holding Gardenzio's arm tightly moved swiftly, glancing at him, asking, "Gardenzio Mattinson?"

Gardenzio looked at John feeling surprised at how he knew his surname, which made him reply asking, "Yes, how did you know?"

Still moving, Raven thought back to Louise and Kirk, replying, "I've heard stories."

Gardenzio produced a puzzled look, which made Raven say, "Don't ask! Now is not the time!"

Cairns had arrived back and saw the devastation the Iranian military base had suffered. It was worse than he could have imagined. He looked up feeling angry when he saw the U.S. F35 fighter planes and Stealth Bombers leaving to return to Kuwait. Most Iranian people were shouting and bawling in retaliation with what the U.S. had done. He turned his face of anger to President Modarres, and then at Colonel Mihailov ordering him to send soldiers to search for any member of Unit Expendable that may be still somewhere inside the military base.

President Modarres climbed out of the truck, staring at the ruined Iranian base, which made him turn to Cairns and say, "You said that your plan was unbreakable!"

Cairns held his head low, thinking for a few seconds, and then raised it showing his anger at Colonel Mihailov. He slowly turned his head to face the Iranian president, listening to him say, "Your plan is destroyed my friend!"

Cairns nodded his head agreeing, feeling disgust at what President Modarres had just said. He climbed out of the truck noticing the Iranian and Russian soldiers running past him. He walked up to President Modarres and said, "I ought to kill you now!"

President Modarres looked into the evil eyes of Cairns replying, "Kill me and the hostile crowd you see here will most likely kill you, because after all you're an American!"

Colonel Mihailov climbed out of the truck noticing the discussion between President Modarres and Cairns had become heated. He interrupted them assuring them that they would get more military weapons from Russia when they will later have their revenge. Cairns while still looking stern at President Modarres said, "Now that's what I like to hear, a man with a positive attitude."

He turned to Colonel Mihailov and with a stern voice said, "Make it happen!"

They all heard gunfire, which made the three men look towards the sounds of the bullets. Cairns said, "It has to be Raven!"

Cairns pulled his gun out saying, "I'm going to find this son of a bitch!"

As he moved away to join the Iranian and Russian soldiers, he saw members of Unit Expendable, which made him start to fire at them. All members of Unit Expendable took cover for their lives and fired back in retaliation when they had the chance. They were becoming surrounded by the enemy, which made Colonel Wareing ask, "Where's Tyler and Seager?"

President Berry and Sarah Johnson kept their heads down feeling scared at being hit from bullets fired close by to them. Sarah Johnson saw Captain Weller firing her weapon at the enemy and said to Susan, "Somebody is out for revenge."

Susan looked across closely watching Captain Weller manoeuvre, killing enemy soldiers and replied, "With what she has been through, I'm not surprised."

Lieutenant Parr and Williams were next to President Berry and Sarah Johnson, aware these people hadn't to be left alone in what was now a dangerous warzone.

Cairns could be heard shouting at his own soldiers close by, giving orders to kill the U.S. soldiers. He became frustrated and started to manoeuvre, firing his weapon. Captain Weller saw him, where she could only feel deep hatred for what he had done to her. She watched him move and was about to pull the trigger, when Colonel Wareing grabbed her arm to move her immediately to take cover from the enemy soldiers who were closing in around her. Colonel Wareing while assessing the situation said, "It's not all about one man! For now it's about staying alive!"

Captain Weller took her position with other members of Unit Expendable and fought back against the enemy gallantly. Colonel Wareing looked across at Lieutenant Parr and Williams, waving for them to move towards him, but remain low.

In the distance, a loud hum of propellers could be heard with Tyler and Seager flying back to see if Unit Expendable had managed to free President Berry and Sarah Johnson. They searched through the smoke listening to gunfire on the ground. They saw Colonel Wareing lying low, but still waving his hand eagerly at them. Seager started to fire the machine gun at the allied enemy soldiers, killing them instantly with blood spurting out of their bodies. Some took cover, waiting to retaliate by firing back at Tyler and Seager.

Tyler saw Lundgren carrying what seemed like a U.S. prisoner of war and decided to fly low near him, as Seager sprayed the enemy with bullets from the machine gun, killing more enemy soldiers. Lundgren placed the American P.O.W. down on the floor, where he crouched down and tapped his face gently asking with some concern, "Are you still with me?"

The U.S. soldier opened his weary eyes nodding his head yes at him. Lundgren shouted at Sarah Jane, where she carried on firing at the enemy as she made her way across to him. He saw Tyler and Seager coming closer, making him quickly signal and point to a position for them to land. Sarah Jane had seen, in the distance, a watchtower with two Russian soldiers who were pointing rocket launchers at the U.S. helicopter. She changed direction and headed for the truck Lundgren had been driving, which made Lundgren shout, "Weller!"

Lundgren turned back to look at the U.S. soldier, becoming concerned for him. He saw Lerner and shouted across to him, where he immediately made his way over to him. Lundgren told him to watch the American P.O.W. and get him aboard the helicopter, as soon as he had the chance, while he went back to look for Raven.

Tyler and Seager hadn't noticed the soldiers in the watchtower with so much going on around them. Sarah Jane, however, had seen them, which made her rush to the truck Lundgren had been driving earlier and climb into the back of it. She searched frantically for the one weapon she needed to use and have the utmost impact. She threw weapons about becoming angry knowing their only route of escape was in serious jeopardy. Feeling anxious for her life, she heard the propellers of the helicopter close by suspecting that it was about to land. As Sarah Jane fired her weapon at the padlocks on the crate, she looked out to see Lerner dragging the U.S. soldier to the helicopter. Tyler climbed out of his seat, rushing to help Lerner bring the P.O.W back to the helicopter.

Sarah Jane came running out holding the rocket launcher, screaming at Luke to get the helicopter back into the air. Luke glimpsed back at Sarah Jane for a few seconds and saw that she was pointing the rocket launcher at the watchtower. He soon realised why, which made him quickly help Lerner with the U.S. soldier and jump inside the craft, telling Seager to get them in the air as fast as possible. Sarah Jane released the trigger with the rocket travelling at a high speed through the air. The Russians had already released their rocket, which was travelling at a speed towards the U.S. helicopter. Tyler said in a stern voice, "Get it higher!"

The rocket crashed with the watchtower with a huge explosion occurring killing the enemy soldiers instantly. A huge fireball erupted into the sky, when seconds later the rocket the Russians had fired hit the ground where the U.S. helicopter had landed moments before. It produced an almighty explosion knocking Sarah Jane from her feet and close to the military truck carrying weapons. Colonel Wareing and other members of Unit Expendable looked back at the huge inferno, and then saw the truck carrying the weapons also explode and rise into the air. Templeton sprinted across after seeing Sarah Jane, just lying on the floor. He frantically dragged her away before the truck landed back on the ground. When it did, he smothered her to try to protect her from the debris and smaller explosions that followed.

Colonel Mihailov ordered more tanks to enter the warzone where Unit Expendable was now at. Cairns stopped one of the tanks, wanting to climb inside to take over from the driver's position, and start constantly firing at Unit Expendable. Colonel Wareing glanced at President Berry and Sarah Johnson, fearing for their lives, and then at Captain Weller. She looked away, noticing to her relief John Raven with Steve Lundgren helping another U.S. Prisoner of War. Cairns saw Raven, stopped the tank from travelling and said to the soldier sitting beside him, "Now there is the man I do want to make suffer!"

He revved his engine again with the three tanks behind following, still firing their guns at Unit Expendable. Cairns had steered the Russian tank close to Templeton, where he diversified and rolled with Sarah Jane, who he suspected was now unconscious from the blast. Cairns drove the tank over them, which made Captain Weller watch in anguish.

Raven saw a fuel tanker, which made him hurry and turn the tap to release fuel splashing onto the ground. He then looked up to see Tyler and Seager in the air. He waved to them, where they immediately flew back into the warzone releasing a couple of missiles at the Russian tanks, which made them explode with huge fireballs rising into the sky. The flames ignited with the fuel spilling onto the ground, which made another explosion, creating another large inferno when they had reached the fuel tanker. With fire, flames and explosions occurring everywhere, Raven and Lundgren were running as fast as they could while trying to help Gardenzio, the lost seal. Nearby, Raven saw President Berry and Sarah Johnson taking cover holding their heads with their hands while they were next to Lieutenant Parr and Williams. Lieutenant Parr had one sole incentive, which was to protect the First Lady, nothing else mattered. Aware that they were in extreme danger, he waved his arm frantically to the U.S. pilots in the helicopter.

Tyler and Seager saw Lieutenant Parr waving frantically at them, and then noticed Raven at times performing the same action. The Russians had sent a couple of Gunships into the warzone, which made Seager pick the radio up to contact the control centre at the Kuwaiti military base, where they confirmed that Womack and Jackson will be there within minutes. Seager shouted, "We don't have minutes, and we're almost out of ammunition!"

Colonel Armstrong asked in a concerned manner, "Do you have the President of the United States and the Secretary of State with you?"

Seager while looking at Tyler, pointed at the Russian Gunships in the distance, where he nodded anxiously agreeing. Tyler said, "It's never like this in simulation!"

Seager ignored Tyler's comment to answer Colonel Armstrong by saying, "President Berry and Sarah Johnson are free, but are still on the ground with members of Unit Expendable and John Raven."

Colonel Armstrong produced a stern look replying, "I suggest you get both V.I.P's into your craft as soon as possible!"

Seager answered the Colonel back by saying, "Sir. We have been a little preoccupied!"

The F35 fighter planes flew by at a speed attacking the Russian Gunships that were about to attack Tyler's craft. Both Womack and Jackson released two missiles each that travelled through the air colliding with both Russian Gunships in seconds and creating even more destruction and carnage.

On the ground Raven held his arm up waving frantically at the U.S. pilots, with Tyler saying, "It's now or never!"

He started to descend, which made Cairns stop the tank, rotate the gun and fire at the U.S. helicopter. Womack and Jackson could see what Tyler and Seager had to do and decided to bank and fly low to attack the Russian tank Cairns was now controlling with their last missile. Cairns quickly opened the hatch, leaping away from the tank as it exploded in the air. Womack contacted Tyler, "Go and get them! They're all yours."

Tyler flew, landing the battered helicopter once more inside the warzone. Raven ran with Lundgren just wanting to get Gardenzio inside the craft. He looked back at other members of Unit Expendable, waving to them frantically to hurry to the helicopter. They did as he had commanded where he saw Williams and Lieutenant Parr sprint with President Berry and Sarah Johnson. Both women ran for their lives through the warzone, ignoring what their eyes could now see. Enemy soldiers opened fire again, making Raven stare and retaliate by firing back at them. With his menacing eyes, he saw the F35 fighter planes' circle once more waiting to escort the helicopter as he fired at more oncoming enemy soldiers. He shouted to Colonel Wareing and Captain Weller, "Come on!"

He waved his arm frantically again, shouting, "Come on!"

Colonel Wareing and Captain Weller kept firing bullets at the enemy as they made their way back to the helicopter. Tyler and Seager were becoming impatient wanting to be up in the air again. They watched Womack and Jackson fly by in their F35 fighter planes. Tyler becoming anxious at the position they were in looked back at everybody in the back. He knew Sarah Jane hadn't arrived yet and with this asked Seager, "Any sign of Sarah Jane and Templeton?"

Seager scanned the area and saw first, Captain Weller and Colonel Wareing battling their way back to the helicopter. In the distance, he then saw Templeton dragging Sarah Jane, where he replied, "There's Templeton, pulling Sarah Jane."

Luke looked at Templeton feeling despair at the thought of Sarah Jane being badly injured, or even worse, lying dead. His emotions took over when he climbed out of his seat and went into the back of the helicopter taking a weapon. The other soldiers seemed bemused by his actions. He jumped out of the craft which made Raven say, "Tyler, what are you doing?"

Tyler ran past Raven firing his weapon at the enemy shouting, "I'm helping Templeton with your daughter!"

Raven, still firing his weapon at the enemy, turned to see Templeton dragging his daughter. He started to run behind Tyler, which made Captain Weller ask with concern as she passed Raven, "Where are you going?"

Raven ignored her, carrying on running behind Tyler. Captain Weller then saw Templeton dragging Sarah Jane and placed her hand to her mouth fearing the worst. Colonel Wareing, still firing at the enemy, glimpsed at what had shocked her. He grabbed her arm, making her swiftly move towards the helicopter and climb inside, where she looked back in anticipation waiting for Raven and members of Unit Expendable to bring her daughter on board.

Colonel Wareing ordered Seager to get the helicopter in the air and fly close to Templeton. Tyler arrived immediately wanting to help Templeton, and with deep concern asked, "Is she still alive?"

Templeton replied, "She has a pulse, but remains unconscious."

Tyler started to drag Sarah Jane with Templeton, enabling them to move much more quickly. More enemy soldiers were starting to surround them, which Raven had noticed. Explosions were occurring all around as Seager flew low precariously managing to get close to Templeton and Tyler. Raven stared across and saw they were lifting his daughter inside the helicopter. Not sure whether she was alive or not, he wanted to release some hypertension and started to fire his machine gun at the enemy.

Tyler climbed inside the craft, quickly taking up his position. Seager patted his shoulder and said, "Good work."

Captain Weller took the position at one of the machine guns positioned at the door and started firing at the enemy, occasionally looking back at her daughter, Sarah Jane, who was unconscious. Womack and Jackson flying in their F35 fighter planes could see the U.S. helicopter was in a vulnerable position.

Colonel Wareing shouted, "Get us up and fly towards Raven!"

The enemy soldiers were surrounding Raven, where they were ready to start firing at him. With the bullets, he was spraying back at the enemy, he was piercing their bodies that made them fall to the floor and die instantly. Captain Weller and Lieutenant Parr was also firing at the enemy from the helicopter, backing Raven up in his quest to finally board the craft. Aware that he was in a vulnerable position, she shouted to Tyler and Seager, "We have to get Raven aboard and fast!"

Captain Weller, still firing at the enemy, shouted to Templeton, "How is Sarah Jane?"

Templeton who was attending to her replied, "She's still unconscious!"

With all the gunfire below, Colonel Wareing went to stand at the door to see John Raven pumping bullets at the enemy. Then, in the distance, another couple of Russian trucks had arrived carrying enemy soldiers. Jackson left Womack in flight formation to begin firing the machine guns on both wings at the truck, resulting in most of the Russian and Iranian soldiers being killed, and the military truck blown to smithereens.

The enemy soldiers were getting close to Raven, where he was becoming low on ammunition. One of the Russian soldiers brought out a rocket launcher, which made Captain

Weller, shout at the top of her voice, "Get us out of here! They're going to launch a rocket!"

Stones were being thrown at the U.S. helicopter from the hostile crowd. One of the stones hit the front windscreen, cracking it. Tyler banked to take the craft in the opposite direction, which made Raven look back in despair. Lundgren came to the door to stand next to Lieutenant Parr, shouting, "John, run!"

Raven, threw the machine gun down that had no more bullets left and started sprinting after the helicopter. Cairns could see what was happening and waved his soldiers to follow him. As John ran, the U.S. helicopter pulled away from him. The rocket that had been launched by the Russian soldier just missed them. Raven kept sprinting after the helicopter with the pain showing on his face, where he had one sole incentive, to be inside with members of Unit Expendable.

Captain Weller moved to the other side of the helicopter to stand next to Lundgren, watching John running for his life, and willing him on to make it aboard their helicopter. Tyler made things a whole lot worse when he could see enemy soldiers also approaching Raven, realising he now had them coming at him from all directions. Tyler shouted, "Enemy soldiers!"

Colonel Wareing stared feeling anguish, and then looked at Captain Weller, shouting, "If he is close enough, tell him to jump!"

President Berry said to Sarah Johnson, "If ever one soldier deserved to be aboard this craft, then it's him."

Colonel Wareing stared at them replying, "This is just where I didn't want him to be because this time it could be *One Time Too Many.*"

Captain Weller heard what the Colonel had just said to President Berry and the Secretary of State and shook her head from side to side refusing to accept it. She saw the huge presence of Raven running and shouted, "Jump John! Jump now!"

Raven glanced at the U.S. helicopter, starting to descend slightly and reached out knowing he had only one chance to leap onto the legs of the helicopter. He listened to the hum from the propellers as he glanced at the enemy soldiers now coming for him. With not having much choice, he decided to jump and just about grabbed the legs of the helicopter. Captain Weller placed her arm out to him, but Lundgren moved her with him being much stronger. Colonel Wareing shouted, "Take us up Tyler!"

Lundgren shouted to other members of Unit Expendable, "Hold my legs!"

Williams was the first to grab Lundgren's legs tightly so he wouldn't be pulled out of the helicopter. He called to the others for help, which made Captain Weller, Colonel Wareing, President Berry and Sarah Johnson all hold onto Lundgren to ensure he didn't fall out of the helicopter.

He reached out, gripping Raven's hand, and using all his strength slowly started to pull him up. The enemy soldiers fired bullets at Raven, who was in a vulnerable position. He was grazed on the leg with a bullet, which made him jerk and break his grip with Lundgren. He was hanging onto the craft with one hand noticing that one of the enemy soldiers below was pointing a rocket launcher at them all. He looked up at Lundgren, shook his head saying no. Lundgren stared back feeling as though Raven was going to give up. Raven, wanting to make sure everybody on board was safe, made the decision to release his grip on the leg of the helicopter and take the consequences for his actions. It went frantic inside the helicopter, when John released his grip and fell to the ground. Captain Weller released her grip on Lundgren's leg and saw John lying there on the ground, where she screamed at the top of her voice, "John!"

Raven saw the enemy soldiers coming to take him and just waved them away to freedom. The F35 fighter planes flew by to escort the badly damaged U.S. helicopter climbing rapidly, leaving President Berry, Sarah Johnson and members of Unit Expendable looking down to who was the main man and the reason they were now free to live another day.

Sorrow & Disagreements

$\mathcal{C}$aptain Weller stared wide-eyed at the thoughts of what Cairns and his accomplices would do to John Raven. She turned to President Berry asking, "Do you think we should go back and make one final try to help Raven?"

Lundgren replied before the president by saying, "Yeah, we should do what is right and go back for him because he would have done the same for us?"

President Berry paused for a few seconds knowing that he was the man who had saved her life again. She then looked at her good friend, Sarah and replied, "If that is what you want to do, you have my blessing."

Lundgren shouted to Tyler and Seager at the front of the helicopter, "Turn the craft around. We're going back for Raven!"

Colonel Wareing intervened by saying, "Carry on travelling back to the Kuwaiti military base and that is an order!"

Steve Lundgren wasn't happy, saying, "This is not right!"

Colonel Wareing closed his eyes thinking about what the enemy will do to John Raven when they have him in their grasp. Slowly, he opened his eyes staring in the face of President Berry and said, "With having you on board, you know I can't perform this action."

Williams joined in the conversation by saying, "Can't or won't?"

Colonel Wareing looked at Williams and said, "Williams! Remember who you're speaking to!"

Lundgren turned to look at Williams with his sudden outburst and watched him reply to the Colonel, "When I was in your office, I called that guy down there an American bum."

Lundgren raised his eyebrows at what Williams had just mentioned and asked, "And you're still living?"

Williams didn't answer Lundgren's question, instead he carried on speaking to the Colonel by saying, "I was wrong about Raven because after seeing him in action, he is the ultimate fighting machine."

Lundgren moved his eyes, while watching Williams and listened to him say, "We should go back and at least try!"

Colonel Wareing, feeling pressure, started to frown knowing the helicopter hardly had any ammunition left. Sarah Jane was still unconscious; President Berry and her Secretary of State were aboard, making the U.S. helicopter become Air Force One. President Berry, aware Colonel Wareing was under pressure, looked up to him and said, "Go back, but make sure the F35's don't leave our side."

Captain Weller, who was beside her daughter still lying unconscious, looked up to Colonel Wareing hoping he would follow President Berry's request. After pausing for a few seconds, he shook his head from side to side saying no. With his eyes starting to water, he said, "As much as I would like to go back into the warzone to get my man, I can't because I have to take you and Sarah Johnson to where it's safe."

Lundgren sat down noticing Colonel Wareing didn't feel particular good in himself with having to make such a huge decision. Colonel Wareing saw him staring at him annoyed, they hadn't turned back to get Raven. Colonel Wareing leaned forward, patted Lundgren's leg and said. "Raven will either find a way out, or we go back for him later, on a new mission."

Lundgren nodded his head slowly, agreeing with the Colonel's proposal. Williams, also listening said, "If you're going back on another mission to get him, then you should involve Unit Expendable."

Colonel Wareing placed his head back thinking of the previous battles Raven had been involved in and then replied to Williams, "I wouldn't have it any other way."

Captain Weller looked down at her daughter, Sarah Jane, fighting back the tears. Not sure whether she would gain consciousness again, and not sure whether she would see John Raven again, she started to sob quietly, with the tears falling onto Sarah Jane. President Berry went across to hold and comfort her. Luke Tyler sitting in the front of the helicopter turned to look behind noticing that Sarah Jane was still unconscious. He banged his hand on the dials in frustration, which made Lee Seager turn to him and say, "She'll be okay. She's John Raven's daughter. The Raven's don't die."

Captain Weller lifted her head after hearing those words from Lee and repeated them, where she turned to members of Unit Expendable to say, "You're right, Raven's don't die! They just get even!"

Templeton looked at a battered, bruised and bloody Captain Weller, where he held her hand. With what Cairns had done to her she pulled it away sharp, while saying, "I'm sorry."

President Berry turned to Templeton to say, "She had a rough time inside that hellhole we have just left and probably won't want to be touched by a man for a long time."

Templeton nodded his head agreeing, trying to reassure her by saying, "I'm sure John will make it."

Captain Weller closed her eyes replying, "He has to because I was going to retire from the military . . ."

Colonel Wareing interrupted asking, "What?"

Captain Weller turned to the Colonel and carried on saying, "I spoke to John before I left the United States, telling him that I was going to retire and spend the rest of my life with him."

Colonel Wareing frowned with the thought of losing Captain Weller. President Berry saw his facial expression and said, "With what she has experienced, you couldn't blame her."

Captain Weller looked down at her daughter once more and then said, "I don't know what the future holds anymore."

As the helicopter was being escorted back to Kuwait with the roar of F35 fighter planes at either side, she listened to the hum of the propellers wishing Raven was at least on board one of these aircraft. She placed her hand onto Sarah Jane's forehead while gazing at her, hoping that she would open her eyes for her. She didn't, which made Captain Weller place her other hand to her own forehead starting to feel the stress of everything that had just happened.

Colonel Wareing was still feeling dumbfounded at Captain Weller's decision to quit her military career after her traumatic time, which made him ask, "Debbie?"

She looked around to face the Colonel, replying in a low voice, "What."

The Colonel looked into her eyes before speaking, paused and said, "Think about your decision before leaving your military career."

Captain Weller replied, "My decision was made even before I had left for U.S.S. Abraham Lincoln."

Colonel Wareing placed his head down, feeling bitterly disappointed, reluctantly saying, "You'll be missed."

Sarah Johnson joined in with the conversation, saying, "After what she has experienced, which will probably haunt her for the rest of her life, she deserves a break from the military force."

Colonel Wareing listened hard to Sarah Johnson, which made him look at President Berry, and watch her nod her head agreeing. Captain Weller said in a solemn voice, "There's only one person I'll miss and that's John Raven, where you owe him."

Colonel Wareing frowned, while saying, "He once mentioned those very same words to me, when I was compelled to be there by his side at the time he needed me the most."

President Berry placed her head down thinking back to *America In Conflict* and how John Raven had almost died.

She slowly lifted her head ruling out the possibility Raven would be killed and said, "We have to believe John Raven will make it through the terrible ordeal that beckons."

She placed her hand out to hold Captain Weller's hand, as she looked into her sorrowful eyes just trying to reassure her by saying, "Trust me, John will come home."

Captain Weller, nodded her head slowly, agreeing and replied, "He has to because we need him."

Williams, who was sitting with other members of Unit Expendable said, "The first chance I get, I will be there with Unit Expendable to help bring him home."

Colonel Wareing smirked, saying, "The difference between Unit Expendable and John Raven is that you need him. John Raven doesn't need anybody. He is the ultimate soldier the United States is proud to call up on, on many occasions."

Lundgren listened hard to everything being discussed and said, "The first chance I get, I'm going back for him when dying is not an option!"

Colonel Wareing stared at Lundgren with concern replying, "Lundgren! The Russians and Iranians are going to be ready for us to return at some point to collect who is our main man. It will be like lambs being taken to the slaughter, and I can't allow that to happen!"

Williams just as before, said, "Can't or won't! Don't you forget Pomfret and Ashworth are still somewhere down there?"

Colonel Wareing, replied, "I've told you once Williams!"

Williams replied, "I'm with Lundgren. The first chance Unit Expendable receives, we should go back to rescue a man whom we admire and who should be I think standing behind President Berry when she is performing her duties."

Captain Weller turned around, gently took hold of Williams' hand and said, "Thank you."

After listening to what Williams had just said, President Berry spoke by telling everybody, "I will most certainly give that opinion of yours some thought."

Sarah Jane slowly started to gain consciousness again groaning a little, which made everybody in the helicopter turn to look at her. Captain Weller produced a smile of glee, feeling thankful that she still had her daughter. Colonel Wareing looked down at her, asking, "Are you okay kid?"

Sarah Jane nodded her head wearily, and then looked to her mother asking, "Where's Dad?"

Captain Weller looked down at her and couldn't answer her question immediately because her eyes started to form tears once more. Still lying down, Sarah Jane said, "Mum?"

Other members of Unit Expendable closed their eyes fearing the worst, which made Sarah Jane slowly struggle to sit up, while ignoring the pain she was in and say to the Colonel, "Sir. We have to go back."

Colonel Wareing's eyes started to glaze over slightly, which made him turn away and say, "We've already been through this."

Lundgren leaned forward, with his hair hanging into his face. He touched Sarah Jane's arm wanting to reassure her, and said, "I promise you, I will bring your father home. He's our blood."

Sarah Jane frowned; feeling confused at what Lundgren had just told her. She couldn't understand why Lundgren had used the expression, our blood. Lundgren pulled his arm away slowly, which made Sarah Jane reply, "Thank you. It's going to take something more than you, Unit Expendable, or even members of Unit Invincible to help my father escape from wherever he is."

Listening to her daughter speak like this, Captain Weller gave a wry grin, saying, "Perhaps it's time to contact your brother."

With John Weller's name being mentioned, brought back memories to President Berry, which made her smile as she remembered what he had once done for her.

Lundgren asked, "Does Raven's son fight like the John Raven I know?"

President Berry visualised Weller, replying to his question by saying, "Oh yes, because he is John Raven through and through."

Lundgren turned to the Colonel and said, "Call this man, because together we will bring John Raven home."

Sarah Jane looked at the Colonel waiting anxiously for a response. He looked at Captain Weller, where she too was waiting, which made him reluctantly ask, "Would you like me to call him?"

Colonel Wareing remained quiet for a few seconds and then spoke by saying, "When we get to base, "Call Ricky Stevens."

Captain Weller replied, "Okay."

Colonel Wareing glanced across at Lundgren sitting opposite him and carried on saying, "Then call John Weller."

Lundgren couldn't resist from asking, "When do we begin?"

Colonel Wareing thought back to his good friend, John Raven, and then looked at President Berry and replied, "Soon!"

Sarah Jane couldn't resist from saying, "I told my Dad, don't make it one time . . . ."

Colonel Wareing interrupted her by saying, "Don't even think that! Somehow, someway, we will bring your father home."

All the members of Unit Expendable gave a huge cheer feeling united at the prospect of being able to release their mentor. They couldn't wait to start planning their dangerous mission once Raven's son arrives at the U.S. military base in Kuwait. All they had to do was contact him. Although Captain Weller started to feel renewed hope, inwardly she wondered what Louise's reaction would be when she eventually finds out about the bad news.

Infliction

$\mathcal{A}$s the U.S. helicopter flew back to Kuwait, John Raven was standing alone looking at the carnage he had created, while listening to the jeering crowd clenching their fists and hurling insults at him. He glanced and then held his head low feeling disappointment. The enemy surrounded him, leaving him to slowly look up and watch them pointing their weapons at him. In a strong tone, they shouted, "Drop your weapon!"

Raven turned his head, moved his eyes to look through his hair at the hostile enemy, and then turned back feeling deflated. The allied enemy soldiers shouted to him once more, "Drop your weapons!"

They fired bullets close to his feet, which made him glare at the enemy soldiers. Reluctantly, while still glaring at the enemy, he decided to release his grip and drop his weapon to the ground and give himself up. The allied enemy soldiers ran to him, grabbed him hard, and dragged him to Cairns and President Modarres who were rapidly approaching the man who had been the instigator of the devastation that had been created.

Cairns laughed when he saw the soldiers had now captured Raven and said to President Modarres, "I have to give something back to Raven, he had once given to me at the point of my downfall."

President Modarres asked, "What might this be?"

Cairns decided to quick stride replying, "Watch this!"

As he passed by Russian and Iranian soldiers waiting in anticipation at what he was about to do to Raven, he approached the two Russian soldiers holding each arm as he clenched his fist tight. Raven saw him clench his fist, making him recall when he had punched him in the face after uncovering espionage activities. Raven moved his eyes, staring in the face of Cairns, while watching him lift his arm to hit Raven in the face hard. Cairns hit him that hard, he would have fallen over if it hadn't been for the soldiers holding him. The crowd cheered at Cairns' actions and celebrated by starting to light fires. Others would throw stones at Raven feeling hatred, which made the Russian soldiers point their guns at them when they were also being hit with stones. Raven looked back at Cairns, spat the blood out of his mouth and just stared at him. President Modarres walked, wanting to stand beside Cairns and placed his hand on his shoulder, listening to Cairns say, "That felt good! I've waited a long time to give him back what he once gave to me!"

President Modarres noticed that Raven still had his knife and went to take it from Raven's holster. When he pulled it out, Cairns looked at it and then weaved it around in front of his face. He held the handle tightly, lunging forward with the tip of the blade resting onto Raven's throat. With evil showing in his eyes he said, "You don't how good this feels to have you in such a vulnerable position!"

Raven didn't move a muscle; although the adrenalin was still flowing through his body, he remained calm just staring into the face of Cairns. Cairns produced an evil grin, while pulling the knife away from his throat, which made Raven say, "I'm going to kill you next time!"

Cairns moved his head to look at President Modarres, and then spontaneously lashed out using Raven's knife to slice open his chest. The knife had touched the clotted wound Raven had received earlier, making it bleed once more. He watched the blood drip down Raven's chest and then looked at Raven's knife where it had become blood stained. He held the knife up, placed it to his mouth licking the blood of Raven. Raven watched, but could do nothing. Cairns moved his eyes to glance at the Iranian crowd, while holding the knife up in the air shouting, "I have the blood of John Raven!"

The crowd cheered, starting to shout and bawl once more. A member of the hostile crowd threw a picture of him burning, which made Raven take notice of. Cairns pointed at the picture, while shouting to the Iranian crowd, "This is what will happen to America's finest soldier! He will burn, and then go to hell!"

Raven moved his eyes, staring at Cairns, after listening to his last remark and watched him place his face into Raven's face and say, "Not before you've received infliction!"

President Modarres turned around to watch the burning buildings, the smoke, and the destruction Raven and Unit Expendable had created, which made him want to ask, "Why have you done this to us?"

Raven frowned at President Modarres's question, spat more blood out of his mouth and replied in a deep voice, "You threatened the United States with nuclear war!"

President Modarres replied, "Correct, where you have only delayed the inevitable from happening. When more missiles are transported from Russia it will only be a matter of time before the rest of your nation joins you in hell!"

Cairns laughed as he turned to President Modarres to say, "He didn't only come to fight for his country. He came for the good looking Captain Weller, who I have to say, is quite the shag!"

Raven lunged forward in anger at Cairns, making the soldiers hold him much more tightly, and pull him back. Cairns smirked, saying, "I'm sorry John, did I hit a raw nerve?"

Raven staring into the eyes of Cairns replied, "Fuck you!"

Cairns moved forward, placed his hand onto Raven's wound and watched him pulling his face feeling the pain rush through his body from Cairns' grip. Cairns laughed, saying, "John, John! I guess I'm just going to have to teach you some manners!"

He looked at the knife he was still holding and then decided to clench his fist with his other hand and thump Raven in the stomach hard, winding him badly. With Raven bending down, President Modarres placed his leg up and put his boot onto his head, which made Raven slowly stand up and give a menacing stare at the Iranian President, and shout, "You're a fucking dead man!"

President Modarres looked stern, but remained silent. As he watched Raven, he said to Cairns, "We should take him back to my palace."

Cairns nodded agreeing with the president. President Modarres turned to the soldiers and carried on saying. "Put him in the truck!"

Cairns held his hand up holding Raven's knife and said, "Do you think this man is worthy of being able to travel in our vehicles after he has destroyed so many?"

President Modarres narrowed his eyes asking, "What do you mean?"

Before answering he looked into the eyes of Raven, replying, "He can walk!"

Cairns shouted to Colonel Mihailov to bring the handcuffs and a rope from one of the military vehicles. President Modarres frowned once more, which made him ask, "What are you going to do?"

Cairns, still looking into the eyes of Raven replied, "Later I'm going to kill John Raven, but for now he's going to suffer from the infliction I intend to place on him!"

Colonel Mihailov walked up to Cairns with the handcuffs and the rope, and listened to him say, "Place the handcuffs on him, and then wrap the rope around his waist."

Colonel Mihailov did as Cairns had ordered and then asked, "Now what?"

Cairns, who hadn't taken his eyes away from Raven, replied; "Now you fasten the rope to my vehicle! We will travel through Iran passing the Iranian people, who will be free to do what they want to this U.S. soldier as we travel to President's Modarres's palace."

The Iranian crowd standing close by to Cairns had heard what he had said, which made them cheer and spread the word among themselves. Cairns told the Russian soldiers to bring Raven to his own vehicle he would be travelling in, and tie the rope to the back bumper. Raven was helpless; he couldn't do anything to protect himself from the actions being instructed by Cairns. When the soldiers had tied the rope to the military vehicle, Cairns told all the allied enemy soldiers to climb back into their vehicles and follow him to President Modarres's palace. President Modarres smirked and patted Cairns on the shoulder feeling pleased, which made him say, "This has just been a temporary setback, which can be fixed."

Raven spat more blood out of his mouth and then turned to Cairns to say "You haven't got a fucking prayer!"

Cairns, holding Raven's knife, stood still choosing not to reply. After giving a stern look at Raven, he turned to walk down the side of his truck and climbed into the passenger seat, telling the soldier sitting in the driver's seat to drive. The soldier obeyed Cairns by starting the engine, placing the gearstick into gear and released the clutch and handbrake to make the truck slowly move. The rope started to take the strain, which meant Raven having no choice but to move with the truck. Armed soldiers walked alongside Raven, when at times, they would prod him with their weapons. The Iranian truck travelled outside the military base, which made the crowd run up to Raven. The Russian soldier's pointed their weapons at them, making them think twice about their actions. It didn't stop them from throwing stones and burning flags at him. Some hit him on his back, which made him look at the hostile Iranian crowd in anger. Cairns wound the window down and placed his head out to see what was happening behind the truck. He laughed when he saw him being attacked by the Iranian people. Cairns placed his head back inside the cab, turned to President Modarres sat behind and said, "Your people hate Raven more than me!"

President Modarres replied, "We stand united, achieving our objective by not letting any U.S. soldiers stand in our way."

Cairns smirked, feeling proud and replied, "Soon you will have it all."

President Modarres laughed and said to the driver, "Drive faster!"

The driver sped up making Raven run to keep up with the truck. Struggling to remain standing, he fell down with the truck dragging him on the road.

With what had happened in Iran and who it had involved, it didn't take the media long to start broadcasting the news. They were announcing that President Berry, the Secretary of State, Sarah Johnson, Captain Weller and soldiers that had been forgotten had been freed by John Raven and Unit Expendable. Live pictures showed President Berry climbing out of the U.S. helicopter at the Kuwaiti military base, which made it almost a happy day for every single U.S. citizen. When pictures showed John Raven being dragged through the streets of Iran, it made their faces change to despair knowing what he had done for them previously.

Colonel Wareing walked inside the control centre to greet General Hardaker and Colonel Armstrong. General Hardaker said, "Good work Colonel."

Colonel Wareing replied, "I disagree. We're a few men down."

General Hardaker frowned when he couldn't see John Raven, but did notice President Berry and Sarah Johnson. He decided to walk across and escort them to where they could now get cleaned up. One of the workers inside the control centre shouted, "Sir!"

The sudden outburst from the communications worker made all the officers stop in their stride. President Berry and Sarah Johnson turned around to see that on the huge screen, John Raven being dragged through the streets of Iran in a cruel sadistic way. Captain Weller walked inside the control centre with a weak frail Sarah Jane, helped by Steve Lundgren and Luke Tyler. Lieutenant Parr was behind with other members of Unit Expendable and saw John Raven on the screen and said, "Look at what they're doing to John Raven!"

Captain Weller looked at the screen feeling sadness in her heart. Sarah Jane glared at the screen saying, "We have to go back for him!"

Lundgren agreed by replying, "I agree!"

Colonel Wareing produced a sombre look as he saw his good friend being dragged down the road. Starting to regret his decision about not going back after President Berry had authorised him to do so, he brought out his mobile phone to dial John Weller's mobile number. Standing there, still watching the horrific scenes when the Iranian people were throwing stones, chanting and raving at Raven, Colonel Wareing waited for Weller to answer his phone. Captain Weller saw that he was using his phone, which made her ask, "Who are you ringing?"

Colonel Wareing replied, "John Weller-Raven, only he isn't answering his phone!"

Captain Weller closed her eyes feeling the stress of it all. She opened them after hearing Sarah Jane say, "With it being the Christmas holidays, Louise will have made him turn his phone off!"

Captain Weller watched Raven on the big screen scamper to his feet and replied, "Your brother will be just enjoying his Christmas with Louise. He wasn't to know all this was about to occur."

Colonel Wareing joined in the conversation saying, "He was aware of the nuclear threat Iran and Russia had made to the U.S. though!"

Captain Weller sighed, with her eyes starting to water, forming tears once more. Sarah Jane took a few paces to stand by her wanting to give her mother a hug. Staring at John on the screen she said, "We can only hope that your brother has seen this report in the U.S. and will want him to make the right decision."

President Berry walked back to stand beside Colonel Wareing, saying, "You should have gone back when I said so!"

Captain Weller moved her head to listen to the president's comments, and then listened to the Colonel reply, "With having you and Sarah Johnson on board, you know I couldn't have done this."

President Berry, with a sharp tongue said, "We should have at least tried, because the Raven's have always been there for me!"

Colonel Wareing, while watching Raven being dragged through the streets of Iran, started to feel guilty. Feeling angry at what he was witnessing on the screen, made him bawl to one of the work operatives to contact John Weller-Raven. He turned to Captain Weller and Sarah Jane to say in a solemn voice, "I'm sorry."

Colonel Wareing then turned around and passed a dumbfounded President Berry walking away feeling dejected, which made Lundgren shout, "Sir!"

The Colonel stopped in his stride to look back at Lundgren, to listen to him say, "We'll get him out."

Colonel Wareing reluctantly nodded his head agreeing and then turned around to walk away, when Sarah Johnson stopped him to say, "He'll make it! He's John Raven!"

In a sombre voice, Colonel Wareing replied, "Sometimes we ask too much of him, and we only realise it when it's too late."

He then walked by her to go to Colonel Armstrong's office just wanting to be alone.

As John Raven was being dragged, at times he glanced at the Iranian crowd, wondering how people can behave like this towards another human being. He scampered back to his feet and saw in the distance, Afshin cheering with the hostile crowd, which disappointed him. Ignoring all the shouts and the taunts, he saw Farrin and Delroba standing there watching, suspecting that they had been made to come against their wishes. Feeling surprised at seeing these two genuine Iranian people once again, he stumbled and fell to the ground with the military truck still pulling him along the road. Farrin ran out into the road, making the Russian soldiers aim their weapons at her. She shouted, "Please. I mean no harm."

Afshin watched his wife running out into the road to help Raven and stopped cheering with the rest of the crowd, producing a face of anger. Raven saw her and scampered to his feet where he bent down for her to wipe away the blood from his face and chest. With all the pain he was feeling, he looked down at her, saying in a solemn voice, "Thanks."

Afshin wasn't happy with his wife's actions, which made him run up to her and slap her, immediately knocking her to the ground. Raven shouted in anger and raised both of his arms, but knew he couldn't do anything with his hands handcuffed. Afshin ran to kick Raven, making the Iranian crowd become more hostile and start to break through the enemy soldiers. Cairns stopped the truck, while Russian soldiers climbed out of several other military vehicles, aiming their weapons at the hostile crowd. Cairns climbed out of the truck, walked to the rear, ordering the soldiers to place Raven inside the back of the truck. With the instructions Cairns had just given, Raven asked, "Are you going soft suddenly?"

Cairns replied, "No! I want to relish the opportunity to kill you when nobody is going to take that away from me!"

The Russian soldiers grabbed Raven, and threw him into the back of the truck. They followed, and sat down next to him still pointing their weapons at him, suspecting that he was still a threat because of whom he was. Raven rested his arms onto his legs looking at both of his hands handcuffed. He glanced at the soldiers sitting opposite who were pointing their fingers at him while sniggering at the same time. With knowing he couldn't do anything, he placed his head back letting it rock from side to side with the bumps in the road. As the Iranian crowd chanted outside the truck, John could only think of his family and begin to wonder how he was going to re-join them once more. Slowly, his eyes softened as he thought back to Christmas Day, spending time with members of the family. Then his soft look became stern when he recalled the event leading up to Captain Weller's kidnap and one reason for him becoming involved in yet another war. The Russian soldiers spoke among themselves and laughed at what they were about to do. One of the soldiers raised his elbow and hit Raven hard in the face. Raven retaliated by kicking the soldier, which made him lean towards Raven, feeling the pain. Raven moved forward and head butted him hard, making blood gush down his face. The other Russian soldiers watching, pointed their guns at him, which made Raven glare at them all and retreat, with him saying, "You're all dead, the first chance I get!"

The Russian soldiers laughed at Raven's outburst, starting to realise they were slowing down to stop. Two Russian soldiers grabbed Raven and threw him out of the truck, which made him land awkward on the ground. He sighed, as he lifted his head, taking notice of President Modarres palace, and then felt the clutching hand of Cairns grab his hair and pull him up. Cairns looked at him and said, "You're hardly the warrior now!"

Raven held his head low with Cairns still holding his hair with a tight grip. He moved his eyes to look at Cairns with hatred, which made Cairns say, "Admit it, you hate me don't you?"

Raven spat blood out of his mouth, replying, "That much so, I'm going to kill you the first chance I get!"

President Modarres climbed out of the truck and went to stand next to Cairns. Cairns, noticing the Iranian president had now stood beside him said, "These U.S. Green Berets never seem to understand when they're beaten."

He pushed down on Raven's head and lifted his knee up and hit him in the side of his face using his kneecap, which made Raven fall to the floor. Cairns walked by him and told the Russian and Iranian soldiers to take him to the courtyard, unlock his handcuffs and place his hands around the pole and then put the handcuffs back on him where he could not escape.

The Russian soldiers did as they were told, leaving John alone trapped around a pole wondering what the enemy was about to do to him. He rested his head against the pole and closed his eyes beginning to notice the pain rushing through his body. In the distance he heard sounds from the enemy approaching feeling pleased that they had captured one of America's legendary Green Berets. Russian soldiers joined them, feeling content with watching the Iranians do what they had to do. Raven moved his head back starting to watch one of them carrying a whip, which made him, close his eyes, suspecting that he was now going to endure even more pain. One of the Iranian soldiers walked up to Raven to taunt him and begin pulling his hair tightly, eventually placing his face into his saying, "You come into our country and create all of this devastation and expect to live?"

Raven glared with his menacing eyes at the Iranian soldier, choosing not to reply. The conscript soldier threw his head forward where it hit the pole and then stepped aside for another soldier to step up and start whipping him on his back. Raven moved his head back yelping in pain. The Russian soldiers cheered, encouraging the Iranians to carry on whipping him. The Iranians would look back laughing knowing that they were placing Raven in great pain. After several lashes of the whip, Raven leant sideways on the pole feeling as though his body couldn't take anymore. President Modarres and Cairns were watching from the balcony feeling pleased with themselves. Cairns fired his gun up into the air making the soldiers in the courtyard look up to him. He shouted, "Enough!"

Raven, still leaning sideways on the pole, looked back at Cairns and President Modarres standing on the balcony holding just one thought, which was, if I have to die, somehow someway I'm going to take you two with me.

Cairns saw Raven staring up at him and moved his finger to one of the Iranian soldiers to give him one final lash of the whip, making Raven fall to the ground and lay there on his stomach. One of the Russian soldiers threw a bag of salt to one of the Iranian soldier's, which made others laugh as they watched him pick it up and open it. Looking at Raven lying on the floor, he produced an evil grin as he started to walk over to Raven. He placed his hand up into the air to his colleagues, while pouring salt onto his wounds produced from the lashes he had just received. This made

Raven arch his back with feeling even more pain than before and made him casually look at the ground saying in a low voice, "I'm done."

One of the Iranian soldiers heard him say something and asked, "You say something you American piece of trash?"

Raven sighed, as he felt the boot of an Iranian soldier hit him in the kidneys. Cairns came outside to join all the soldiers and walked on Raven's back and then crouched down to him and said, "Welcome to Iran John!"

Raven didn't reply, instead he just produced a prolonged blink, while looking at the ground relishing the thought about the first chance he may have when he would then kill them all for what they had done to him. Cairns grabbed John's hair tightly, which made him have no choice but to have to stand up. Cairns released his grip on Raven's hair and walked around to face him, which made Raven ask in a weak voice, "What happened to you?"

Cairns produced an evil grin, replying, "I know how to get well paid for my actions, obviously you don't!"

Still giving a sombre look toward Cairns, Raven asked, "You're an American, how can you do this to your own people?"

Cairns chuckled, producing an evil face as he pulled Raven's hair, which made his head hang to one side. Cairns placed his face into Raven's and replied, "I'm no American and never will be again!"

He released his grip on Raven's hair and then called some of the Iranian soldiers over to him, ordering them to take him to a cell below the palace. Cairns watched closely as the soldiers went to collect the keys from the Russians to release the handcuffs. As he waited for them to walk back to Raven, John shook his head in disgust, asking the same question, "What happened to you Cairns?"

Cairns, was watching the Iranian soldiers walking back to him with the keys. He turned to face Raven after hearing the same question being asked again, deciding to remain silent by choosing not to reply. He told the soldier to hurry and take off the handcuffs, which made two more soldiers come and pull him away from the pole. The Iranian soldier holding the handcuffs asked Cairns, "Have I to place these back on to him?"

Before answering, Cairns assessed Raven to see whether he would still be a danger. Noticing that he was weak and badly injured, he took the handcuffs from him, replying, "No, we won't need these anymore, take him to the cell!"

Cairns watched the soldiers start to drag Raven, where he produced an evil smirk and shouted, "Raven! I'm going to give the Iranians what they want, because tomorrow I'm going to send you to hell by burning you at the stake!"

Raven heard what Cairns had just said and turned his head to look at him in the corner of his menacing eyes. Just as before, he remained silent, quietly thinking about how he will have his revenge.

Cairns laughed out aloud as he watched Raven being taken away. President Modarres, who was still standing on the balcony, applauded his actions. As the soldiers took Raven inside the palace and down a flight of stairs, Cairns stopped laughing and said, "When you're gone, the real game begins!"

He turned to the Russian soldiers to tell them to prepare the courtyard for the Iranian people to attend and be able to watch John Raven burn tomorrow. They immediately followed Cairns' orders feeling pleased that one of America's finest soldiers was going to die in a way like no other had ever experienced before.

The Iranian soldiers arrived at Raven's cell. One of the soldiers following his colleagues walked in front and kicked the cell door open. The two soldiers, who were holding Raven, threw him inside the cell, where he fell to the ground deciding not to move. The Iranian soldier slammed the cell door shut and locked the door with the keys. Before moving away, he looked through the bars to see a badly wounded Raven still lying in the same position, which made him laugh, especially with now knowing he would burn to death the following day.

Raven was alone in the cell not wanting to move a muscle after the pain he had endured. With his hair hanging into his face, he looked at the ground starting to think of Captain Weller and Sarah Jane, thankful that they were now out and free from all this torture and infliction. He closed his eye's feeling despair when he thought of his father, and those words, one time too many, which made him say in a low voice, "I'm coming home."

Slowly, he started to crawl forwards to the stone wall, deciding to sit upright wanting to rest his back against it. Resting his back against the stone wall made him move forward after feeling the pressure of the pain resting on to his wounds. Occasionally, he would lean back on to the stone wall still feeling the pain, but deciding to absorb it. He sighed, raised his head and looked at the cell door, thinking of Louise and his son, John Weller-Raven, wondering what they must now be doing. He turned away, starting to breathe heavy thinking back to the time when he had told his son, John that he will know when the time is right when he has to make the right decision. Unknown to John Weller-Raven, that time has now come.

Decisions

$\mathcal{T}$he people of the United States realised the initial threat of war made by Iran and Russia, had stopped with the nuclear missiles being destroyed while in transit by John Raven and Unit Expendable. The Vice President of the U.S. remained in constant contact with the President of Russia, who kept confirming he had nothing to do with what Iran had been conspiring to with his own nation. It was only a part of Russia that had broken away wanting to form their own allegiance with Iran, with the help of Colonel Mihailov. For now, at least a New Year could beckon when peace may prevail, which made everybody in different parts of the world want to celebrate the New Year with renewed hope.

Louise and John had planned an evening out, looking forward to enjoying a meal and having a few drinks, and then later, go back home to spend the rest of the evening with her father, Kirk. John drove Louise's Mini Cooper S, where they talked about everything, except the one subject John would have liked an answer to, which was the proposal. Inwardly, he became agitated at the fact Louise had not yet given him an answer to his proposal. Wisely, he chose not to linger on the subject has it could have repercussions later when one, possibly both, may regret saying the wrong thing. He turned to glance at Louise, noticing she was beautifully dressed. He smiled at her, saying, "You look good."

Louise smiled, looked back at him with her fringe hanging onto her forehead and replied, "Thanks. You don't look so bad yourself."

As John was changing gear, Louise gently placed her hand onto his and said, "Thanks John for being here this Christmas."

John replied, "I've enjoyed spending time with you."

Louise said, "It could always be like this, if you weren't in the military anymore."

John ignored Louise's comment and just looked through the front windscreen, which made Louise ask, "Did you hear me John?"

John in a solemn voice replied, "I heard you."

Louise watched him place the signal on and turn into the restaurant to park the car and asked, "So what do you think?"

Although John knew, he replied to Louise with a question, "About what?"

Louise narrowed her eyes, slapping John's leg gently and said, "You know very well what about."

After John parked the car, they climbed out, and walked together to the restaurant entrance. Louise, aware that John hadn't answered her question, reminded him by asking him the same question again. This made John reply, "What do I do if I leave the military?"

Louise started to feel hidden glee suspecting John could be at least thinking about what he will do if he decides to leave the military. With this, she replied, "I'm sure you will find something."

They took their seats at the table, with John staring at the roaring fire, watching the flames flickering beside the Christmas tree, while thinking about what Louise had just said to him. The waitress came to their table, and gave them a menu each; to choose drinks and their meal. When they had chosen what they wanted to eat and drink, the waitress came back to the table, took the order and went to process it. As they waited for their food and drinks, John asked Louise,

"If I left the military tomorrow for good, what would your answer be to my proposal?"

Louise looked starry-eyed at John, feeling as though she was winning the battle in being able to persuade him to leave the U.S. military for good. She smiled, replying, "You leave the military force tomorrow and my answer will be a definite yes."

The waitress came back to their table to give them their drinks and tell them that their meal wouldn't be long. Louise thanked her as John thought about her reply. When she turned to speak with John, he asked, "What if I can't leave the military?"

Louise's smile started to disappear, making her reply, "I don't want to think about that."

She picked up her glass of wine, taking a sip while looking across the table at John, wishing she could read his thoughts. The waitress came back to give them their mixed grills, which made John say, "There is plenty of food on those plates."

In a low voice, Louise mumbled, "Yes and I'm eating for two."

John didn't hear what she had said, which made him say with concern, "Pardon?"

Louise looked back across at him smiling and replied, "I just said I'm famished."

They picked up their knives and forks, and started to eat their food while making polite conversation. The television in the corner of the room was showing the news channel, making John at times glance at it. His face changed when he saw for the first time, a replay of his father dragged through the streets of Iran. Louise was speaking to him when he was only half listening because periodically he kept looking at the television at his father. When the replay of John's father had ended, the newscaster broadcasted, "This man John Raven freed the President of the U.S, the Secretary of State and two U.S. soldiers from Iran where they are now safe in Kuwait. Who's going to help the one man who has done it all?"

The broadcast ended with the credits scrolling over a picture of John Raven burning, which made the people inside the restaurant become somewhat quiet and sombre. Louise carried on speaking to John, noticing that something or someone had distracted him. Suspecting it could be another woman; she asked, "Who are you looking at?"

John was churning thoughts over in his mind, making him start to rotate his thumbs. Louise looked behind her to see a couple of good-looking women. One of the women had brunette hair, and the other had blonde hair. She turned back to John and said, "Why did you ask me to marry you when you're looking at those two tarts over there?"

John nodded his head from side to side replying, "No! I wasn't looking at them. I was watching television."

Louise turned around again, noticing the television and saw the next movie starting. She narrowed her eyes, saying, "I don't believe you!"

Doubting John was the worst thing she had ever done because he gave her an evil stare, which made her say, "I'm not your enemy, so don't look at me like that again!"

John listened to Louise's outburst, while sitting there trying to contain his anger. Louise noticed John had become quiet, making her say harshly, "I'm going home!"

John frowned, looked at her, but still said nothing. He sat there churning thoughts over in his mind about his father, while watching Louise pick up her handbag and shout, "Have one of them! You're welcome to them!"

Her sudden outburst made people close by, glance at her with concern. She rushed past people and out of the restaurant, only to stop outside and look through the window to see what John does with the two women she thinks he was watching. They noticed John was now sitting alone amid his own thoughts, and decided to walk over to his table where he looked up at them both. The blonde woman asked him, "Can we join you?"

Tears started to form in Louise's eyes as she watched John take a sip of his drink, suspecting that he had rejected them when they turned to walk away. Realising she was wrong, she came back inside the restaurant sheepishly, took off her jacket and sat back down opposite John and said, "I'm sorry."

John moved his head slowly, giving her a solemn look reluctantly saying, "It's okay."

Louise shook her head disagreeing, replying, "No it's not okay because I've behaved like an ass. I now know you're not interested in those two women, but what were you watching?"

John replied, "As I said before, the television."

She turned to look at the television, saying "Something had caught your eye, what was it?"

John, feeling disappointed, sighed. Taking a sip of lager, he looked at the television at the report being replayed, after the film stopped for the interval. Louise turned and saw on the television, John Raven being dragged through the streets of Iran, which made her slowly look back to John and say, "I'm sorry."

John watched the report and replied to Louise, "It looks as though I have a big decision to make."

Louise put her hand out and placed it on John's, asking, "Do you want to become involved?"

John gave a solemn look at Louise, replying, "I have to do what I feel is right?"

Louise closed her eyes at the thought of John going back into a warzone, which made him ask, "Will you still be there for me when I get back?"

Louise took another sip of her wine, paused for a few seconds and later replied, "What if you don't make it back?"

John brought out his mobile phone from his pocket and turned it on. He scrolled through his list of contacts and sent a text to Ricky Stevens. Louise watched with intent, knowing no matter what and because of who had been captured, he had to go, which made her ask, "What if you don't come back John?"

John left his phone switched on and put it on to the table. Seeing Louise becoming concerned, he answered her question by saying, "I have to make it back for you."

Louise's fringe fell down onto her forehead as she gave a half smile replying, "What about all the anxiety I'm going to go through?"

John placed out his hand to hold hers, replying, "I'm sorry to have to put you through this, but I have to do this for my father."

John's mobile phone rang, which made him let go of Louise's hand to pick up the phone and answer it. After Colonel Wareing was informed by the operative that John Weller-Raven had been contacted, he was put through, waiting for John to answer the phone. John pressed the button and said, "Hello."

Colonel Wareing replied, "Hello John, how are you?"

John suspected what Colonel Wareing was ringing him about and waited for him to mention his father had been captured and brutally tortured by the Iranians. Louise remained quiet fearing the worst and watched, starting to show sadness in her face, aware that it was only going to be a matter of time before John leaves her to do whatever it is he has to do.

Colonel Wareing spoke to John about his father admitting he had seen reports this evening on television, asking who was now going to help the one soldier who had done it all. Colonel Wareing told him that he had performed to the highest level by helping to free President Berry, Sarah Johnson, and two U.S. soldiers, when if he ever makes it home, he will receive another Purple Heart and Medal of Honour. John visualised the pictures of his father being pulled down the Iranian streets and said, "He's in the worst possible place you could imagine!"

Colonel Wareing in a sombre voice asked, "Will you help us to free your father from President Modarres's palace?"

John, feeling mixed up looked down and then slowly at Louise. She suspected what John was going to be asked, making a tear roll down her cheek. Feeling for Louise, he turned away asking Colonel Wareing, "Who is us?"

Colonel Wareing replied, "You will join Unit Expendable on this mission, when the enemy will no doubt be waiting for us to try to free John Raven. It will be dangerous, but just like a younger version of your father, I'm sure you will succeed."

John went quiet, while looking across the table at Louise. She was sitting in the chair feeling upset at losing her boyfriend to the military once more. He placed out his other hand and gently held Louise's hand saying, "I'll do it, but it has to be my way!"

Colonel Wareing replied, "Excellent, report to the U.S. military base. Instructions will be given to you to fly out to Kuwait as soon as possible."

Louise pulled her hand away from John and placed it to her mouth starting to worry about John returning to war. She placed her other hand on her stomach thinking about whether the baby she was carrying, that John didn't yet know about would have a father it could depend on.

John carried on speaking with Colonel Wareing, telling him that he had already contacted Ricky Stevens from Unit Invincible to meet him at the U.S. military base. Colonel Wareing raised his eyebrows, replying, "Unit Invincible and Unit Expendable working together as one, we should call you Unit Dispensable."

John didn't care what the unit name was called; he had just one sole purpose, which was to be able to free his father from the Iranians and Cairns. He was about to hang up when Colonel Wareing said, "John, if you're sitting nearby to Louise, tell her that your father managed to free her brother Gardenzio."

They ended their call, with Louise looking to her side away from John. He looked across at her wanting to tell her the good news about her brother and said, "Louise."

Although she had heard him, she refused to look at him with now having to accept, he was going to enter another warzone. With Louise's reaction, John decided not to tell her about her brother. Convincing her that he was doing the correct thing seemed much more important, which made him say again, "Louise."

She turned her head to face him, and listened to him carry on saying, "I have to do this and would prefer to do it with your blessing."

Louise took another sip of her wine, placed the glass back onto the table and replied, "I don't have much choice do I?"

John stood up, looked down at Louise while placing his jacket on and said, "We ought to go now."

Louise stood up to place her jacket on and asked, "Do you have to go now?"

John nodded his head saying yes, which made Louise feeling sad walk on by him and say, "Well! We had better go then hadn't we?"

John followed her to the car where he unlocked it and climbed into the driver's seat to start travelling back to Louise's house, aware he had to pack up his belongings and leave straight away. Louise was quiet in the car, which made John ask her on several occasions, "Are you okay."

She became irritated with John asking the same question and snapped, "Will you stop repeating the same question over and over!"

John sighed, realising he was in a no-win situation and chose to remain silent for the rest of the trip home. When they arrived home, John climbed out of the car and went inside the house, which made Kirk ask, "Where's Louise?"

As John walked by Kirk, he replied, "She's still sat in the car."

Kirk stood up, concerned for his daughter. He went outside and saw Louise weeping, which made him walk down the steps to her car and open the passenger door. Louise with her make-up smudged, glimpsed up at her father, saying. "John has to go back to the military on a mission to help free his father."

Kirk looked down feeling sorry for her as he placed his hand out to pull her up from the car seat. He closed the car door, placed his arm around her and walked up the steps to enter the house.

John was packing his belongings where nothing else mattered to him now, only his father. He came into the kitchen with his green bag to see Kirk and Louise talking while drinking a cup of coffee. Louise stopped talking to her father and said, "Is this it, is this where it ends?"

John dropped his bag to the floor replying, "I have to do this, you know I have no choice!"

Louise replied, "We have choices! It's how we see fit to use them."

With John almost giving up on his proposal to Louise, he asked, "Will you take me to the railway station?"

Louise started to cry once more nodding her head from side to side saying no. John gave her a sorrowful look, walked across to her to hold her hand and said, "You take care, Louise."

He let go of her hand and turned to look at Kirk with a casual blink trying to hide the emotions he was now feeling. He picked up his bag and opened the door, which made Kirk say, "Wait."

John stood there refusing to turn around to face Louise and Kirk, which made Kirk walk up to him and say, "I'll take you to the railway station."

John replied in a solemn voice, "Thanks."

Kirk looked back to Louise to ask, "Are you sure you don't want to come?"

Louise replied, "I'm sure."

Kirk nodded his head agreeing with her and walked through the door and down the steps behind John. Louise ran to the door, shouting, "John!"

Kirk watched him ignore her and carry on walking to his car. Louise shouted again, "John!"

Kirk looked once more and said, "For Christ's sake, answer her."

John looked at Kirk sternly, and then turned around to look at Louise, where she shouted, "I will always love you John. I just hate the soldier in you."

John paused by lowering his head to look at the ground before replying to her. Feeling as though he had no choice, he raised his head giving her a solemn look and replied, "You've always been the highlight of my day."

Louise closed her eyes remembering those words and then re-opened them to see that her father was driving John away to the railway station to start what he feels he now has to do. She stood there on the steps weeping, and placed her hand slowly onto her stomach saying, "You could have had it all John."

With John and her father now gone, she turned to go back inside the house where she went into the lounge to sob her heart out. The television had been left on showing two U.S. soldiers being interviewed. Louise carried on sobbing holding her head in her hands until she heard one of the soldiers on television say, "I owe John Raven my life."

Slowly, she lifted her head to watch the television and saw her brother Gardenzio, answering questions, which made her say, "Enzio, you're alive, thanks to John Raven."

She wiped her eyes, immediately wanting to tell John and her father what she was watching on television. With hearing such good news about her brother made her want to be with John before he boarded his train to thank him and now say yes to his proposal. She collected her jacket and put it on while looking at her brother once more on television and said, "I'll see you soon Enzio when you arrive home."

She then knew it was the right time to start wearing the engagement ring John had given to her. Aware that she was over the drink driving limit, she picked up the car keys left on the worktop and rushed outside to her car. After placing the keys into the ignition, she reversed quickly and then placed the gearstick into first gear and accelerated away wanting to catch her father and John up before he left on the next train.

John and Kirk arrived at the railway station, making their way to the platform to the train John was going to travel on.

Kirk couldn't resist from asking, "What's going to happen with you and Louise?"

John visualised Louise and replied, "I don't know what the future holds anymore."

He placed his hand out to shake Kirk's hand and said, "I have to tell you something."

Kirk watched the train about to leave and said, "Forget it. Board the train before you miss it."

John let go of Kirk's hand to hurry and board the train. When John had placed his bag above the seats, he sat down at the window, looked back at Kirk and gave him a casual wave. The train slowly started to move with Louise seen to be running down the platform, where she passed her father, which made him look stunned and shout, "Louise!"

Louise was running after the carriage John was now sitting in screaming John's name at the top of her voice. Some passengers, who were travelling on the same train as John, looked out of the window making comments that she did indeed look like a woman in distress. She could see John, which made her scream his name, but all John could do was hold his head low wondering what the future has in store for him. As she ran down the platform after the train starting to pick up speed, she constantly shouted John's name, holding her hand up showing that she was now wearing the engagement ring she had been given. A passenger sitting across from John said, "That woman on the platform is deeply distressed."

John turned to look out of the window and saw Louise holding her hand up to show that she was wearing the engagement ring, which made him produce a wry smile realising that she had now accepted his proposal. He placed the palm of his hand onto the window, leaving Louise to watch him disappear and hope that one day he will come back for her.

Kirk walked up to her and could now see she was wearing the engagement ring and asked, "Did you realise something when it was too late?"

Louise turned to her father and said, "Thanks to John's father, Enzio is now free."

Hearing this good news, Kirk gave Louise a hug and asked, "How do you know this?"

Louise lifted her hand to look at her engagement ring remembering John, and replied, "He was being interviewed at the U.S. Kuwaiti military base."

Kirk produced a huge smile and said, "This is good news."

Louise nodded her head agreeing with her father as she turned to watch the train disappear into the distance. Watching the train become smaller made her think what John has now to go through before she will see him again. She brought out her phone and sent him a text, but after failing to receive one, her father said, "He probably has his phone turned off."

Louise replied, "Yes probably."

Kirk put his arm around her as she looked at the railway line, imagining the train, she had just seen leave, and asked, "Have things just got better or worse?"

Kirk looked in the same direction as Louise replying, "He'll be back because the Raven's are a different breed. They don't die."

Louise brought a wry smile to her face as she placed her hand on her stomach knowing that she now had one of her own growing inside her and replied, "Oh, they're a different breed."

As she stroked her stomach, she hoped that none of the Raven's is killed in action, because after all they're only human.

Day of Reckoning

*J*ohn Weller had arrived back at the U.S. base with military personnel starting to look at him, feeling sorry for him. As he made his way to his own living accommodation, several soldiers would come up to him to apologise after hearing the news about his father being captured in Iran. There wasn't a lot he could say to them, only thanks for their concern.

Weller changed into military uniform, where he pulled out the knife that had once belonged to his father. He held it tightly with the light reflecting in the blade. Ricky Stevens knocked once on his door and walked inside to notice John was holding his knife tightly. Watching him becoming focused, he asked, "Are you planning to use that?"

John grinned as he put the knife down to welcome him, choosing to ignore the question put to him, deciding to ask, "Are you set for what we have to do?"

Ricky was prepared and ready to leave for Kuwait, replying, "I have to do this because your father was there for me when I needed him the most."

John still gathering his equipment said, "That was when my father and mother came to see you at N.A.S.A when you were traumatised with the death of Ashworth."

Ricky nodded his head agreeing, saying yes remembering his good friend, Lee Ashworth replying; "Now it's my turn to be there for your father."

John collected his weapons, walked past Ricky and said, "Mine too, let's go!"

They walked outside with Alison Colquhoun noticing them. Knowing that they were under orders to travel to Kuwait, she walked across to them saying, "Colonel Wareing is aware that you have arrived at the U.S. military base. You will be travelling to Kuwait in the next fifteen minutes."

She gave them papers to give to the Colonel once they had landed in Kuwait and then asked, "Would you like me to take you to the plane?"

John looked at her replying, "Yeah because time is of the essence."

John jumped in the military jeep to sit next to Alison while Ricky jumped in the back. They spoke casually at times, where Alison could see both men were focused in what they were about to do. When she reached the holding area for the plane that would be transporting them to Kuwait, Alison shouted to them, which made them turn around and listen to her say, "Bring John Raven home where he belongs."

John stared at Alison, while watching what was going on around him. Stevens glanced at him and then at Alison replying, "We'll try."

John then added to Stevens comment by saying, "We will!"

They turned around, leaving her to watch them make their way to the huge military plane and board it. She knew conflict with Iran was about to happen, when all that mattered was the freedom of John Raven.

As the plane started to taxi around to the runway, John said to Ricky, "When we arrive in Kuwait, we don't report to Colonel Wareing. We take a fully armed U.S. helicopter to fly into Iran to President Modarres's palace and take whatever is thrown at us."

Stevens was unsure, which made him ask, "Wouldn't we be better with backup?"

Weller focusing on only his father replied, "Yes, which they will have no choice but to do when we have already left for the warzone."

Stevens wasn't sure about John's decision, but reluctantly decided to agree, aware of whom it was they were going after.

Unknown to President Modarres and Cairns, Raven's son and colleague from Unit Invincible were travelling to try and free John Raven from the nightmare he was now going through. Cairns had different plans because on this same day, the stand outside in the courtyard was prepared with bushes placed around it ready to burn Raven alive.

Cairns went outside onto the balcony to see plenty of Iranian people attending what they would remember as a momentous occasion. He chuckled as he walked back inside to join President Modarres saying, "Today is going to be a day remembered when I will go down in history for killing the legendary soldier, John Raven."

President Modarres produced an evil smirk replying, "I think we should go and collect our guest and place him outside in the courtyard."

Cairns feeling pleased said, "He that waits will enjoy the moment."

As he walked across the office, he said to President Modarres, "Come, let's go and collect our guest and burn him alive!"

President Modarres moved from behind his desk to walk with Cairns, while saying, "Perhaps when the Raven saga is over, we can concentrate on destroying the United States and conquer Kuwait."

Cairns chuckled replying, "All good things come to those that wait."

He patted President Modarres on the back carrying onto say, "After the mishap with the previous nuclear missiles, Colonel Mihailov has confirmed that more nuclear missiles are being transported here from Russia."

President Modarres liked what he had just heard and replied, "Soon my friend, we will just as you had said once before, rule the world."

As the men walked side by side, Cairns said, "You've just got to have a little faith."

President Modarres smirked replying, "You're a dangerous man."

Cairns moved his eyes to look at the Iranian President and said, "I would never have guessed."

When they arrived at Raven's cell, they asked the guard to unlock the door and open it for them. Cairns and President Modarres walked inside, followed by two Iranian guards. Raven was sitting on the floor, where he moved his eyes to look at Cairns. Cairns standing close by him said in a stern voice, "Stand up!"

Raven focused on the Iranian guards pointing their weapons at him, deciding to stand up. Cairns became sarcastic by saying to Raven, "You look a mess!"

Raven replied, "No shit Cairns, although you're full of it!"

Cairns turned to the guards, telling them to take him outside to the courtyard and fasten him securely to the stand. President Modarres watched and said, "Raven is co-operating well."

Cairns gave out a burst of laughter replying, "When you rough them up a little they tend to do what I ask, even when it's John Raven."

President Modarres said, "I will watch this memorable death from my balcony."

Cairns replied, "You do that. Take the best seat in the house because today is a good day when I get to finish something I've wanted to do for a long time."

Cairns and President Modarres went their separate ways to prepare for what they thought was going to be a momentous occasion. Cairns arrived outside noticing the Iranian guards tying Raven to the stand, while President Modarres went to stand on the balcony above the courtyard at his palace. Cairns saw people gathering with some deciding to throw stones at Raven, which made him laugh. As he approached Raven, he placed his hand up to the Iranian people warning them to stop throwing stones, which they did, watching in anticipation at what he was about to do. He pulled from his pocket Raven's knife, where he now trotted to a helpless

Raven and placed it onto his throat saying, "I should cut your throat here and now!"

Raven stared back menacingly at Cairns replying in a stern voice, "Go on then! What's stopping you?"

Cairns without hesitation sliced Raven's neck where blood started to pour out. Raven could feel the blood running down onto his shoulder and down his chest, which made him say, "You bastard!"

Cairns stared back in the face of Raven, replying, "You're lucky it wasn't the jugular vein!"

Raven retaliated by saying, "You haven't got the bottle because you're all mouth and no action!"

Cairns produced a stern look at Raven asking, "Is that right?"

He turned away waving the knife to the Iranian crowd making them become even more hostile. Some people set alight pictures of Raven and threw them into the courtyard, which made Cairns place the knife into the fire and leave it. He then walked quickly over to Raven and hit him in the stomach with his knee that made him cower slightly, which meant that Cairns could produce a fist and hit Raven hard in the face.

The cruel actions being performed by Cairns were repeated again and again where the Iranian people just wanted to see the main event, which was to see Raven burn alive. It was up to Cairns when he chose to do this when nothing and nobody would force him into it. He wanted to enjoy being able to see Raven in pain. What he didn't envisage was members of Unit Invincible were travelling hoping to free him from the precarious position, he now found himself in.

Weller and Stevens had arrived at Kuwait with the newly appointed Paul Burn going to meet them in a military jeep. He asked, "Do you want me to take you to Colonel Wareing?"

Weller replied, "No! Take us to the U.S. helicopters immediately."

Burn looked at Weller concerned, aware that he was serious in what he had just said and asked, "Are you guys on a mission?"

Weller replied, "You could say that."

Burn, feeling worried said, "With what you're about to do, I can't authorise it!"

Stevens replied, "Stop being a wuss and just take us! It will be no fault of yours because we will take full responsibility."

Burn looked flustered saying, "Yeah, but you've involved me now! I'm a part of it all."

Weller, who was listening had heard enough, saying, "Paul! You do want to see my father back in the U.S?"

As Paul drove, he glanced at Weller saying, "Yeah but . . . ."

Weller interrupted him saying, "Put your foot down and move."

Burn wasn't happy, thinking about what the consequences could be when they had left the U.S. base in the fully armed helicopter. He made a point of saying, "You two could get me into trouble!"

Weller grinned as Stevens replied, "You worry too much Burn!"

Burn, feeling flustered said, "When you two are here, you're right. I do worry."

Weller smirked, saying, "You'll be okay."

Burn replied, "All I can say is, you better be right, or else I'm coming to look for you."

Stevens glanced at Weller grinning and replied, "Okay."

Burn said, "This is serious!"

Weller replied, "You're right! That's why we have to get my father, John Raven out of Iran as soon as possible!"

Colonel Wareing was speaking with Captain Weller after she had cleaned herself up to look more respectable. Feeling concerned for her, he said, "You can travel to the U.S. if you like and take leave."

Captain Weller looked out of the window, noticing Paul Burn shaking Weller's and Stevens' hand and then board one of the fully armed U.S. helicopters. Becoming concerned with what was happening, made her reply, "Thanks but no thanks. I have to see this through until the end, which by the looks of things, isn't too far away."

Colonel Wareing frowned at her reply as he walked across to the window to see, in the distance, John Weller and Ricky Stevens starting to take off in the U.S. helicopter. He looked at Captain Weller saying, "We have a situation here."

He rushed out of the office and went straight to the control centre where Paul Burn was coming to report what had just taken place. Colonel Wareing and Colonel Armstrong listened to Burn telling them he couldn't do anything with Weller's mind being made up. Captain Weller walked out of the Colonel's office to join General Hardaker as they made their way to the control centre to see harsh words being said. General Hardaker becoming concerned at the friction being created asked, "What's going on here?"

All three people looked at General Hardaker with Colonel Armstrong replying, "Weller and Stevens have arrived, failed to report, and taken a fully armed U.S. helicopter."

President Berry heard part of what Colonel Armstrong had just told General Hardaker and joined in the conversation by saying, "John Weller-Raven is doing what he feels he must!"

Colonel Wareing, standing nearby, replied, "That's all well and good, but you still need a plan."

Sarah Johnson went to stand next to President Berry replying to the Colonel's comment by saying, "President Berry, and I, was involved in traumatic situations, when the Raven's came to save us. I'm sure President Berry will agree with me when I say that those two soldiers have our full support for the actions they have taken and for the actions yet to be performed."

General Hardaker, also listening was standing there stony faced, watching Wareing and Armstrong look at each other in dismay, and then back at Sarah Johnson. Colonel Wareing was about to ask another question but President Berry stopped him when she said, "There isn't time for a discussion! I suggest you call a red alert and have Unit

Expendable, and whoever else you may seem fit to finish the job from the original first attack!"

General Hardaker called a red alert for members of Unit Expendable to be airborne in the next fifteen minutes. Pilots, Aindow, O'Brien, and Simpson were to be also airborne in their Stealth Bombers with a squadron of F35 pilots who included, Stuart Wareing, Jackson, Burton, and Womack to supply support if needed.

President Berry watched General Hardaker's actions, with Sarah Johnson saying, "You better place this military base on full alert for fear of attack by the enemy."

General Hardaker glimpsed at both high influential people knowing that he could not argue with what they had just sanctioned. Colonel Wareing looked around the control centre for Captain Weller, which made him ask, "Has anybody seen Captain Weller?"

One of the operatives saw her climbing aboard one of the U.S. helicopters with Sarah Jane, replying, "Sir. They are over there boarding the fully armed helicopters with Unit Expendable."

Colonel Wareing looked across, immediately saying to the operator, "Give me that headphone."

He spoke to Tyler and Seager, telling them to put Captain Weller on the radio. Before answering the Colonel, he looked back at Captain Weller, where she refused to take the radio from him, distinctly telling him, "Get us up in the air Tyler!"

Tyler placed the radio on the hook and started to make the helicopter rise. Colonel Wareing slammed the headphones down onto the operative's desk saying, "Captain Weller and Sarah Jane are not in a fit state to fly back into a warzone!"

President Berry knew what Captain Weller had gone through during her time spent in the Iranian cell. Aware of what she was about to do, she said, "With what she has gone through, and believe me, you don't want to know. I wouldn't blame her for wanting to put a few things right."

Colonel Wareing narrowed his eyes feeling annoyed events were happening without authorisation. Sarah Johnson walked over to him, saying, "This is a unique situation."

Colonel Wareing replied, "When John Raven is involved it always is!"

President Berry detected a tone in the Colonel's voice saying, "They're doing what is right for themselves, their nation, and their mentor, John Raven."

Colonel Wareing found it hard to accept the truth, but deep down, knew both women were correct in what they were saying. He heard the rumble of the Stealth Bombers speed down the runway, eventually taking off and ascending into the sky, to start travelling into another warzone. General Hardaker passed Colonel Wareing to pick up the headphone wanting to make radio contact with all three Stealth pilots. He told them that Iran was always going to be a threat and suggested that they bomb strategic positions, which would be confirmed by Colonel Armstrong and uploaded to their cockpits. He placed the headphone down and turned to Colonel Armstrong to say, "What are you waiting for? It's happening now!"

Colonel Armstrong immediately moved away to work with more of his colleagues, telling the Stealth pilots what they had to bomb to ensure Iran didn't become a threat to the rest of the world again. Operatives started to send the same information using wireless technology, which each pilot received inside their cockpit about what they had to bomb and destroy with minimum civilians being killed or injured. President Berry, watching with concern said, "I hope the nuclear power station is on the list of priorities."

Colonel Wareing looked dumbfounded, which made him ask, "You cannot be serious about bombing the nuclear plant?"

He heard the rumble of the F35 fighter planes take off one by one while listening to President Berry reply, "You don't get to pick and choose in war! You should know better than anybody! What I want is a New Year with the world knowing they can live their lives in peace, instead of listening to the likes of Cairns and his big ideas."

Colonel Wareing knew President Berry was right again in what she had said and chose to remain silent. Her tone changed slightly, which made her carry on saying, "You ought to think about being with Unit Expendable, because you may live to regret it if you don't join them this time."

Colonel Wareing produced a half grin, using a solemn voice, by replying, "Raven once told me that I owed him. I thought I had paid him back the last time when I managed to save his life in North Korea."

President Berry walked over to hold the Colonel's arm gently while replying, "Follow your heart this time, and not your brain. It will all become clear."

After listening to what President Berry had just said, Colonel Wareing walked away to the window starting to imagine what John Raven must be going through, knowing that Cairns despised him. He then recalled everything being a competition between him and Cairns, when they never got on together, resulting in bitter arguments and sometimes fights. Staring at the sky, Colonel Wareing remembered the time Cairns had been found out performing espionage. It was the start of his downfall with the U.S. military and the start of John Raven having to come back to fight another war, when this time, it was for the son he never knew. He held his hand to his mouth as he recalled different memories, which made him turn to see General Hardaker speaking with President Berry and Sarah Johnson. He then looked around the room watching everybody performing their rightful duties and decided that he should do what is right. He turned to leave the building, which made President Berry while speaking with the General watch, and slowly produce a smile knowing he had made the right decision.

Inside the Iranian courtyard, Cairns enjoyed inflicting pain on Raven's body, but suddenly stopped when he heard huge explosions. President Modarres became startled suspecting that his country was under attack again, which made him look down at the Iranian crowd, and then Cairns with concern. Louder explosions were heard, in the distance, which made Cairns run to collect Raven's knife. He held it tightly and hurried back to Raven, pointing the blade at his eyes. The heat from the blade made Raven look away, but Cairns grabbed his hair with his other hand, pulling his head closer to the blade making his eyes feel the heat once more. Raven immediately closed his eyes with not wanting to go blind from the heat. In the distance, he heard a hum, suspecting it could be a U.S. helicopter. Cairns also heard the constant hum, which made him take the knife away from Raven's eyes, turn and start shouting to the allied enemy soldiers, alerting them the Americans were coming once more. He threw Raven's knife to the ground and ordered Colonel Mihailov to bring out the scuds. The Iranian people in the courtyard had suddenly become quiet, but refused to leave. Raven somehow produced a smirk that Cairns had taken notice of. He picked up a flamethrower and ran back to Raven, grabbing his throat tightly, which made him feel more pain from where his neck had been cut earlier with the knife. He looked into Raven's face saying, "They're coming for you John! The cavalry is coming only you're going to be dead!"

Simon Ashworth and Hayley Pomfret, who were also members of Unit Expendable, were wearing Iranian clothes to disguise the fact of whom they were. Ashworth aware of the people standing close by to him said to Pomfret, "We can't let them do this to John Raven! We have to do something."

Pomfret agreed, replying, "Listen, do you hear that? Let's just wait for a little longer before we make our move."

Cairns turned around to see the Russian soldiers were driving the scud trucks underneath the arch into the courtyard. He then heard the sound of propellers that were much louder and much closer, which made him, hit Raven in the face once more with his fist. He stepped down, shouting to the Iranian people as he ignited the flamethrower. They started to chant and cheer, yet still feeling apprehensive about what they could also now hear, in the distance. Cairns pointed the flamethrower at the wood and bushes below Raven and said, "See you in hell!"

Raven moved his head sideways with his eyes focusing on what Cairns was about to do. Cairns laughed as he ignited the wood and bushes below Raven and shouted, "Burn!"

Weller and Stevens were flying close to President Modarres palace and could see the scud trucks were rotating into position to launch the missiles. Stevens said, "This looks ominous!"

Weller fired two missiles at one of the scud trucks, which knocked it on its side and exploded up into the air. Cairns waved his arm at the other scud truck to hurry so it could retaliate at the U.S. helicopter.

President Modarres looked stern, pointing his finger at Cairns, which made him shout at the Russian soldiers, where they started firing at Stevens and Weller. Pomfret said to Ashworth, "Look at Raven, he's going to burn to death! We have to do something and now!"

Ashworth looked at Raven feeling concerned and said, "For something or nothing, what I do is for you. Come on!"

They covered their faces, quickly making their way to the front of the crowd without being noticed, as Stevens and Weller kept firing at the enemy soldiers, with bullets piercing their bodies, killing them instantly.

Raven was trying to move his body away from the intense heat of the flames. At times, he struggled to wriggle free from the heat. His legs were burning from the heat of the flames, but after seeing the U.S. helicopter, he refused to accept the pain. Stevens and Weller kept firing at the enemy, with Cairns becoming frustrated, telling the Russian soldiers to hurry up raising the missiles. Stevens, suspecting it was Raven, asked, "Who's that down there fighting the flames? Is it Raven?"

Weller looked to see that it was his father. He left his seat, which made Stevens ask, "Where are you going?"

Weller wrapped the headband his father had once given him around his head and fastened it tightly, replying, "For my father!"

Stevens looked at the man trying to avoid the flames at the stand realising for sure, it was Raven. He watched him turn his head to look up at Stevens with his facial expressions pleading with him to get him out of the flames before they burn him to death. Weller feeling angry held the rocket launcher, pointing it at the second scud truck. He didn't hesitate in pulling the trigger and firing a rocket creating a huge explosion, followed by a fireball that created a large inferno. Flames appeared that made the Iranian people start to run in fear of their lives. Cairns turned to look at the flames burning Raven's legs, and then ran to take cover from all the falling debris.

Ashworth and Pomfret were making their way closer to Raven, who was now beginning to fear for his own life with the flames starting to take hold. Weller could see he was in the worst position imaginable and said to Stevens in a stern voice, "Take us down!"

Stevens immediately started to take the helicopter down, while President Modarres fired his gun at him, where one of the bullets cracked the windscreen. Stevens, starting to feel apprehensive, kept his finger on the button, constantly firing bullets at the enemy soldiers. Cairns, feeling annoyed, shouted to Colonel Mihailov, "Launch the missiles now!"

Colonel Mihailov gave the signal for more scud trucks to enter the courtyard without delay. As they approached the courtyard, they were now rotating and raising the missiles into position as they moved ready to fire at the U.S. soldiers.

Weller, realising what was happening below, took a machine gun, paused for a few seconds by holding the necklace his father had once worn and said in a low voice, "Hold on. I'm coming."

He jumped from the helicopter landing on the ground aiming his gun at the enemy and started firing at them. Stevens was spraying bullets everywhere knowing he had landed the helicopter in a precarious position.

Unit Expendable had almost arrived on the scene and could see, in the distance, that John Weller and Stevens had landed, which made Captain Weller shout, "Take your positions!"

Steve Lundgren and Sarah Jane were standing at the machine guns positioned at both doors ready to shoot at the enemy. Tyler and Seager looked through the front windscreen in disbelief. They saw Raven with a huge fire blazing below him. Tyler shouted, "Captain Weller! You might want to look at this!"

Captain Weller moved to watch her son, John Weller, sprinting to his father standing at the stake about to burn. Fearing the worst, she looked sharply back at Sarah Jane suspecting she must have seen her father for her to start firing bullets at the enemy.

Weller was still running to his father to try to save him but was held back by the flames. Missiles were launched from Tyler's helicopter, which made more explosions. The burning stand Raven was standing on fell over, which made Pomfret react by running over to him, while pulling out her knife to cut Raven free. Weller thought she was the enemy, where he fired his weapon again, but lucky for her his gun was out of bullets. In temper, he threw down his weapon, and brought out his knife still running to his father and the person he thought was going to kill him. Before Hayley could use her knife, Weller grabbed her arm and threw her to the ground. Thinking that she was the enemy, he lunged down at her with his left arm holding her neck and his right hand in position holding the knife ready to kill her. She quickly moved the gown from her face revealing who she was before Weller could kill her. As soon as Weller saw her face, he remembered her from the flower shop and said, "Don't do that!"

He pulled her to her feet quickly, and let go of her, where they both used their knife, to cut one of Raven's hands free from the stand and pull him away from the flames. Cairns saw what they had done, which made him snatch one of the Russian soldier's weapons and fire it at them. Unit Expendable was leaping from their helicopter to support Weller and Pomfret. Some of the crowd that had decided to stay, started to throw stones and petrol bombs at the U.S. soldiers, which made Lundgren shout, "Try not to fire at any Iranian civilians!"

Weller and Pomfret pulled Raven away, noticing his legs were badly burned. Hayley looked at Weller while picking up Raven's knife that had been left on the ground, and said, "He doesn't look good."

Raven looked up at his son and Pomfret, while slowly climbing to his feet and said, "Remember, no pain!"

For a few seconds Weller and Pomfret were surprised at Raven's perseverance. Pomfret placed her hand out to give Raven his knife back, where he snatched it from her. One of the members of Unit Expendable shouted at them, "Look out!"

A hand grenade had been thrown at them, which made the Raven's and Pomfret move quickly to take cover. Ashworth ran for the flamethrower, ducking and diving bullets being fired at him. The firing of bullets became so frequent; he dived to the floor crawling along the ground for flamethrower that was in his grasp. When he was close enough, he reached out his hand to pull the weapon closer to him. In all the carnage, he stood up pointing it at the enemy, quickly releasing the trigger to burn many of them alive. Cairns saw the tanks arriving with more scud trucks behind aiming their missiles at the helicopter in the courtyard. Captain Weller ordered Tyler to circle the warzone, when she and her daughter would fire at the enemy from above. The hand grenade exploded sending the Raven's and Pomfret up into the air where they all landed on the ground close by to more enemy soldiers. Ashworth saw that they were vulnerable and pointed the flamethrower in their direction. The three soldiers sprung to their feet quickly, using their knives against the enemy soldiers by killing them using just one strike of the weapon. They started to hurry to the U.S. helicopter for their lives, as Raven saw Cairns disappearing away from the courtyard. Pomfret saw Stevens standing at the doorway at the side of the helicopter waving his arms frantically for them to get back aboard his craft. Stones and petrol bombs were thrown by the disruptive Iranian crowd at the U.S. soldiers with some hitting the windscreen, which cracked and shattered a large part of it. Stevens glanced at the Iranian people, deciding that needs must and pulled the pin from a hand grenade, immediately throwing it at the enemy nearby to them. When he saw Raven, Weller and Pomfret running to his helicopter, he pulled the pin from another hand grenade, throwing it towards the enemy. He waved his arm frantically shouting, "Come on!"

Raven stared when he heard his own words being shouted. As he ran past killing Iranian and Russian soldiers feeling the pain he had suffered, he saw members of Unit Expendable fighting the enemy in their own groups while trying to make their way to Stevens' helicopter.

The Russian tanks raised their guns at Tyler and Seager flying back into the warzone, to fire shells, which made them bank quickly to avoid being hit. Captain Weller and Sarah Jane kept firing their machine guns positioned at both sides of the helicopter. Tyler fired more missiles, destroying buildings and military vehicles nearby. Captain Weller shouted, "Try to save some missiles. We may need them!"

Sarah Jane saw Raven fall with him starting to feel so weak. Tyler fired another missile at the Russian tank making it explode into another huge inferno. Cairns could see he was on the losing side, which made him move further away from the warzone. Captain Weller spotted him, which made her jump off the helicopter flying low, wanting revenge for what he had done to her. Weller and Pomfret looked back, only to find that Raven had fallen. Weller scanned the area noticing Templeton, Parr and Williams close by. He shouted to Pomfret, "Go over there with them!"

Pomfret did as she was told with other members of Unit Expendable grabbing her and dragging her down to take cover. They saw Sarah Jane firing at the enemy realising that she was running to her father. Parr, Williams and Templeton fired at the enemy to give Sarah Jane more cover.

The roar of the F35 fighter planes flew low, starting to bank ready to attack. Lundgren looked at some of the members of Unit Expendable near him and said, "We have to get out of here, and fast!"

Weller ran back to help his father up and looked at his sister. Raven looked up at the apple of his eye where she said, "Come on. You have to make it!"

Raven from somewhere found the strength to stand again with Weller helping him. Lundgren ran out firing his weapon at the enemy, wanting to make his way to Raven, and grab his arm, which made Raven say, "Not this time."

Lundgren ignored him by dragging him with the help of his son into the helicopter. Stevens rushed into the damaged cockpit wanting to get it off the ground and back into the sky. A Russian scud truck placed its holder in a position to launch a missile at the helicopter. Stevens shouted at the top of his voice, "Jump!"

They didn't need telling twice, Weller, Lundgren and Sarah Jane jumped from the helicopter onto the ground. John Raven leaped up and away from the helicopter towards the balcony using what strength he had left to climb over it. The missile hit the helicopter making it explode and come crashing down, which created another almighty explosion. All the soldiers rolled out of the way as debris hit different parts of the ground. One of the blades from the rear propeller flew through the air and hit Sarah Jane, which pierced her stomach and made blood pour out of her body. Her brother, John, shouted, "No!" at the top of his voice not wanting to accept that his sister and his good friend Stevens had been killed. He wanted to go to her and collect her but Steve Lundgren stopped him for fear of getting shot. Lerner and Ashworth frantically made their way across the warzone to them still firing at the enemy as Parr and Pomfret came to help try to recover Sarah Jane's body, hoping to be able to take it home.

Tyler and Seager knew they had to fly in and get the remaining members of Unit Expendable out before they were killed. Seager looked down at the flames burning, and the destruction created watching Iranian people run away in fear for their lives. Tyler made the helicopter move and fly in where he fired two more missiles at the enemy. The Russians retaliated by firing shells from the military tanks and scud missiles, which made Tyler have to weave and fly like never before to avoid becoming like Stevens. Seager commented, "This isn't good!"

Tyler replied, "Take the machine gun at the door!"

Seager rushed to the back starting to fire bullets at the enemy, which made him shout, "Where are they all coming from?"

Tyler replied, "There are no rules for engagement. Kill them all including the conscripts, and then we rescue our mates down there from Unit Expendable after the aftermath!"

Seager moved as bullets were fired back at him. He shouted to Tyler, "We're getting low on ammunition!"

Tyler replied, "When you are pushed!"

He pressed the button to release another missile knowing he only had one left. He flew into the carnage below while firing at the Iranians and Russians with members of Unit Expendable frantically waving their arms to come and get them. Tyler fired the machine gun and saw the F35 fighter planes, in the distance, coming into attack with a vengeance.

Raven rushed from the balcony and through the French doors to see Cairns and President Modarres arguing. He watched the Iranian President throw the laptop computer from his desk in temper while still listening to the aftermath of the war outside. Raven held his knife tightly glaring at both men as he walked towards them. President Modarres sensed Raven, which made him turn to point his gun at him and pull the trigger. There were no bullets left in the barrel, which made the badly wounded Raven walk closer to the two people that had instigated this war. Cairns shouted, "Still fighting until the end, eh Raven!"

Raven stared with his menacing eyes, angry with what they had done to him. They started to feel intimidated when President Modarres shouted at Cairns, "Do something!"

Cairns had no weapon making him feel vulnerable as he watched the power of Raven approaching him, especially with the brutality and punishment he had inflicted on him. President Modarres fearing for his life ran to the door that had been left open, which made Cairns turn and notice

Captain Weller. He moved quickly to grab her arm trying to prevent her from using her weapon. Although she wasn't in the best of positions, she diversified still able to fire her weapon twice at President Modarres, making him fall to the floor in a pool of blood while saying, "You bitch!"

Attacking Captain Weller made Raven move much faster to try to protect her. Cairns struggled with her, trying to take her weapon. With being stronger he had the advantage by managing to take it from her and point it straight at Raven, who was still holding his knife ready to use. Captain Weller ran at him and thumped Cairns, which made him grab her and say, "You should have stayed away because now I am going to rape you when I've killed him standing there!"

He threw her to the ground, which made Raven produce a face of anger. He lunged at him to strike him using his blood stained knife. Cairns immediately turned and was about to pull the trigger when Captain Weller pulled a knife from the side of her trousers and threw it at Cairns, stabbing him in his thigh, which made him cower slightly. He turned to shoot Captain Weller, which made Raven rush up to slice his waist and back, making blood gush out onto his hand as he pulled the knife from him. Cairns fell to the ground dying next to Captain Weller, where she kicked him away and then grabbed Raven's hand, noticing how his body had become badly battle scarred. With his hair hanging into his battle scarred face, he moved his eyes slowly, listening to her say, "You don't look good."

Raven gave her the thousand yard stare, replying, "No!"

Raven turned when he heard the F35 fighter planes suspecting that they were coming into finish what Unit Expendable had started. He rushed back to the French doors to see Tyler's helicopter moving up for him and Captain Weller. He shouted to Captain Weller, "Come on!"

Womack in one of the F35 fighter planes ordered Tyler to move from the front of the palace next to the balcony or take the consequences. Tyler glimpsed through the smoke and flames at the enemy soldiers still firing at them shouting on the radio, "We haven't got Raven!"

Weller and members of Unit Expendable were aboard the battered helicopter, where he shouted to Tyler, "We have to wait for my father!"

Tyler, feeling angry replied, "I have to move the helicopter, or else we're all going to die. The pilots in the F35 fighter planes have received orders to destroy the palace."

Weller looked down at his dead sister feeling anguish at the thought of being alone. Tyler received another warning from Womack telling him to move. Without hesitation he did, while looking back at the palace thinking about what will happen to Raven. All the pilots in the F35 fighter planes released missiles to destroy President Modarres's palace to smithereens.

When Tyler had left the front of the palace, Raven and Captain Weller arrived on the balcony where they saw what was heading for them. John took hold of Captain Weller's hand and shouted, "Jump!"

Colonel Wareing had arrived in his U.S helicopter with Ron Crenna, noticing Raven and Captain Weller leaping out of a huge fireball down to the ground. The palace crumbled in flames with a vast amount of dust and smoke rising into the sky. Colonel Wareing looked in dismay at what Raven and Captain Weller had just done saying, "Please God. No!"

He saw Tyler's battered helicopter about to be attacked from a watchtower, which made him release a couple of missiles to destroy the watchtower and enemy soldiers standing inside it, up in an inferno. He then ordered Tyler and Seager to fly back to the Kuwaiti U.S. military base, immediately leaving Weller standing at the door with his headband displaying the stars and stripes of the U.S. blowing in the breeze. He placed his hand onto the green emerald stone while glaring at what the Colonel was about to do wondering if his father will make it out. Colonel Wareing ordered the F35 fighter planes to back him up, while he tried to land and collect Raven and Captain Weller. All the pilots obeyed circling the perimeter of the palace still firing at what was left of the enemy. Colonel Wareing landed the U.S. helicopter, rushed into the back, collected a machine gun and then saw through the smoke Captain Weller trying to help and pull the huge physique of John Raven to his craft. Colonel Wareing closed his eyes for a few seconds, and then chose to ignore the worst, deciding to run and help her to bring Raven back to the helicopter that still had its propellers spinning. Raven moved his head to look at Colonel Wareing and said in a weary voice. "Mission accomplished."

Colonel Wareing helped him and the injured Captain Weller back to the helicopter saying, "Don't talk!"

Raven nodded his head slowly, replying, "Heard those words . . . ."

Captain Weller looked up at Raven and then said to Colonel Wareing, "I think . . ."

She paused for a few seconds feeling her eyes starting to water and said after trying to contain herself, "I think he's dying!"

Raven moved his head to look at her, sighed a few times struggling to eventually reply, "It has to happen even to the best."

Colonel Wareing ignored Raven, saying to Captain Weller, "Get him inside the helicopter!"

They helped Raven into the helicopter by sitting him on the floor next to the weapons to rest his battered body. Raven kept opening and closing his eyes, where he could only look outside at the carnage, devastation and destruction created. Captain Weller turned to see what he was looking at, where she too saw the carnage through the smoke and fire, and then went to sit down next to him. Colonel Wareing started to make the helicopter climb when at times he would look back at John with his eyes closed. Feeling concerned, he shouted, "John!"

Crenna left his seat wanting to attend to Raven, hoping he could at least save this soldier who had seen it all, and done it all to prevent him from dying. Staring at his wounds his battered body had taken, he looked at Captain Weller, who was feeling distressed with the way John appeared. At times Colonel Wareing glanced behind to John just sitting there with his eyes closed. Just as before Colonel Wareing shouted, "John!"

Raven still didn't open his eyes, which made him shout, "Raven!"

Raven opened his eyes slowly saying, "Sir. You owe my father."

Colonel Wareing listened to what Raven had said has he started to fly back to Kuwait wondering if Raven would live through this war he had just been involved in. He looked back once more to see tears forming in Captain Weller's eyes and then took notice of the F35 fighter planes rapidly approaching to fly alongside him. The Stealth Bombers followed, with all the pilots feeling honoured in being able to escort one of the bravest U.S. legendary soldiers they could ever call up on, John Raven.

Flashbacks

$\mathcal{A}$s they travelled back to Kuwait, Colonel Wareing shouted to Captain Weller. "How is he?"

Captain Weller fought back the tears, placing her hand on his forehead and then looked at the serious wounds on his body, replying, "He isn't good."

After listening to Captain Weller's reply, it made Colonel Wareing glance once more behind him, and listen to her say while still fighting the tears back, "I hate to say this, but I think he's dying."

Colonel Wareing turned back to look through the huge windscreen not wanting to accept what Captain Weller had just told him. Captain Weller moved John's head and said, "John."

John remained sat still, which made her say again a little more assertive, "John!"

John opened his eyes, looking wearily at Captain Weller and asked in a solemn voice, "What?"

Captain Weller couldn't help herself from starting to cry quietly with tears starting to roll down her cheeks. John moved his head slightly and then his eyes and said, "I never said it when I should have done, but somewhere inside me, I've always loved you."

Hearing Raven speak like this, Colonel Wareing frowned and glanced back, shouting, "Hey soldier, you'll live to fight another day."

Raven swallowed a lump in his throat, looked at Captain Weller and then Crenna, replying to the Colonel's comment by saying, "Not this time. It's over."

Captain Weller remained silent choosing to just gently take hold of his hand and then heard Colonel Wareing, who was in denial shout, "That's not what I want to hear Raven!"

John gave a casual blink to Captain Weller, swallowed another lump in his throat and said in a tired voice, "They're coming for me."

Captain Weller, reluctantly started to accept that Raven was dying, which made her ask in a solemn voice, "Who's coming to meet you John?"

John struggling to breathe replied, "I can't make them all-out. Their faces are blurred."

Captain Weller while still holding John's hand placed her other hand to her forehead and then heard him while struggling to breathe in a weary voice, "I can see Colonel Lewis."

Captain Weller slowly took her hand away starting to accept she was losing John forever, which made her cry as if her heart had been broken. John's eyes were almost closed when he said, "I can see."

Captain Weller wanting to help, asked, "What can you see?"

Colonel Wareing sat in the cockpit not wanting to believe that this could be the final conversation he will hear from John Raven. Feeling anguish, he fought back tears realising that this time it was one time too many.

John moved his eyes slowly to face Captain Weller, and listened to her ask the same question again to him, "What can you see?"

Raven, who was fighting for every breath replied, "You don't want to know this, but you will soon."

He closed his eyes, which made Captain Weller still frowning at his last comment say, "John!"

He just about opened them while thinking about his father's last words to him, which were come home and replied, "You take care Debbie. You take care."

He closed his eyes letting out his final breath and rested his head in Debbie's hands, watching his life flash before his eyes. From the day, he had been born when his mother was holding him, to the days when he was at school playing American football. Girls and soldiers he had met in his life flashed by where they were young and old. Captain Weller appeared many times with different appearances, with his father Richard, once seen to have been having a furious argument with her when they were both much younger. He saw himself travelling to Vietnam with his friends and how that occurred from arguing with Captain Weller about their careers causing them to split up. He saw death; carnage, destruction and devastation, a tank and helicopter go head-to-head when each person had just one passion. To win! Colonel Lewis could be heard saying "It's over Raven. It's over!"

Raven saw himself sitting there speaking to Colonel Lewis, telling him the story about how he and some of his friends were going to cruise until the tyres fell off their car. Shortly afterwards he was holding his best friend when he was trying to put him together again. Colonel Lewis could be seen standing at a fence telling John that he had a mission that involved taking just photographs. Then words shouted by him, "Nothing is over!" and "Let it go!" where he visualised his father in the barn grabbing the knife he had made.

The image of his father changed to Sarah, the missionary he had met during his stay in Burma, when he said, those same words to her, when she was pleading with him holding onto what John had been holding. With his hair falling down into his rugged face while staring at her, he said, "Let it go!"

The police flashed by where he saw one king shit cop wanting to run him out of town eventually making him ask, "Why are you pushing me?"

The necklace holding the green emerald appeared where he saw the beautiful oriental girl and how she lost her life making him want to treasure this item. Words previously spoken passed him by, "I don't make the rules Raven!"

He saw himself standing there holding his bow and arrow just wanting to get even with the enemy after they had killed a beautiful oriental girl who was close to him. Those words echoed, "You make a good choice."

Then he saw himself pulling his hands away on the ground after burying her when she had been killed. The necklace appeared again, where he gave it to a small boy named Azar, for his bravery with helping him fight against the Russians. The image of the same boy changed to show Azar as a full grown adult and a high ranking officer in the Afghan terrorist group Hermes. Raven snatched the necklace back from him many years later after finding out what he had become.

Weapons he had used flashed by where he saw himself holding them and performing elite kills. He stood there with an arrow pointing to a mercenary soldier who kept calling him the boatman. After a disagreement, he distinctly told him that he knows what we are, and ended with saying, "Die for something or live for absolutely nothing!"

The question kept repeating again and again, "What's your call?"

Raven replied, "Let's move!"

He saw himself walking out of the U.S. military base in Kuwait feeling angry with Captain Weller, leaving her to watch and shout, "That's it John, walk away again!"

In desperation, she had no choice but to have to tell him about the son he never knew existed. Finding out the truth made him accept he had to come back into battle once more to fight the enemy for his own blood. Espionage resulted in flashbacks showing Raven hitting Cairns hard in the face and then the same flashbacks being reversed when he was having the same blows given from Cairns in Iran. Fire and smoke were all around, which made him wonder if he was on his way to hell. Many conflicts were shown while *America In Conflict* stood out with President Berry claiming we will prevail. He saw President Berry in many ways, just recently inside the Iranian cell and then with his son when they were in North Korea fighting against General Kwan and Azar Sajadi.

He saw himself answering the same question to different people using the same words. A small Iraqi girl listened to him say, "I don't make the rules."

Then the girl changed into what seemed like a wise old Korean gentleman when he replied to him in the same way by saying, "I don't make the rules."

The words he had once spoken "somewhere in between" kept coming back to him as he spoke with the wise old Korean gentleman. Then he saw him give the material to him and listened to him say, "If you lived here, you would most probably have become a samurai. Take this, as a gesture of our country and let it remind you that we're not all bad."

He saw himself wearing different headbands, and then feeling the pain from previous wars. Gunpowder was placed into a serious wound, leaving him no choice but to light it to kill the infection. He yelped in agony with the pain that travelled through his body. Falling from a cliff and into trees that helped break his fall made him relive the time when a large piece of the twig had become trapped inside his body. He saw his facial features change in a matter of seconds as he spoke to different people during his life. Those words nothing is over echoed once more.

Then he saw two mercenary soldiers standing there listening to their superior officer saying. "God can you feel the damn heat, get me a cold drink."

Pulling the ring back he took a huge gulp, starting to tell John his own birthday, 07/06/47. The date he joined the military, 08/06/64. His achievements, including being awarded with two silver stars, four bronze, four Purple Hearts, a Distinct Service Cross and the Medal of Honour where he threw the file down while saying "You get around didn't you."

With being awarded with these medals made him see President Berry awarding him and his son with the same medals when he had finally returned from his war in North Korea.

Colonel Wareing and Captain Weller were seen visiting when they told him the sad news about when Colonel Lewis had died of a heart attack. They wanted him to take over the training of Unit Invincible from Colonel Lewis when this was the only time he ever doubted himself. Different flashbacks of Colonel Wareing and John Raven occurred, when most were good, but at times others were bad when they were seen to be disagreeing.

The crucifix given to him by a missionary was in his hand, when he saw himself sitting down thinking about whether to enter another war. The bench slowly changed, where he was sitting on a different bench looking up to the sky at Colonel Lewis, feeling sad that he had left this world. The crucifix came into his hand again, after reliving the moment when he was standing in the Korean jungle alone for a few seconds perhaps dazed amid his own thoughts. It was the same crucifix; he had given to his daughter when he had first met her lying on the ground. He knew the mission had just become twice as big. Not only was he there to protect his son, who didn't know he had embarked on this mission, and the U.S. President he accompanied, he would once again have to save *His Own Blood!* Only this time, it was the apple of his eye, his beautiful daughter Sarah Jane.

From seeing the crucifix, back to the necklace, and then to the knife made him see him giving his famous weapons to his daughter and son. He heard Sarah Jane saying, "Promise me that it won't be one time too many." He stood there replying, "I can't promise that."

Meeting his family he saw a much more gentle side to him where he enjoyed the time spent with his daughter, Sarah Jane and his son John. His father could be heard saying these words from different time zones once more, "Come home!"

Gradually, his father's face changed into his own, saying to a missionary asking for help, "Go home."

He saw himself pouring petrol on a boat and setting it alight and then leaping from another boat onto Colonel Wareing's Harrier wing when he was almost at death's door. He fired the tank buster in the direction of General Kwan and Azar Sajadi. The vision rapidly turned into a Russian patrol boat approaching him inside yet another boat when he struggled to break free from a pirate after rescuing a U.S. prisoner of war. After stabbing the pirate in the stomach, he didn't hesitate in jumping into the water away from the badly damaged patrol boat on a collision course he had fired a rocket at moments before. When he came out of the water, he had one sole intention, to escape and travel to his pickup point.

It suddenly went calm, where he could see himself speaking with a beautiful Oriental young woman when they were telling stories. She asked, "What brings you luck?" After scraping the deck, he held his knife up and replied, "I guess this."

The Oriental young woman started to disappear where he could hear her saying repeatedly, "Raven, you're not expendable."

Sarah Jane was coming to meet John on his new journey, has his life flashed by him in what seemed like a few seconds. It was time to say goodbye to our famous soldier, because he placed out his hand for Sarah Jane waiting for him to take. She held her father's hand and started to walk, deciding to look back at Captain Weller, who sadly, doesn't yet know that she has also lost her daughter sobbing over John Raven's dead body.

Captain Weller was heartbroken with losing John where she struggled to get her words out, but when she could, she finally said to Colonel Wareing, "He's gone."

Colonel Wareing closed his eyes trying to hold back the tears and said in a humble voice, "One time too many."

Captain Weller, still sobbing nodded her head agreeing and replied, "I'll never forget him for getting me out of that hellhole in Iran."

Colonel Wareing closed his eyes again trying to hold back the tears. He picked up the radio wanting to tell the military personnel at the Kuwaiti control centre what had happened to John Raven and found that he too had a lump in his throat where he couldn't do it. He placed the radio back down and said to Captain Weller, "Today a legend has left us who will never be forgotten."

Ron Crenna, feeling deeply saddened placed his arm around Captain Weller, who was still sobbing her heart out. She pulled away from Crenna, who was trying to console her, wanting to agree with the Colonel. She looked down with tears rolling down her cheeks, at the battered body of John Raven sleeping, knowing he will be never awake again. She went to lean across, moving his long hair to kiss his cheek and replied, "He will always be somewhere in my heart. I love you John and always will."

Captain Weller paused, while pulling away, but still kept looking at him. She had to accept, he had gone, when this time, it was for good. Feeling heartbroken, she gazed at the man who had done it all and achieved it all, and said, "No matter what, you were always the best of the best!"

Truth Hurts

----

*W*hen Colonel Wareing had arrived back at the Kuwaiti military base, from his cockpit, he saw Tyler and Weller carrying Sarah Jane onto a stretcher for the medics to take her away in a military ambulance. Suspecting his worst nightmare, he turned feeling sorry for Captain Weller crying over John Raven. Seeing Captain Weller so upset, made him think that today was the worst day of his life after losing two sought after elite soldiers.

President Berry, Sarah Johnson, and the military officers came outside, watching the medics wheel away Sarah Jane's dead body. President Berry gave a look of despair, realising that Sarah Jane had passed away. She recalled events from when she spent time with her in North Korea, when she had no choice but to share a cell and help each other to survive and be able to live another day.

Sarah Johnson looked sad, which made her say to President Berry, "She had everything to live for."

President Berry still watching them take Sarah Jane away, in the distance, replied, "With being a Raven, maybe she had more to die for."

Sarah Johnson seemed surprised at Susan's comment as she looked away to notice the F35 fighter planes and Stealth Bombers circling before landing on the runway. President Berry saw a despondent Weller stood next to Tyler and other members of Unit Expendable where his headband showing the stars and stripes of the U.S. was blowing in the breeze. Remembering what he had once done for her, she walked down the steps to him, placed her arm around his waist and looked up to him. John, feeling despondent, gave a solemn look at Susan, but couldn't find any words to say. Although she knew, his expression said it all. They stood there watching Colonel Wareing climb out of his helicopter waving frantically to members of Unit Expendable for help. President Berry and Weller frowned with concern as they watched members of Unit Expendable rush to help. Colonel Wareing and a distraught Captain Weller started to bring John Raven's dead body from the helicopter, which made Steve Lundgren immediately take over from her with him being so heavy to carry. Another military ambulance arrived, with the shock starting to penetrate through that John Raven hadn't survived his latest war.

His son stood there next to the U.S. President, where she placed her hand to her cheek to wipe away her tears. She looked up at John, deciding to take his hand and hold it tightly, trying to reassure him. He watched intensively, ignoring President Berry trying to comfort him while feeling shivers go through his body with not wanting to believe that his father has now died.

Captain Weller looked across at her son, standing there in shock, not wanting to move. President Berry, while watching Raven being wheeled away, said, "Go to your mother, she needs you."

Weller didn't reply to President Berry. He just rushed over to his mother, Captain Weller, to console her while trying to remain strong for them both. Captain Weller, sobbing said, "He's gone."

Weller watched Sarah Johnson trot past President Berry towards the stretcher to see for herself if it was true that John Raven had died. Weller looked back at his mother, placed his arm around her, wondering how he could find the right words to tell her about Sarah Jane. He swallowed a lump in his throat knowing there would be no easy way to tell her about his sister, and decided to say in a solemn voice, "I know. He's with Sarah Jane now."

Captain Weller pulled away from John to see him looking away from her, which made her ask, "John, not Sarah Jane too?"

John, still looking away from his mother, closed his eyes where she knew now for sure that she had to accept, she had lost her daughter too. She lunged forward, placing her head onto his blood stained shirt and sobbed her heart out. John fought back the tears trying to remain strong. Everything around became a haze for him as he comforted his mother.

General Hardaker and Colonel Armstrong walked over to President Berry, where she said to them in a solemn voice, "Today a legend has died."

General Hardaker watched the military ambulance drive John Raven away and replied, "Today is a sad day for us all."

Colonel Wareing walked up to John Weller, and placed his hand onto his shoulder saying, "I'm sorry John."

John gave a casual blink like his father would once have done choosing not to reply to the Colonel. He was in denial, blaming himself for not doing more to ensure his father could have lived to see another day. Captain Weller pulled away from her son, which made John let go of her while watching her look up at him and say, "Be strong John, be strong for both of us."

John lowered his head not wanting to speak to anybody. Colonel Wareing gently took her away from John, placing his arm around her to comfort her and started to walk away. Captain Weller looked back at her son standing alone fighting his emotions and said once more, "Be strong."

President Berry saw John standing alone with his hair blowing in the breeze. She gazed at him, remembering the combat fighting machine he has become. Concerned for him, she walked over to him saying, "Another Air Force One plane will arrive this evening, where I would like you and members of Unit Expendable to fly back with me back to the United States."

John turned to look at Susan, asking, "What about my father and sister?"

President Berry held his blood stained hand, replying, "It's an honour to take your father and sister home and have them back on our own soil."

President Berry watched John's reaction and then carried on saying, "With what's happened there will never be a right time to say this to you. For your bravery I'm going to award you with a Purple Heart and Medal of Honour."

John replied, "Give them to my father!"

President Berry could see that John was hurting and said in a solemn voice, "I intended to give them to your father and sister too."

John looked down at President Berry replying, "Medals are only material items. It's life that is precious."

Colonel Wareing walked back to them wanting to give his father's knife to him. John received it graciously, and then placed his hand out to receive his watch and headband. Susan looked at the headband, closing her eyes wishing the truth didn't have to hurt. Colonel Wareing watched John's reaction, which made him say, "He was the best."

John managed to bring a wry smile to his face has he stroked his father's headband and replied in a solemn voice, "He always will remain the best of the best."

Colonel Wareing patted his arm and then asked President Berry to join him, deciding to leave John alone to capture his own thoughts and memories and be able to relive them once again.

John, now standing alone could see the military personnel carrying on with their duties, which made him look at his father's knife, he had made on Christmas Day. He tied his father's headband to the handle as he walked over to a bench close by to sit down. He placed the knife down next to him and put on his father's watch. With bringing back memories, he brought out his own knife that once belonged to his father and looked at it. A wry smile appeared on his face when he recalled the time his father had given it to him when he claimed that he no longer wanted to be known as John Weller, it had to be John Weller-Raven.

Steve Lundgren saw him sitting alone and decided to walk over to ask him if he could sit down with him to talk. Although John wasn't in the mood for a conversation, he listened to him telling him stories how he and his father once had a severe fight. John grinned while rotating the knife looking at his own reflection asking, "What was the fight about?"

Lundgren replied, "I made the mistake of betraying him, which took a long time for him to gain my trust again."

With concern, John asked, "What did you do?"

Lundgren replied, "Perhaps I will tell you someday."

John turned away, looking at the sky, visualising only his father. Lundgren picked up the knife on the bench, also visualising John Raven. Weller turned to look at Lundgren, and listened to him say, "I see your father in you, where you will become a legend just has he once did."

For a few seconds John thought back to Louise knowing what she wants from him and asked, "Do you think so?"

Lundgren stood up, bent down and patted his arm and said, "I know so!"

Watching Lundgren walk away, John frowned knowing that Cairns had performed serious acts of betrayal, which made him call out, "Lundgren!"

Lundgren turned around, to listen to John asking him again, "What was the betrayal you performed against my father?"

Lundgren narrowed his eyes while looking down at him and replied, "It's ancient history now, but maybe one day I will tell you the full story."

John stood up pointing his finger at him asking, "You're not like Cairns are you, a weasel in disguise?"

Lundgren laughed replying, "Give me some credit will you! No I'm not like him at all, but one day when you're in the right frame of mind I will tell you the full story."

John grinned, replying, "I'll hold you to that."

Lundgren said, "You do that."

John then sat down to watch the sun set while visualising his father and sister, wishing that they were still here with him and his mother, Captain Weller. He felt a shiver go through his body as he looked into the sky, causing a tear to roll down his cheek. He brought out his mobile phone to look at the picture of Louise, and him sat in the back of Tony's car. At the time, they were going to watch the American football game between the Arizona Cardinals and the New York Giants. He remembered Louise running by the side of the train, when she had decided to put on the engagement ring; he had given to her, which made him smile. He looked back at the red sky feeling his father and sister's presence close by and decided to send Louise a text. About to use his phone to text, he was distracted with the rumble of Air Force One, which could be heard in the distance. It landed on the runway at the Kuwaiti military base to take President Berry, Sarah Johnson and Unit Expendable back to the United States. He glimpsed at the huge 747, and then carried on typing his text to Louise, which said. *I'm safe. We will be home sometime tomorrow when we travel on Air Force One when I will need you, because to some, home is now a different place.*

Home Coming

$\mathcal{T}$he next morning, President Berry and Sarah Johnson were ready to fly back to the United States with members of Unit Expendable. She thanked General Hardaker and Colonel Armstrong for their hospitality and most of all her life. The military officers walked beside her and the Secretary of State towards Air Force One with Colonel Wareing and Captain Weller following. They saw John sat alone on the bench, where he had stayed all-night. Captain Weller walked away from the group, which made them watch, while taking notice who she was walking over to. President Berry looked over to see Captain Weller speaking with her son, while Colonel Armstrong spoke to her. She interrupted him by saying, "I'm sorry to interrupt you Colonel, but I need to make sure that he is one person that does board this flight."

Colonel Armstrong glanced at Captain Weller speaking with John and said, "Let's hope, he won't board it from the wheels."

President Berry sniggered, understanding what the Colonel meant replying, "Not this time."

John stood up holding his father's knife and started walking with Captain Weller towards President Berry. Concerned for him she asked, "Are you okay?"

John replied to President Berry in a solemn voice, "I've been better."

She then walked with them as they made their way to board Air Force One and join the rest of their colleagues by taking their seats. Lundgren was waiting for John, where he handed to him, his green bag containing his belongings, which made him say, "Thanks."

Lundgren watched John walk by him carrying his bag and said, "John."

He looked back at Lundgren, listening to him say, "Put the knife away."

John raised his arm slowly, turned his hand to look at what were once his father's knife and then his headband tied to the handle. Flashbacks came back from when he had been wearing it during previous conflicts. He put down his bag, untied the headband from the knife handle, and crouched down to unzip his bag, placing the knife inside it. He looked at his name on the green bag, wishing his father could have also been aboard Air Force One alive. It made him show his own thoughts by slowly taking off his own headband showing the stars and stripes of the United States, and place it into his bag. Still crouched down, he held his father's headband, caressing it, wishing that he was still here beside him. Lundgren watched his actions, but said nothing. John held the headband tightly, stood up, and wrapped it around his head, tying it tightly while giving a menacing stare at Lundgren. Lundgren gave a stare back, and said, "In you, your father now lives!"

He walked past John patting his arm, saying in a solemn voice, "He was the best."

John moved his head slightly to his left after hearing those words nodding his head agreeing. He turned to follow with Lundgren asking John to sit next to him because he had something important to ask him.

When the pilots knew President Berry was aboard, Air Force One received clearance to taxi around to the runway, take-off and travel back to the United States of America.

When they were in the air Lundgren said, "This is probably not the right time."

John moved his head to face Lundgren, intrigued at what he was about to say. Lundgren, aware that he seemed interested carried on saying, "Why don't you think about joining my team of elite soldiers, because you would be an asset?"

John sighed, thinking of only Louise, and replied, "Maybe."

Lundgren, frowning at John, asked with concern, "What's stopping you?"

John thought about Louise again, and replied, "Before I do anything, I want to take Ricky Stevens' belongings back to his parents."

Lundgren agreed with his decision telling him that Ashworth had collected Stevens' belongings, which made him look down the plane at him.

As they travelled back to the U.S. people watched the news being broadcasted on television around the world that John Raven had been killed while freeing President Berry, the Secretary of State and U.S. soldiers from past and present. John didn't want to listen to the report anymore because he knew the truth, and it hurt him hugely. He stood up, making Lundgren ask, "You will think about my offer?"

John glanced at the screen showing different images of his father, and then thought about his girlfriend, Louise, replying, "What if I'm done, finished, after all this?"

Lundgren sighed and said, "Inside yourself, you know what you are. You know what you have become, and you know what you have to do."

John, realising that he was being pulled in two directions, knew that he had a big decision to make. He looked at the screen again, while placing his fingers onto the headband resting on his shoulder and replied, "Perhaps."

Lundgren listened to John's reply, feeling as though it wasn't good enough. With this, he said, "You owe your father this!"

John narrowed his eyes at Lundgren, choosing not to discuss this matter anymore. He turned, starting to walk to another part of the plane. He stopped to say a few words to Ashworth, telling him that he would take Stevens' bag when they had landed back in the United States. When Ashworth agreed with his request, John moved away, wanting to look at his girlfriend once more on his mobile phone. Gardenzio walked by him and saw the picture of Louise and John on his phone, which made him ask, "May I?"

John hadn't met Gardenzio yet and frowned, causing him to look intimidating at him. Gardenzio said, "I think it's my sister Louise, but I can't be sure with not having seen her for seven years."

John remembered the conversation at Louise's house about her brother, which made him ask, "Are you Enzio?"

Enzio replied, "I am."

John produced a smirk saying, "This here is my fiancée and your sister, Louise."

He handed the phone to Enzio, looking at her closely. He grinned with recognising her and replied, "You have made a good choice."

John said, "I know I have. This picture was taken when we were travelling to see an American football game, which didn't go as planned."

He held the emerald stone, thinking of Louise, when she had given the necklace to him at Tony's grave. His father, watching agreed to the actions she had performed. Turbulence distracted John's thoughts, making him look down the plane at Lundgren, thinking about the offer he had made, and then said in a low voice. "People always die around me."

Enzio, still looking at his sister on his phone, looked up to ask, "Did you say something?"

Although many thoughts were churning around in John's mind, he replied, "No."

Enzio, while looking at his sister on John's phone, became intrigued with what had happened at the American football game John had mentioned. He gave the phone back to him asking, "What happened at the American football game?"

John looked at President Berry, and replied to Enzio, "It's a long story."

Enzio said, "It's a long flight."

As Air Force One travelled back to the U.S. John refused to go into detail about previous missions. Most of the time he spoke about his sister, Sarah Jane, his father John Raven, and Louise, when they couldn't wait to see her once again. After what had happened to Captain Weller, who was still feeling the hurt from losing John Raven, she felt relieved that her son was at least talking and starting to accept that his father had now sadly gone.

The media became aware that President Berry was travelling home on Air Force One with John Raven's son, and members of Unit Expendable, making people hurry to the airport to welcome them home like heroes.

Louise and her father Kirk saw the news report on television. Without any hesitation, it made Louise say, "We have to meet John and Enzio when Air Force One lands."

Kirk agreed with her, immediately stopping what he was doing. He went to collect his jacket and walked outside to his car with Louise following. They were feeling elated at being able to see not only John once more, but Enzio, after John's father had managed to free him from the clutches of Iranian torture.

Richard Raven also saw the television report. At the time he was trying to accept that his son and granddaughter would no longer be around him. Standing there watching television, he felt mixed emotions. Part of him felt sad at the thought of losing his son. Another part of him felt angry; when he told the military that John had done his time, and that they should leave him alone. They ignored Richard on several occasions; leaving him to dwell on his last words when John left with President Berry and Sarah Johnson, telling him, don't make it one time too many. He walked over to the television, turned it off and went to collect his jacket, deciding to travel and watch Air Force One land when he would see for himself what the military had done to his son.

A huge crowd had gathered wanting to see Air Force One approaching. The growing crowd waved U.S. flags rejoicing at the return of President Berry and Unit Expendable. When they saw Air Force One, in the distance, an almighty cheer was heard. Richard Raven, standing in the crowd felt a shiver while watching Air Force One land and taxi to its docking bay. The media, positioned nearby with restricted access, had been waiting in expectation to report and take photographs of President Berry's return to the U.S.

The steps were positioned at the doors of Air Force One, with the crowd waiting in expectation. When the door opened, President Berry, followed by Sarah Johnson and Unit Expendable stepped out to a huge cheer from the crowd. They were greeted by relieved friends, family and members of her cabinet. Louise and Kirk watched in expectation at being able to see Enzio for the first time in years. At first they saw members of Unit Expendable, watching friends and family greet them. When Enzio finally showed, it made Louise look and run to him wanting to greet him, thankful he was still alive. Enzio saw Louise, and hurried to her, where they hugged each other. Grateful to be standing on American soil again, he said, "I'm indebted to John Raven for getting me out of Iran."

Louise smiled, feeling pleased at being able to see her brother again. Kirk, feeling excited rushed over to Enzio, placing his hand on his shoulder. Enzio let go of his sister to shake his father's hand and then hug him, and say, "It's good to be home."

Louise replied, "It's good you're back, because there is much to tell."

Enzio, feeling elated, replied, "It's good to be back."

Louise moved forward to give him another hug and saw Captain Weller and elite soldiers from Unit Expendable leaving Air Force One carrying a coffin that had the U.S. flag displayed over it, which made her stand back and watch. Enzio turned to watch with her as well, while Kirk placed his arm around him feeling thankful that his son was still alive.

Richard Raven, in the distance looked down at the ground suspecting it was either his granddaughter or his son. President Berry saw him, and walked over to him to say, "I'm sorry about your family."

Richard didn't speak at first, which made President Berry start to move away knowing that whatever she said to Richard, no words could express how he was feeling. Richard turned and gave a stare only his son could have once given and said to the U.S. President, "The military got what they wanted where I warned them!"

President Berry feeling sorry for Richard replied, "I owe your son and grandson my life twice over, which I will always be eternally grateful for. I'm sorry for what has happened to John. He was and always will be the best the military has ever produced, which is why we probably asked too much of him."

Richard sighed, containing his anger and decided to reply, "Don't ever forget him, do you hear?"

President Berry raised her eyebrows slightly with Richard's abrupt tone towards her. She ignored it knowing that he must be grieving from the loss of his son and replied, "I don't intend to."

Captain Weller helped to place the coffin holding her daughter into a hearse and then turned to see Louise who was starting to shed tears. She ran over to her, where they hugged each other and then looked back to see, John Weller, Steve Lundgren, Colonel Wareing and Hayley Pomfret carrying another coffin displaying the U.S. flag. Starting to cry once more, she said to Louise, "John Raven and Sarah Jane are gone."

Richard moved forward wanting to be close to the coffin. Captain Weller saw him, reluctantly saying, "Richard, I'm sorry."

He looked at her, paused for a few seconds and later replied, "I'm glad he could get you out."

He then carried on walking towards the coffin holding his son, with John Weller noticing his grandfather approaching. He told the others helping him to hold the coffin and wait while Richard approached them. He looked at his grandson, and then at Lundgren a little longer, and said to them, "I'm glad you made it home."

John frowned, glancing at Lundgren as Richard placed his hand onto the U.S. flag displayed on the coffin. He looked down and could only imagine his son with what he must now look like. Still containing his anger, Richard saw Louise and Captain Weller standing beside him. Noticing Louise was wearing an engagement ring; it made him say to John, "You ought to think about doing what is right, because believe it or not you're not expendable."

Louise rested her hand showing her engagement ring on the coffin, weeping at the loss of John Raven. Lundgren saw Louise's engagement ring and glimpsed at Weller, starting to understand why he stalled at the offer put forward to him earlier. Captain Weller rested her hand on the coffin, sobbing and reminded them all that John Raven was indeed the best of the best.

They had been instructed to move away while the coffin was placed inside the hearse, knowing it will be at the funeral when they say their last goodbye. John walked over to Louise wanting to give her a hug, feeling glad that she had come to meet him this time. Simon Ashworth saw them and walked over to give him his own bag and Ricky Stevens' bag. When Louise saw the bags, with concern, it made her ask, "Where's Ricky?"

John shook his head from side to side, gritted his teeth and replied, "He's with my father now."

Louise gave him another hug and said in a humble voice, "It could have so easily have been you, think about what we discussed and let's start a new life."

Richard heard what Louise had just said and added to her comment by saying, "You ought to listen to her because life can be short."

John turned to watch the hearse's driving away, nodding his head agreeing, and replied, "Maybe, just maybe I will."

Louise smiled and kissed his cheek as John watched Lundgren walk by, making him think back to the offer made to him earlier to join his group of elite soldiers. John and Louise had a secret. It was just a matter of finding the right time to discuss the new life growing inside her and the prospect of fighting in what could be another war.

Last Goodbye

$\mathcal{P}$eople from all over, came to John Raven's and Sarah Jane Weller-Raven's funeral. Each person wanted to say goodbye in their own way. President Berry and Sarah Johnson with their bodyguards came to say their last goodbye, remembering a soldier that always said, " . . . then I die."

Sadly, he has now died, when he will be remembered for always performing for his country at the highest level. This made different people come up to Captain Weller, Richard, John and Louise and say he died for something. Captain Weller had to be careful with her replies because Richard was like a volcano ready to erupt. Richard could never forgive the military for what they had done, by keep asking his son to come back and fight once more. He suspected there may come a time when he didn't return home alive. Sadly, for him and other members of the family that day had arrived, when it was time to lay a legend to rest.

John Raven and his daughter Sarah Jane were lowered slowly into the ground, making people standing nearby shed tears with the loss of two people that were close to their hearts. Louise, supporting John throughout this sad day, looked radiant even when she was dressed in black. Colonel Wareing was there to support Captain Weller. Feeling sad, she noticed Richard standing alone, when this was not a day to be left on your own. She left the Colonel, starting to walk over to him, wanting to comfort him with his huge loss. He put his arm around her saying, "I meant what I said when I told you previously, that I feel glad that John managed to get you out of Iran."

Captain Weller looked down at the coffins, remembering her time in Iran and replied, "It's time for me to leave the military."

Richard said, "Good! Learn to enjoy life."

As she looked down at the coffin visualising John, she thought about what she had discussed with him, when they were getting back together. A tear rolled down her cheek, as she recalled saying she would look forward to this, after finishing her task aboard U.S.S. Abraham Lincoln. She told Richard, which made him reply, "With the Iranians capturing you. He had no choice but to have become involved. Christmas Day, when he should have been with his family, he was in the barn making a lethal weapon. He became frustrated at what to do for the best."

Captain Weller listened to Richard speaking, and replied, "I feel as though it's my fault, he is where he is."

Richard shook his head in disagreement saying, "No! Don't blame yourself because he would have performed in the same way for any one of us. What if it had been Louise? Although my grandson would probably have been there, you can bet that his father would also have been there too."

Captain Weller wiped the tears away from her eyes. She looked at Richard, pausing before replying. Reflecting on her loss, later in a sad voice she said, "You're right when you say he would have done it for anyone of us. At least Louise's brother, Enzio, has the chance now to live a normal life."

Richard glanced across at Enzio, glad that he was now safe and replied, "I just wished the military had listened to me more."

Captain Weller watched Steve Lundgren walk over to her son, noticing he had taken a considerate approach to him. Richard also noticed, watching closely as everybody paid their last respects to John and Sarah Jane. President Berry walked to the graveside, gently taking hold of John's arm and said, "I'm sorry for your loss."

She moved away wanting to say a few words about two soldiers who had risked their lives, so she and others can still live with theirs. Captain Weller and Richard listened to President Berry praise Sarah Jane, but more so, John Raven. At times, Richard was watching Steve Lundgren closely. Captain Weller, while still listening to President Berry making her brief speech, asked Richard, "Why do you keep staring at Lundgren?"

Richard narrowed his eyes replying, "Sometimes things are better left not mentioned."

They watched President Berry throw a Purple Heart and a Medal of Honour onto each coffin. Captain Weller then replied, "With the secret I had kept for many years, maybe I'm not the right person that should be asking this question."

Richard looked down at her, saying, "None of us are perfect, but there comes a time when the truth has to come out later."

Captain Weller frowned at what Richard had said. She recalled the time when she had no choice, but to have to tell John about the son he never knew existed, making him come back and fight once more for the sake of his own blood. Noticing President Berry was now stepping away from the graveside, Captain Weller asked Richard, "What has this got to do with Lundgren?"

Richard replied, "When you get the chance, look at him closely, and you may see some of John's features and characteristics."

Captain Weller, with concern, asked, "What are you trying to say?"

Richard, in a stern tone said, "I'm trying to tell you that Steve Lundgren is John's half-brother, who is using his mother's surname."

Louise and John heard what Richard had just told Captain Weller. John turned around sharply to face Steve, who placed out his hand and said to John, "In you not only do I see your father, I see my half-brother."

John, in shock, slowly placed his hand out to shake Steve's hand, making him ask, "So you're my Uncle?"

Steve replied, "I guess so."

Louise watched Steve release John's hand, and shake his father by the hand realising that another Raven had come on the scene. She gave a wry smile, knowing that she was also carrying one too.

People left the graveside, by going inside to eat the buffet arranged for the military, friends, and family. Colonel Wareing discussed the life of John Raven with General Hardaker. He told him that he will hang the picture of John Raven backup on the wall next to Colonel Lewis where it will always remain. As he spoke, he looked around the room noticing that Captain Weller wasn't available. He saw her standing alone sobbing at the graveside of her daughter and John Raven, making him say, "Excuse me General."

Louise had also noticed and said, "Colonel, let me go because I have something to say to her."

Reluctantly, Colonel Wareing agreed, watching her walk outside across to her. Louise placed her arm tenderly around her, and listened to Captain Weller say, "I miss them."

Louise replied, "I know what you're going through because when I had lost my brother in Iran, it was like he had died."

Captain Weller wiped away her tears, saying, "I've decided to leave the military, this time has just been too much."

Louise replied, "I wish John would leave the military."

Captain Weller looked back, in the distance, at members of Unit Expendable and John Weller speaking with them. She remained quiet thinking about what Louise had told her, and then replied, "John is his own man."

Louise, feeling renewed hope that he is at least considering a new life, explained to Captain Weller what he was now considering. Seeing Steve Lundgren come outside and place his arm around John made Captain Weller look at the gravestone and say, "I wouldn't be so sure about that."

Louise starting to feel deflated, replied, "He has to!"

Captain Weller, with concern asked, "You have always known what he is and what he has to do. I don't think you will be able to change him."

A tear rolled down her cheek, making her glance at the birth date showing on John Raven's gravestone 07/06/47 and reply, "I'm carrying his child."

Captain Weller, feeling pleased, smiled, and went towards her to give her a hug wanting to ask, "Does John know?"

Louise replied, "Not yet. I can't find the right time to tell him."

After hearing Louise's answer, Captain Weller thought back to when she had to tell John about their son and said, "That comment sounds familiar, but don't leave it as long as I did, or you will live to regret it."

Captain Weller put her arm around her and said, "Come on let's go inside."

Louise made Captain Weller promise that she wouldn't tell John about the child she was expecting. She wanted to do it when she felt the time was right. Captain Weller agreed, where she was starting to look at her as a daughter and not John's girlfriend. Louise held out her hand showing her engagement ring to her, which made Captain Weller say, "It's a sparkler."

John noticed them, deciding to leave the conversation he was having with some of the members of Unit Expendable, and casually walk across to them. He asked them if they were okay, which Captain Weller after hearing Louise's news replied, "I feel a little better."

John said, "That's good."

He noticed the graveside had nobody standing next to it, which made him say, "I'm just going to spend a few moments with my father and sister."

Captain Weller understood, replying, "You go, spend as much time as you need."

Louise gave a starry-eyed look towards John, asking, "Would you like me to come with you?"

John, while looking at his father's gravestone from a distance, replied, "I want to be alone."

Captain Weller, after hearing Louise's news, produced a stern face and said, "Don't shut her out John."

John turned to face them and replied, "Okay, give me a few minutes alone and then come and join me."

Captain Weller smiled at him, saying, "That's better."

They walked inside to re-join family and friends, as John went to walk to his father's graveside. Standing there looking down at the gravestone amid his own thoughts, Hayley came wanting to pay her respects by placing a yellow rose onto his grave. Feeling concerned for John, she said, "I'm sorry about the loss of your father."

John thanked her by slowly nodding his head at her. She patted his arm and walked away, leaving him looking down remembering his family. He took off his black tie, placing it into his pocket. Thinking back to when his father had worn his necklace, he undid a couple of shirt buttons to pull out the emerald stone that had much history with it. He held the stone tightly, closed his eyes for a few seconds, while pulling it away from his neck and laid it where it should rightfully remain. He felt a cold shiver go through his body when he stood back up, which made him look to the sky and say, "I'll know when the time is right."

He saw Templeton from Unit Expendable coming to his father's graveside, wanting to pay his respects in his own way. He pulled from his pocket; the photograph John's father had once given to his mother, and placed it down below the necklace so it wouldn't blow away. Before turning to leave, he said, "You can say he has come full circle now."

Templeton walked away, leaving John to bend down, graciously pick up the photo and look at the picture of his father standing next to his own friends with Unit Storm. Looking at the photograph, a tear rolled down his cheek. Louise, concerned for John, quietly walked up to him and placed her arm around his waist. She too saw the photograph John was studying, making her ask, "Are you okay?"

John, thinking about his father paused for a few seconds, and later replied, "Yes."

He gently pulled away from Louise to place the photograph back down with the necklace. Louise saw the emerald stone, but before she could say anything, John said, "It's back where it always belonged."

He pulled a photograph from his own pocket, looking at members of Unit Invincible, knowing he had to take Stevens' belongings back to his home. He glimpsed at the photo on the grave showing a young John Raven, and then turned to Louise to put his arm around her, asking, "Is history about to repeat itself?"

Captain Weller was walking back up to John's graveside with Rachel, remembering Tony having no choice, but to leave her in the same circumstances, when he left this world. Captain Weller acknowledged Louise and John and looked down at the photograph Templeton had left earlier. It made her upset, knowing it was how she remembered John before they went their separate ways. Rachel comforted her as she wept, having to accept he had now gone. Her son, John, remained standing there looking down at the graves thinking about what his sister could have been and his father who had taught him everything he now knew. As his hair blew back in the breeze, Louise noticed that he had become despondent, which made her hold his arm knowing he was grieving inwardly. Captain Weller, still crying found it hard to speak, which made John say, "It's okay Mum. I'm here."

Captain Weller ignored what John had just said. Louise let go of him, wanting to comfort his mother with Rachel and listened to her say, "John Raven was always the best of the best."

John contained his sorrow, starting to hide his feelings and feel strong while looking down at his father and sister. He could only focus on the necklace that had plenty of history. The breeze blew his hair as he watched his mother weep with Louise and Rachel. She looked down at John Raven, and then across to her son, wanting to say, when she could finally get the words out, "It's time for a new era."

The End